The path of true love will lead to three...

Innocent Brides To Be

by

BETTY NEELS

This international bestselling write[r] [one] of the
world's best-loved romance author[s] [w]e are
proud to bring back three charm[ing] [stor]ies
in one special collection[.]

BETTY NEELS

Innocent Brides To Be

Containing

A SUITABLE MATCH
A GIRL TO LOVE
& RING IN A TEACUP

*M&B™ and M&B™ with the Rose Device
are trademarks of the publisher.
Harlequin Mills & Boon Limited, Eton House,
18-24 Paradise Road, Richmond, Surrey TW9 ISR*

INNOCENT BRIDES-TO-BE © by Harlequin Books S.A. 2008

A Suitable Match, A Girl to Love and *Ring in a Teacup* were first
published in Great Britain by Harlequin Mills & Boon

A Suitable Match © Betty Neels 1986
A Girl to Love © Betty Neels 1982
Ring in a Teacup © Betty Neels 1978

ISBN: 978 0263 86668 1

009-0508

Printed and bound in Spain
by Litografia Rosés S.A., Barcelona

A Suitable Match

Betty Neels spent her childhood and youth in Devonshire before training as a nurse and midwife. She was an army nursing sister during the war, married a Dutchman, and subsequently lived in Holland for fourteen years. She moved with her husband to Dorset, and has a daughter and grandson. Betty started to write after she retired, incited by a lady in a library bemoaning the lack of romantic novels.

Over her thirty-year writing career, Betty Neels wrote an astonishing one hundred and thirty-four novels and was published in more that one hundred international markets. She continued to write into her ninetieth year, remaining as passionate about her characters and stories then as she was in her very first book. She will always be remembered as a truly delightful person who brought great happiness to many.

In Mills & Boon's centenary year, Betty Neels features in two very special collections:

As one of our Queens of Romance in
Summer Engagements
out in August 2008;

And Betty Neels also features in our 100th Birthday Collection with
The Doctor's Girl
in July 2008.

CHAPTER ONE

EUSTACIA bit into her toast, poured herself another cup of tea, and turned her attention once again to the job vacancies in the morning paper. She had been doing this for some days now and it was with no great hope of success that she ran her eye down the columns. Her qualifications, which were few, didn't seem to fit into any of the jobs on offer. It was a pity, she reflected, that an education at a prestigious girls' school had left her quite unfitted for earning her living in the commercial world. She had done her best, but the course of shorthand and typing had been nothing less than disastrous, and she hadn't lasted long at the boutique because, unlike her colleagues, she had found herself quite incapable of telling a customer that a dress fitted while she held handfuls of surplus material at that lady's back, or left a zip undone to accommodate surplus flesh. She had applied for a job at the local post office too, and had been turned down because she didn't wish to join a union. No one, it seemed, wanted a girl with four A levels and the potential for a university if she had been able to go to one. Here she was, twenty-two years old, out of work once more and with a grandfather to support.

She bent her dark head over the pages—she was a pretty girl with eyes as dark as her hair, a dainty little nose and a rather too large mouth—eating her toast absentmindedly as she searched the pages. There was nothing... Yes, there was: the path lab of St Biddolph's Hospital, not half a mile away, needed an assistant bottle-washer, general cleaner and postal worker. No qualifications required other than honesty, speed and cleanliness. The pay wasn't bad either.

Eustacia swallowed the rest of her tea, tore out the advertisement, and went out of the shabby little room into the passage and tapped on a door. A voice told her to go in and she did so, a tall, splendidly built girl wearing what had once been a good suit, now out of date but immaculate.

'Grandpa,' she began, addressing the old man sitting up in his bed. 'There's a job in this morning's paper. As soon as I've brought your breakfast I'm going after it.'

The old gentleman looked at her over his glasses. 'What kind of a job?'

'Assistant at the path lab at St Biddolph's.' She beamed at him. 'It sounds OK, doesn't it?' She whisked herself through the door again. 'I'll be back in five minutes with your tray.'

She left their small ground-floor flat in one of the quieter streets of Kennington and walked briskly to the bus-stop. It wasn't yet nine o'clock and speed, she felt, was of the essence. Others, it seemed, had felt the same; there were six women already in the little waiting-room inside the entrance to the path lab at the hospital, and within the next ten minutes another four turned up. Eustacia sat there quietly waiting, uttering silent, childish prayers. This job would be nothing less than a godsend—regular hours, fifteen minutes from the flat and the weekly pay-packet would be enough to augment her grandfather's pension—a vital point, this, for they had been eating into their tiny capital for several weeks.

Her turn came and she went to the room set aside for the interviews, and sat down before a stout, elderly man sitting at a desk. He looked bad-tempered and he sounded it too, ignoring her polite 'Good morning' and plunging at once into his own questions.

She answered them briefly, handed over her references and waited for him to speak.

"You have four A levels. Why are you not at a university?'

'Family circumstances,' said Eustacia matter-of-factly.

He glanced up. 'Yes, well…the work here is menial, you understand that?' He glowered across the desk at her. 'You will be notified.'

Not very hopeful, she considered, walking back to the flat; obviously A levels weren't of much help when applying for such a job. She would give it a day and, if she heard nothing, she would try for something else. She stopped at the baker's and bought bread and then went next door to the greengrocer's and chose a cauliflower. Cauliflower cheese for supper and some carrots and potatoes. She had become adept at making soup now that October was sliding into November. At least she could cook, an art she had been taught at her expensive boarding-school, and if it hadn't been for her grandfather she might have tried her luck as a cook in some hotel. Indeed, she had left school with no thought of training for anything; her mother and father had been alive then, full of ideas about taking her with them when they travelled. 'Plenty of time,' they had said. 'A couple of years enjoying life before you marry or decide what you want to do,' and she had had those two years, seeing quite a lot of the world, knowing only vaguely that her father was in some kind of big business which allowed them to live in comfort. It was when he and her mother had been killed in an air crash that she'd discovered that he was heavily in debt, that his business was bankrupt and that any money there was would have to go to creditors. It had been frightening to find herself without a penny and an urgent necessity to earn a living, and it had been then that her grandfather, someone she had seldom met for he'd lived in the north of England, had come to see her.

'We have each other,' he had told her kindly. 'I cannot offer you a home, for my money was invested in your father's business, but I have my pension and I believe I know someone who will help us to find something modest to live in in London.'

He had been as good as his word; the 'someone' owned property in various parts of London and they had moved into the flat two years ago, and Eustacia had set about getting a job. Things hadn't been too bad at first, but her typing and shorthand weren't good enough to get a job in a office and her grandfather had developed a heart condition so that she had had to stay at home for some time to look after him. Now, she thought hopefully, perhaps their luck had changed and she would get this job, and Grandfather would get better, well enough for her to hire a car and take him to Kew or Richmond Park. He hated the little street where they lived and longed for the country, and so secretly did she, although she never complained. He had enough to bear, she considered, and felt nothing but gratitude for his kindness when she had needed it most.

She made coffee for them both when she got in and told him about the job. 'There were an awful lot of girls there,' she said. 'This man said he would let me know. I don't expect that means much, but it's better than being told that the job's been taken—I mean, I can go on hoping until I hear.'

She heard two days later—the letter was on the mat when she got up, and she took it to the kitchen and put on the kettle for their morning tea and opened it.

The job was hers—she was to present herself for work on the following Monday at eight-thirty sharp. She would have half an hour for her lunch, fifteen minutes for her coffee-break and tea in the afternoon, and work until five o'clock. She would be free on Saturdays and Sundays but once a month she would be required to work on Saturday, when she would be allowed the following Monday free. Her wages, compared to Grandfather's pension, seemed like a fortune.

She took a cup of tea to her grandfather and told him the news.

'I'm glad, my dear. It will certainly make life much

easier for you—now you will be able to buy yourself some pretty clothes.'

It wasn't much good telling him that pretty clothes weren't any use unless she had somewhere to go in them, but she agreed cheerfully, while she did sums in her head: the gas bill, always a formidable problem with her grandfather to keep warm by the gas fire in their sitting-room—duvets for their beds, some new saucepans... She mustn't get too ambitious, she told herself cautiously, and went off to get herself dressed.

She got up earlier than usual on Monday, tidied the flat, saw to her grandfather's small wants, cautioned him to be careful while she was away, kissed him affectionately, and started off for the hospital.

She was a little early, but that didn't matter, as it gave her time to find her way around to the cubby-hole where she was to change into the overall she was to wear, and peep into rooms and discover where the canteen was. A number of people worked at the path lab and they could get a meal cheaply enough as well as coffee and tea. People began to arrive and presently she was told to report to an office on the ground floor where she was given a list of duties she was to do by a brisk lady who made no attempt to disguise her low opinion of Eustacia's job.

'You will wear rubber gloves at all times and a protective apron when you are emptying discarded specimens. I hope you are strong.'

Eustacia hoped she was, too.

By the end of the first day she concluded that a good deal of her work comprised washing-up—glass containers, dishes, little pots, glass tubes and slides. There was the emptying of buckets, too, the distribution of clean laundry and the collecting of used overalls for the porters to bag, and a good deal of toing and froing, taking sheaves of papers, specimens and the post to wherever it was wanted. She was tired as she went home; there were, she supposed, pleasanter ways of earning a living, but never mind that, she was already looking forward to her pay-packet at the end of the week.

She had been there for three days when she came face to face with the man who had interviewed her. He stopped in front of her and asked, 'Well, do you like your work?'

She decided that despite his cross face he wasn't ill-disposed towards her. 'I'm glad to have work,' she told him pleasantly, 'you have no idea how glad. Not all my work is—well, nice, but of course you know that already.'

He gave a rumble of laughter. 'No one stays for long,' he told her. 'Plenty of applicants when the job falls vacant, but they don't last...'

'I have every intention of staying, provided my work is satisfactory.' She smiled at him and he laughed again.

'Do you know who I am?'

'No. I don't know anyone yet—only to say good morning and so on. I saw Miss Bennett when I came here—she told me what to do and so on—and I've really had no time to ask anyone.'

'I'm in charge of this department, young lady; the

name's Professor Ladbroke. I'll see that you get a list of those working here.'

He nodded and walked away. Oh, dear, thought Eustacia, I should have called him 'sir' and not said all that.

She lived in a state of near panic for the rest of the week, wondering if she would get the sack, but pay-day came and there was nothing in her envelope but money. She breathed a sigh of relief and vowed to mind her Ps and Qs in future.

No one took much notice of her; she went in and out of rooms peopled by quiet, white-coated forms peering through microscopes or doing mysterious things with tweezers and pipettes. She suspected that they didn't even see her, and the greater part of her day was concerned with the cleansing of endless bowls and dishes. It was, she discovered, a lonely life, but towards the end of the second week one or two people wished her good morning and an austere man with a beard asked her if she found the work hard.

She told him no, adding cheerfully, 'A bit off-putting sometimes, though!' He looked surprised, and she wished that she hadn't said anything at all.

By the end of the third week she felt as though she had been there for years—she was even liking her work. There actually was a certain pleasure in keeping things clean and being useful, in however humble a capacity, to a department full of silent, dedicated peo-ple, all so hard at work with their microscopes and pipettes and little glass dishes.

She was to work that Saturday; she walked home,

shopping on her way, buying food which her grand-father could see to on his own, thankful that she didn't have to look at every penny. In the morning she set out cheerfully for the hospital. There would be a skeleton staff in the path lab until midday, and after that she had been told to pass any urgent messages to who-ever was on call that weekend. One of the porters would come on duty at six o'clock that evening and take over the phone when she went.

The department was quiet; she went around, chang-ing linen, opening windows, making sure that there was a supply of tea and sugar and milk in the small kitchen, and then carefully filling the half-empty shelves with towels, soap, stationery and path lab forms and, lastly, making sure that there was enough of everything in the sterilisers. It took her until mid-morning, by which time the staff on duty had arrived and were busy dealing with whatever had been sent from the hospital. She made coffee for them all, had some herself and went to assemble fresh supplies of dishes and bowls on trays ready for sterilising. She was returning from carrying a load from one room to the next when she came face to face with a man.

She was a tall girl, but she had to look up to see his face. A handsome one it was too, with a com-manding nose, drooping lids over blue eyes and a thin mouth. His hair was thick and fair and rather untidy, and he was wearing a long white coat—he was also very large.

He stopped in front of her. 'Ah, splendid, get this checked at once, will you, and let me have the result?

I'll be in the main theatre. It's urgent.' He handed her a covered kidney dish. 'Do I know you?'

'No,' said Eustacia. She spoke to his broad, retreating back.

He had said it was urgent; she bore the dish to Mr Brimshaw, who was crouching over something nasty in a tray. He waved her away as she reached him, but she stood her ground.

'Someone—a large man in a white coat—gave me this and said he would be in the main theatre and that it was urgent.'

'Then don't stand there, girl, give it to me.'

As she went away he called after her. 'Come back in ten minutes, and you can take it back.'

'Such manners,' muttered Eustacia as she went back to her dishes.

In exactly ten minutes she went back again to Mr Brimshaw just in time to prevent him from opening his mouth to bellow for her. He gave a grunt instead. 'And look sharp about it,' he cautioned her.

The theatre block wasn't anywhere near the path lab; she nipped smartly in and out of lifts and along corridors and finally, since the lifts were already in use, up a flight of stairs. She hadn't been to the theatre block before and she wasn't sure how far inside the swing-doors she was allowed to go, a problem solved for her by the reappearance of the man in the white coat, only now he was in a green tunic and trousers and a green cap to match.

He took the kidney dish from her with a nice smile.

'Good girl—new, aren't you?' He turned to go and then paused. 'What is your name?'

'Eustacia Crump.' She flew back through the swing-doors, not wanting to hear him laugh—everyone laughed when she told them her name. Eustacia and Crump didn't go well together. He didn't laugh, only stood for a moment more watching her splendid person, swathed in its ill-fitting overall, disappear.

Mr Brimshaw went home at one o'clock and Jim Walker, one of the more senior pathologists working under him, took over. He was a friendly young man and, since Eustacia had done all that was required of her and there was nothing much for him to do for half an hour, she made him tea and had a cup herself with her sandwiches. She became immersed in a reference book of pathological goings-on—she understood very little of it, but it made interesting reading.

It fell to her to go to theatre again a couple of hours later, this time with a vacoliter of blood.

'Mind and bring back that form, properly signed,' warned Mr Walker. 'And don't loiter, will you? They're in a hurry.'

Eustacia went. Who, she asked herself, would wish to loiter in such circumstances? Did Mr Walker think that she would tuck the thing under one arm and stop for a chat with anyone she might meet on her way? She was terrified of dropping it anyway.

She sighed with relief when she reached the theatre block and went cautiously through the swing-doors, only to pause because she wasn't quite sure where to go. A moot point settled for her by a disapproving voice behind her.

'There you are,' said a cross-faced nurse, and took the vacoliter from her.

Eustacia waved the form at her. 'This has to be signed, please.'

'Well, of course it does.' It was taken from her and the nurse plunged through one of the doors on either side, just as the theatre door at the far end swished open and the tall man she had met in the path lab came through.

'Brought the blood?' he asked pleasantly, and when she nodded, 'Miss Crump, isn't it? We met recently.' He stood in front of her, apparently in no haste.

'Tell me,' he asked, 'why are you not sitting on a bench doing blood counts and looking at cells instead of washing bottles?'

It was a serious question and it deserved a serious answer.

'Well, that's what I am—a bottle-washer, although it's called a path lab assistant, and I'm not sure that I should like to sit at a bench all day—some of the things that are examined are very nasty...'

His eyes crinkled nicely at the corners when he smiled. 'They are. You don't look like a bottle-washer.'

'Oh? Do they look different from anyone else?'

He didn't answer that but went on. 'You are far too beautiful,' he told her, and watched her go a delicate pink.

A door opened and the cross nurse came back with

the form in her hand. When she saw them she smoothed the ill humour from her face and smiled.

'I've been looking everywhere for you, sir. If you would sign this form…?' She cast Eustacia a look of great superiority as she spoke. 'They're waiting in theatre for you, sir,' she added in what Eustacia considered to be an oily voice.

The man took the pen she offered and scrawled on the paper and handed it to Eustacia. 'Many thanks, Miss Crump,' he said with grave politeness. He didn't look at the nurse once but went back through the theatre door without a backward glance.

The nurse tossed her head at Eustacia. 'Well, hadn't you better get back to the path lab?' she wanted to know. 'You've wasted enough of our time already.'

Eustacia was almost a head taller, and it gave her a nice feeling of superiority. 'Rubbish,' she said crisply, 'and shouldn't you be doing whatever you ought instead of standing there?'

She didn't stay to hear what the other girl had to say; she hoped that she wouldn't be reported for rudeness. It had been silly of her to annoy the nurse; she couldn't afford to jeopardise her job.

'OK?' asked Mr Walker when she gave him back the signed form. He glanced at it. 'Ah, signed by the great man himself…'

'Oh, a big man in his theatre kit? I don't know anyone here.'

Mr Walker said rather unkindly, 'Well, you don't need to, do you? He's Sir Colin Crichton. An honorary consultant here—goes all over the place—he's specialising in cancer treatment—gets good results too.' He looked at his watch. 'Make me some tea, will you? There's a good girl.'

She put on the kettle and waited while it boiled and thought about Sir Colin Crichton. He had called her Miss Crump and he hadn't laughed. She liked him, and she wished she could see him again.

However, she didn't, the week passed and Saturday came again and she was free once more. Because it was a beautiful day—a bonus at the beginning of the winter—she helped her grandfather to wrap up warmly, went out and found a taxi, and took him to Kew Gardens. Supported by her arm and a stick, the old gentleman walked its paths, inspected a part of the botanical gardens, listened to the birds doing their best in the pale sunshine and then expressed a wish to go to the Orangery.

It was there that they encountered Sir Colin, accompanied by two small boys. Eustacia saw him first and suggested hastily to her grandfather that they might turn around and stroll in the opposite direction.

'Why ever should we do that?' he asked testily, and before she could think up a good reason Sir Colin had reached them.

'Ah—Miss Crump. We share a similar taste in Chambers' work—a delightful spot on a winter morning.'

He stood looking at her, his eyebrows faintly lifted, and after a moment she said, 'Good morning, sir,' and, since her grandfather was looking at her as well, 'Grandfather, this is Sir Colin Crichton, he's a consultant at St Biddolph's. My Grandfather, Mr Henry Crump.'

The two men shook hands and the boys were introduced—Teddy and Oliver, who shook hands too, and, since the two gentlemen had fallen into conversation and had fallen into step, to stroll the length of the Orangery and then back into the gardens again, Eustacia found herself with the two boys. They weren't very old—nine years, said Teddy, and Oliver was a year younger. They were disposed to like her and within a few minutes were confiding a number of interesting facts. Half-term, they told her, and they would go back to school on Monday, and had she any brothers who went away to school?

She had to admit that she hadn't. 'But I really am very interested; do tell me what you do there—I don't mean lessons…'

They understood her very well. She was treated to a rigmarole of Christmas plays, football, computer games and what a really horrible man the maths master was. 'Well, I dare say your father can help you with your homework,' she suggested.

'Oh, he's much too busy,' said Oliver, and she supposed that he was, operating and doing ward rounds and out-patients and travelling around besides. He couldn't have much home life. She glanced back to where the two men were strolling at her grandfather's pace along the path towards them, deep in talk. She wondered if Sir Colin wanted to take his leave but was too courteous to say so; his wife might be waiting at home for him and the boys. She spent a few moments deciding what to do and rather reluctantly turned back towards them.

'We should be getting back,' she suggested to her grandfather, and was echoed at once by Sir Colin.

'So must we. Allow me to give you a lift—the car's by the Kew Road entrance.'

Before her grandfather could speak, Eustacia said quickly, 'That's very kind of you, but I daresay we live in a quite opposite direction to you: Kennington.'

'It couldn't be more convenient,' she was told smoothly. 'We can keep south of the river, drop you off and cross at Southwark.' He gave her a gentle smile and at the same time she saw that he intended to have his own way.

They walked to the main gate, suiting their pace to that of her grandfather, and got into the dark blue Rolls-Royce parked there. Eustacia sat between the boys at the back, surprised to find that they were sharing it with a small, untidy dog with an extremely long tail and melting brown eyes. Moreover, he had a leg in plaster.

'This is Moses,' said Oliver as he squashed in beside Eustacia. 'He was in the water with a broken leg,' he explained and, since Eustacia looked so astonished, said it for a second time, rather loudly, just as though she were deaf.

'Oh, the poor little beast.' She bent to rub the unruly head at their feet and Sir Colin, settling himself in the driving-seat, said over his shoulder, 'He's not quite up to walking far, but he likes to be with us. Unique, isn't he?'

'But nice,' said Eustacia, and wished she could think of a better word.

It was quite a lengthy drive; she sat between the boys, taking part in an animated conversation on such subjects as horrendous schoolmasters, their favourite TV programmes, their dislike of maths and their favourite food. She found them both endearing and felt regret when the drive was over and the car drew up before their flat. Rolls-Royces were a rarity in the neighbourhood, and it would be a talking-point for some time—already curtains in neighbouring houses were being twitched.

She wished the boys goodbye and they chorused an urgent invitation to go out with them again, and, conscious of Sir Colin's hooded eyes upon her, she murmured non-committally, bending to stroke Moses because she could feel herself blushing hatefully.

She waited while her grandfather expressed his thanks for the ride, and then she added her own thanks with a frank look from her dark eyes, to encounter his smiling gaze.

'We have enjoyed your company,' he told her, and she found herself believing him. 'The boys get bored, you know; I haven't all that time at home and my housekeeper is elderly and simply can't cope with them.'

'Housekeeper? Oh, I thought they were yours.'

'My brother's. He has gone abroad with his wife, a job in Brunei for a few months. They are too young for boarding-school...'

They had shaken hands and he still held hers in a firm grasp.

'They like you,' he said.

'Well, I like them. I'm glad I met them and Grandfather has enjoyed himself. He doesn't get out much.'

He nodded and gave her back her hand and went to open the rickety gate, and waited while they went up the short path to the front door and opened it. Eustacia turned as they went inside and smiled at them all, before he closed the gate, got back into his car and drove away.

'A delightful morning, my dear,' said her grandfather. 'I feel ten years younger—and such an interesting conversation. You are most fortunate to be working for such a man.'

'Well, I don't,' said Eustacia matter-of-factly. 'I only met him because he came down to the path lab for something. He goes to St Biddolph's once or twice a week to operate and see his patients, and as I seldom leave the path lab except when there is a message to run we don't meet.'

'Yes, yes,' her grandfather sounded testy, 'but now that you have met you will see more of each other.'

She thought it best not to argue further; she suspected that he had no idea of the work she did. Sir Colin had been charming but that didn't mean to say that he wished to pursue their acquaintance; indeed it was most unlikely. A pity, she reflected as she went to the kitchen to get their lunch, but they occupied different worlds—she would probably end up by marrying another bottle-washer. A sobering thought even while she laughed at the idea.

It was December in no time at all, or so it seemed, and the weather turned cold and damp and dark, and the shops began to fill with Christmas food and a splendid array of suitable presents. Eustacia did arithmetic on the backs of envelopes, made lists and began to hoard things like chocolate biscuits, strawberry jam, tins of ham and a Christmas pudding; she had little money over each week and she laid it out carefully, determined to have a good Christmas. There would be no one to visit, of course. As far as she knew they had no family, and her grandfather's friends lived in the north of England and her own friends from school days were either married or holding down good jobs with no time to spare. From time to time they exchanged letters, but pride prevented her from telling any of them about the change in her life. She wrote cheerful replies, telling them nothing in a wealth of words.

On the first Saturday in December it was her lot to work all day. Mr Brimshaw arrived some time after she did, wished her a grumpy good morning and went into his own office, and she began on her chores. It was a dismal day and raining steadily, but she busied herself with her dishes and pots, made coffee for Mr Brimshaw and herself and thought about Christmas. She would have liked a new dress but that was out of the question—she had spent more than she could afford on a thick waistcoat for her grandfather and a pair of woollen gloves, and there was still something to be bought for their landlady, who, although kindly disposed towards them as long as the rent was paid on time, needed to be kept sweet. A headscarf, mused Eustacia, or perhaps a box of soap? She was so deep in thought that Mr Brimshaw had to bawl twice before she heard him.

'Hurry up, girl—Casualty's full—there's been an accident in Oxford Street and they'll be shouting for blood before I can take a breath. Get along with this first batch and then come back as fast as you can.'

He had cross-matched another victim when she got back, so she hurried away for a second time with another vacoliter and after that she lost count of the times she trotted to and fro. The initial urgency settled down presently and Mr Brimshaw, crosser than ever because he was late for his lunch, went home and Mr Walker took over, and after that things became a little more settled. All the same, she was tired when the evening porter came on duty and she was able to go home. It was still raining; she swathed her person in her elderly raincoat, tied a scarf over her hair and made for the side entrance. It being Saturday, there wouldn't be all that number of buses which meant that they would be full too. She nipped smartly across the courtyard, head down against the rain, and went full tilt into Sir Colin, coming the other way. He took her considerable weight without any effort and stood her on to her feet.

'Going home?' he wanted to know gently.

She nodded and then said, 'Oh…' when he took her arm and turned her round.

'So am I. I'll drop you off on my way.'

'But I'm wet, I'll spoil your car.'

'Don't be silly,' he begged her nicely. 'I'm wet too.'

He bustled her to the car and settled her into the front seat and got in beside her.

'It's out of your way,' sighed Eustacia weakly.

'Not at all—what a girl you are for finding objections.'

They sat in a comfortable silence as he turned the car in the direction of the river and Kennington. That he had only just arrived at the hospital intent on having a few words with his registrar, when he saw her, was something he had no intention of revealing. He wasn't at all sure why he had offered to take her home; he hardly knew her and although he found her extremely pretty and, what was more, intelligent, he had made no conscious effort to seek her out. It was a strange fact that two people could meet and feel instantly at ease with each other—more than that, feel as though they had known each other all their lives. Eustacia, sitting quietly beside him, was thinking exactly the same thing.

He smiled nicely when she thanked him, got out of the car and opened the gate for her and waited until she had unlocked the door and gone inside before driving himself back to the hospital, thinking about her. She was too good for the job she was doing, and like a beautiful fish out of water in that depressing little street.

He arrived back at St Biddolph's and became im-

mersed in the care of his patients, shutting her delightful image away in the back of his mind and keeping
it firmly there.

CHAPTER TWO

THE path lab would be open over Christmas; accidents and sudden illness took no account of holidays. Eustacia was to work on Christmas Day morning and again on Boxing Day afternoon, sharing the days with the two porters. She went home on Christmas Eve much cheered by the good wishes and glass of sherry she had been offered before everyone left that evening. Once there, she opened the bottle of claret she had been hoarding and she and her grandfather toasted each other before they sat down to supper. She had bought a chicken for their Christmas dinner, and before she went to bed she prepared everything for the meal so that when she got back home the next day she would need only to put the food in the oven. In the morning she got up earlier than usual, laid the table and put the presents they had for each other beside the small Christmas tree, took her grandfather his breakfast and then hurried off to work. There was no one there save the night porter, who wished her a hasty 'Merry Christmas' before hurrying off duty. He hadn't had to call anyone up during the night, he told her, and hoped that she would have a quiet morning.

Which indeed she did. Mr Brimshaw, arriving shortly afterwards, wished her a mumbled 'Happy Christmas' and went along to his office to deal with

27

the paperwork, and Eustacia set about putting the place to rights, turning out cupboards and then making coffee. The telephone went incessantly but there were no emergencies; at one o'clock the second porter took over and Mr Brimshaw handed over to one of the assistants. Eustacia went to get her outdoor things, wished the porter a civil goodbye and made for the door just as one of the hospital porters came in with a parcel.

'Miss Crump?' he enquired. 'I was to deliver this before you left.'

'Me?' Eustacia beamed at him. 'You're sure it's for me?'

'Name's Crump, isn't it?'

He went away again and she tucked the gaily packed box under her arm and went home, speculating all the way as to who it was from.

But first when she got home there was her present from her grandfather to open—warm red slippers; just what she needed, she declared, during the cold months of winter. After he had admired his waistcoat and gloves she opened her package. It had been wrapped in red paper covered with robins and tied with red ribbons, and she gave a great sigh of pleasure when she saw its contents: an extravagantly large box of handmade chocolates, festooned with yet more ribbons and covered in brocade. There was a card with it, written in a childish hand, 'With Love from Oliver and Teddy.'

'Well, really,' said Eustacia, totally surprised. 'But

I only met them once, remember, Grandfather, at Kew...'

'Children like to give presents to the people they like.'

'I must write and thank them—only I don't know where they live.'

'They're with their uncle, aren't they? And with luck someone at the hospital will surely know his address.'

'Yes, of course. What a lovely surprise. Have one while I start the dinner.' She paused on her way to the kitchen. 'It must have cost an awful lot, and they're only children.'

'I dare say they've been saving up—you know what children are.' Her grandfather chose a chocolate with care and popped it into his mouth. 'They're delicious.'

They had their dinner presently and afterwards Eustacia went to church, and went back home to watch television until bedtime. Without saying anything to her grandfather she had hired a set, to his great delight, for he spent a good part of the day on his own and she guessed that he was sometimes lonely. If, later on, she couldn't afford it, she could always return it— although, seeing the old man's pleasure in it, she vowed to keep it at all costs. It was an extravagance, she supposed, and the money should perhaps be saved against a rainy day or the ever-worrying chance that she might lose her job. On the other hand, it was their one extravagance and did much to lighten their un-eventful lives.

She went back to work the next day after their

lunch. There were two of the staff on duty, cross-matching blood for patients due for operations the following day, doing blood counts and checking test meals. Eustacia made tea for them both, had a cup herself and busied herself restocking the various forms on each bench. That done, she put out clean towels, filled the soap containers and cleaned the sinks which had been used. She was to stay until six o'clock when the night porter would take over, and once the others had gone it was very quiet. She was glad when he came to spend a few minutes in cheerful talk before she took herself off home.

Everyone was short-tempered in the morning—too much to eat and drink, too little sleep and a generally jaundiced outlook on life cast gloom over the entire department. Miss Bennett found fault with very nearly everything, until Eustacia felt like flinging a tray of dishes and bottles on to the floor and walking out for good. She held her tongue and looked meek, and to her great surprise at the day's end Miss Bennett rather grudgingly admitted that on the whole her work was quite satisfactory, adding sternly that there was to be no more slackness now that the festive season was over. 'And a good thing it is,' she observed. It was obvious to Eustacia that the poor woman found no joy in her life. Such a pity, one never knew what was round the corner.

It was halfway through January when she got home one evening to find, to her great astonishment, Sir Colin Crichton sitting all at ease opposite her grandfather's armchair by the open fire. He got up when she went in and wished her a polite good evening, and she replied with a hint of tartness. She wasn't looking at her best; it had been a busy day and she was tired, and, conscious that her hair was untidy and her face badly needed fresh make-up, the frown she turned upon him was really quite fierce and he smiled faintly.

'I came to talk to you,' he said to surprise her, 'but if you are too tired...?'

She took up the challenge. 'I am not in the least tired,' she assured him, and then said suddenly, 'Oh—is it about my job?'

He had sat down again and she glanced at her grandfather, who, beyond smiling at her when she kissed him, had remained silent.

'Er—yes, to a certain extent.'

She took an indignant breath. She had worked hard at a job she really didn't like and now she supposed she was to get the sack, although why someone as exalted as Sir Colin had to do it was beyond her.

He said in his quiet, deliberate voice, 'No, it is not what you think it is, Miss Crump, but it would please me very much if you would give up your job in the path lab and come to work for me.'

'Come to work for you?' she echoed his words in a voice squeaky with surprise. And then added, 'Why?'

'My nephews,' he explained. 'They have both had flu, tonsillitis and nasty chests. It is obvious that London doesn't agree with them, at least until they are fit again. I feel responsible for them while their mother and father are away, but I am rarely at home during the day and there is no question of their going back to school for several weeks. I have a home at Turville, just north of Henley. A very small village and quiet— I don't go there as often as I would wish. I should like the boys to go there and I would be glad if you would go with them. They have taken to you in a big way, you know.' He smiled his charming smile. 'There is a housekeeper there, her husband does the garden and the odd jobs but they are both elderly and the boys need young company—a kind of elder sister? I think that you would fill that role exactly…'

Eustacia had her mouth open to speak and he went on calmly, 'No, don't interrupt—let me finish… I am not sure how long it might be before my brother returns—but at least two months, and at the end of that time you would have sufficient experience to get a post in a similar capacity. There is plenty of room for everyone; the Samwayses have their own quarters on the ground floor at the back of the house and adjoining it is a bedroom which Mr Crump could use. You yourself, Miss Crump, would have a room next to the boys on the first floor. Now as to salary…' He mentioned a sum which made Eustacia gape at him.

'That's twice as much as I'm getting,' she told him.

'I can assure you that you will earn every penny of it. Do you know anything about little boys?'

'No, I'm afraid not.'

He smiled. 'But I believe that you would do very well with them. Will you consider it?'

She looked at her grandfather, and although he

didn't say anything she saw the eagerness in his face. 'This flat?' she asked. 'It's—it's our home.'

'You could continue to rent it. Naturally I do not expect you to pay for your rooms and food at Turville.' He sounded disapproving and she blushed.

'It is a very generous offer...' she began, and he laughed then.

'My dear girl, this is no sinecure. The boot will be on the other foot if you agree to take charge of the boys. Would you like time to think it over?'

She caught sight of her grandfather's face again. 'No, thank you, sir, I shall be glad to come.' She was rewarded by the look on the old man's face. 'I shall have to give my notice. I don't know how long...?'

'Give in your notice and I'll have a word. And don't call me sir, it makes me feel old.' He got to his feet. 'I am most grateful for your help. You will hear from me as soon as the details are settled.'

She saw him to the door. 'You're quite sure...? she began as she opened it.

'Quite sure. The boys will be delighted.'

She stood in the doorway and watched him drive away and then went back to her grandfather.

He quickly dispelled any vague doubts floating around in her head. 'It couldn't be better,' he declared. 'It is a splendid start; when you leave the boys you will have a good reference and plenty of experience. You will be qualified for an even better post.'

'But Grandfather, what about you?' She sat down at the table.

'We still have this flat—there must be a job such

as this one where one can live out.' He allowed himself to dream a little. 'You might even get a post in the country where there is a cottage or something similar where we might live.'

She had her doubts, but it would be unkind to throw cold water over his pleasure. She let him ramble on happily and hoped that she had done the right thing. After all, her job, although not to her liking, was, as far as she knew, safe enough, and she had earned enough to make their life a good deal easier than it had been. On the other hand, she wouldn't need to buy food, they would live rent-free and she would be able to save a good deal of the money she earned.

'I hope I'm doing the right thing,' she muttered as she went to the kitchen to get their supper.

She went to see Miss Bennett the next morning and was surprised to find that that lady knew all about it. 'You will have to work out your week's notice,' she told Eustacia, and her usually sharp voice was quite pleasant. 'There will be no difficulty in replacing you—I have a list of applicants ready to jump into your shoes.' She added even more surprisingly, 'I hope you will be happy in your new job. You will have to see the professor before you go. You are on Saturday duty this week, are you not?' And when Eustacia nodded, 'So you will leave at six o'clock on that day.'

She nodded dismissal and Eustacia escaped to the quiet of the little cubby-hole where she washed the bottles and dishes and, while she cleaned and polished, she allowed her thoughts to wander. Sir Colin hadn't said exactly when they were to go, but she hoped it wouldn't be until Monday so that she would have time to pack their things and leave the flat pristine.

There was a letter for her the following morning. If her grandfather and she could be ready by Sunday afternoon directly after lunch, they would be fetched by car and driven to Turville; he trusted that this arrangement would be agreeable to her. The letter was typewritten, but he had signed it with a scrawl which she supposed was his signature.

She could see no reason why they should not go when it was suggested, so she wrote a polite little note saying that they would be ready when the car came, and went off to tell her grandfather.

She packed their clothes on Saturday evening, got up early on Sunday morning and did some last-minute ironing, shut the cases and set about seeing that the flat was left clean. There wasn't time to cook lunch, so she opened a can of soup and made some scrambled eggs and was just nicely ready when the doorbell was rung.

She was surprised to find Sir Colin on the doorstep. He wished her good-day in his placid voice, exchanged a few words with her grandfather, helped him into the front seat and put their luggage in the boot, ushered her into the back and, without more ado, set off.

There was little traffic on the road. Just before they reached Henley, Sir Colin turned off on to a narrow road running between high hedges which led downhill into Turville. Eustacia saw with delight the black and white timbers of the Bull and Butcher Inn as they reached the village, drove round the small village green with its fringe of old cottages, past the church and down a very narrow lane with meadows on one side and a high flint wall on the other. The lane turned abruptly and they drove through an open gateway into a short, circular drive leading to a long, low house with many latticed windows and a stout wooden door, the whole enmeshed in dormant Virginia creeper, plumbago and wistaria. It would be a heavenly sight in the summer months, she thought; it was a delightful picture in mid-winter with its sparkling white paint and clay-tiled roofing. Sir Colin stopped the car before the door and it was immediately thrown open to allow the two boys to rush out, shouting with delight.

Sir Colin got out, opened Eustacia's door and helped her out, and left her to receive the exuberant greetings of the little boys while he went to help her grandfather. A grey-haired man came out of the door to join him. 'Ah, Samways, here are Mr and Miss Crump.' And, as he smiled and bowed slightly, Sir Colin went on, 'Pipe down, you two, and give a hand with the luggage.'

He had a quiet, almost placid voice and Eustacia saw that they did as they were told without demur. They all went indoors to the hall, which was wide and long with pale walls and a thick carpet underfoot. The graceful curved staircase faced them, flanked by a green baize door on the one side and on the other a glass door with a view of the garden beyond. It was

pleasantly warm and fragrant with the scent of the hyacinths in the bowl on a delicate little wall-table.

Sir Colin said in his quiet voice, 'Samways, if you
would show Mr Crump to his room…' He paused as
the baize door opened and a small, stout woman bustled through. 'Ah, Mrs Samways, will you take Miss
Crump to her room? And if we all meet for tea in ten
minutes or so?'

Eustacia watched her grandfather go off happily
with Samways and then, with Mrs Samways leading
the way and the two boys following behind, she went
up the staircase. There was a wide landing at its top
with passages leading from it, and Mrs Samways took
the left-hand one, to open a door at its end. 'The boys
are just next door,' she explained. 'They have their
own bathroom on the other side.' She led the way
across the large, low-ceilinged room and opened another door. 'This is your bathroom, Miss Crump.'

It was all quite beautiful, its furniture of yew, the
walls and carpets the colour of cream, the curtains and
bedspread of chintz in pale, vague colours. Eustacia
was sure that she would sleep soundly in the pretty
bed, and to wake up each morning with such a glori-
ous view from her windows…

'It's lovely,' she murmured, and peeped into the
bathroom, which was as charming in its way as the
bedroom with its faintly pink tiles and piles of thick
towels. She gave a sigh of pure pleasure and turned to
the boys. 'I'm glad you're next door. Do you wake
early?'

'Yes,' said Oliver, 'and now you're here, perhaps we can go for a walk before breakfast?'

'Just listen to the boy,' said Mrs Samways comfortably, 'mad to go out so early in the day. Not that I've anything against that, but what with getting the breakfast and one thing and another I've not had the time to see to them...'

'I'm sure you haven't,' said Eustacia, 'but if Sir Colin doesn't mind and we won't be bothering you, we might go for a quick walk as long as it doesn't upset the way you like to run the house, Mrs Samways.'

'My dear life, it'll be a treat to have someone here to be with the boys. Now I'll just go and fetch in the tea and you can come down as soon as you're ready.' She ushered the boys out ahead of her and left Eustacia, who wasted five minutes going round her room, slowly this time, savouring all its small luxuries: a shelf of books, magazines on the bedside table with a tin of biscuits and a carafe of water, roomy cupboards built into the wall, large enough to take her small wardrobe several times over, a velvet-covered armchair by the window with a bowl of spring flowers on a table by it. She sat down before the triple mirror on the dressing-table and did her face and hair and then, suddenly aware that she might be keeping everyone waiting, hurried down the stairs. The boys' voices led her to a door to one side of the hall and she pushed it open and went in. They were all in there, sitting round a roaring fire with Moses stretched out with his head on his master's feet, and a portly ginger cat sitting beside him.

Sir Colin and the boys got to their feet when they saw her, and she was urged to take a chair beside her grandfather.

'You are comfortable in your room?' asked Sir Colin.

'My goodness, yes. It's one of the loveliest rooms I've ever seen.' She beamed at him. 'And the view from the window…'

'Delightful, isn't it? Will you pour the tea, and may I call you Eustacia? The boys would like to call you that too, if you don't mind?'

'Of course I don't mind.'

She got up and went to the rent table where the tea things had been laid out, and her grandfather said, 'This is really quite delightful, but I feel that I am imposing; I have no right to be here.'

'There you are mistaken,' observed Sir Colin. 'I have been wondering if you might care to have the boys for an hour each morning. Not lessons, but if you would hear them read and keep them up to date with the world in general, and I am sure that there have been events in your life well worth recounting.'

Mr Crump looked pleased. 'As a younger man I had an eventful life,' he admitted. 'When I was in India—'

'Elephants—rajas,' chorused the boys, and Sir Colin said blandly,

'You see? They are avid for adventure. Will you give it a try?'

'Oh, with the greatest of pleasure.' Mr Crump accepted his tea and all at once looked ten years younger. 'It will be a joy to have an interest…'

Eustacia threw Sir Colin a grateful glance; he had said and done exactly the right thing, and by some good chance he had hit on exactly the right subject. Her grandfather had been in India and Burma during the 1940-45 war, and as a young officer and later as a colonel he had had enough adventures to last him a lifetime. He had stayed on in India for some years after the war had ended, for he had married while he'd been out there, and when he and her grandmother had returned to England her father had been a small schoolboy.

'I am in your debt—the boys won't be fit for school for a week or two. I hope they won't be too much of a handful for you both. It is a great relief to me that they can stay here in the country.' He looked at Eustacia. 'You won't find it too quiet here?'

She shook her head. 'Oh, no, there's such a lot to do in the country.'

They finished their tea in an atmosphere of friendly agreement, and when the tea things had been cleared away by Samways they gathered round the table and played Scrabble until Sir Colin blandly suggested that the boys should have their supper and go to bed. A signal for Eustacia to go with them, to a small, cosy room at the back of the rambling house and sit with them while they ate it. It seemed obvious to her that she was expected to take up her duties then and there, and so she accompanied them upstairs to bed after they had wished their uncle and her grandfather goodnight.

Getting ready for bed was a long-drawn-out business with a great deal of toing and froing between the bathroom and their bedroom and a good deal of laughing and scampering about. But finally they were in their beds and Eustacia tucked them in, kissed them goodnight and turned off all but a small night-light by the fireplace.

'We shall like having you here,' said Oliver as she went to the door. 'We would like you to stay forever, Eustacia.'

'I shall like being here with you,' she assured him. To stay forever would be nice too, she reflected as she went to her room and tidied her hair and powdered her flushed face. She was a little surprised at the thought, a pointless one, she reminded herself, for as soon as the boys' parents returned she would have to find another job. It would be a mistake to get too attached to the children or the house. Perhaps it would be a good idea if she didn't look too far ahead but just enjoyed the weeks to come.

She went back to the drawing-room and found Sir Colin alone, and she hesitated at the door. 'Oh, I'll go and help my grandfather unpack...'

'Presently, perhaps? I shall have to leave early tomorrow morning, so we might have a little talk now while we have the opportunity.'

She sat down obediently and he got up and went over to a side-table. 'Will you have a glass of sherry?' He didn't wait for her answer, but poured some and brought it over to her before sitting down again, a glass in his hand.

'You are, I believe, a sensible young woman—keep your eye on the boys, and if you aren't happy about them, if their coughs don't clear up, let me know. Make sure that they sleep and don't rush around getting too hot. I'm being fussy, but they have had badly infected chests and I feel responsible for them. You will find the Samwayses towers of strength, but they're elderly and I don't expect them to be aware of the children's health. They are relieved that you will be here and you can call upon them for anything you may need. I shall do my best to come down at weekends and you can always phone me.'

He smiled at her, and she had the feeling that she would put up with a good deal just to please him. She squashed it immediately, for she strongly suspected that he was a man who got his own way once he had made up his mind to it.

She said in her forthright way, 'Yes, Sir Colin, I'll do my best for the boys too. Is there anything special you would want me to know about them?'

He shook his head. 'No—they're normal small boys, full of good spirits, not over-clean, bursting with energy and dreadfully untidy.'

'I've had no experience—' began Eustacia uncertainly.

'Then here is your chance. They both think you're smashing, so they tell me, which I imagine gives you the edge.'

He smiled at her very kindly and she smiled back, hoping secretly that she would live up to his good opinion of her.

Her grandfather came in then and presently they crossed the hall to the dining-room with its mahogany table and chairs and tawny walls hung with gilt-framed paintings. Eustacia sat quietly, listening to the two men talking while she ate the delicious food served to her. Mrs Samways might not be much to look at but she was a super cook.

They went back to the drawing-room for their coffee and presently she wished them goodnight and took herself off to bed, first going in search of her grandfather's room, a comfortable apartment right by the Samwayses' own quarters. He hadn't unpacked so she did that quickly, made sure that he had everything that he might need and went upstairs to her own room.

The boys were asleep; she had a bath and got into bed and went to sleep herself.

She was wakened by a plump, cheerful girl, who put a tray of tea down by the bed, told her that it was going to be a fine day and that her name was Polly, and went away again. Eustacia drank her tea with all the pleasure of someone to whom it was an unexpected luxury, put on her dressing-gown and went off to see if the boys were awake.

They were, sitting on top of their beds, oblivious to the cold, playing some mysterious game with what she took to be plastic creatures from outer space. Invited to join them, she did so and was rewarded by their loud-voiced opinions that for a girl she was quite bright, a compliment she accepted with modesty while at the same time suggesting that it might be an idea if they all had their breakfast.

She made sure that their clothes were to hand and went away to get herself dressed, and presently returned to cast an eye over hands and hair and retie shoelaces without fuss. They looked well enough, she decided, although they were both coughing. 'I'd quite like to go for a walk after breakfast,' she observed casually. 'I mean a proper walk, not on the road.'

Breakfast was a cheerful meal, with Samways hovering with porridge, bacon and scrambled eggs, and her grandfather, after a good night's sleep, willing to recount some of his youthful adventures. Eustacia left them presently, went upstairs and made their beds and tidied the rooms, did the same for her grandfather and then went to remind the boys that they were going to take her for a walk.

'There's a windmill,' she reminded them. 'It doesn't look too far away—I'd love to see it.'

She had hit on something with which to interest them mightily. Had she seen the film *Chitty Chitty Bang Bang*? they wanted to know, because that was the very windmill in it. They walked there briskly and returned to the house for hot cocoa and an hour's reading before lunch. The afternoon was spent with her grandfather and she was able to spend an hour on her own until Mrs Samways suggested that she might like to look round the house. It was quite large and rambled a good deal. 'Rather a lot to look after,' observed Eustacia, peering at family portraits in the library.

'Ah, but there's two good girls who come up from the village each day, and Sir Colin comes mostly at weekends and then not always... He brings a few guests from time to time and we have Christmas here, of course. He's not all that keen on London. But there he's a clever gentleman and that's where he works. I dare say if he were to marry—and dear knows I hope and pray he does, for a nicer man never stepped—he'd live here most of the time. London isn't a place for children.'

Eustacia murmured gently; she realised that Mrs Samways was doing her an honour by talking about her employer and she was glad that the housekeeper seemed to like her. It hadn't entered her head that making the beds and tidying up after the boys had endeared her to Mrs Samways' heart. 'That's a nice young lady,' she had informed her husband. 'What's more she gets on with the boys and they listen to her, more than they ever did with me.'

They had their tea in a pleasant little room at the back of the house and gathered round the table afterwards to play cards until the boys' supper and bedtime. Eustacia tucked them in finally, listening rather worriedly to their coughs, although neither of them were feverish. They had certainly eaten with youthful gusto and, by the time she had got out their clean clothes for the morning and gone to her own room to tidy herself, they were sound asleep, their nice, naughty-little-boy faces as peaceful as those of small angels.

After dinner she sat with her grandfather in the drawing-room, listening to his contented talk. He hadn't been so happy for a long time, and it reminded her of his dull existence at their flat in London; this was like a new lease of life to him. Her thoughts flew ahead to the future when the boys' parents would return and she would know that she was no longer needed. Well, she reflected, she would have to find another job similar somewhere in the country and never go back to London. She had said goodnight to her grandfather and had seen him to his room and was on the point of going upstairs when the phone rang as she was turning out the drawing-room lights.

She picked it up hesitantly, not sure if this was something the Samwayses would consider to be their prerogative, and indeed Mr Samways appeared just as she was lifting the receiver.

'I'm sorry—I should have left it for you.'

He smiled at her in a fatherly fashion. 'That's all right, miss, I dare say it will be Sir Colin.' He took the receiver from her and said in a different, impersonal voice, 'Sir Colin Crichton's residence,' and then, 'Good evening, sir. Yes, Miss Crump is here.'

He smiled again as he handed her the phone.

Sir Colin's voice came very clearly over the line. 'Eustacia? You don't mind if I call you that? The day has gone well?'

'Yes, thank you, sir. They have been very good and they went to bed and to sleep at once.' She gave him a brief, businesslike resumé of their day. 'They both cough a great deal...'

'Don't worry about that, that should clear up now they're away from London. I'll look them over when I come down. You and your grandfather have settled in?'

'Yes, thank you. Grandfather has just gone to his room. I think that he is a very happy man, sir…'

'And you, Eustacia?'

'I'm happy too, thank you, sir.'

'Good, and be kind enough to stop calling me sir with every breath.'

'Oh, very well, Sir Colin. I'll try and remember.'

He sounded as though he was laughing as he wished her goodnight and rang off.

The week went by, delightful days filled with walks, visits to the village shop, an hour or so of what Eustacia hoped was useful study with the boys and afternoons spent helping Mrs Samways with the flowers, the linen and such small tasks that the housekeeper didn't allow the maids to do, while the boys spent a blissful hour with her grandfather.

It was, thought Eustacia, too good to be true. And she was right.

Sir Colin had phoned on the Saturday morning to say that since he had an evening engagement he wouldn't be down until Sunday morning.

'I expect he's going to take Gloria out to dinner,' said Oliver. 'She's keen on him…'

Eustacia suppressed a wish to know more about Gloria and said quellingly, 'I don't think we should discuss your uncle's friends, my dear. You can stay up an hour later this evening because you always do, don't you? But no later. I dare say he'll be here quite soon after breakfast.'

The boys complained, but only mildly; she swept them upstairs to bed with only token arguments against the harshness of her edict and, with the promise that she would call them in good time in the morning just in case their uncle decided to come for breakfast, she left them to go to sleep. Her grandfather went to bed soon after them and, since there was no one to talk to and the Samwayses had gone out for the evening and wouldn't be back until late, she locked up carefully, mindful of Mr Samways' instructions about leaving the bolts undone on the garden door so that he could use his key to get in, and took herself off to bed.

She didn't hurry over her bath, and finally when she was ready for bed she opened one of the books on her bedside table, got into bed, and settled down for an hour of reading. It was an exciting book, and she was still reading it an hour later when she heard the telephone ringing.

It was almost midnight and the Samwayses weren't back yet; she bundled on her dressing-gown and went silently downstairs to the extension in the hall. She was in two minds as to whether to answer it—it was too late for a social call and it could be one of those heavy-breathing types... She lifted the receiver slowly and said austerely, 'Yes?'

'Got you out of bed?' enquired Sir Colin. 'Eustacia, I'm now on my way to Turville. I'll be with you in half an hour. Are the Samwayses back?'

'No.' There had been something about his voice. 'Is there something the matter? Is something wrong?'

'Very wrong. I'll tell you when I get home. If you have locked up I'll come in through the garden door.'

He hung up before she could say anything more.

She left the light on in the hall and went along to the kitchen, where she put the coffee on the Aga and laid up a tray with a cup and saucer, sugar and cream, and while she did that she wondered what could have happened. An accident with his car? A medical report about one or both of the boys?

She shuffled around the kitchen, peering in cupboards looking for biscuits—he would probably be hungry. She had just found them when she heard the car, and a moment later his quiet footfall coming along the passage towards the kitchen.

He was wearing a dinner-jacket and he threw the coat he was carrying on to a chair as he came in. He nodded to her without speaking and went to warm his hands at the Aga, and when she asked, 'Coffee, Sir Colin?' he answered harshly,

'Later,' and turned to face her.

It was something terrible, she guessed, looking at his face, calm and rigid with held-back feelings. She said quietly, 'Will you sit down and tell me? You'll feel better if you can talk about it.'

He smiled a little although he didn't sit down. 'I had a telephone call just as I was about to leave my London house this evening. My brother and his wife have been killed in a car accident.'

CHAPTER THREE

EUSTACIA looked at Sir Colin in horror. 'Oh, how awful—I am sorry!' Her gentle mouth shook and she bit her lip. 'The boys…they're so very small.' She went up to him and put a hand on his arm. 'Is there anything that I can do to help?'

She looked quite beautiful with her hair loose around her shoulders, bundled into her dressing-gown—an unglamorous garment bought for its long-lasting capacity—her face pale with shock and distress, longing to comfort him.

He looked down at her and then at her hand on his arm. His eyes were hard and cold, and she snatched her hand away as though she had burnt it and went to the Aga and poured the coffee into a cup. She should have known better, of course; she was someone filling a gap until circumstances suited him to make other arrangements. He wouldn't want her sympathy, a stranger in his home; he wasn't a man to show his feelings, especially to someone he hardly knew. She felt the hot blood wash over her face and felt thankful that he wouldn't notice it.

She asked him in her quiet voice, 'Would you like your coffee here or in your study, Sir Colin?'

'Oh, here, thank you. Go to bed, it's late.'

She gave a quick look at his stony face and went

without a word. In her room she sat on the bed, still in her dressing-gown, going over the past half-hour in her mind. She wondered why she had been telephoned by him; there had been no need, it wasn't as if he had wanted to talk to her—quite the reverse. And to talk helped, she knew that from her own grief and shock when her parents had died. It was a pity that he had no wife in whom he could confide. There was that girl the boys had talked about, but perhaps he had been on his own when he'd had the news.

She sighed and shivered a little, cold and unhappy, and then jumped with fright when there was a tap on the door and, before she could answer it, Sir Colin opened it and came in.

He looked rigidly controlled, but the iciness had gone from his voice. 'You must forgive me, Eustacia—I behaved badly. I am most grateful for your sympathy, and I hope you will overlook my rudeness—it was unintentional.'

'Well of course it was, and there's nothing to forgive. Would you like to sit down and talk about it?' Her voice was warm and friendly, but carefully unemotional. 'It's the suddenness, isn't it?'

She was surprised when he did sit down. 'I was just leaving the house—I had a dinner date—we were standing in the hall while Grimstone, my butler, fetched my—my companion's handbag. When the phone rang I answered it but I wasn't really listening; we had been laughing about something or other. It was a long-distance call from Brunei. Whoever it was at the other end told me twice before I realised...' He paused, and when he went on she guessed that he was leaving something out. 'I had to get away, but I wanted to talk about it too. I got into the car and drove here and I'm not sure why I phoned you on the way.'

'Tell me about it,' said Eustacia quietly, 'and then you can decide what has to be done. Once that's settled you can sleep for a little while.'

'I shall have to fly there and arrange matters.' He glanced at his watch. 'It is too late now…'

'First thing in the morning.'

His smile shook her. 'What a sensible girl you are. I have to tell the boys before I go.' He looked at her. 'You'll stay?'

'As long as I'm needed. Tell me about your brother and his wife.'

'He was younger than I, but he married when he was twenty-three. He was an architect, a good one, with an international reputation. He and Sadie, his wife, travelled a good deal. The boys usually went with them, but this time they weren't too happy about taking them to the Far East. They were to go for three months and I had the boys—their nanny came with them but her mother was taken ill and she had to leave. Mrs Samways has done her best and so has my cook, Miss Grimstone. It was most fortunate that we made your acquaintance and that the boys took to you at once.'

'Yes. It helps, I hope. Now, we are going to the kitchen again and I'm going to make a pot of tea and a plate of toast and you will have those and then go to bed. When you've slept for a few hours you will be able to talk to the boys and arrange whatever has to be arranged.'

'You are not only sensible but practical too.'

It was after two o'clock by the time she got to bed, having made sure that Sir Colin had gone his room. She didn't sleep for some time, and when she got up just after six o'clock she looked a wreck.

The boys were still sleeping and the house was quiet. She padded down to the kitchen and put the kettle on. A cup of tea would help her to start what was going to be a difficult day. She was warming the teapot when Sir Colin joined her. He was dressed and shaved and immaculately turned out, and he looked to be in complete control of his feelings.

'Did you sleep?' asked Eustacia, forgetting to add the 'Sir Colin' bit. And when he nodded, 'Good—will you have a cup of tea? The boys aren't awake yet. When do you plan to tell them?'

He stood there, drinking his tea, studying her; she was one of the few girls who could look beautiful in an old dressing-gown and with no make-up first thing in the morning, and somehow the sight of her comforted him. 'Could we manage to get through breakfast? If I tell them before that they won't want to eat— we must try and keep to the usual day's routine.'

'Yes, of course. May I tell Grandfather before breakfast? He is a light sleeper and there's just the chance he heard the car last night and he might mention it and wonder why you came.'

'A good point; tell him by all means. Samways will be down in a few minutes, and I'll tell him. He was fond of my brother...' He put down his cup. 'I shall be in the study if I'm wanted.'

She did the best she could to erase the almost sleepless night from her face, thankful that her grandfather had taken her news quietly and with little comment save the one that he had heard the car during the night and had known that someone was up and talking softly. Satisfied that she couldn't improve her appearance further, she went to wake the boys.

'Have you got a cold?' asked Teddy.

'Me? No. I never get colds. But I didn't go to sleep very early. I had such an exciting book...'

They discussed the pleasures of reading in bed as they dressed, and presently the three of them went downstairs and into the dining-room.

Sir Colin was sitting at the table, a plate of porridge before him, reading his post; her grandfather was leafing through the Guardian. The scene was completely normal and just for a moment Eustacia wondered if she had dreamed the night's happenings.

The boys rushed over and hugged their uncle, both talking at once. When he had come? they wanted to know. And how long was he going to stay and would he go for a walk with them?

He answered them cheerfully, begged them to sit down and eat their breakfast, bade Eustacia good morning, asked her if she would like coffee or tea and got up to fetch it for her.

Eustacia, pecking away at a breakfast she didn't want, wondered how he did it. That he was grief-stricken at the death of his brother and sister-in-law had been evident when he had talked to her but now, looking at his calm face, she marvelled at his self-control. The meal was a leisurely one and it wasn't until they had all finished that Sir Colin said, 'Eustacia, bring the boys along to the study, will you? We'll leave Mr Crump to read his paper in peace.'

He told them very simply; she marvelled at the manner in which he broke the awful news to them with a gentle gravity and a simplicity which the boys could understand. Teddy burst into tears and ran and buried his head in her lap and she held him close, but Oliver asked, 'Will they come home, Uncle?'

'Yes. I am going to fetch them.' He smiled at the child and Oliver went to him and took his hand. 'Will you look after us, Uncle? And Eustacia?'

'Of course. This will be your home and we shall be a family...'

'Mummy and Daddy wouldn't mind if you and Eustacia look after us?'

'No.' The big man's voice was very gentle. 'I think they would like that above all things.'

He put an arm round the little boy and held him close, and Eustacia, unashamedly crying while she comforted Teddy, accepted the future thrust upon her. The boys liked her, and for a time at least she could in some small way fill the immense gap in their lives. Further than that she wouldn't look for the moment.

Presently Sir Colin said, 'You know, I think a walk would do us all good. Don't you agree, Eustacia? I must get to Heathrow by two o'clock, so we can have an early lunch. I shall be gone perhaps two or three days, but you will be quite safe with Eustacia and when I get back we will have a family discussion.'

'They're safe in heaven?' Teddy wanted to know.

'Of course they are,' Sir Colin answered promptly. 'It's rather like going into another room and closing the door, if you see what I mean.'

They walked briskly up to the windmill and back again and he kept the talk deliberately on their mother and father, using a matter-of-fact tone of voice which somehow made the sadness easier to bear. Presently they sat down to an early lunch and then they waved him off in his car.

He had taken a few minutes of his time to speak to Eustacia. 'You can manage?' It was more a statement than a question. 'Very soon it will hit them hard.' His eyes searched her face. 'I believe you will be able to cope.'

She said steadily, 'Oh, yes. My parents died in a plane crash a few years ago, so I do know how they feel.'

'I didn't know. I'm sorry. You are sure…?'

'Quite sure, Sir Colin. I hope your journey will go well.'

He said softly, 'You are not only beautiful, you are a tower of strength.'

She reminded herself of that during the next few days, for just as he had warned her the boys were stricken with a childish grief, with floods of tears and wakeful nights, sudden bursts of rage and no wish to eat. It was on the third day after he had gone that he telephoned while they sat at lunch. Samways had brought the telephone to the table and given her a relieved smile. 'It's Sir Colin, Miss Crump.'

She hadn't realised just how much she had been hoping to hear from him. His voice was calm in her ear. 'Eustacia? I'm flying home in an hour's time. I'll be with you some time tomorrow. How are the boys?'

'Absolute Trojans. You'd be proud of them. Can you spare a moment to say hello?'

When they had spoken to their uncle and he had rung off, Oliver asked, 'What's a Trojan, Eustacia?'

'A very brave, strong man, my dear.'

'Like Uncle Colin?'

'Exactly like him. Aren't you lucky to have him for an uncle?'

'When I grow up,' said Teddy, 'I shall be just like him.'

'What a splendid idea, darling.'

'And I shall be like Daddy,' said Oliver, and although his lip trembled he didn't cry.

'Of course, he'll be proud of you.' She glanced at her grandfather. 'It's still raining, so how about a game of Scrabble? Let's see if we can beat Grandfather.'

She was becoming adept at keeping the boys occupied and interested. Walking, she had quickly found out, was something they liked doing, and since she had spent a good deal of her childhood in the country she was able to name birds, tell weeds from wild flowers and argue the difference between a water-vole's hole and that of a water-rat. Even on a wet morning such as it had been she managed to keep them amused, first with Scrabble and then after lunch with painting and drawing until teatime. They spent the time before bed cleaning their bikes while Eustacia did the same to Mrs Samways' elderly model, which she had been allowed to borrow. She wasn't too keen on cycling— it was years since she had ridden a bike and, although Samways had assured her that once one had learned to ride one never forgot, she wasn't too happy about it. She wasn't too happy about the skateboards either; if it was a fine morning, she had promised to try one out under the expert eyes of the boys and, although she was prepared to do anything to keep them from the grief which threatened to engulf them from time to time, she wasn't looking forward to it. But there would be no one to see her making a fool of herself, she reflected, and if she made the boys laugh so much the better.

As it turned out, she did rather better than she had expected; the boys were experts, turning and twisting with the fearlessness of the young, but they were patient with her while she wobbled her way down the slope at the back of the house, waving her arms wildly and tumbling over before she reached the bottom. They yelled and shrieked and laughed at her and did a turn themselves, showing off their expertise, and then finally she managed to reach the end of the slope still upright on her board and puffed up with pride. She did it again, only this time she began to lose her balance as she reached the end of the slope. Waving her arms wildly with the boys shouting with laughter, she fell into the arms of Sir Colin, who most fortuitously appeared at that moment to block her path. He received her person with ease, set her upright and said, 'What a nice way to be welcomed home.'

Eustacia disentangled herself, red in the face. 'Oh, we didn't know—good afternoon, Sir Colin, we're skateboarding...' She stopped, aware of a pleasant surge of delight at the sight of him and, at the same time, of the inanity of her remarks.

He didn't answer her, for the boys had rushed to meet him, and thankfully she collected the skateboards and started to walk back to the house. They would have a lot to say to each other and it would give her time to regain her normally calm manner.

Sir Colin left again on the following day; his brother had lived in London when he hadn't been travelling abroad, and his affairs had to be set in order and the funeral arranged. He told Eustacia this in an impersonal manner which didn't allow her to utter anything warmer than a polite murmur. In his calm face there was no trace of the man who had come to her room and talked as though they were friends.

'When I return we must have a talk,' he told her. 'The boys' future must be discussed.'

She was surprised that he should wish to discuss it with her; she had already said that she was willing to stay with the boys until such time as permanent arrangements had been made. Perhaps he no longer wanted her and her grandfather to remain at his house; it had been a temporary arrangement and he could hardly have envisaged their permanent residence there.

She said, 'Very well, Sir Colin,' and watched him drive away in his Rolls-Royce. There was no point in speculating about the future until he chose to tell her what he intended to do.

He returned three days later, and not alone. A middle-aged couple, his sister-in-law's parents, were with him as well as an older lady who greeted the boys with affection and then held out her hand to Eustacia.

'You must be Eustacia. My son has told me what a great help you have been to him during these last few days.'

She was tall and rather stout, but not as tall as Eustacia. She was elegantly dressed and good-looking and her eyelids drooped over eyes as blue as her son's. Eustacia liked her, but she wasn't sure that she liked the other guests. They greeted the boys solemnly and the woman burst into tears as she embraced Teddy, who wriggled in her arms.

'Mother, you have already introduced yourself—Mrs Kennedy and Mr Kennedy, my sister-in-law's parents. They will be spending a day or so here before they go back to Yorkshire.'

Clearly they regarded her as a member of the staff, nodding hastily before they turned back to the boys. Mrs Kennedy uttered little cries of, 'My poor darling boys, motherless. Oh, my dearest Sadie—the awful shock—how can I go on living? But I must, for someone must look after you...'

Mrs Crichton tapped her briskly on the shoulder. 'Dry your eyes, Freda, and endeavour to be cheerful.' She eased the two boys away from their maternal grandparents and marched them into the house. 'I'd like my tea,' Eustacia heard her say and Samways, as if on cue, appeared with a loaded tray.

Mrs Samways led the ladies away to their rooms and then Eustacia, bidden by Sir Colin, poured the tea, settled the boys with sandwiches and cake and handed plates. Mrs Crichton evinced no surprise at the sight of Eustacia sitting behind the teapot, but Mrs Kennedy raised her eyebrows and made a moue of disbelief. 'I thought this was to be a family conference,' she observed.

Sir Colin glanced at her, his face blandly polite, his eyes hidden by the heavy lids. 'Which it is, but I think we might have tea first. Mr Baldock will be here very shortly with Peter's will. In the meanwhile shall we hear what the boys have been doing with themselves?' He glanced at Eustacia. 'Any more walks to the windmill?'

She nodded. 'Oliver, do tell about the rabbits…'

He embarked on a long account of the animals they had seen and Teddy, his tears forgotten, joined in. 'And we had another go with the skateboards,' said Oliver. 'Eustacia stayed on twice, she's not bad for a girl.'

Mrs Kennedy drew a deep breath. 'But surely, today of all days, they should have been—?'

She wasn't allowed to finish—Mrs Crichton said rapidly, 'I've always wanted to go on one of those things. Is it difficult, Eustacia?'

'Very, Mrs Crichton, but such fun. The boys are very good, I don't know who showed them how—Sir Colin, perhaps?'

She hadn't meant the question seriously, but he answered at once. 'Indeed I did. I consider myself pretty good. Once we have perfected Eustacia's technique I think we must persuade Mr and Mrs Samways...'

A remark which set the boys rolling around with laughter, and Mrs Kennedy's expression became even more disapproving. She looked at her husband, who cleared his throat and began, 'The boys—' but got no further, for Samways announced Mr Baldock.

He was elderly, tall and thin and wore old-fashioned pince-nez attached to his severe black coat by a cord, but his eyes were very alive and he had a surprisingly loud voice. Sir Colin got up to greet him while Samways fetched fresh tea. 'You know everyone, I believe, except Miss Eustacia Crump, who is my right hand and a tower of strength and common sense.'

He shook her hand and took a good look at her. 'A very pretty name and certainly a very pretty girl,' he observed. 'You are indeed fortunate.' He added thoughtfully, 'Small boys can be the very devil.'

She agreed composedly. 'But they are great fun too—they see things one overlooks when one is grown-up.'

'Intelligent, too.' He sat down, accepted a cup of tea and made light conversation about this and that, never once alluding to the funeral they had all attended earlier that day. Not an easy matter, for Mrs Kennedy tried her best to turn the cheerful tea-party into a wake.

Tea things cleared, Eustacia rose, intent on making an unobtrusive exit with the boys. She was hindered, however, by Sir Colin. 'Take the boys along to Mrs Samways, Eustacia, and come back here, will you?'

She gave him an enquiring look and he smiled and added, 'Please?'

She slipped back into the room and Sir Colin looked round and smiled again as she sat down a little to one side of the gathering.

'Good. Will you start, Mr Baldock?' Sir Colin sat back, his long legs stretched out before him, and smiled at his mother.

The will was brief and very much to the point. Sir Colin was to be the legal guardian of Oliver and Teddy, assisted as he might think fit by some suitable person or persons and should he marry it was hoped that his wife would become a guardian also. The bulk of the estate went to the boys in trust, but there were legacies for members of the family and various directions as to the selling of property.

Mr Baldock smoothed the pages neatly and took off his pince-nez. 'A very sensible document, if I may be allowed to say so. And quite straightforward.'

'But it's ridiculous,' exclaimed Mrs Kennedy. 'I have every right to have the boys, they are my grandchildren—'

'They are also mine,' said Mrs Crichton briskly, 'but I don't consider that any of us has a right to them. Colin is very well fitted to bring them up, and if he should marry they will have brothers and sisters as any normal child would like to have.'

'But Colin has no time—he's at that hospital all

hours of the day and he's always travelling from one place to another; the boys will be left to servants—'

'They will be in the care of Eustacia, whom they happen to have developed a deep affection for. She has promised to stay and care for them and, despite my work, I do spend my evenings and nights at home. As soon as they are perfectly fit they will go back to school like any other small boys, and if it is possible they will come with me should I have a lecture tour or seminars.'

'And this—this Eustacia? Will she go with you?' Mrs Kennedy was plum-coloured with temper.

He gave her a cold look from eyes suddenly icy. 'Of course. Much as I enjoy their company, I am not conversant with their wants. If Mr Baldock agrees to this arrangement as the other executor of the will, I think that it will work perfectly.'

'Do you intend to marry in the foreseeable future?' asked Mr Kennedy.

Sir Colin said, 'Yes,' without a moment's hesitation, and Eustacia felt a distinct pang of regret. And very silly too—she gave herself a metaphorical shake—there was no earthly reason why she should concern herself with Sir Colin's private life.

'And until such time as this should occur,' said Mr Baldock, 'you are willing to remain as surrogate mother to Oliver and Teddy?' He studied her over his glasses and gave a little nod of approval.

'Yes, I told Sir Colin that I would stay as long as I am needed, and if you wish me to do so I will repeat my promise.'

'No need, my dear young lady. I perceive that you are eminently suitable for the post.' He glanced across to Mrs Crichton. 'You agree with me, Mrs Crichton?'

'Absolutely. And I am sure that Mr and Mrs Kennedy will give their approval. The boys are fortunate in having grandparents living in such a lovely part of Yorkshire—think of the holidays they will enjoy...'

Mrs Kennedy dabbed her eyes with a handkerchief. 'I still think that it is against human nature...'

Everyone looked rather puzzled until Sir Colin said kindly, 'But you must agree that Peter—and I'm sure that Sadie would have agreed with him—was thinking of the boys and their future. I must state the obvious and point out that when they are still young men I shall, hopefully, be here to act as their guardian, whereas you may no longer be with us.'

'Well, really,' exclaimed Mrs Kennedy, 'what a thing to say.' She caught her husband's eye. 'Though that may be true enough. They must come to us for holidays.'

'Of course, and you both know that you are always welcome at my home. I was fond of Sadie and it is a consolation to know that they were devoted to each other and the boys. We must all do our best to continue that devotion.'

From anyone else it would have sounded pompous, reflected Eustacia, but Sir Colin had uttered the words in a calm and unhurried voice and moreover had sounded quite cheerful.

'Eustacia, would you fetch the boys here, please?

And how about a drink before dinner? You'll stay, of course, Mr Baldock? Samways will drive you back to town.'

Eustacia ushered the boys into the drawing-room and slid away to find her grandfather. He was in his room, sitting before a cosy little fire, enjoying a late tea. He bent a patient ear to her account of the family gathering and agreed with her that she had no option but to stay with the boys.

'Their granny and grandpa from Yorkshire don't like the idea,' she explained, 'they don't like me; they want the boys with them but they had to agree to the will. I don't think Sir Colin's mother minds; she's nice and she's sad, but she didn't let the boys see that...'

She went away presently to be told that as a great treat the boys were to stay up for dinner. Sir Colin, when he told her, didn't mention that Mrs Kennedy had expressed annoyance at the idea of Eustacia's dining with them; she had made the mistake of saying so in front of the boys, who had instantly chorused that if Eustacia couldn't be there, they didn't want to be there either.

Sir Colin, a tactful man, smoothed frayed tempers and presently they all sat down to dinner, during which he kept the conversation firmly in his hands, aided by his mother, not allowing Mrs Kennedy to dwell on the unhappy circumstances which had brought them together that day. And after the meal, when Eustacia had bidden everyone goodnight and borne the boys off to their beds, he played the perfect host until Mr Baldock declared that he must go home and Mr and Mrs

Kennedy retired to bed, for they were to stay the night. Only when he was alone with his mother did Sir Colin allow his bland mask to fall.

'Not the happiest of days, my dear,' he observed. 'I would wish that we could have been alone—there has been no chance to talk about Peter. I shall miss him and so will you. You have been very brave, Mother, and a great help. It is a pity that the Kennedys can't see that the boys are more important than anything else.'

'I never liked the woman,' said Mrs Crichton forthrightly. 'I like that young woman, Eustacia, and the boys like her too. She will be able to give them the comfort they'll need. I must get to know her.' She stood up. 'I'm going to bed now, my dear—don't sit here grieving.'

He stood up and kissed her cheek. 'You'll stay a few days? I'll be free at the weekend, and I'll run you back to Castle Cary—the boys will enjoy the ride.'

At breakfast he was his usual pleasant self, joking with the boys, exchanging opinions with Mr Kennedy about the day's news and listening courteously to Mrs Kennedy's advice about the boys' coughs. Eustacia, watching him when she could, saw the tired lines in his face and the tiny muscle twitching in his cheek. Probably he had slept badly and no wonder, he had had a wretched week and hadn't complained once. That bland, cheerful manner must have cost him something... He looked up and caught her eye and smiled warmly and her heart gave a lurch and she glanced away, feeling uncertain and not knowing why.

The Kennedys went presently after a protracted farewell to the boys, a chilly one to Sir Colin and his mother and a frosty nod to Eustacia. Quite definitely she wasn't liked.

With their departure it was as though a cloud had lifted from the house. Sir Colin stayed for lunch and then went back to the hospital, saying as he went that he would be back at the weekend. 'We'll take Granny back home and see about Moses's leg on Sunday—that plaster is due to come off.'

He kissed his mother, gave the boys an avuncular hug and opened his car door, then turned back to where they were standing outside the door to wave him on his way.

'You will phone me if you are in the least worried about anything, Eustacia.' She was surprised when he went and kissed her swiftly, then he got into his car and drove away.

Eustacia had gone delightfully pink, but a quick glance at her companions showed her that they had either not noticed or they found nothing strange in Sir Colin's behaviour. They went into the house and she told herself that he had been acting out of kindness, not wishing her to feel left out. He had certainly noticed Mrs Kennedy's coldness towards her although he had said nothing.

Mrs Crichton took the boys to the village shop to buy sweets, and Eustacia went along to see her grandfather. He looked up with a smile as she joined him.

'Sir Colin gone? But back at the weekend, he tells me. You are quite happy about this job, my dear? I must say that Mrs Kennedy didn't seem too pleased about it, but really it is a most sensible arrangement at least until such time as the boys are over their grief. Thank heaven that children are so resilient. Am I to continue with our little sessions or are they to be free?'

Eustacia sat down beside him. 'I should think that an hour in the afternoon would be a good idea. Mrs Crichton will be here for the rest of the week and I think she might like to have them to herself in the mornings. She's very fond of them and they love her.'

'A fine woman, and she has a fine son.'

The week passed pleasantly and Eustacia took care to fill the days so that the boys had no time to mope. There were moments of sadness, but comforting and some small treat mitigated those and Mrs Crichton was a great help; she had her son's calmness and a capacity for inventing interesting games. She and Eustacia liked each other and, with her grandfather and the faithful Samways backing them up, Eustacia felt that they had come through a trying two weeks very well.

Sir Colin arrived home on Friday evening. The boys were already in bed but Eustacia, crossing the hall on the way to the dining-room with a tray of glasses as he came in, paused to say that they were still awake and waiting for him.

He crossed the hall, took the tray from her and said, 'Good. How are they?'

'Recovering well. Mrs Crichton has been marvellous with them and they love her very much, don't they?'

'Yes. Why are you carrying trays?'

'Just one tray, Sir Colin. Samways is in the cellar and Mrs Samways can't leave the stove just at the moment.' She took the tray back. 'Your mother is in the drawing-room.'

He nodded and looked faintly amused. 'You will join us with your grandfather? He is well?'

'Yes. Thank you. The boys have had their reading lessons and they're starting on a map of India.'

'Splendid.'

He let her go then and went unhurriedly into his drawing-room where his mother and Moses waited for him.

She was told at breakfast the next day that she would be going to Castle Cary with the boys—something she hadn't expected. 'We'll leave directly after we have had coffee, stop for lunch on the way, have tea there and drive back in the early evening.'

An announcement hailed with delight by the boys and uncertainty by Eustacia.

'Oh, very well, Sir Colin, but I thought you might like to have the boys...'

He smiled his kind smile. 'I'm delighted to have the boys; I'm not sure if I'm qualified to cope with their various needs. Your grandfather assures me that he will very much enjoy a day on his own. The Samwayses will take good care of him.'

They drove down to Henley-on-Thames, through Wokingham and on to the M3, and presently they were on the A303. At Amesbury they stopped for lunch at the Antrobus Hotel, a pleasantly old-fashioned hotel where the boys were listened to with sympathy when they requested sausages and some chips in preference to the more sophisticated menu.

It was a cheerful meal, and they drove on in high spirits until they reached Wincanton and turned off to Castle Cary. Eustacia had never been there and she was enchanted by the mellow stone cottages and the narrow high street lined with small shops.

Mrs Crichton lived in the centre of the small town, in a large Georgian house with a vast front door with its brass knocker and bell. There was no garden before it but the windows were just too high for passers-by to peer in. In any case, Eustacia thought, it was such a dignified house, no one would dare to stare in even if they could.

The door was opened as they got out of the car and a small, stout woman ushered them in, beaming from a rosy-cheeked elderly face.

'Well, madam dear, it's nice to see you back and no mistake. And the two young gentlemen too, and how is Mr Colin?'

'All the better for seeing you, Martha.' He placed a kiss on her cheek. 'This is Eustacia Crump, who is looking after the boys. Eustacia, this is Martha, who has lived with us forever.'

They shook hands and liked each other at once. 'Now, isn't that nice?' observed Martha in her soft Somerset voice.

The house was warm and very welcoming; it was furnished with some lovely old pieces and yet it was lived in and comfortable. Mrs Crichton led the way into a high-ceilinged room overlooking the street. 'I know you can't stay long, but tea will only be a few minutes.'

Eustacia took the boys' coats and caps, took off her own coat and went with them to look at the garden from the big bay window of a room leading out of the sitting-room. It was rather grandly furnished and a Siamese cat was sitting on the rent table by the window. It got up sedately and went to meet Mrs Crichton and they all gathered by the window to look at the garden. It was large, charmingly laid out and walled. Even with local traffic going to and fro the house was very quiet.

'You must come and stay when the weather is warmer,' said Mrs Crichton. 'The Easter holidays, perhaps?' An invitation accepted with enthusiasm by the boys. Eustacia shared their enthusiasm but she didn't say so—she wasn't sure if she was included in the invitation.

They had their tea in a small room at the back of the hall, at a round table near the open fire. The kind of tea little boys liked: muffins swimming in butter, Marmite on toast cut in little fingers, fruit cake and sandwiches and a plate of chocolate biscuits to finish. The boys ate with gusto and so, for that matter, did Sir Colin.

They left soon after tea and this time the boys were strapped into the back seats and Eustacia was bidden to sit in front.

The boys were sleepy by the time they got back; they ate their supper quickly, full of their day and the pleasure of taking Moses to the vet in the morning, but they were too tired to protest when Eustacia bade them say goodnight to their uncle and whisked them upstairs to baths and bed. When she got down again, it was to find Sir Colin gone. An urgent call from St Biddolph's, Samways told her, and he would see her at breakfast. She dined with her grandfather, recounting details of their trip while they ate.

'You didn't mind being on your own, Grandfather?'

'My dear child, it was delightful. I had the leisure to read and write and eat the delicious meals Mrs Samways cooked. I have never been more content. I realise that it cannot last forever, but I am grateful for these weeks of pleasant living.'

They went to the vet's in the morning and Moses had his plaster removed and was allowed, cautiously, to walk on all his legs. After lunch, since Sir Colin said that he had work to do in his study, Eustacia took the boys for a ride on their bikes, mounting guard upon them from the elderly bike which Mrs Samways had lent to her.

They all had tea round the fire and then a rousing game of Snap before the boys had supper and went to bed. Eustacia came down presently to find Sir Colin and her grandfather discussing the boys' schooling, but they broke off when she joined them and Sir Colin got up to fetch her a drink.

'I think that the boys might go back to school in another two weeks,' he told her. 'There is a good prep school on the other side of Turville Heath, only a mile or so away. Can you drive, Eustacia?'

'Yes, but I haven't for several years.'

'Well, there is a Mini in the garage—take it out once or twice and see how you get on. Samways will go with you if you like.'

'I'd rather go alone.'

'I shall be away all this next week but here for the weekend. The following week I have to go to Leiden to give a series of lectures. I'll leave a phone number in case of an emergency but you will find Samways a tower of strength. Your grandfather has most kindly suggested that he should have the boys each morning for easy-going lessons so that they won't feel too strange when they start school.'

They dined in a leisurely fashion, and later when she said goodnight he said, 'I shall be gone by the time you get down in the morning. Enjoy your week, Eustacia.'

She did; the boys had recovered their good spirits and she kept them occupied when they weren't at their lessons. She thought the lessons weren't very serious, for she heard gales of laughter coming from the room where they studied with her grandfather. She told Samways that she was to drive the Mini and he got it from the garage for her and told her of the quietest roads. After the first uncertain minutes, she found that she was enjoying herself hugely. After the first day or two she ventured on to a nearby main road and then drove to the school where the boys were to go, quite confident now.

When Sir Colin came at the weekend she assured him that she felt quite capable of driving the boys, and he said at once, 'Good. Get your coat, we'll go over to the school—I want to see the headmaster.'

Something she hadn't bargained for, but she got into the driver's seat, and since she was a big girl and he was an extremely large man the journey was a cramped one—indeed she found it rather unsettling.

At Sir Colin's request, she went with him and was introduced. 'So that you are known here when you come to fetch the boys,' explained Sir Colin. They went back home presently; the boys were to start school in two weeks' time—after half-term—and she would fetch them each day and ferry them to and fro.

The weekend went too quickly and on Monday morning Sir Colin left again. 'I'll be away for a week, perhaps a little longer—I have friends in Holland and I may stay a day or two with them.'

He hugged the boys, promised that he would bring them something Dutch when he got back, shook Mr Crump's hand and, rather as an afterthought, kissed Eustacia's cheek before he drove himself off.

The house seemed empty without him; he was a quiet man but somehow, reflected Eustacia, one felt content and secure when he was there. The days ahead looked empty. She was vexed with herself for feeling discontented—the calm routine of their days was something to be thankful for.

It was towards the middle of the week that the calm was disrupted.

Mrs Kennedy telephoned quite late one evening; the boys were long since in bed and her grandfather had gone to his room.

'I wish to speak to Sir Colin,' said Mrs Kennedy. 'Is that the maid?'

'Eustacia,' said Eustacia with polite coolness.

Mrs Kennedy gave a nasty little laugh. 'Well, fetch him, will you?'

'He isn't here, Mrs Kennedy.'

'Oh, where is he? In town?'

'He's abroad.' The moment she had said it, Eustacia would have given anything to recall her words.

'Do you mean to say that he has left you in charge of my grandsons? You're not capable of looking after them. I simply won't have it.' She was fast working herself into a temper. 'I don't know how long he will be away but I intend fetching them to stay with us until such time as he returns. It was made clear in my son-in-law's will that they should live with their guardian, but obviously Sir Colin chose to ignore that. Expect me some time tomorrow and have the boys ready to leave with us.'

She hung up abruptly and Eustacia replaced the receiver.

It was time-wasting to call herself a fool, but she undoubtedly was. What was more she was shaking with fright and rage. She must do something about it, and quickly. She went to Sir Colin's study and took the slip of paper from his desk, and picked up the phone and dialled the number on it.

She was answered very quickly but she had to wait until he was found. His 'Yes, Eustacia?' was uttered in a calm voice which checked her wild wish to burst into tears and, while she was struggling for a normal voice, he said, 'Take your time and try not to cry.'

She took a deep breath and, in a voice squeaky with battened-down emotions, began to speak.

CHAPTER FOUR

'MRS KENNEDY,' said Eustacia in a voice she was pleased to hear sounded normal. 'She telephoned about ten minutes ago; she asked to speak to you and I said you weren't here, so she asked where you were.' She gulped. 'I said that you were abroad, and do call me fool if you want to because that's what I am… She said that I wasn't fit to look after the boys and they should be living with her because you weren't at home, and she is coming to fetch them tomorrow…'

'Dear me, what a tiresome lady, and don't reproach yourself, Eustacia, you weren't to know that she was going to turn nasty. Now please stop worrying about it; I'll be home in time to deal with the matter. Go to bed, there's a good girl.' He sounded just as he did when he was talking to his nephews: firm but kind.

'But you're in Holland—it's miles away…'

'Have you never heard of aeroplanes, Eustacia? Are you crying?'

'Well, a bit—I've let you down.'

'Don't be silly; now go to bed. Oh, and unbolt the garden door again, will you? Leave it locked and take the key out of the lock.'

She dealt with the door and went obediently to bed where, surprisingly, she slept until the early morning. She lay and worried for a while and then got up, show-

ered and dressed and crept downstairs with the vague
idea that, if Mrs Kennedy should arrive unexpectedly,
she would at least be ready for her. She gained the
bottom of the staircase and the study door opened and
Sir Colin came out. He was dressed with his usual
elegance and from where she was standing he appeared to be a man who had had a good night's sleep
in his bed.

She surged across the hall, delight and relief making
her beautiful face a sight to linger over. 'Oh, you're
here, I'm so very glad to see you.'

He smiled down at her. 'Good morning, Eustacia.
Why are you up and dressed at six o'clock in the
morning?'

She answered him seriously. 'Well, I thought if Mrs
Kennedy arrived unexpectedly I'd be ready for her.'

'I told you I would be home in time to see her.'

'Yes, and I believed you, but you might need help.'

His eyes gleamed with amusement but he said
gravely, 'That was most thoughtful of you. Do you
suppose we might have a cup of tea?'

'Of course, I'll bring you a tray. Would you like
some toast with it?'

'Yes, I would. We will have it in the kitchen while
we make our plans.'

The kitchen was warm, and Moses opened a sleepy
eye and thumped his tail with pleasure at seeing his
master. Eustacia put the kettle on the Aga and fetched
cups and saucers while Sir Colin cut the bread.

'Is there any of Mrs Samways' marmalade?' he
wanted to know, and loaded the toaster. She found the

marmalade and the butter and got plates and knives and presently they sat down opposite each other at the big scrubbed table with Moses sitting as close as he could get to Sir Colin.

'How did you get here so quickly? There aren't any planes during the night, are there?'

'I chartered one.' He took a bite of toast.

'Oh, I see. You didn't mind me phoning you, Sir Colin? It hasn't made a mess of your seminar—or was it lectures?'

He smiled. 'Both, and the lectures were finished— the seminar isn't all that important.' He passed his cup for more tea. 'No, I didn't mind your phoning, Eustacia; indeed, I would have been very angry if you hadn't.'

'It was silly of me…'

'Why? You were not to know what Mrs Kennedy intended.'

'What shall you do?' She passed the marmalade. 'She can't take the boys away, can she?'

'Of course not.' He sounded placid. 'And there is a simple solution to the problem.'

'Oh—good.' She bent to give Moses a piece of buttered toast.

'We could marry.'

She almost choked on her toast. 'Marry? You and me? Me? Marry you?'

'A very sensible idea,' he pointed out smoothly. 'You will then be a guardian of the boys and there can never be a question of their being taken away from us.'

'But I don't—that is, you don't…' She came to a stop searching for the right words.

'I hardly see that that comes into it. We get on well together, do we not? We should be able to provide a secure background for the boys without getting emotionally involved with each other. After all, there won't be any difference if you become my wife; we get along well, as I have just said, and I see no reason why we shouldn't continue to do so. I am a good deal older than you and there is always the hazard that you may meet someone with whom you will fall in love, in which case the situation can be dealt with reasonably. I assure you that I wouldn't stand in your way.'

It sounded very cold and businesslike. 'Supposing you fall in love?' she asked him.

'But I already have, so you need not concern yourself with that.'

'Grandfather…?'

'A delightful old gentleman, welcome to live here for the remainder of his days.'

'I—I would like to think about it.' There was a panicky excitement inside her.

'By all means,' he glanced at his watch, 'I doubt if the Kennedys will get here for another two hours at the earliest.'

'You mean I have to decide before then?'

'It would make things much easier.' He smiled across the table; he was tired but he knew exactly what he was doing. 'Do you suppose your grandfather is up yet? I should like to talk to him.'

She was glad to have an excuse to get away. Her

head was in a turmoil and she simply had to have time to think. 'I'll go and see. I think he may be in the library—he likes to read before breakfast.'

She left the two men there and went to get the boys out of their beds.

'You look funny,' said Oliver as she brushed his hair. In case she hadn't understood, he added, 'You're pretty, I don't mean that—you look excited.'

'Probably the thought of breakfast. I'm hungry, aren't you?'

'Yes!' shouted Teddy. 'Bacon and eggs and sausages and mushrooms and toast and marmalade...'

The three of them hurried downstairs.

Over breakfast Mr Crump suggested that since their uncle was home and might want to take them out later it would be a good idea if they did some reading first.

'What a splendid idea,' observed Sir Colin, for all the world as though he hadn't just arranged that, and smiled at Eustacia. He looked pleased with himself and confident, as though he was certain that she would consent to his preposterous idea. She would have to talk to him about it once the boys had gone with her grandfather, but as it turned out she had no chance— they had left the table, the boys and Mr Crump to go to the library, she to make the beds upstairs, Sir Colin presumably to go about his own business, when there was a demanding peal on the doorbell.

Sir Colin caught her by the arm as Samways went to answer it.

'Mrs Kennedy?' she heard him say to Samways, who nodded with dignity and a knowing look. So Sir

Colin had found time to tell Samways too… Eustacia allowed herself to be drawn into the drawing-room. 'Sit there,' said Sir Colin and urged her into a small easy-chair facing the door, 'and don't say a word unless I ask you something.' He smiled suddenly. 'Will you marry me, Eustacia?'

She opened her mouth to explain that she must have time to think about it, but now there were voices, rather loud, in the hall—any moment Mrs Kennedy and Mr Kennedy with her would be in the room. She said snappily, 'Oh, all right, but I haven't—' She felt the quick kiss on her cheek and then he was gone, to the other end of the room away from the door, where he wouldn't be seen at once.

Samways opened the door and Mrs Kennedy and her husband surged past him, ignoring his announcement.

'It has been no easy matter driving here, Miss—er—Crump, but I know my duty. If Sir Colin feels unable to make a suitable home for the boys then I must sacrifice my time and leisure and bring them up as befits my daughter's children. Be good enough to send for Oliver and Teddy at once; they will return with us. When Sir Colin chooses to return we can discuss the matter further. For them to remain here with nothing but a parcel of servants is quite—' She stopped, her cross face assuming a look of utter astonishment, her eyes popping.

Sir Colin had advanced a few steps so that he had come into her line of vision. His voice was blandly polite. 'Mrs Kennedy, you must have had a very tiring journey—you travelled through the night? May I offer you both breakfast?'

Mrs Kennedy made a gobbling noise. 'She,' she nodded at Eustacia, 'told me that you were abroad.'

'Eustacia spoke the truth; when you telephoned I was. It seemed to me to be necessary to come home and put your mind at rest about the boys. Let me allay your doubts—Eustacia and I are to be married very shortly so that, when I need to be away from home, they will have a guardian in her.'

'Marry her?' Mrs Kennedy had gone an unbecoming plum colour.

Sir Colin's voice was as steely as his eyes. 'Eustacia has done me that honour.'

'It's a put-up job, she's no more—'

'I beg your pardon, Mrs Kennedy?'

Mr Kennedy spoke for the first time. 'My wife didn't mean that,' he said hastily. 'I did explain to her that everything was quite satisfactory as regards the boys.' He added awkwardly, 'My congratulations, I hope you will be very happy.'

Mrs Kennedy had pulled herself together. 'Yes, yes indeed. I spoke hastily. One forgets how quickly one can travel these days. Aeroplanes, you know, and hovercraft and so on.' She looked around her a little wildly and Eustacia, much as she disliked her, decided that it was time to rescue her from an awkward situation.

'Won't you sit down, Mrs Kennedy and Mr Kennedy? And shall I fetch the boys, Colin?'

She uttered this in what she hoped was a sufficiently loving voice and got answered in her own coin.

'Will you, darling? And ask Samways to bring coffee, would you?'

The smile which went with it was full of tender charm as he went to open the door for her. She didn't dare to look at him. He must be a splendid actor, she reflected, hurrying across the hall; she had read somewhere that surgeons very often had a strong artistic streak, and his must be acting.

The boys weren't exactly enthusiastic. 'Must we?' asked Oliver. 'Mr Crump was just telling us about the Aztecs and it's really very interesting.'

'Yes, I'm sure it is,' agreed Eustacia, 'and you won't need to stay long. I'm sure Grandfather will be delighted to continue when you get back. He's going to have a cup of coffee now.'

The boys behaved beautifully, offering hands and cheeks and answering politely when they were questioned. They pretended not to notice when their grandmother started crying, and Eustacia suggested that she might like to freshen up after her drive. A sudden imp of mischief prompted her to add, 'Perhaps you would like to stay the night?' She turned her beautiful face towards Sir Colin. 'Don't you think that is a good idea, Colin?' She gave him an innocent look, and he turned a sudden laugh into a fit of coughing.

'By all means, darling.' He sounded the perfect host, anxious to do all he could for his guests.

However, the Kennedys didn't wish to stop. Mrs Kennedy was shepherded away to repair her face and tidy herself, and presently they made their farewells and drove away with the assurance, not over-enthusiastically received by them, that Sir Colin, Eustacia and both the boys would spend a day or two with them as soon as the warmer weather arrived.

They stood on the steps, waving, and the two boys scampered back to Mr Crump. 'I had no idea that you had it in you, Eustacia,' said Sir Colin.

'Had what, Sir Colin?'

'This ability to be a loving fiancée at a moment's notice, although I could have wished for a few more melting glances.'

'Well, I didn't want to overdo it.'

'That would be impossible.' He turned her round and took her arm and walked her into the house. 'Now, when shall we get married?'

She turned to face him. 'You aren't serious?' She studied his face and decided that he was.

'Am I to be jilted before we are even engaged? I had thought better of you, Eustacia.'

She stammered a little. 'I thought—well, I thought that it was just an emergency.'

'Certainly not—an expediency, perhaps. You must see, since you are a sensible girl, that if we marry it ensures a secure and happy future for the boys with no further interference from the Kennedys. Of course, they have every right to see the boys as often as they wish, and have them to stay for holidays, but this will be their home and you and I will be, in effect, their parents.'

She had nothing to say; it all sounded so logical and businesslike.

Sir Colin eyed her thoughtfully. 'Naturally our marriage will be one of convenience. We have, I think, a mutual liking for each other which is more than can be said of a good many marriages these days. Should you meet a man you truly love, then I will release you—'

'And what about you?' asked Eustacia sharply. 'You're just as likely to meet another woman.'

He said seriously, 'I'm thirty-six, my dear, I have had every opportunity to meet another woman...'

'What about Gloria?'

She wished she hadn't said it, for his face became as bland as the voice with which he echoed her. 'Gloria?'

She muttered, 'It was something I heard, and I thought that she was—'

'Set your mind at rest, Eustacia. Gloria was—still is—a friend of long standing and the very last woman I would marry.'

She went pink but met his look candidly. 'I'm sorry, it isn't my business—it was impertinent of me.'

The bland look which she didn't much care for disappeared and he smiled at her, the kind smile which made her feel that everything was all right between them. He said gently, 'I am a good deal older than you, Eustacia—if you do have second thoughts I shall understand.'

'Well, I hadn't thought about it,' she told him, 'and it doesn't matter. I do like you very much and I think that I could love the boys, really love them, and I should be very happy living here with them…'

He chuckled. 'I do come home at weekends and sometimes during the week. Besides, from time to time I should like you to come up to town. I have many friends and I like to entertain them occasionally. Have you any objection to that?'

'Me? No, it sounds exciting. You don't mind Grandfather being here? Would you like him to go back to the flat? I dare say—'

'Certainly not. I find him a delightful man and the boys like the time they spend with him and are fond of him. I believe he is happy here, is he not? And he is performing a yeoman service teaching them to play chess and answering all their questions, and I suspect that when they go to school he will be roped in to help them with their homework.'

They had been standing in the hall, and at Samways' little cough they both looked round.

'I thought perhaps some fresh coffee, sir?'

'Excellent, Samways. And please fetch up a couple of bottles of champagne—we will have some at lunch. Miss Crump and I have just become engaged.'

Samways was delighted; he offered congratulations with suitable gravity, mentioned that Mrs Samways would be more than pleased to hear the news, and went away to fetch the coffee.

'I think,' said Sir Colin, sitting in his chair with a coffee-cup in his hand, 'that you had better come up to town with me; I have a small house there, and I should like you to meet Grimstone who runs it for me—his sister does the cooking. We must decide on a date for the wedding too.' He sat thinking. 'I'm rather busy for the next few days but I will send Samways down to fetch my mother—she can stay here and help your grandfather to keep an eye on the boys so that you may spend a few days shopping. Would you object to marrying here in the village? The church is rather nice…'

Really, thought Eustacia, he's arranged everything in a couple of sentences. She said calmly, 'I think that would be delightful—being married here, I mean. And if you want me to come up to London with you then I will. The boys will be all right?'

'Perfectly all right. We will drive up this afternoon and I'll bring you back this evening. I have a list in the morning but not until ten o'clock, so I can spend the night.' He glanced at her. 'Am I going too fast for you?'

'Yes, but I'll catch up. Will your mother mind?'

'No. She likes you. Shall we go and tell your grandfather and the boys?'

Their news was received with boisterous delight by the boys and quiet satisfaction by her grandfather.

'You'll never go away?' asked Teddy. 'You'll look after us?'

She hugged him. 'Of course I will, we'll all have such fun…'

'And when you're an old lady,' said Oliver, 'if you need looking after, you and Uncle Colin, we'll take care of you both.'

'I think we shall both be very glad to have you

around and it is very kind of you to think of us, my dear.'

'We call Uncle Colin Uncle—do we have to call you Aunt?'

'Only if you would like to.'

'You won't mind if we call you Eustacia?'

'I should like it above all things.'

She had sat down at the table with the boys on either side of her, and Sir Colin turned round from the conversation he was having with her grandfather.

'Uncle Colin, we think you are a very lucky man,' said Oliver.

'I know I am, old chap. We shall be married here quite soon and have all our friends at the church.'

'And a cake, and Eustacia will be a bride in a white dress?'

Before she could answer, Sir Colin said positively, 'Yes, to both questions.'

'A party?' asked Teddy, happily.

'A party it shall be.' He spoke to his small nephew but he looked at Eustacia, smiling faintly. Quite carried away by the excitement of the moment, she smiled back, her cheeks pink and her eyes sparkling.

The next hour or so seemed a little hazy, partly due to the champagne and the children's excitement, which made sensible conversation, or sensible thought for that matter, impossible. Presently she found herself sitting beside Sir Colin, in the Rolls, waving goodbye to the little group at the front of the house, and when they were out of sight she sat back composedly, very neat in the elderly suit. There was still a great deal she wanted to know and she supposed she would be told sooner or later; meanwhile there seemed little point in aimless chatter.

Presently Sir Colin said, 'It is the prerogative of the bride to decide what kind of wedding she wants, is it not? There was no chance to explain my high-handed plans, but perhaps you understood?'

'Yes. It's for the boys, isn't it? It will help them to adjust, won't it? If they have something positive to hang on to.'

'Exactly. This afternoon we are going to visit an old friend of my father's. He is a bishop and I hope he will be able to advise us about a special licence and the quickest way to get one. I shall put an announcement in the *Telegraph* tomorrow and invite friends to the wedding. I haven't many relations, but they will come, I'm sure of that. So will colleagues I work with. Is there anyone you would like to invite? I know that you have no family...'

'There isn't anyone—I had friends, but during the last two years I've lost touch.'

'I dare say one or two people from the path lab will want to come.'

They were in London by now, going through Chiswick and Kensington and skirting Hyde Park, up Park Lane and then into the elegant, quiet streets around Portman Square. The street they turned into was short, tree-lined and bordered by narrow, bow-windowed Regency houses. Sir Colin stopped at the end of the terrace where there was an archway leading to a mews behind the houses.

Eustacia studied it from the car window. 'You live here?'

'Yes. It's not too far from St Biddolph's and I've consulting-rooms in Wimpole Street.'

He got out and opened her door and they crossed the narrow pavement together. He let himself in with his key and ushered her into the narrow hall, and at the same time a tall, very thin man came up the stairs at the back.

He answered Sir Colin's cheerful greeting solemnly and then bowed to Eustacia as Sir Colin said, 'This is Grimstone, Eustacia, he runs this house on oiled wheels and his sister is my cook. Grimstone, Miss Cramp has done me the honour of promising to marry me in the very near future.'

Grimstone bowed again. 'I'm sure we are delighted to hear the news, Sir Colin and Miss Crump. My felicitations.'

Sir Colin swept Eustacia across the hall and into a charming room overlooking the street. 'Take Miss Crump's coat, will you, Grimstone, and may we have some tea? We have to go out very shortly but shall be back for dinner if Rosie can manage something. I'll be down at Turville tonight.'

'Very good, sir, I will speak to Rosie.'

When he had gone Sir Colin sat her down in a small armchair by the brisk fire, sat himself down opposite her and observed, 'Grimstone appears severe, but in fact he has a heart of gold and a very wise old head. He'll be your slave but he will never admit to it.'

'He's been with you for a long time?'

'He was with my father and mother. They lived here when my father was alive; when my mother moved to Castle Cary, Grimstone elected to stay here and run the house for me. He doesn't like the country.'

While they had their tea she looked around her. The room wasn't very large but the furniture, mostly Regency and comfortable chairs and sofas, suited it very well for there wasn't too much of it.

'I've hardly altered anything,' observed Sir Colin, almost as though he had read her thoughts. 'My father inherited this house from an aunt and it had been in her family for a very long time. I loved living here when I was a child, although I'm just as fond of the house at Turville. The best of both worlds—it hardly seems fair...'

'If you idled away your days it wouldn't be fair, but you work hard and you help people—save their lives—take away their pain.'

He said without conceit, 'I do my best; my father was a physician, so was his father, and I don't think they ever quite forgave me for taking up surgery.' He put down his cup. 'Shall we go and see this bishop and see what he can do for us?'

He took her to a nice old house in Westminster and the bishop, an old man with bright blue eyes which missed nothing, approved of her. There were certain formalities, he explained, which he would be delighted to arrange, and he could see no reason why they shouldn't marry within about a couple of weeks in Turville Church. 'And I hope I shall be invited to the wedding.'

Eustacia glanced at Sir Colin and saw his faint smile. 'I don't suppose you would marry us?' she ventured.

'My dear young lady, I hoped that you might ask that. I shall be delighted. I will get in touch with your rector, and you of course will be going to see him.'

'It will have to be tomorrow evening…'

They left presently and, as they drove back to the house, Sir Colin said, 'I'll leave you to choose the day, Eustacia. If you could let me know by the weekend I can organise a couple of days free.'

No honeymoon, she reflected, but a honeymoon would be silly in the circumstances; they were entering a kind of business partnership for the sake of the boys, and she mustn't forget that. She agreed pleasantly and later, sitting in the drawing-room drinking her sherry before dinner, she followed his lead and kept the talk impersonal.

They dined deliciously; tomato and basil soufflé, roast lamb with new potatoes and purée of broccoli and a syllabub with ginger biscuits. The white burgundy she was offered pleased her and loosened her tongue too, so that her host sat back with a glint in his eyes, encouraging her to talk.

She was taken aback when, instead of Grimstone, his sister Rosie came in with the coffee-tray. She beamed at Eustacia as she put the tray on the table. 'I'm sorry that I hadn't the time to plan a good dinner for you, seeing as how you're engaged and that. And I'm sure I wish you both very happy. I did the best I could but there weren't no time.'

'It was a delicious dinner,' said Eustacia, and she meant it. 'Those ginger biscuits—you made them yourself, of course.'

Rosie's smile became even wider. 'Indeed I did, Miss Crump. I don't allow Sir Colin to eat any of those nasty cakes and biscuits from the shops. Sawdust and sugar, I always say.'

'I'm sure you look after him beautifully, Rosie, and it really was a super dinner.'

Rosie retired, still smiling, and Sir Colin, who hadn't said a word, drank his coffee and she said uneasily, 'I've annoyed you, haven't I?'

'Now why should you say that, Eustacia? On the contrary, I have been thinking that you have the gift of instant empathy.'

'Oh, have I? I like people—well, most people.' She thought of Mrs Kennedy and hoped that next time they met the meeting would be a happier one, though she doubted it.

They drove back to Turville very shortly afterwards, to discuss their plans with her grandfather, but not before Eustacia had nipped up to the boys' room and made sure that they were sleeping. Oliver opened an eye as she peered at them both by the light of the dim night-light she thought it prudent to allow them.

'You're back? Is Uncle with you?'

She tucked him up and dropped a kiss on the top of his head. 'Yes, dear, but he has to go again after breakfast. Now go to sleep like a good boy.'

She went to bed herself shortly afterwards—the day had been full of surprises and she hadn't been given

time to think about them. Once in bed, she allowed
her thoughts to wander. Her grandfather and Sir Colin
had been so matter-of-fact about the whole thing, she
thought peevishly, as though the kind of upheaval she
had experienced that morning was a perfectly normal
happening—and now she came to think about it, perhaps she had been too hasty. It had all sounded so
sensible when Sir Colin had suggested that they should
marry, but now a hundred and one reasons why she
should cry off reared their heads. An hour later, from
whichever angle she looked at it, the reason for marrying Sir Colin more than cancelled out her own
against. The Kennedys, she felt sure, were quite capable of doing their utmost to have the care of the
boys unless Sir Colin could provide them with a stable
background. And, of course, if she married him the
background would be just that. They were dear children and they had been dealt a bitter blow, and Sir
Colin was so obviously the right person to give them
a home. She slept on the thought.

Sir Colin left after breakfast with the promise of a
speedy return, and it was left to Eustacia to enlarge
upon the plans for the wedding. The rest of the week
was largely taken up with discussions involving the
actual wedding, the prospect of school and what
Eustacia was to wear. It must be white, they told her,
but she drew the line at a train, six bridesmaids and a
diamond tiara. 'Would a pretty hat do?' she wanted to
know. 'And no bridesmaids, but I promise you that
I'll wear white,'

In the quiet of her room she did anxious sums; she

had saved her salary and there was a small amount in the bank. It wasn't just the wedding dress—she simply had to have a suit and some shoes and a dress—one which she could wear if by any chance someone came to dinner or they went out. It didn't seem very likely; she envisaged a quiet future, with her living with the boys at Turville, making a home for them. That was why she was marrying Sir Colin, wasn't it?

He came home at the weekend, swept them all off to church on Sunday morning, took the boys for a walk after lunch and drove her back to London after tea. Over dinner he told her that he would be at the hospital for the next two days, going from there to his consulting-rooms and getting back for dinner in the evening. 'I'll drive you back on Wednesday evening,' he told her. 'Can you get your shopping done in that time?' He smiled his gentle smile. 'Have you enough money?'

'Oh, yes, I think so.'

'How much?'

And when she told him, 'You will have an allowance when we are married. I think it might be a good idea if I give it to you before you start your shopping.' And when she demurred, 'No, please don't argue, Eustacia. I have a number of friends and we shall have social occasions to attend together as well as the occasional weekend when we are away or entertaining guests at Turville. Buy all the clothes you will need and, if you run out of money, let me know.'

She thanked him quietly; there was no point in arguing about it for he made sense—her wardrobe was scanty, out of date and quite unsuitable for the wife of an eminent surgeon.

They didn't talk about it again. He told her that he had arranged for the wedding to take place on the day she had wanted, and there would be fifty or sixty guests coming. 'Short notice, I know, but I know most of them well enough to phone them.'

She went to bed soon after dinner and he made no attempt to keep her up. He opened the door for her and put a hand on her arm as she passed him. 'Don't worry, it will work out perfectly.'

He kissed her cheek and wished her goodnight, and she wondered if he had meant the wedding or their future together.

He had gone when she went down in the morning. She had slept peacefully in the charming room with its pastel colours and silk curtains, and it had been bliss to be roused by Rosie with early-morning tea. There was an envelope on the tray with a note from Sir Colin hoping that she had had a good night's sleep. There was a roll of notes too. Her eyes almost popped from her head when she counted them—she could never spend that in a year... The note bore a post-script: he hoped there was sufficient for her to get the wedding clothes, and he would see that she had the same amount before the following day. 'Well,' said Eustacia, and counted the notes again just to make sure and then, over breakfast, fell to making a list of suit-able clothes for every occasion. She glanced down at her well-worn skirt and wondered if he had minded her shabbiness; never by a glance had he betrayed that fact. He was a kind man and they got on well now that she had got to know him better. She wondered if he had been in love and decided that he had, quite a few times probably—he might still be for all she knew, but that was not her concern—she must remember that they were marrying for the boys' sake and for no other reason. She shook off a sudden feeling of sadness and applied herself once more to her list.

CHAPTER FIVE

EUSTACIA hadn't had the chance to shop with almost unlimited money in her purse for several years—her venue had been the high street stores at sale-time, and even then it had been a question as to whether it was a garment which would stand up to a good deal of wear and still remain at least on the fringe of fashion. Now, clutching what she considered to be a small fortune, she took a bus to Harrods.

She paused for an early lunch, surrounded by dress-boxes and elegant packages, the possessor of a wedding dress, a charming hat to go with it, elegant shoes she felt she would never wear again after the wedding-day, a beautifully tailored suit in a rich brown tweed, sweaters and blouses to wear with it, and two dresses which she hoped would be suitable for any minor social occasion. She scanned her list as she ate her asparagus flan and decided what to buy next. A decent raincoat and stout shoes, and, if there was any money left, a pretty dressing-gown and slippers, and even if there was any money left after that she doubted whether she would be able to carry any more parcels, even as far as a taxi.

It was teatime when she arrived back at Sir Colin's house. Grimstone must have been on the look-out for her for he opened the door as she got out of the taxi, paid the driver and carried her packages inside.

'A successful day, Miss Crump?'

'Oh, very, thank you, Grimstone, I've had a lovely time.'

'I will convey these to your room, miss, and tea will be served in the drawing-room in ten minutes' time if that is suitable to you?'

There seemed an awful lot of boxes and bags, but she resisted the desire to open them and take a look, tidied herself in a perfunctory fashion and went downstairs. Tea had been arranged on a small table before the fire; tiny sandwiches, strips of toast, little iced cakes arranged on paper-thin china, and, to keep her company, Moses and Madam Mop the cat. There was no sign of Sir Colin, so presently she went upstairs and opened the purchases. The wedding dress she hung away in the wardrobe, resisting the temptation to try it on once more. It was of very fine white wool with a satin collar and cuffs and of an exquisite cut, worth every penny of its exorbitant price. Then she took the hat out of its box; it was white mousseline and satin with a wide brim and a satin bow to trim it, not, perhaps, quite what the boys had wanted but definitely bridal. She was head and shoulders in the wardrobe arranging the shoes just so when there was a knock on the door, and she called, 'Come in.'

She backed away, expecting to see Rosie intent on drawing the curtains and turning down the bed, but Sir Colin was standing there, leaning against the door. She said, 'Oh, hello,' and then, stupidly, 'You're home.'

He smiled and agreed; he had started his day just after eight o'clock with a ward round, operated until the early afternoon, eaten a sandwich, spent an hour in Outpatients and then gone to his rooms to keep appointments with his private patients and presently, after dinner, he would go back to St Biddolph's to check on the patients he had operated upon that morning. A long, hard day and he was tired. It struck him that the sight of Eustacia, standing there surrounded by tissue paper and cardboard boxes, was somehow very soothing.

'Had a good day?' he asked, and when she said yes in a shy voice, 'Then let's go down and have a drink and you can tell me all about it.'

The evening, for Eustacia, was quite perfect. They discussed the wedding over dinner in a matter-of-fact manner and later, when she said goodnight, he bent to kiss her cheek again. 'I hope to be home soon after tea tomorrow, so buy a pretty dress and we will go out to dinner.' He smiled down at her and then kissed her again, and when she looked surprised, 'We should put in some practice,' he told her blandly, 'the boys will expect it.'

There was another envelope on her tea-tray in the morning, and this time the money was almost double the amount she had been given on the previous day. She counted it and wondered if she should save some of it, but on the other hand he had told her to buy all the clothes she needed...

She made another list and presently went back to Harrods. A winter coat was a must, even though it was the tail-end of winter. There were still cold days ahead and her coat was old and very shabby—and a pretty dress… She found a brown top-coat which went well with the tweed of her suit, and then she began her search for a dress. She found what she wanted—amber satin swathed in chiffon with very full chiffon sleeves to the elbow and a low neckline, partly concealed by a swathing of chiffon. At the saleswoman's suggestion, she bought an angora wrap to go over it.

There was still plenty of money; she found slippers and a small evening-bag and took herself off to the undies department where she spent a good deal more money on wisps of silk and lace, to her great satisfaction. Gloves and a leather handbag took almost all the money which was left in her purse; she collected her purchases and got into a taxi.

She had forgotten lunch although she had stopped for a cup of coffee, and, since it was three o'clock in the afternoon and Grimstone had doubtless taken it for granted that she had had a meal while she was out, she went to her room, ate all the biscuits in the tin by her bed and examined her new purchases and then put them away tidily. By that time it was after four o'clock and she went downstairs, her thoughts on a cup of tea and some of Rosie's dainty sandwiches. Sir Colin had said that he would be back after tea, and that small meal would fill in the time nicely until he came.

Grimstone was in the hall and went to open the drawing-room door for her, murmuring in his dignified way that tea would be brought at once, and shutting the door firmly behind her.

Sir Colin was sitting beside the fire with Moses beside him and Madam Mop curled up at his feet. He got up as she paused halfway across the room and said, pleasantly, 'Come and sit down. Outpatients wasn't as heavy as usual so I came home early. Have you had a good day?'

She sat down opposite him. 'Heavenly, thank you. And thank you for all that money. I—I've been very extravagant…!'

'Good. There's still tomorrow if you haven't finished getting all you need.'

'Well,' said Eustacia with disarming honesty, 'I've bought all I need and a lot of things I don't, but they were so exactly what I've been wanting, if you see what I mean.'

'Indeed I do. Do you like dancing? I have booked a table at Claridge's for eight o'clock.'

Eustacia beamed at him. 'Oh, how lovely—I bought a dress—I do hope it will do.'

He smiled. 'I'm quite sure it will. I look forward to seeing it. I think we might go back to Turville tomorrow evening. I've one or two patients to see in the late afternoon but I think we might get back in time for dinner there, and to see the boys before they go to bed.'

'They will be pleased. They wanted to know when we would be coming home.' She blushed. 'That is, when we would be going back to Turville.'

'I'll phone them presently. Your grandfather is all right?'

'He's so happy... You're sure, aren't you? I mean, about me and him?'

'Quite sure, Eustacia.' He put down his cup. 'I'm going to take Moses for a gentle trot and then I must do some work. Shall we meet down here a little after half-past seven?'

It was as though he had closed a door between them, very gently, but closed just the same. She said, 'Very well,' and watched him, with Moses walking sedately beside him, go out of the room. She really must remember, she reflected a little sadly, that their marriage was for the boys' sakes and personal feelings wouldn't come into it. Perhaps later on—he was an easy man to like. A small voice at the back of her head added that he would be an easy man to love too, but she refused to hear it.

Not having had lunch, she polished off the rest of the sandwiches and a slice of Rosie's walnut cake and took herself back to her room, where she sat and thought about nothing much in particular until it was time to have her bath and dress. She wanted very much to think about Sir Colin, but it might be wiser not to allow him to loom too large in her thoughts.

The dress did everything asked of it; she had a splendid figure and the satin and chiffon did it full justice. Excitement had given her pretty face a delicate colour and her hair, confined in a French pleat, framed it with its rich dark brown. She took up the wrap and little bag, slid her feet into the high-heeled slippers she had very nearly not bought because of their wicked price, and went downstairs to the drawing-room.

She was surprised to find Sir Colin already there in the subdued elegance of a dinner-jacket, and she said breathlessly, 'Oh, am I late? I'm sorry, I thought you said just after—'

'I am early, Eustacia. How delightful you look; that is a charming gown.' He studied her smilingly and she stood quietly while he did so. 'You are also beautiful—I have already told you that, haven't I?'

She said seriously, 'Yes, at St Biddolph's—but it's this dress, you know.'

'If I remember rightly, you were wrapped in a very unbecoming overall.'

'Oh, yes, well…' She could think of nothing to say and she suspected that he was amused. 'Clothes make a difference,' she added, and her eyes sparkled at the thought of her well-stocked wardrobe.

Sir Colin silently admired the sparkle. 'If you are ready, shall we go?'

As they reached the door he put out a hand to detain her. 'Before we go, I have something for you. I should have given it to you before this, but there has been no opportunity.'

He took a small velvet box from his pocket and opened it. The ring inside was a sapphire surrounded with diamonds and set in gold. 'It has been in the family for a very long time, handed down from one bride to the next.' He picked up her left hand and slipped the ring on her finger—it fitted exactly.

Eustacia gave a gulp of delight—it was a ring any

girl would be proud of. She said slowly, 'It is absolutely beautiful. Thank you very much, Sir Colin—only wouldn't you rather I had a ring that wasn't meant for a—a bride?' She was aware that she wasn't making herself clear. She must try again. 'What I mean is,' she began carefully, 'this ring must have been a token...' She paused—there were pitfalls ahead and this time he came to her rescue.

'In plain words, my dear, you feel that it isn't right to accept a ring which should be given as a token of love.'

'Now why couldn't I have put it as plainly as that?' she wanted to know.

'And another thing—do in heaven's name stop calling me Sir Colin. Colin sounds much nicer, and as for the ring, there is no one else I would wish to give it to, Eustacia.' He bent and kissed her and he took her arm. 'That having been settled, let us go.'

Perhaps it was the ring or the dress or the elegance of Claridge's, but the evening was a success. They dined superbly: mousseline of lobster, noisettes of lamb, biscuit glacé with raspberries and praline, accompanied by champagne and finally coffee, and in between they danced. Eustacia, big girl though she was, was as light on her feet as thistledown, and Sir Colin danced as he did most other things, very well indeed. They made a handsome couple and she, aware that she looked her best, allowed herself, just for once, to pretend that the future would be like this too, happy in each other's company, content and secure. It was one o'clock when they arrived at his home but she felt

wide awake, wanting to prolong the evening's pleasure. She stood in the hall, hoping that he would suggest that they talked for a little while, but as he
shrugged off his coat he said pleasantly, 'A delightful
evening, Eustacia.' He glanced at his watch. 'I have
half an hour's work to do and I shall be gone before
you are down in the morning. Only I'll see you tomorrow afternoon—I thought that we might try to get
to Turville in time to see the boys before they go to
bed.'

He crossed the hall to his study. 'Goodnight,
Eustacia, sleep well.' The smile he gave her was what
she described as businesslike; the warmth of the evening had gone—perhaps it had never been there, perhaps she had imagined it. She went sadly to her room,
hung the lovely dress carefully in the wardrobe, put
the ring carefully back into its little box and finally
got into bed.

It took her a long time to get to sleep. It was too
late for her to back out of their bargain now, and she
wasn't sure that she wanted to. What worried her was
that perhaps Colin had had second thoughts. But he
had seemed so certain that everything would be all
right, and he wasn't a man to change his mind once
it was made up. What had she expected, anyway?

She slept on the thought.

The boys were delighted to see them home again
and Eustacia slipped back into the quiet routine as
though she had never been away—only the lovely
clothes hanging in the wardrobe were there to remind
her. She saw very little of Sir Colin; he spent his

weekends at Turville and came there once or twice in
the week but never long enough for them to talk for
any length of time. That week went by and the boys
started school and she drove them there and back each
day, missing their company although she had enough
to do now, for wedding presents were arriving and she
needed to keep a list so that Colin could see it when
he came home. There were discussions with Samways
about the reception. The caterers would come on the
day before the wedding, but furniture would have to
be moved then the flowers would have to be arranged.

Sir Colin came home on the evening before the
wedding, apparently unmoved by the thought of getting married. He approved of the flowers, conferred
with Samways about the caterers and the drinks, teased
the boys and settled down to a rambling discussion
about the early English poets with her grandfather. His
manner towards her was exactly as it always was, and
she told herself that she was silly to expect anything
else.

That evening his mother arrived and so did the
bishop. The wedding was to be at noon with a reception directly afterwards and, as he had told Eustacia,
he intended to return to London in two days' time.
'We will have a holiday later in the year,' he'd observed, 'and I'm sorry if you are disappointed, but my
lists are made out weeks in advance and I have a back-
log of private patients.'

She had told him matter-of-factly that she hadn't
expected to go away. 'The boys have only just started

school and they're a bit unsettled, although they are happy there.'

She wore one of her pretty dresses at dinner that evening and the meal turned into quite an occasion. The boys were allowed to stay up, and since Mrs Crichton and the bishop were there too there was a good deal of animated conversation. She went with the boys when the meal was finally finished and stayed a while, pottering around until, despite their excitement, they slept. When she went back to the drawing-room she found Mrs Crichton alone.

'The men are in the library,' she observed, 'looking up something or other legal, and I'm glad, for we haven't had a chance to talk, have we?' She smiled at Eustacia. 'Come and sit down, my dear, and tell me what you think of Colin.'

Eustacia sat and did her best to answer sensibly. 'He's a very kind man and good too. He's also generous—I've never had so much money to spend on clothes in my life before, I'm not sure that it's—'

She was cut short. 'Colin is a leading figure in his profession, and besides that he is a rich man. He would expect you to dress in a manner befitting his wife. You are a very pretty girl, my dear, and I am sure that you will make him proud of you.' She shot a glance at Eustacia's doubtful face. 'I dare say you will spend most of your time here. He would prefer to live here himself, I know, but he has always come here for his weekends and any evening that he can spare. I expect you will go up to town sometimes for he has any number of friends and entertains from time to time. I hope that during the Easter holidays he will agree to the boys coming to stay with me, in which case you will be able to go to town and stay there with him. A chance to go to the theatre and do some shopping. The boys are very happy—of course they grieve for their mother and father, but they love Colin and I believe that they begin to love you too.'

'I hope so, for I'm very fond of them both; besides, it will make it all worthwhile, won't it?'

'You have no doubts? No regrets?'

Eustacia shook her head. 'Oh, no. Not any more. I did for a while, you know, but Colin is quite right, it's the boys we have to think about.'

Mrs Crichton agreed placidly.

The men came back presently and after an hour's desultory conversation Mrs Crichton went to bed, and soon after that Eustacia said her goodnights and went to the door. Sir Colin opened it and to her surprise followed her into the hall.

'Cold feet?' he asked blandly.

'Yes—haven't you?'

'No.' His voice was kind now. 'It will be all right, I promise you, Eustacia.'

'Yes, I know that. I'll do my best, Colin, truly I will.'

He put his hands on her shoulders. 'Yes, I know that too, my dear.' He smiled his kind smile. 'Goodnight.' He bent and kissed her lightly, and she started up the stairs. She looked back when she reached the curve in the staircase. He was standing there still, watching her, this large, quiet man who was so soon to be her husband. And quite right and proper too, she thought absurdly, for I love him and even if he never loves me it will be quite all right to marry him. The upsurge of excitement and delight and relief was so great that she actually took a step down again in order to tell him so, but common sense stopped her just in time. It would never do for him to know; the very fact that they were good friends and nothing more had made it easy for him to suggest that they should marry. She managed to smile at him and ran up the rest of the staircase.

Sir Colin stood where he was for a few moments. Eustacia, usually so serene and practical, had looked as though she had just had a severe shock. He must remember to ask her about it.

They were all at breakfast, although Mrs Samways protested vigorously when she saw Eustacia sitting in her usual place. 'You didn't ought to be here,' she objected. 'The bridegroom shouldn't see the bride until she goes to church.'

'I won't look at her,' promised Sir Colin, and everyone laughed. 'Although I was under the impression that the bride took hours to dress.'

'Well, I shan't. I must see to the boys first…'

'What about taking Moses for a walk?' Sir Colin glanced across the table to his mother. 'Will you and Mr Crump keep each other company while we take the bishop as far as the church?'

It wasn't the usual way for a bride and groom to behave. Mrs Samways, clearing the breakfast things, shook her head and muttered darkly and went to the window to watch the pair of them with the two boys and Moses escorting the bishop as far as the church gate.

'And them in their old clothes,' observed Mrs Samways to the empty room.

However, she had to admit a few hours later that there was no fault to find with the bridal pair. Eustacia, walking down the aisle with her grandfather, made a delightful picture; the wide-brimmed hat was a splendid foil for her dark hair and the elegant simplicity of her dress was enhanced by the double row of pearls around her neck. She had found them on her dressing-table when she had gone to her room to dress with a note from Colin, begging her to wear them. There was a bouquet for her too, cream roses and lilies of the valley, freesias in the faintest pink and orange-blossom. Sir Colin was well worth a second look too, thought his devoted housekeeper. He stood, massive and elegant in his grey morning-coat and pale grey stock, and Mrs Samways wiped a sentimental eye and exchanged eloquent glances with Rosie, who had come for the wedding with Grimstone.

Eustacia walked back down the aisle, her hand tucked under Colin's arm, smiling at the rows of faces, his family and friends, of whom she knew absolutely nothing. She had expected to feel different now that she was married, although she wasn't sure why. The calm man beside her showed no sign of overwhelming happiness—indeed, he looked as he always looked: placid, self-assured and kind. She took a quick look at his profile and thought it looked stern too, but then he glanced down at her and smiled. A friendly smile and comforting, although why she needed to be comforted was a puzzle to her. She should be riotously happy, she had married the man she loved…

Photos were taken amid a good deal of cheerful bustle and presently they were driven back to the house, heading the steady flow of guests.

The next hour or two were like a dream; Eustacia shook hands with what seemed to be an unending stream of people, forgetting names as fast as they were mentioned. It was towards the end of the line of guests that she found herself facing a girl not much older than herself and as tall as she was and as splendidly built. She was pretty too, and dressed with great elegance. 'I'm Prudence,' she said cheerfully, 'I'll introduce myself while these two men talk. Haso has known Colin for years; he stays with us when he comes over to Holland, so I hope we shall see a lot of each other…'

'Haso and Prudence ter Brons Huizinga,' said Colin, 'my very good friends and I'm sure yours as well, my dear.'

Haso offered a hand. He was a tall man, fair-haired and blue-eyed and with commanding features, but his smile was nice. 'We are so pleased that Colin has married. I think that he is a very fortunate man, although I do not need to tell him that. When he comes to Holland you must come with him and stay with us.' He looked at Colin. 'There is a seminar in May, is there not?'

They made their way into the drawing-room and

Eustacia said, 'I liked her; have they been married long?'

'Nearly two years. A well-matched pair, aren't they?'

They cut the cake presently and toasts were drunk, and after a while they found the guests began to leave. Eustacia started shaking hands all over again. All the people from the path lab had come; Miss Bennett in an awesome hat bade her a severe goodbye and observed, 'Of course it was obvious that you were quite unsuited for the job.' A remark which left Eustacia puzzled. Professor Ladbroke, on the other hand, gave her a hearty kiss, told her that she might find being married to Colin a good deal more exacting than cleaning bottles, and went on his way with a subdued roar of laughter.

As for Mr Brimshaw, she was touched when he said grumpily, 'Hope you'll be happy, Eustacia, you deserve to be.'

She thanked him, echoing the wish silently.

Prudence and Haso were among the last to leave and Colin and Eustacia accompanied them to their car, a dark grey Daimler. 'We're going back on the night ferry,' said Prudence. 'A bit of a rush, but I wouldn't have missed your wedding for the world.' She kissed Eustacia. 'I'm sure you'll both be very happy, just like us.'

Eustacia saw the tender look that Haso gave his wife and felt a pang of sorrow and a great wave of self-pity, instantly dismissed. She was Colin's wife now

and all she had to do was to give him every opportunity to fall in love with her.

He showed no signs of doing so that evening
though. They sat around, the bishop, Mrs Crichton, Mr
Crump, Colin and herself, drinking tea and discussing
the wedding until they dispersed to get ready for dinner, a meal Mrs Samways and Rosie had planned between them. Colin's best man, a professor of endo-
crinology from St Biddolph's, had driven back to town
but would return for dinner and the party would be
increased by the rector and his wife. The boys were
to stay up and Eustacia urged them upstairs to wash
their faces and brush their hair before going to her
room to tidy herself. Even without the hat and the
bouquet the dress looked charming. She did her hair
and her face and sat studying the plain gold ring under
the sapphire and diamonds. At the moment she didn't
feel in the least married.

They were all there in the drawing-room when she
went down, drinking champagne cocktails, and the
dinner which followed was a leisurely, convivial one.
Rosie and Mrs Samways had excelled themselves: ar-
tichoke hearts, roast duck with ginger, followed by
Cointreau mousse and a chocolate sauce and a splendid selection of cheeses. They drank champagne while
the boys quaffed sparkling lemonade and then, pleasantly relaxed, they went back to the drawing-room
where, after a short while, the boys said goodnight.

'I'll just go up with them,' said Eustacia, conscious
of their wistful, sleepy faces as she ushered them to
the door.

Colin opened it. 'Come down again, won't you?' he asked.

She gave him a quick smile. 'Of course.'

The boys were lively and still excited, but once they were in their beds they were asleep within minutes. She stood looking at them for a moment, the sight of their guileless, sleeping faces making sense of Colin and her marrying; they had lost the two people closest to them in their short lives and now they deserved some kind of recompense.

They sat around talking until late. The Samways and Grimstone and Rosie had been brought in to have a glass of champagne and to be complimented upon the dinner, and no one noticed the time after that. The rector and his wife were the first to go and after that the party broke up slowly until there was only Eustacia and Colin left.

Now, perhaps, thought Eustacia, we can sit quietly for half an hour and talk and get to know each other. She sat down opposite Colin and Moses pottered over to have his ears gently pulled. She was glad of that for she could think of nothing to say for the moment and Colin didn't seem disposed to speak. Presently she said brightly, 'It was a very nice day, wasn't it?'

Hardly the beginning of a scintillating conversation, but the best she could do.

'Delightful. You were a beautiful bride, Eustacia— the boys were enchanted. And it was pleasant to meet friends again; normally there isn't much time... I'm glad Prudence and Haso came; she's a darling.'

'And very pretty,' commented Eustacia, determined to be an interesting companion.

'You must be very tired—don't let me keep you up. Would you like anything else before you go to bed? A drink? Tea?' He gave her an impersonal, kindly smile and she managed to smile back, although her face almost cracked doing it.

'Nothing, thank you, and I am tired; you won't mind if I go to bed?'

He was already on his feet. 'Of course not. I must dictate a couple of letters and ring my registrar, something I should have done earlier.'

She swallowed chagrin. 'Oh, that would never do,' she said, her voice high with suppressed and sudden rage. 'You shouldn't let a little thing like getting married interfere with your work.'

She marched out of the room, whisking past him at the door. She was half-way up the staircase when he caught up with her.

'Now just what did you mean by that?' he wanted to know silkily.

'Exactly what I said; but don't worry, I'll be careful never to repeat it. But that is what I think and what I shall always think, although I promise you I'll not let it show.'

She went on up the stairs and he stayed where he was. At the top she turned round and went back to him. 'I'm sorry. I'm grateful to you for all that you have done for grandfather and me—I wouldn't like you to think that I'm not. But I did mean what I said, though it's my fault; you see, I thought we could be friends, share things… I'm making a muddle of it, though—I should have realised that there's nothing personal—it's as you said, an expediency. I'll remember that and I'll do my best to be a mother to the boys. That's what you want, isn't it?'

She didn't wait for his answer but ran back to the gallery and went into her room, where she stood looking at her trembling person in the pier-glass. For a girl who had set out to attract the man she loved, she had made a poor beginning. She took the pins out of her hair with shaking fingers, unfastened the pearls and took off the sapphire ring. She had made a mistake, she should never have consented to marry Colin, she should have turned and run at the sight of him. She undressed and lay in the bath for a long time; her usual common sense had deserted her, and all she could think of was how much she loved Colin and what she was going to do about it.

The cooling water brought her back to reality. 'Nothing,' she told herself loudly, and got out of the bath. She hadn't expected to sleep, but strangely enough she did.

Breakfast was reassuringly normal in the morning; the boys didn't go to school on a Saturday and they were excited at their uncle being at home until Monday morning and full of ideas as to what they should do.

'Shall we let Eustacia choose?' suggested their uncle and smiled across the table at her, quite at his ease. Not to be outdone, she smiled back.

'Oh, may I?' She glanced out of the window. It was

a surprisingly mild morning. Do you suppose we might drive out to Cliveden and go for a walk in the grounds? I went once, years ago, and I loved it—we could take Moses too.' She looked round her, rather diffidently.

'Splendid,' said Sir Colin without hesitation, 'there are some lovely woods there, I could do with stretching my legs.'

The boys echoed him and Mrs Crichton said, 'It sounds lovely, but you won't mind if I stay here and do nothing?'

Mr Crump nodded at that. 'Yesterday was delightful, but a little tiring; I too would like to remain here.'

The professor was driving the bishop back to London during the morning; they expressed envy, agreed that it sounded a delightful way to spend a morning and accepted invitations to spend a weekend later on so that they could stretch their legs too, and everyone went their various ways.

They left half an hour later, having seen the bishop and the professor on their way, and made sure that Mrs Crichton and Grandfather were comfortably settled until lunchtime, and wrestled the boys into their outdoor things.

Eustacia, determined to fulfil the role she had promised to adopt, joined in the cheerful talk, and if she laughed rather more than usual no one noticed. It wasn't a long drive to Taplow. They parked the car in the grounds of Cliveden, got their tickets and a map of the routes they could take through the woods and set off with Moses on his lead and the boys running off the path to explore. Eustacia, walking beside Colin, kept up a cheerful chatter about nothing in particular— it was more of a monologue, actually, for he had very little to say in reply. Only when she paused for breath did he say quietly, 'I'm sorry if I upset you yesterday. It wasn't my intention. We have had no time to talk, have we? Perhaps this evening...? If we could start again with the same intention we had when we first knew about my brother and his wife?'

He had stopped for a moment, standing very close to her, and she longed to tell him that she had fallen in love with him and ask what she was to do about it. But of course she couldn't. Perhaps they could grow closer to each other through the shared aim of making the boys happy and making a home for them. She looked up into his face and saw that he was tired and worried.

She put a hand on his arm. 'We'll start again,' she told him, 'and I'm sorry too; I dare say it was getting married—it's unsettling.'

He smiled then. 'That is the heart of the matter,' he agreed. 'Perhaps we should forget about being married and return to our friendly relationship, for it *was* that, wasn't it?'

She nodded. 'Oh, yes.' She wanted to say a good deal more but she didn't, and after a moment he bent and kissed her. 'To seal our everlasting friendship,' he told her, and took her arm and walked on to where they could hear the boys calling to each other.

CHAPTER SIX

MONDAY came too soon after a delightful weekend. Eustacia, conscious of her wifely status, got up early in order to breakfast with Colin. He was already at the table when she joined him, immersed in a sheaf of papers, and although he got to his feet and wished her good morning she saw at once that he would have preferred to be alone. She sat silently, drinking coffee, until he gathered up his papers and got to his feet.

'You have no need to come down early to share my breakfast,' he told her kindly. 'I'm poor company, I'm afraid. You've only had coffee, haven't you? You will be able to breakfast with the boys. I'll try and get down tomorrow evening and I'd be glad if you would come back with me—we have to see Mr Baldock and arrange for you to be made the boys' guardian.'

'Very well. How do I get back here?'

'I'll drive you back.' He laid a large hand on her shoulder and gave her an avuncular pat. 'I'll give you a ring this evening before the boys go to bed.'

Her 'very well, Colin' was uttered in what she hoped was the kind of voice a wife would use. 'I hope you have a good day; goodbye.'

His hand tightened on her shoulder for a moment and then he was gone.

The boys were full of good spirits, and she saw to

their breakfast, drove them to school, assured them that she would collect them at four o'clock and drive them home, and then she went back to spend an hour with her grandfather before being led away by Mrs Samways, who, with an eye to the fitness of things, considered that Eustacia should inspect every cupboard in the house.

Colin phoned after tea and the boys talked for some time before calling her to the phone. 'Uncle's coming home tomorrow evening,' said Teddy. 'He wants to talk to you now.'

'It's me,' said Eustacia with a sad lack of grammar.

'The boys sound very happy. You've had a good day?'

'Yes, thank you.' Her loving ear caught the note of weariness in his voice. 'You're tired—you've had a lot to do?'

His chuckle was reassuring. 'No more than usual, and remember that I like doing it.'

She remembered something. 'Shall I have time to do any shopping when I'm in London? Mrs Samways wants some things from Fortnum and Mason...'

'We shouldn't be too long with Mr Baldock, so there should be time enough.' He added, 'I shall be home about six o'clock, Eustacia.'

'Oh, good.' She had no idea how delighted she sounded.

It was nearer seven o'clock by the time he arrived the next day, but the boys, bathed and ready for bed, had their supper while he talked to them until Eustacia shooed them upstairs, to tuck them up and potter quietly around the room until they were asleep.

They drove up to London directly after breakfast, taking the boys to school first, and they went straight to Mr Baldock's office. Eustacia signed papers, listened to what seemed to her to be a long-winded explanation of their guardianship by Mr Baldock, and presently left with Colin.

It was a fine morning even if chilly, and outside the office she paused. 'I can walk from here, it isn't far and it's a lovely day.'

He took her arm. 'I'm coming with you. I can park the car close by and I haven't any patients until eleven o'clock at my rooms.'

'Oh, that'll be nice.' She skipped into the car, feeling happy. It was going to be a lovely day...and not just the weather.

They strolled around Fortnum and Mason and she bought the particular brand of marmalade and the special blend of tea Mrs Samways had asked for, and when her eye caught a box of toffees she bought them too. 'Teddy has a loose tooth,' she explained to Colin, 'and it's the best way of getting it out almost painlessly.'

They were going unhurriedly to the door when they were confronted by a small, slender woman with blonde hair, very blue eyes and a pretty, rather discontented face. She was dressed in the height of fashion and Eustacia thanked heaven that she had chosen to wear the tweed suit with a silk blouse and a pert

little hat, all of them in the very best of taste and very
expensive in an understated way.

Colin had stopped. 'Why, Gloria, how delightful to
see you.'

He sounded far too pleased, thought Eustacia. 'I was
so sorry you couldn't come to our wedding.' He
smiled with charm. 'This is Eustacia, my wife; my
dear, this is Gloria Devlin.'

They shook hands and smiled, and disliked each
other at once. Gloria stared at Eustacia with cold eyes.
'My dear, how exceedingly nice to meet you, I have
wondered what you would be like. Not in the least
like me, but then it wouldn't do to marry an imitation
of me, would it?' She laughed and Eustacia said
gently,

'I should think it would be very difficult to imitate
you, Gloria.' She allowed her gaze to roam over the
woman's person, at the same time allowing her eyebrows to arch very slightly and her mouth to droop in
a doubtful fashion. It had the effect she had hoped
for—Gloria glanced uneasily at her flamboyant outfit
and, since Eustacia's eyes had come to rest on her
scarlet leather boots, bent her gaze on them.

Colin stood between them, a ghost of a smile on his
bland face. He said now, 'You must come and see us
soon, Gloria, must she not, Eustacia? We shall be up
here from time to time—dinner one evening, perhaps?'

Eustacia smiled brilliantly. 'Oh, yes, do say you will
come. Colin has your phone number, of course, and
I'll give you a ring.' She glanced at her watch. 'Colin,

you'll be late for your patient, we must go. It *has* been nice meeting you, Gloria—goodbye.'

'What a very pretty woman,' observed Eustacia, getting into the car. 'I'm only surprised that you didn't marry her.'

'The boys didn't like her.' His reply was most unsatisfactory. 'She is an old friend.'

'So I gather,' said Eustacia coldly.

She didn't see his smile. 'Perhaps you would like to come to my rooms and have a cup of coffee while I see my patients? Miss Butt, my receptionist, and Mrs Cole the nurse were at our wedding, and they would like to see you again.'

So Gloria was a closed book, was she? mused Eustacia, agreeing with every sign of pleasure.

The rooms were on the ground floor of a large Georgian house with several brass name-plates beside its elegant front door. He ushered her inside and Miss Butt, middle-aged, neat and self-effacing, and exuding a vague sympathy which must have been balm to such of his patients who were nervous on arriving or upset on leaving, darted forward to meet them.

'Sir Colin, will you phone the hospital—your registrar? Lady Malcolm is due in five minutes.'

Colin started for the door leading to his consulting-room. 'Thank you, Miss Butt; give Lady Crichton a cup of coffee, will you? And sneak one in to me after the first patient.'

There was a little room behind the waiting-room and Miss Butt ushered Eustacia into it. There was a small table and two comfortable chairs, a minute fridge and a shelf with an electric kettle and a coffee-making machine on it. Miss Butt got cups and saucers, sugar and milk and put them on the table and found a tin of biscuits.

'This is a pleasure, Lady Crichton, Mrs Cole and I did so enjoy your wedding, and, if I say so, you made a beautiful bride. Mrs Cole will be here in a minute or two but she won't be able to stay: she attends the patients while Sir Colin examines them.'

She poured their coffee and got up again. 'There's Lady Malcolm now. I won't be a tick.'

'I expect you have a very busy life here,' said Eustacia as Miss Butt sat down again.

'Indeed I do, and Mrs Cole too. Sir Colin works too hard, but I'm sure you know that. Going from a busy morning here to operate at St Biddolph's and then flying off heaven knows where to lecture or consult or address a seminar... There is no end to it.' She beamed at Eustacia over her spectacles. 'I dare say now that he is a married man he will cut down on some of these since he will want to be at home with you.'

'And Oliver and Teddy,' said Eustacia. 'They adore him and he's very fond of them.'

'The poor little boys. What a terrible thing to happen, but how wonderful that they have a home and two people to love them.'

She got up again as Lady Malcolm was shown out by the nurse, saying, 'I'll just pop in with Sir Colin's coffee,' and as she went out Mrs Cole came in. A small, stout lady in an old-fashioned nurse's uniform and apron, a starched cap on her greying hair.

'Well, this is nice,' she declared. 'We saw you at the wedding, of course, but there were such a lot of people there—Sir Colin has so many firm friends…'

The next patient came and went and Colin put his head round the door and said, 'Come and see my consulting-room, Eustacia.'

It was a restful place, like the waiting-room, soothing greys and a gentle green with a bowl of spring flowers by the window. His desk was large and piled with papers and she imagined him sitting at it, listening patiently to whomever was sitting in the chair on the other side of it.

This was a side of him she didn't know and she suddenly wished that she did. 'May I come to St Biddolph's one day—just to see where you work? The wards and the outpatients and the operating theatre, if that's allowed.'

'Of course it's allowed, if I say so.' He gave her a thoughtful look. 'You would really like to see everything there?'

She nodded. 'Yes, please. You see, if I know where you are, I can—' She stopped; it wouldn't do to let him think that she was deeply interested in everything he did.

He smiled a little. 'It is a strange thing, but I feel as though you have been my wife for a long time…'

'Oh, why do you say that?'

He grinned, sitting on the edge of his desk, his long legs stretched out before him. 'You behave absolutely exactly as one imagines a wife would behave. You have slipped into the role very neatly, Eustacia.'

That brought her up short. Of course, to him it was a role, not the real thing. She couldn't think of the right answer to that and presently he went on, 'We're invited to drinks at St Biddolph's—the medical staff and the cream of the nursing staff. Next Saturday—I accepted for us both. I thought we might bring the boys up in the morning and stay the night.'

'They would love that.'

'And you, Eustacia? Will you love it too?'

'Oh, yes. Although I am a bit nervous about meeting your colleagues.'

'Don't be. I'm sorry I can't take you to lunch. I'm operating this afternoon. Do you want a dress for the party on Saturday? I'll drop you off wherever you want to go...'

'Oh—well, yes, perhaps I'd better get something. Will it be very formal?'

'If you mean black ties, no, but the women will be wearing short party dresses. You know what I mean?'

She nodded, remembering the few happy years she had had after she had left school and travelled with her parents. There had been parties then...

'You will need some money. I'll arrange with Harrods so that you have a charge account, but perhaps you have some other shop in mind?' He gave her a roll of notes.

'I'm costing you an awful lot,' said Eustacia guiltily.

He smiled. 'Get something pretty, you have excellent taste.' He waited while she stowed the money away. 'Shall we go?'

She elected to get out at Harrods. It was a shop which had everything and she was sure to find something she liked; besides, she could have a snack lunch there.

'I'll be home around five o'clock,' said Colin as she got out of the car.

'Will you have had tea?'

'Oh, I'll get a cup at the hospital. Have yours when you like.'

He drove away without a backward glance and she had the lowering feeling that he had already forgotten her.

She took her time looking for a dress. It was after her lunch that she found it. Coppery autumn leaves scattered over a misty grey silk, its full skirt cleverly cut so that it swirled around her as she walked, the bodice close-fitting with a simple round neckline cut low, and very full elbow-length sleeves. It took almost all the money Colin had given her and was worth every penny of it. She bore it back to the house, tried it on once more, packed it carefully into its tissue paper, and went down to have her tea. Grimstone had set it on a small table by the fire and Rosie had made some little chocolate cakes to follow the strips of buttered toast.

She eyed everything happily. 'What a lovely tea, Grimstone, and how delightful those little cakes look.'

Grimstone allowed himself the luxury of a smile. 'Rosie thought you might like them, my lady. I'm told you will be here for the weekend with the young gentlemen. If there is anything special you would like to have you have only to say.'

'I'm sure Rosie must know better than I do what the boys like to eat, but I'll come and see her presently, shall I?'

She spent half an hour in the delightful kitchen, sitting at the table with Rosie while they discussed the merits of potatoes roasted in the oven and those baked in their skins. 'I'm sure the boys will eat them if they're smothered in butter,' said Eustacia. 'How about Sir Colin?'

'Well, he likes a nice roast potato, my lady, but I could do some of each...' They settled on a menu to suit everybody and Eustacia went back to the drawing-room, reflecting that, although she had found being called 'my lady' very strange at first, now she hardly noticed it. One could get used to everything, given time, even being married to a man who didn't love one.

Colin got back just before six o'clock. 'Give me fifteen minutes to shower and change,' he begged her. 'You're ready to leave?'

The traffic was heavy, but they got back to Turville before the boys' bedtime. Eustacia took her purchases to her room, did things to her face and hair and went downstairs to find Colin playing Snakes and Ladders with the boys and her grandfather. They looked up and smiled as she went in but returned to the game immediately, so that after a minute or two she went to the kitchen to see Mrs Samways and take her the things she had wanted.

'I'll keep dinner back until Sir Colin has gone, shall I?' asked Mrs Samways. 'Pity he can't stay the night. Always on the go, he is.'

Eustacia said faintly, 'Yes, isn't he? Do wait until he is gone if you can do so without spoiling anything. The boys will still have to go to bed…'

She went back to the drawing-room and found that the game was finished and Colin was standing with his back to the fireplace, his hands in his pockets. 'Ah, there you are,' he observed cheerfully. 'I'll be off again.'

'So Mrs Samways has just told me,' said Eustacia waspishly.

'The hospital board of governors are meeting this evening and they have asked me to look in—'

'Oh, yes? Where will you dine?'

'Rosie will find something for me.' He was still infuriatingly cheerful. He bade the boys goodnight, reminded them that he would be back on Friday evening, wished Mr Crump goodnight too and went to the door, sweeping her along with him. In the hall he asked, 'You're cross—why?'

'I am not in the least cross. After all, there is no reason why I should be told of your plans.' She made the remark with a cold haughtiness which would have shrivelled a lesser man.

He actually laughed. 'Oh, I am sorry, Eustacia. I am so used to a bachelor's way of living. I promise you I'll try to remember that I'm married now. No hard feelings?'

'No,' said Eustacia, loving and hating him at the

same time, wondering if it would be possible to be out of the house with the boys when he got back on Friday evening. Serve him right. What was sauce for the goose was sauce for the gander.

'Expect me on Friday evening.' He gave her an avuncular pat on the shoulder and went out to his car and drove away with a wave of the hand as he went.

Standing in the doorway, she waved back, quite unable to see him clearly through the tears she was doing her best not to shed. She wiped them away roughly; the boys would have to be put to bed and they had sharp eyes.

It was during dinner that her grandfather asked, 'What's the matter, Eustacia?'

'The matter? Nothing, Grandpa.' She smiled at him. 'I expect I'm a bit tired—it was quite a long day and I went shopping and then Colin took me to his consulting-rooms...' She enlarged upon this for some minutes and her grandparent said,

'I dare say it is as you say, my dear. It is so peaceful here after Kennington, although I dare say Colin's house is quiet enough.'

'Oh, it is, not at all like the London we lived in.' She began to tell him about the house there and presently they parted for the night.

She was still determined to be out of the house when Colin got home on Friday evening. She was being unreasonably unkind, she knew that, but she wanted to do something to make him aware of her and chance was on her side. There was a bazaar in the village in aid of the church and at the end of the afternoon there was to be a conjuror, a treat the boys didn't want to miss.

'But will it be over before Uncle gets home?' asked Oliver.

'I'm not sure, but I don't think he will mind if we're home a bit late.'

Sir Colin got back earlier than he had expected; indeed, he hadn't stopped for the usual cup of tea after his list, aware of a desire to get to Turville as quickly as possible. He had told his registrar to phone him if it was necessary, made his excuses to Theatre Sister who had a tray of tea waiting in her office, and had driven himself off.

'Well, I've never known him miss his tea,' said Sister, much aggrieved.

'He's never been married before,' observed his registrar. 'She's a beauty—you'll see her on Saturday.'

The house was quiet as Sir Colin let himself in, and the drawing-room was empty. Mr Crump was in the library enjoying a good book, which he put down as Sir Colin walked in. He said in a pleased voice, 'Ah, you are home again. A busy few days, I expect?'

Sir Colin agreed amiably. 'Where is Eustacia? And where are the boys?'

'Oh, I dare say that they will be back at any moment; there was a conjuror's show in the village hall and she took them to see it.' He added, 'A treat, since they have done well at school this week.'

Sir Colin replied vaguely. He had telephoned Eustacia on the previous evening and she hadn't said a word about the conjuror. He began to smile and Mr

Crump asked, 'You are pleased that they have done well?'

'Oh, most certainly. You'll forgive me if I go to my study and do some phoning?'

He was sitting in his chair, reading a newspaper with Moses lying on his feet when they got home. He received the boys' boisterous welcome with calm good humour, observing that they appeared to have had a most entertaining evening. 'And you enjoyed yourself too, Eustacia?'

'Oh, very much,' she assured him and smiled for the boys' benefit although her eyes were cool. 'Have you been home long?'

'I was early.' His smile was placid and she reflected that it had been a waste of time planning to annoy him. She doubted very much if she would ever get the better of him, and it was mortifying to realise that he had seen though her efforts to pay him back in his own coin.

The rest of the evening passed pleasantly enough. The boys had their supper, stayed up for an extra half-hour in order to play a boisterous game of Scrabble and went to bed, in due course, nicely tired and looking forward to their weekend in London. As for Eustacia, she entered into the conversation at the dinner table and then sat in the drawing-room, knitting sweaters for the boys while the two gentlemen went away to play billiards.

'For all the world as though we'd been married for half a lifetime,' she muttered to the empty room.

She was knitting, the outward picture of contented

composure, when Sir Colin and her grandfather joined
her. She looked up as they went in and enquired
sweetly if they had had a good game. 'Would you like
coffee? I asked Mrs Samways to leave some ready…'

They declined, and after ten minutes or so she stuck
her ball of wool on to the ends of the needles and got
to her feet. 'Then I'll go to bed.' She flashed them a
brilliant smile and made for the door.

Colin got there first and laid a hand over hers. 'Will
you spare a moment? I thought we might leave about
eleven o'clock, have an early lunch and take the boys
to Madame Tussaud's, and then go somewhere for tea.
We'll need to leave the house at half-past six for the
party—can you get them to bed and dress in an hour?'

'Just about.'

He nodded. 'Good.' He bent and kissed her cheek
and then opened the door. 'I am so glad that you enjoyed the conjuror,' he murmured as she went past
him.

The next morning went according to plan; a fore-
gone conclusion, reflected Eustacia—plans made by
Colin went smoothly and exactly as he wished. A light
lunch was enjoyed by them all at the London house
and very shortly afterwards the four of them piled into
a taxi and were driven to Madame Tussaud's, a highly
successful outing despite the frustrated wishes of the
boys to view the Chamber of Horrors. The prospect
of a splendid tea made up for this and they did full
justice to the meal, served with great elegance in
Claridge's Hotel; sandwiches, buns and small cream
cakes were polished off with the assistance of a sym-

pathetic waiter who produced an unending supply of delicacies and orange squash.

'Did we behave well, Eustacia?' asked Oliver as they got out of the taxi and went indoors.

'You were both quite perfect,' she declared. 'I was proud of you—weren't you, Colin?'

She turned to him and found him watching her with an expression which puzzled her. She forgot it once she was engulfed in the bustle of getting the boys to their beds, arranging for them to have milk and sandwiches once they were there and then going off to dress.

She had ten minutes to spare before they needed to leave; she went along to the boys' room and found them in their beds, demanding their supper. She promised to see Rosie on her way and hurry her up, kissed them goodnight and then, since they wanted it, paraded up and down the room in the new dress, twirling round so that the skirt billowed around her.

'Oh, very nice,' said Colin from the door, 'you will be a sensation.'

She came to a sudden halt. 'Don't be absurd,' she told him severely. 'I shall be very dignified…'

'Why?' He sounded amused.

'Well, consultants are dignified, aren't they? So I imagine their wives are too.' She added slowly, 'I think I'm a little nervous of meeting them.'

'No need. You look exactly as a consultant's wife should look.' He walked towards her and deliberately added, 'Elegantly dressed, beautiful and charming. I shall be the envy of all the men there.'

She blushed charmingly but looked at him uncertainly. He was probably being kind and bolstering up her ego. She said hesitantly, 'As long as I'll do...'

For answer he turned to the boys. 'Will Eustacia do, Oliver—Teddy? Will she be the prettiest lady there?'

They shouted agreement and he said, 'You see? Unanimous. We'll tell you all about it in the morning.'

The party was being held in the large room adjoining the consultant's room, a high-ceilinged apartment used for social occasions, meetings of hospital governors and other solemn events, and as they went in Eustacia had the impression that it was packed to the ceiling with people.

She felt Colin's hand, large and reassuring, on her arm as they made their way to where the hospital governors and his colleagues were waiting. After that, she began to enjoy herself. The men were plainly interested in her and their wives were kind. Presently she found that Colin had been surrounded by a group of older men and she was taken under the wing of the hospital secretary and passed from group to group. There were even a few people she knew: Miss Bennett and Mr Brimshaw and Professor Ladbroke, and in a little while Colin joined her, introducing her to a bewildering number of medical staff as well as the matron and several of the senior sisters. When the medical director called for silence, Colin took her hand and held it fast, which was a good thing, for the medical director, elderly and forgetful and of a sentimental turn of mind, made a long speech about the joys of marriage and young love before presenting them with a wedding gift. A silver rose-bowl which Eustacia received with a shy smile and a murmured thank you. It was left to Sir Colin to reply and anyone listening to him, she thought, would think that he was head over heels in love and blissfully happy. Indignant colour flooded her cheeks and everyone looked at her and smiled kindly, thinking that she was shy.

She smiled in return, while she reflected with something like dismay on a future full of pitfalls. Marrying Colin for a sensible and good reason was one thing, but to have to enact a loved and loving wife for the rest of her days was suddenly unendurable, since he had shown no desire to have a loving wife, only a surrogate mother for his nephews.

They left soon after with enough invitations for morning coffee and dinner parties to keep them occupied for weeks to come. As they got into the car Eustacia said, 'You're very popular, aren't you, Colin?'

'I have been working at St Biddolph's for years,' he told her, as though that were sufficient answer, and then he added placidly, 'I dare say I should not have received half as many invitations if you hadn't been with me. I can see that you will be a great asset to me, Eustacia.'

She glanced at his calm profile. 'I shouldn't have thought that you needed assets.' She sounded very slightly cross.

'For some reason patients are much more at ease with their medical adviser if he is a married man.'

'What a good thing,' declared Eustacia sharply. 'I must bear that in mind.'

'Yes, do,' said Colin at his most bland.

The boys were still awake when they got back, so they said goodnight for a second time and then sat down to their dinner. 'Would you like to go out this evening?' Colin asked. 'A night-club or dancing?'

She took a mouthful of Rosie's delicious asparagus soup and thought about it. 'Unless you want to, no, thank you…'

'Oh, good. I seldom get a quiet evening at home. I can catch up on my reading, there may be something worth watching on TV, and there are several new novels you may like to dip into.'

But no conversation, thought Eustacia. 'It sounds delightful,' she said with what she hoped was suitable wifely acquiescence, and she quite missed the gleam of amusement in her husband's eye.

They went to the drawing-room and had their coffee and she chose a book and opened it, and Sir Colin, with what she imagined was a sigh of contentment, unfolded the evening paper. She had read page one and embarked on page two when the front doorbell pealed and she heard Grimstone's measured tread crossing the hall and then the murmur of voices. A moment later he opened the drawing-room door and announced, 'Miss Gloria Devlin.'

She came tripping into the room, a brilliant figure in a magenta silk trouser-suit with a black camisole top, and had begun to talk before Sir Colin had cast aside his newspaper and risen to his feet.

'My dears, I heard you were in town for the week-end and after that dreary drinks party at the hospital I knew you would be longing for a lively evening.' She paused as a youngish man came into the room. 'So Clive and I put our heads together and came round to collect you both. We can go to a night-club...' She looked at Eustacia. 'You haven't met Clive, have you? He's a scream and such good fun.'

'How delightful to see you, Gloria,' Sir Colin was at his most urbane, 'and so kind of you to think of us.' He nodded at her companion. 'Do come in and have a drink. Unfortunately we have other plans for the evening, so we must refuse your invitation, but stay for a while. Sit here, by the fire, Gloria. What will you drink?'

'Oh, my usual, vodka—you surely haven't forgotten after all these months?' She gave a little tinkling laugh and Eustacia wanted to box her ears.

Sir Colin made no answer to this but poured her drink and turned to the man. 'And you, Stevenson?'

'Whisky, thanks.'

'You haven't met my wife, I believe?' went on Sir Colin smoothly. 'Eustacia, this is Clive Stevenson, he runs a clinic for plastic surgery.' He added, 'Would you like a drink, darling?' He smiled across the room at her. 'Perhaps you had better not, since we're going out again.'

She smiled back. 'I don't want anything, thank you, dear.' She turned to Gloria. 'I didn't see you at St Biddolph's this evening.'

'Me? Go there? It's the last place that I'd set foot

in. Clive heard about it from one of the doctors there—
he anaesthetises for him. Clive has a huge practice
making tucks and face-lifting. He alters shapes too…'
She gave Eustacia's person a penetrating look, but
since there was nothing wrong with it she remained
silent, but Stevenson chimed in with a laugh,

'No good looking at our hostess, Gloria, she looks
perfect to me.'

Eustacia gave him a look to freeze his bones and
glanced at Sir Colin. His face was without expression
but his mouth had become a thin line.

'You must forgive us,' he said in a voice which
conveyed the fact that he had not the least interest in
their forgiveness. 'We are due to leave in a very short
time and I must phone to the hospital first.'

Gloria pouted. 'Oh, Colin, how dull of you to go
off on your own, just the two of you—we could have
had such a good time.' She cast a sly look at Eustacia.
'As we used to…'

Sir Colin took no notice of this remark and she
shrugged her shoulders and got up. 'Oh, well, we
might as well go and leave you to your domestic bliss.'

Eustacia got up too. 'So kind of you to call in,' she
said sweetly, 'I hope you will have a pleasant evening.'

'I'm sure we shall.' Gloria's voice was just as
sweet. 'Though I rather think our ideas of a pleasant
evening aren't the same.' She tripped over to Sir Colin
and leaned up to kiss him, then grabbed Clive's arm.
He had gone over to say goodbye to Eustacia and
Gloria gave him a tug. 'Come on, Clive, it's me you

are taking out.' She gave another of her irritating trills of laughter. Eustacia watched them go and stood listening to them talking to Colin in the hall, wondering what they were saying. A pity the door was almost closed...

Sir Colin came back presently and picked up his paper. Eustacia addressed the back of it. 'I am sorry if it's inconvenient to you, but I do not like your friends,' she observed waspishly, 'at least, some of them.'

He lowered the paper and looked at her over it. 'Hardly friends—I don't care for Stevenson—'

'She kissed you...' She hadn't meant to say that and she frowned furiously.

'I have yet to meet a man who didn't enjoy being kissed by a pretty woman.' He spoke with maddening calm, but his eyes beneath the heavy lids were watching her cross face with hidden amusement.

It seemed impossible to get the better of him; there was no answer to that. She put down her book and rose with dignity. 'The prospect of looking at the back of your newspaper for the rest of the evening leaves me with no alternative but to go to bed. Goodnight, Colin.'

She sailed to the door and most unfortunately tripped up as she reached it; he was just in time to set her on her feet again, making no effort to let her go. 'Thank you,' she said coldly. He smiled down at her.

'Crosspatch.' The kiss he gave her would, in the right circumstances, have been very satisfying.

CHAPTER SEVEN

EUSTACIA lay awake for a long time; a good weep had done very little to relieve her feelings, and the evening's events were going round and round in her head until they were in such a muddle that she had no clear idea of what she was thinking about any more. She slept at last and woke in the morning with the lowering feeling that she had behaved badly. She dressed and went to see how the boys were getting on and presently they all went down to breakfast. There was no one at the table but, looking out of the window, they could see Sir Colin in his small garden. He had Moses with him and Madam Mop was sitting on the edge of a stone bird-bath, watching them. The garden was charming, ringed around by a variety of small trees and a high brick wall, with a patio outside the house, a small lawn in its centre and flower-beds bordering the narrow paths. In another week or so there would be daffodils everywhere and, later, tulips. Sir Colin was crouching over a centre bed, planting bulbs, and the boys lost no time in opening the french window and rushing out to join him.

Eustacia watched while they gave him a hand; they were talking nineteen to the dozen and getting in the way of their uncle, and she very much wanted to join them. She was feeling awkward about meeting Colin

again after the previous evening; she had been insuf-
ferably rude and, not only that, his kiss had taken her
by surprise, leaving her uncertain and more in love
with him than ever, a state of affairs which wouldn't
do at all. She was roused from her unhappy thoughts
by Rosie's voice.

'Catch their deaths out there,' she said, 'and breakfast all but on the table, too.'

'I'll call them in,' said Eustacia hastily, 'but it's not
cold, is it?' She turned to smile at the housekeeper.

'Well, not so's you'd notice, my lady, but there's
good hot porridge waiting to line their stomachs.'

Eustacia said, 'Oh, good, Rosie,' and opened the
french windows again and yelled, 'Breakfast—now,
this instant!'

She watched them go in through the garden door
and presently they came into the dining-room. 'Did
you wash your hands?'

They chorused a yes and Sir Colin said meekly, 'I
washed mine too. Good morning, Eustacia.'

Her good morning was drowned by the boys' de-
mands to know what they were going to do all day.
'Sit down, eat your porridge and I'll tell you,' said Sir
Colin. 'Church?' He cocked an eyebrow at Eustacia,
who nodded without hesitation. 'St Paul's, I think,
don't you? And afterwards we'll cross the river and
drive and find somewhere for coffee before we come
back here for lunch. How about an hour or two at the
zoo before tea? And then we'll go back to Turville.'

This programme was greeted with approbation by
the boys and, after they had made a hearty breakfast,

Eustacia led them away to be tidied and fastened into their coats, while Sir Colin wandered off to appear in a short time suitably attired in a dark grey suit and beautifully polished shoes.

'I like that outfit,' he told Eustacia, who was waiting for him in the hall, and to her great annoyance she blushed.

The vastness and magnificence of St Paul's Cathedral did much to soothe her. She listened to Teddy's shrill voice piping up when he knew the hymns, Oliver's more assured treble and Colin's deep rumbling bass and, since it was expected of her, joined in with her own small, clear voice.

They found somewhere to have coffee after the service, and then went home to Rosie's Sunday dinner of roast beef, Yorkshire puddings, roasted potatoes and sprouts, cooked to perfection, and followed by a trifle which was sheer ambrosia.

They wasted no time in going to the zoo, and Eustacia was glad of that. There had been no opportunity to be alone with Colin, let alone talk to him; they had the boys with them all the time and when they got home they had tea together, a substantial meal of Marmite on toast, sandwiches and chocolate cake.

It was as they were on the point of leaving after this meal that Grimstone asked, 'At what time will you be back, Sir Colin? Rosie will have a meal ready for you...'

'No need,' he replied, shrugging himself into his coat. 'I'll have dinner at Turville. Go to bed if I'm not

back, Grimstone, but see that I'm called at seven
o'clock tomorrow morning, will you?'

Grimstone inclined his head in a dignified manner,
wished them all a safe journey and they got into the
Rolls and drove away.

The boys, in the back with Moses, carried on the
kind of conversation normal for small boys, but
Eustacia sat silent, racking her brains for a suitable
topic of conversation and, since the man beside her
remained silent too, presently she gave up searching
for a harmless subject, so that they gained Turville
with no more than the odd remark exchanged. But
once in the house there was a welcome bustle and a
good deal to talk about for Mr Crump wanted to know
about their weekend and Mrs Samways wanted to
know about the boys' supper.

That attended to, Eustacia went to her room, tidied
herself and went back downstairs to warn Mrs
Samways that Sir Colin would be staying for dinner.

'I thought he might, my lady. Me and Rosie, we're
used to him coming and going, as it were, though I
dare say now he's settled down he'll get a bit more
regular in his ways, if you don't mind me saying so.'

Eustacia assured her that she didn't mind in the
least. 'Though I dare say it will take a little time to
adjust, Mrs Samways.'

'No doubt, my lady, but you'll attend to that, I'll be
bound.'

Eustacia agreed, thinking that it would be very unlikely, and went to preside over the boys' supper and
then to get them bathed and into their beds. They were

tired and went willingly enough after protracted good-nights to their uncle.

Once they were settled she went along to her room and changed her clothes. There was a rather nice Paisley-patterned dress hanging in the wardrobe which hadn't been worn yet. She put it on and was pleased with the result; Colin might even notice...

They had drinks and then dined, the three of them, and the conversation was of nothing in particular; indeed, she had the suspicion that Colin was encouraging her grandfather to reminisce so that conversation between the two of them was unnecessary, and very soon after they had had coffee he declared that he had to get back. 'I've a round at eight o'clock tomorrow,' he explained, 'and a list after that, but I'll try and get down in a couple of days.'

Eustacia went out into the hall with him and stood watching him while he got into his coat.

'We're bound to get some invitations to dine,' he told her cheerfully, 'but I'll ring you each evening and we can decide what to do about them.'

'Very well. And if there are any messages for you?'

'Oh, let Grimstone know, he'll find me and pass them on.' He broke off as Samways came into the hall. 'Samways, tell Mrs Samways that dinner was excellent, will you? Lady Crichton will let her know when I'm coming down again—in a day or so, I hope.'

Samways inclined his head gravely, wished him a good journey and withdrew discreetly.

Eustacia waited until he had shut the door behind him. 'I cannot think,' she declared pettishly, 'how it is that you manage to have such willing staff at both your homes. Some of the wives I met at the party were saying that they couldn't get anyone, not even cleaning ladies.'

He ignored the pettishness and answered her seriously. 'I pay them well, I house them well, I give them due credit for work well done, just as I hope that my patients give me credit when I succeed in making them better.' He grinned suddenly. 'And I inherited Grimstone.'

She felt foolish and muttered, 'Oh, yes, so you did,' and looked away from his amused glance and raised eyebrows. She had been silly to talk like that and now she suspected that he was laughing at her.

'Take care of the boys,' he said gently, 'and take care of yourself.'

She nodded, hoping that he would kiss her, but he smiled again and opened the door and was gone.

She went to bed presently, a prey to highly imaginative doubts as to where Colin had gone and what he was doing. Gloria loomed large, set against a background of exotic night-clubs and restaurants with pink-shaded table-lamps. After all, she told herself worriedly, Colin had never actually said that he hadn't been, at some time, in love with Gloria—he might still be, although she was quite sure that now he was married he would give her up—although in this modern world, she reflected gloomily, it would be quite permissible for him to continue to be friends with the woman. From what Gloria had said, they had known each other for a long time. She went to sleep at last, having convinced herself that the pair of them were in some remote restaurant, looking into each other's eyes and breaking their hearts silently. She woke once in the night and it all came flooding back, more highly coloured then ever. 'I hate the woman,' said Eustacia angrily before she went to sleep again…

The day seemed endless; she did flowers, talked to her grandfather, discussed the meals with Mrs Samways and ferried the boys to and from school. By eight o'clock, she had given up hope of Colin telephoning.

It was almost ten o'clock when he did, and quite forgetful of her role of concordant partner she snapped, 'It's almost ten o'clock—you're late.'

Sir Colin thought of his busy day, not yet over, but all he said was, 'Is there something worrying you?' and that in the mildest of voices.

'No, but you said—'

He said smoothly, 'I am not always able to keep to an exact timetable, Eustacia.'

She said recklessly, common sense quite drowned in vivid imagination, 'I suppose you've been out to dinner with—with someone?'

Sir Colin, who had got through his day on a sandwich and a beer and a cup of tea forced upon him by his theatre sister, said equably, 'If that is what you think, my dear, who am I to deny it?' He laughed suddenly. 'You have Gloria in mind?'

Eustacia put down the receiver with a thump and burst into tears.

She felt terrible about it in the morning; she had

been a fool and behaved like a silly, jealous schoolgirl, probably he would never want to see her again, she was utterly unsuitable as his wife and she had made a hash of being married to him. With a great effort she managed to behave normally towards the boys, listening to their ideas about the Easter holidays, now looming. 'It would be nice to go away on holiday,' said Teddy, 'but it might be cold at the seaside.'

She agreed that it certainly would be. 'But there are heaps of other things we can do,' she promised. 'Perhaps your uncle will be able to spare the time to take you to see your Granny.'

Teddy liked that idea. 'But perhaps we'll have to go and stay with Granny and Grandpa Kennedy,' he said worriedly. 'I don't want to.'

'I dare say you would have a lovely time—'

'Only if you and Uncle Colin are there too.'

'Well, no one has said anything about it, my dear, so we don't need to think about it, do we?'

'All right, when is Uncle Colin coming home?'

Eustacia said in an animated voice, 'Oh, he rang up last night, quite late, and he had been very busy—he didn't say.'

'I hope he'll come soon,' said Oliver, 'in time for the end-of-term concert.'

'He'll come just as soon as he can,' said Eustacia, dreading the idea and longing to see him just the same.

He came that evening, between tea and dinner, while Eustacia was sitting at the small table in the sitting-room, helping Oliver with his history and encouraging Teddy to write tidily in his copy-book. The three of them were so engrossed that they didn't hear Sir Colin's quiet entrance until his equally quiet, 'Hello, there.'

The boys flew to greet him, both talking at once, and he listened patiently to a jumble of information about school and the holidays and the last day of term, and would he be there because Oliver had to recite a poem and Teddy was singing a song with six other little boys?

Eustacia had time to look at Colin as he bent his height to the little boys' level. He was tired, and his handsome looks showed lines of fatigue, but he answered the boys' excited questions, came to the table to look at their homework and bent to drop a quick kiss on her cheek. 'Perhaps the boys could go and tell Mrs Samways that there will be one more for dinner,' he suggested placidly. 'I don't need to go back until tomorrow morning.'

They pranced off with Moses in close attendance and he sat down at the table facing Eustacia.

'You and I have to talk,' he said quietly, 'but not now. Perhaps we can present a suitable front for the sake of the boys in the meanwhile.' And as they came running back again, 'I shall certainly be here for the end of term and I heard from Mother yesterday—she would like us to spend a few days with her during the holidays. I can manage four or five days.'

Teddy had climbed on to his knee and Oliver had got on to the chair beside him. 'Your Granny and Grandpa Kennedy have asked if you would go and stay with them. I said that I would ask you. I know you don't want to go very much, but it might be fun, and Eustacia and I will drive you up and come to fetch you home, so will you go?'

They looked at him and then at Eustacia. 'Just a week?' she coaxed.

They nodded reluctantly and Sir Colin said, 'Good chaps.' Then he added, 'And when you come home we'll do something really exciting—you shall choose.'

'May we stay up and have our supper with you?' asked Teddy.

'I think that's a splendid idea, if Eustacia agrees.' He looked at her with raised eyebrows and a smile and she said at once,

'Oh, I don't see why not, but it might be a good idea if they have their baths now and get into their pyjamas and dressing-gowns so that they can pop into bed directly after dinner.' She got up. 'I'll let Mrs Samways know...' She smiled at the three of them, not quite looking Colin in the eye.

Dinner over and the boys in bed and the three of them in the drawing-room, she handed Colin several envelopes. 'These came—invitations—two for dinner and one for drinks; they're all in town. What would you like me to reply?'

'Oh, we'll accept, shall we?' He glanced at them in turn. 'The dates won't interfere with our visit to Castle Cary. I met Professor Ladbroke this morning and I told him that a couple of weeks' time would suit us—the boys will be in Yorkshire and we can stay in town if we feel like it.' He looked at Mr Crump. 'You won't mind, sir?'

'My dear Colin, I am in my seventh heaven here.'

'I'm glad.' He handed the invitations back to Eustacia. 'Will you answer them? I dare say there will be more. It might be a good opportunity to give a dinner party while the boys are in Yorkshire—in town, I think, don't you? You too, of course, sir.'

'That would be delightful, but I wouldn't wish you to feel compelled to invite me.'

'You need have no fear of that; I don't see enough of you—of any of you.'

His glance lighted upon Eustacia who, with her knitting in her lap, had been watching him. They stared at each other for a long moment before she picked up her needles and began to knit furiously.

The house came alive when he was at home, but once he had gone again in the morning it sank back into its peaceful state. Eustacia was glad when the boys were back from school in the afternoon, taking her attention so that she had little time to think.

School was to break up at the end of the week, and the evening before Sir Colin came home. He would have to go again on the Monday morning, he explained, but only for a few days and then they would all go to Castle Cary. His manner towards Eustacia was exactly as usual, placid and friendly, and she did her best to respond for the sake of the boys.

They all went along to the school in the morning, Sir Colin in one of his sober, beautifully tailored suits and Eustacia very smart in a new grey suit and a silk blouse and, since it was an occasion, a grey felt hat with a small brim turned up at one side. Before they left she was inspected by the boys, who pronounced her very nicely dressed. 'You'll be just like all the other Mums,' said Teddy, and his small lip quivered.

Eustacia flung an arm round his narrow shoulders. 'Oh, good, darling, and just look how smart your uncle looks. We both mean to be a credit to you, and I can't wait to hear you sing.'

Teddy sniffed. 'I do love you,' he whispered.

'And I love you, Teddy...'

'And do you love Oliver and Uncle Colin too?'

'Yes. That's what a family is, you see, people living together and loving each other, just like all of us.'

She kissed the upturned face and Sir Colin, who had heard every word, sighed gently.

The day was a great success; Teddy sang in his choir, Oliver recited his poem and they all watched the short play put on by the older boys before the buffet lunch. Once home again, their reports were studied and discussed and suitably rewarded with loose change from Sir Colin's pocket. 'Eustacia and I are very proud of you both,' he told them.

When Oliver asked, 'As proud as Daddy and Mummy would have been?' he answered at once.

'Just as proud, are we not, darling?'

He looked at Eustacia, who blushed because he had called her darling even though he hadn't meant it. 'Oh, rather—I've been thinking, on Monday suppose we drive over to Henley and buy the Easter eggs? We shall need to make a list—a secret list, of course.'

They had tea round the fire for the days were still

chilly, and after the boys were in bed they dined and made plans for the next week or two.

'I'll be back here on Thursday,' said Sir Colin. 'We can go to Mother's on Friday and stay until the middle of the week, perhaps a little longer. The Kennedys expect the boys on the Sunday after that, we'll drive them up and have lunch on the way and go straight back home for the night so that I can check on one or two things. Shall we say Monday evening for our dinner party?' He fished in a pocket and studied the list in his hand. 'Eight guests, I thought, if you're agreeable.' He read out names: colleagues and their wives and the hospital matron to partner Mr Crump. Eustacia, who had half expected to hear Gloria's name, sighed with relief.

Sunday went too swiftly and she watched the Rolls slide round the corner of the drive with a pang of unhappiness which she shook off at once. The little boys had had enough unhappiness of their own, and it behoved her to show a cheerful face.

Surprisingly the days went by quickly, and Sir Colin was back once more and this time for a week at least. She packed happily, bade her grandfather goodbye and got into the car with the boys and Moses in the back, and with them there it was easier to be on friendly terms with Colin. There was a good deal of talk and giggling as they travelled and it would have been impossible not to have joined in the fun. They stopped in Hindon at the Lamb Inn for their lunch and, because Colin said it would be good for them to stretch their legs, they walked Moses down the village street and back again before driving on. It was a matter of half an hour later they drew up before Mrs Crichton's house in Castle Cary. Martha had been watching out for them and had the door open before they could reach it, and their welcome from Mrs Crichton was full of warmth. There was a good deal of milling around and happy chatter before Eustacia was led upstairs with the boys darting to and fro and following at their heels.

'You are in your usual room, my dears,' said Mrs Crichton. 'Eustacia, you are next door to them.' She led the way into a charming, moderately sized room overlooking the garden at the back of the house. 'The bathroom is through that door and Colin's dressing-room is beyond that. I do hope you will be comfortable. It's so delightful having you all. Are the boys happier now? Have they settled down?'

Eustacia was looking out of the window; Colin was in the garden with Moses. 'Very nearly. Oliver seems to have got over it better than Teddy, but, of course, Teddy's younger. Sometimes they wake in the night, you know...'

'And what do you do, my dear?'

'Cuddle them and let them cry if they want to, and then we talk about their mother and father and all the nice things they remember.'

Mrs Crichton nodded. 'I understand they are to go to Yorkshire next week. A pity.'

'Mrs Kennedy is anxious to have them. We're going to take them up and then fetch them again.'

'You and Colin will have a few days together—that will be very nice.'

'Oh, very,' said Eustacia, and some of the happiness she felt at the thought bubbled up into her voice so that her companion gave her a quick, thoughtful glance.

The next few days were sheer delight; Mrs Crichton was a splendid granny, mixing mild authority with a grandparent's legitimate spoiling. They all went out every day—Cheddar Gorge and the caves, Cricket St Thomas to see the animals and sample the simple amusements for the children, Glastonbury and its Tor. Mrs Crichton declined to climb its steep height but the boys, with Eustacia and Colin following more sedately, did. When they got home each afternoon Martha had a magnificent tea waiting for them and that was followed by an hour or so in the drawing-room, with Moses dozing at Colin's feet while they played Snakes and Ladders and Beat your Neighbour and the memory games. Sir Colin always won—he seemed to know exactly where the cards were. Eustacia, regrettably, was quite unable to remember where the cards were, but that was because her thoughts weren't on the game but centred on Colin sitting, large and relaxed, so close to her.

The last day of their visit came, and they bought presents for the Samways and the maids, and for Grimstone and Rosie, presented Mrs Crichton with an armful of roses and Martha with a box of chocolates, had a last walk down the high street and got into the car with the promise that they would pay another visit just as soon as it could be arranged. Half-term, as Sir Colin pointed out in his placid way, was a bare two months away, and it would be early summer. The boys brightened at the thought, hugged their grandmother once more and settled down in the car with Moses perched between them.

They were home in time for tea, and Eustacia, mindful of their trip to Yorkshire in three days' time, disappeared as soon as the meal was over to confer with Mrs Samways about washing and ironing and the clothes the boys should take with them—something which suited her very well, for she was becoming far too fond of Colin's company.

He drove himself up to the hospital the next morning, saying he would be back that evening. But five o'clock came and then six o'clock, and just as she was getting the boys ready for bed he telephoned. Something had come up, he told her; he would be delayed, and it might be better if he stayed in town for the night.

'Very well,' said Eustacia in a matter-of-fact voice which hid her disappointment, 'I'll explain to the boys.'

'And you?' enquired Sir Colin gently. 'Am I to explain to you, Eustacia?' And when she remained silent, 'Or don't you want to know why I'm staying here?'

She said primly, 'I'm sure if it is necessary for you to stay that is sufficient reason—you have no need to tell me anything you don't wish to.' Upon which unsatisfactory conversation she hung up, after wishing him goodnight in a voice straight from the deep-freeze.

The unwelcome shadow of Gloria hung over her as she prepared for bed and caused her to lose quite a lot of sleep so that she was hard put to it to be her usual cheerful self in the morning. Luckily she was fully occupied for most of the day, seeing to the boys' clothes ready for their journey to Yorkshire, and they spent a good deal of their time with her grandfather, but by teatime there was nothing left to do and she was sitting with them in the drawing-room, watching Samways setting out the tea, when Sir Colin walked in.

He crossed the room to her chair and bent to kiss her cheek before returning to the boys' excited welcome and her grandfather's sober one.

Eustacia was grateful for the excited talk from the boys so that there was no need for her to say much, which was a good thing for she could think of nothing to say. She had been longing for Colin to come home and, now that he was here, she was dumb. She thought with excited pleasure of the week ahead—a whole week, the greater part of it in London. She would have the opportunity of getting to know him, perhaps.

They had tea, had a rousing game of Scrabble with the boys before the youngsters went off for their supper and bed and then she went back to the drawing-room. Sir Colin was alone.

'Can you spare half an hour?' he asked her. 'About tomorrow—it will take about five hours to drive to Richmond. We'll go up on the A1, I'll cut across country to Bedford and pick it up a few miles further on from there. The M1 would be quicker but it's very uninteresting for the boys to be on it all day. We'll stop for lunch on the way and get there around teatime. Would you be too tired if we drove back that evening? We can come back straight down the M1 and be home by midnight. We can stop on the way for a meal.'

Eustacia agreed quietly and hoped she didn't look as excited as she felt. He poured drinks and came and sat down again. 'The dinner party is on Monday, isn't it? We'll fetch your grandfather up to town in the afternoon, and if he doesn't want to stay I'll drive him back the same night. I dare say you might like to stay in town for a couple of days? I have a list on the Tuesday, one I can't put off, but I thought we might go to a theatre on the Wednesday if you like and drive back to Turville that evening and stay there until we fetch the boys back on Sunday.' He was watching her carefully. 'Unless there's anything else you would rather do?'

'It sounds delightful, and I shall enjoy a day's shopping.' She added silently, But not half as much as I shall enjoy being with you, my dear.

They were away before nine o'clock the next morning, stopping for coffee just before they joined the M1 and then driving fast up the motorway. They stopped in Wetherby and had lunch at the Penguin Hotel and, since the boys had grown a little silent at the idea of parting, the meal was a leisurely one with the talk centred on what they would all do when they got back home again, with a few tactful remarks about the pleasures in store for them with their grandparents.

The children had been there before with their parents, brief visits of a day or so, but they had no lasting memories of them.

'Isn't there a castle there?' asked Eustacia. 'A ruined one, I mean. Did you go there?'

Oliver nodded. 'We went twice. I liked it...'

'So did I,' said Teddy. 'Mummy and me found a little hole like a cave and we hid.' He gave a prodigious sniff and Eustacia said cheerfully,

'It sounds fun. Will you buy a postcard and write to us? There'll just be time before we come again. I'm sure your granny will help you with the address. I dare say she will have all kinds of surprises for you.'

The Kennedys lived in a Victorian redbrick house on the edge of the town; it had high iron railings and a short drive to the front door, and the curtains at its sashed windows were a useful beige of some heavy material. The front door was large and had coloured-glass panels and was opened by a thin woman with an acidulated expression who gave them a grudging good-day and led them across the dark brown hall.

The Kennedys were waiting for them in a large, high-ceilinged room, as brown as the hall and filled with heavy furniture. Eustacia, snatching a quick look, thought that everything had cost a great deal of money and was of the very best quality even if gloomy.

They were welcomed with meticulous politeness before Mrs Kennedy swooped upon the boys to hug and kiss them and then burst into tears. Eustacia stole a look at Colin's face and saw that he was angry, although he said nothing, only when there was a chance suggesting that the boys might like to see their rooms before they had tea. 'Eustacia will unpack for them,' he added. 'I'm sure that you have enough to do, Mrs Kennedy.'

Mrs Kennedy wiped her eyes with a wisp of handkerchief. 'Oh, indeed I have; the planning and shopping I have had to do, you have no idea. The boys are in the room at the back of the house if you'd like to take them up…'

They were shown the way by the thin woman, who opened a bedroom door for them and went away again without a word and Eustacia, making the most of things, went over to the window and said, 'Oh, look, what a lovely view of the town, and surely that's the castle? And what a lovely big room.'

She sounded enthusiastic but her heart sank at the sight of the two small faces looking up at her. She sat down on one of the beds and caught them close. 'Darlings, this time next week we'll be in the car and Uncle Colin will be driving us all home. Don't forget to write, and do you suppose you could send a post-card to Grandfather Crump?' She opened her handbag. 'And here's some pocket-money; I know Uncle has given you some already, but you'll want to buy presents—don't forget Mr and Mrs Samways and Rosie and Grimstone.'

They helped her unpack and then the three of them went downstairs again.

Tea had been set on a table on Mrs Kennedy's right, and her husband and Sir Colin were sitting opposite her. Colin got up as they went in and Mrs Kennedy uttered an awkward little laugh. 'Oh, I hadn't expected

Oliver and Teddy to have tea with us, but of course they shall if they like to. I'm not used to small children. Come and sit down, dears.' She looked at Eustacia. 'Perhaps you would ring the bell there by the fireplace and we'll have more cups and plates.'

The boys sat one on each side of Eustacia, balancing plates on their small, bony knees, and she was thankful that they had had a hearty lunch, for tea was a genteel meal of thin bread and butter and slices of madeira cake.

'The boys will have their supper before they go to bed,' observed Mrs Kennedy. 'I'm sure Cook has something special for them.' Eustacia hoped so too.

They said goodbye presently with a false cheerfulness on Eustacia's part and near tears on the part of the boys. Sir Colin put a great arm around their shoulders. 'Look after each other,' he begged them, 'and remember about all the things you see so that you can tell us next week.'

His goodbyes to the Kennedys were very correct and he listened with every sign of attention to Mrs Kennedy's gushing account of the pleasures in store for the boys. 'They won't want to leave us,' she cried playfully, and then said a cold goodbye to Eustacia. Her husband had very little to say; Eustacia hoped that he would let himself go a bit and be good company for the boys.

She sat very still beside Sir Colin as the Rolls slid out of the drive. She hated leaving the boys and she wanted quite badly to cry about it.

She said in a rather shaky voice, 'They're not going to like it there. I do hope their granny doesn't keep crying over them, and the house is so—so very brown.'

Sir Colin laid a large hand briefly on the hands in her lap. 'I know. I hate the idea of their being there, but we have no right to prevent them going to stay with their grandparents; they must get to know them as well as they know my mother.'

'Yes, but she loves them and they love her, you know they do.'

She sniffed dolefully, and he said comfortably, 'A week soon passes, my dear.'

They were on the A1 again and then the M1, travelling fast. At Lutterworth they stopped at the Denbigh Arms and had dinner, then they drove on. The motorway was fairly empty and they made good time; well before midnight he stopped the car outside their home and Samways, appearing silently, opened the door and offered hot drinks and sandwiches.

Sir Colin glanced at Eustacia. 'Ah, Samways, good of you to wait up. A pot of tea, I think, and one or two sandwiches. We'll be in the small sitting-room.'

Samways made his way to the kitchen where Mrs Samways was waiting, ready dressed for bed in a red woolly dressing-gown. 'Tea,' said Samways, and gave his wife an old-fashioned look. 'Mark my words, Bessie, Sir Colin's head over heels even though he may not know it. Tea—I ask you—him drinking tea at this hour of the night?'

'And very right and proper too,' said Mrs Samways, arranging sandwiches on a plate. 'It's time he was a family man.'

Sir Colin put an arm round Eustacia's shoulders. 'Tired? It has been a long day.'

'I enjoyed it, though I hated leaving the boys. Do you suppose they'll be all right?'

They sat down opposite each other with Moses in between them.

'Provided Mrs Kennedy doesn't weep all over them. I know she must miss her daughter and grieve for her, but it is hardly fair to inflict her grief upon the two small boys.'

They drank their tea, not talking much, and presently Eustacia said goodnight and took herself off to bed. 'It was a lovely day,' she told him. She would have liked to have said a great deal more than that, but the bland look upon his face stopped her just in time.

They drove up to town after lunch the next day and after they had telephoned the Kennedys. The boys were out walking, they were told, and had settled down very well.

'They slept well?' asked Eustacia.

'Of course they slept well.' Mrs Kennedy sounded quite put out and Eustacia felt it necessary to make soothing sounds by way of apology. With that they had to be content.

Grimstone admitted them, assured them that everything was in train for the dinner party and bore Mr Crump off to his room while Sir Colin disappeared into his study and Eustacia, after tidying herself and unpacking her overnight bag, went to talk to Rosie in the kitchen. They had discussed the menu at some length and now she was assured that everything was going well. The sorrel soup, the grilled trout with pepper sauce, the fillets of lamb with rosemary and thyme and the chestnut soufflé with chocolate cream were in various stages of cooking and Rosie herself would see to the dinner table. In the meantime tea would be taken into the drawing-room whenever it was wanted.

'Oh, then now, I think, Rosie, and you and Grimstone have yours before you have to go back to the cooking.'

The guests had been bidden for eight o'clock. Eustacia, wearing a new dress—a pleasing mixture of blues and greens in soft silk—went downstairs to check the dining table and then join the men in the drawing-room.

'Nervous?' asked Sir Colin as she went in. 'You shouldn't be, you look quite delightful.'

A remark which seemed a good augury for the evening. As it was, Eustacia went to bed that night feeling pleased with herself; it had been highly successful, conversation had never flagged and she had liked her guests. Moreover Colin had been pleased with her and her grandfather proud of her. The two gentlemen had driven off to Turville after the guests had gone and she had waited up until Colin had come back. His casual, 'Still up?' rather dampened her good spirits, but she said in her usual quiet way, 'I was just going to bed. Will you be at the hospital all day tomorrow?'

'Yes, it's quite a heavy list and I've one or two private patients I must see first.'

She nodded and smiled in what she hoped was a wifely fashion. She had hoped that he might have remembered his promise to take her round the hospital one day, but obviously that wouldn't be possible. She wished him goodnight, agreeing pleasantly that if he found himself unable to get home in time for dinner she was to dine alone.

'You won't mind too much?' he wanted to know.

'Me, mind? Not at all.' She smiled charmingly as she escaped upstairs, but he didn't miss the sharp edge to her voice.

She went shopping in the morning and got home for a late lunch. She had put away her purchases and sat down with a book until teatime when the phone rang. Mrs Kennedy's voice, thick with emotion, shrilled in her ear. 'He's run away, the silly child—you should have sent a governess or someone with them, I've never—'

Eustacia cut her short, ice-cold fingers running up and down her spine. 'Teddy or Oliver? And when? Mrs Kennedy, pull yourself together and tell me plainly what has happened.'

'That is no way to speak to me... Teddy, of course—oh, some time this morning, he had been rude and I corrected him,' her voice rose, 'and Oliver slapped me—he's in his room, the naughty boy.'

'Who is looking for Teddy?'

'My husband is searching the streets. Of course the child isn't far—he can't be, probably he's just hiding.'

Eustacia choked back a rage she didn't know she possessed. 'You are to let Oliver out of that room at once, Mrs Kennedy. Tell him I'm on my way to you and so is his uncle.' She put down the receiver since there was no point in wasting time with Mrs Kennedy, and then she dialled St Biddolph's. Sir Colin wasn't available, she was told, he was in theatre, but the porter obligingly put her through to the theatre block. A rather timid voice answered her and, when she said who she was, vouchsafed the information that Sir Colin had just started to operate and was expected to be in theatre for at least another three hours.

'The same case?' asked Eustacia.

'Yes, Lady Crichton. Do you want me to get hold of someone? I mean, I'm only a first-year student.'

'He mustn't be disturbed, but when he is finished I want you to tell him to ring his home the minute he is free, tell him it's urgent. Don't forget, will you?'

She went in search of Grimstone next and thanked heaven that he was quick to understand. 'I want a car,' she told him, and, 'When Sir Colin rings please tell him exactly what I have told you. If he wants to call the police he'll do that. Now, a car—'

'The Mini is in the garage, my lady, I'll fetch it round while you collect up your things. Which way will you go?'

'Up the M1 as far as possible.' She flew up to her room and found a coat and stuffed money into her handbag, and when she got down to the hall there was Rosie with a Thermos flask and some scones in a bag. 'No time for any sandwiches,' she explained as

Eustacia got into the Mini. Eustacia glanced at her watch as she drove away. She had only one thought: to get to Richmond.

CHAPTER EIGHT

EUSTACIA concentrated on getting out of London as
quickly as possible, not allowing herself to think of
anything else, but once clear of the city she had time
to reflect. She began to wonder if she had done the
right thing. Should she have told the police? But surely
Mr Kennedy would do that? And would Colin be angry with her for not letting him know immediately?
On the other hand, he couldn't stop in the middle of
an operation and just walk away from the patient, and
it must have been major surgery if it was going to last
for so long. In any case, there was no point in indulg-
ing in hindsight now; she was committed to drive to
Richmond and find Teddy, and hopefully Colin, when
he learned of what had happened, would know exactly
what to do. 'Oh, my darling, if only you were here,'
she said loudly. 'And I'll shake that awful Mrs
Kennedy until her dentures rattle when I see her—
shutting Oliver up. She has absolutely no idea how to
be a granny.'

The Mini scooted along and thankfully the tank was
full; upon reflection she decided that Colin's cars
would always be ready to get into and drive. A splendid man, she thought lovingly, only she wished she
knew what he was thinking sometimes behind that
calm face of his. Perhaps it was as well that she didn't.

She was on the M1 now, keeping the little car at seventy but driving carefully too. She glanced at the clock and was surprised to see that it was almost six o'clock—it had been some time after half past three when Mrs Kennedy had telephoned and it would be another hour before Colin came out of theatre, and in that time she would be well on her way. If she could keep up the pace until she reached Leeds she had a good chance of getting to Richmond soon after dark. The thought cheered her and she began to think about Teddy. He might, as his grandmother seemed to think, have hidden in some nearby garden or shed, or he could have wandered into a shop... She frowned—as far as she could remember there had been no shops close to the house. At least it wasn't on a main road and the traffic along it had been light. The moment she got there she was going to question Oliver, since he was the most likely to know where Teddy had gone. A faint memory stirred at the back of her head and became all at once very clear. They had been talking about the castle at Richmond and Teddy had told her about a cave there where he and his mother had been. If he was lonely and unhappy, might he have tried to find it? It was a shot in the dark but at least it was something to start with. Possibly the police would have found him by now, in which case should she take the boys back with her? But then Colin would have telephoned... She had told Mrs Kennedy that he would drive up to Richmond, but that had been a spur of the moment remark as much to give herself comfort as Mrs Kennedy. If he were free he would have come, she was sure of that, but he had a responsibility to his patients too.

It had been a dull day and dusk was falling early, but she was nearing Leeds and there were only around seventy miles left to go. She had to slow down now for it had begun to rain from low-lying clouds, but it was no good getting impatient; she kept on steadily, watching the miles go by with what seemed like maddening slowness. When she reached the outskirts of Richmond it was nine o'clock and quite dark. She couldn't remember exactly where the Kennedys lived—she had to stop twice and ask the way, and it was with a great sigh of relief that she finally turned into the short drive and stopped before the door. There were lights on in the downstairs rooms but the curtains were drawn. She thumped the knocker and the thin woman came to the door.

Eustacia walked into the hall. 'Where is Mrs Kennedy? Is Teddy found?'

'In the dining-room.' The woman opened a door and ushered her in.

Mr and Mrs Kennedy were seated at the table, eating their supper. There was no sign of Oliver. It was no time for good manners. 'Where is Teddy? And Oliver…?'

Mr Kennedy had got to his feet but his wife remained seated. She said, 'Oliver is in bed, of course. Teddy hasn't come back yet but he can't be far away—several people have seen him during the afternoon. Mr Kennedy has been out all day looking for him—he is exhausted, and although I mustn't complain I am severely shocked.'

Eustacia let that pass. 'The police? Are they searching for Teddy?'

'We thought we would wait until the morning,' said Mr Kennedy. 'After all, they can't do much now that it is dark, and since Teddy has hidden away twice already in the garden and across the road in the house opposite, that's where he'll be now.'

'How can you sit there—?' Eustacia choked back rage and walked out of the room and upstairs to the room where the boys slept. Oliver was there, a small, wretched heap in his bed, and she went straight to him and put her arms around him. 'It's all right, love, I'm here and I'll find Teddy and I'm quite sure that your uncle will be here just as soon as he can. Have you any idea where Teddy could be?'

Oliver shook his head, and his voice was tear-sodden. 'He ran away and hid twice and Grandmother was very cross...'

'Why did he run away, darling?'

'Grandmother keeps talking about Mummy and crying and saying how we couldn't have loved her because we're happy with you and Uncle Colin. We do love her, but we love you too.'

'You can love any number of people for the whole of your life, that's the nice thing about it. So, now we know why he ran away—you were shut up, weren't you? Was that after he disappeared?'

'I tried to go after him, but you see Grandmother was so unkind to Teddy and I smacked her, so I was shut up here and then someone came and unlocked the door.'

Eustacia got off the bed. 'Now, love, I want you to be very brave and stay here and if—no—when your uncle comes tell him that I've gone to the castle. I've an idea, perhaps it's a silly one, but it's worth a try. Don't tell anyone else where I've gone.' She kissed him. 'Are you hungry?' and when he nodded, 'So am I—famished. As soon as Teddy and Uncle Colin are here we'll find something to eat.'

She tucked him into bed and slipped quietly out of the house. Apparently no one was in the least interested in her movements. She didn't take the car—it was a small town and it didn't take her long to walk to the other end and take the path to the castle, a gloomy pile against the cold night sky. She had had the wit to take the torch from the car, and she was glad of its cheerful light as she approached the ruins. Nasty ideas concerning ghostly figures, tramps and thieves on the run flitted through her head but she kept on, moving into the shadow of the ancient walls.

She hadn't the least idea where to look. She crept around, her teeth chattering with cold and fright, and finally came on to an outer wall overlooking the river below. There was a railing, but she swallowed panic and started to walk its length. Halfway along, a narrow opening led to an inner wall and then a whole series of ruined walls, and she stood there still shining her torch and calling Teddy softly by name. There was no answer and she stood irresolute, wondering what to do next, where to go. She swept the beam of her torch around her and then held it steady. A little to one side of her there was a low opening, and through it she could just glimpse a small foot clad in a red sock and a stout little shoe. Teddy.

He was asleep, the deep, sound sleep only small children enjoyed—she could have walked round blowing a trumpet and he wouldn't have stirred. But he was cold and he had been crying. She wedged herself in beside him and put a careful arm round him while she thought what to do.

She would have to wake him up and probably carry him to start with until he had warmed up a little. When she got him back to the Kennedys, should she put him to bed? And would they let her stay the night? And perhaps give her some supper? Her insides were woefully empty.

She caught her breath at a whisper of sound somewhere out there in the ruins and clutched Teddy more tightly. It could be a tramp, a desperate man hiding, a ghost—there must be hundreds in a place as old as this, she thought wildly and then gave a great gulp of relief as a voice she longed to hear said placidly, 'Hello, my dear. Oliver gave me your message.' He crouched down beside her and dropped a kiss on her cheek and laid a gentle hand on Teddy.

Eustacia sniffed away a great lump of tears in her throat. 'They said you'd be hours in theatre…didn't you operate after all?'

'Oh, yes. I flew up here.'

Her tired, grubby face broke into a wide smile. 'Oh, Colin…'

He smiled slowly. 'Yes, well—later. Let us get this young man into his bed and reassure Oliver.'

'Can't we go home?'

'In the morning, my dear. There is a good deal of talking to be done first. We must talk too, you and I.' He scooped up the sleeping Teddy. 'Can you manage? Take the torch and go ahead of us.'

Going back was easy because Colin was there. They left the dark ruins behind them and went through the quiet town until they were back at the Kennedys' home.

Mrs Kennedy met them in the hall. 'Well, where did you find him? Not far away, I'll be bound. Bring him in here—'

'He needs to go to bed at once,' said Sir Colin in a firm, detached voice which Eustacia had never heard before. 'Will you send someone up with warm milk for the boys? Are there electric blankets? No? Then hot-water bottles if you please.'

He went upstairs with the sleeping Teddy and Eustacia trailed behind. Oliver was awake, sitting on top of his bed wrapped in a blanket.

'You said Uncle Colin would come and he did,' he told Eustacia. 'Can we have supper now that Teddy's back? He must be awfully hungry.'

'He will be when he wakes up. I'll find something as soon as I can, my dear.'

Sir Colin had put Teddy on his bed and was taking off the boys' shoes. Teddy began to sit up and stir and then whimper, and Eustacia said matter-of-factly,

'Hello, there. Wake up, darling, we're all dying for our supper.'

Someone knocked on the door and the thin woman handed her a tray with two glasses of milk on it.

'Well, it's a start,' said Eustacia and gave one to Oliver before starting to undress Teddy.

There was another knock on the door; this time it was Mrs Kennedy. 'There's nothing wrong with him, is there? He ran away to annoy us, I have never been so upset—'

'Could we have something to eat?' asked Eustacia baldly.

'It's gone ten o'clock, Cook will be in her bed and Mary only stayed up to oblige me—just in case you came back, as I knew you would. Such a fuss—'

'We shall do our best not to inconvenience you, Mrs Kennedy. Eustacia and I will sleep here with the boys and leave in the morning, for that seems the best thing to do, does it not? Perhaps later, in a month or two when you feel stronger, they can pay you another visit.' Colin spoke pleasantly but Mrs Kennedy took a few steps back to the door. 'Don't worry about food, we shall be quite all right.'

When she had gone Eustacia said with a hint of peevishness, 'It may be all right for you, but the boys and I are starving— '

'So am I. Get the boys sorted out, I'm going off to buy fish and chips.'

He was a man in a thousand, she reflected, watching his broad back disappear through the door. She had the two boys in their beds by the time he returned, carrying a large newspaper parcel and with a bottle under one arm. He sat down on Teddy's bed and portioned out the food, found two tooth-glasses in the bathroom and opened the wine. Eustacia gave a rather wild giggle. 'If you read this in a book you wouldn't believe it...'

'Who wants books?' Sir Colin handed her a glass. 'Drink up. The boys can have some too.'

She ate a chip with enormous pleasure. 'Look, what do we do? I mean, tonight? And isn't anyone going to explain anything?'

He waved a fishy hand. 'You are, for a start. Try and begin at the beginning and tell me everything.'

Between mouthfuls she gave him a brief and sensible account of what had happened. He nodded when she had finished. 'Now, you, Oliver, tell us just what went wrong.'

Oliver was sleepy, but he managed very well. Eustacia kissed him and told him what a good, brave boy he was and he fell asleep with the suddenness of a child. Teddy, awake now and eating his supper with gusto, was rather more difficult to understand but presently Sir Colin said, 'I think I have enough now. I'm going downstairs to talk to Mr Kennedy.' He put a hand on Eustacia's shoulder. 'I'll be back.'

Teddy was asleep before she had tidied away the fishy newspaper. She perched on his bed, leaning her head against the headboard, and since she was tired out she closed her eyes.

It was almost an hour later when Sir Colin returned. He stood looking down at Eustacia, dead to the world, her head lolling sideways against the bedhead, her pretty mouth half open. He put out a hand and shook her gently awake and she shot upright at once, letting out a protest at a stiff neck and a stiff shoulder.

'Sorry,' said Sir Colin, 'but you can't sleep like that all night. I've had a talk with Mr Kennedy; he agrees with me that perhaps the best thing is for us to take the boys home in the morning.' His voice was dry and she wondered what had passed between the two men. 'I suggested that we might all come up again later in the year,' and at the look on her face, 'Yes, I know, but we have to try again. In the meantime that sour-faced woman has been prevailed upon to make up the beds in a guest room. I'll sleep there with Oliver, you stay here with Teddy.'

'Yes, but I haven't anything with me—no tooth-brush, or soap or nightie…'

He brushed this protest to one side. 'There will be soap in the bathroom, you can clean your teeth with the children's toothpaste and your finger and you don't need a nightie…' He bent down and kissed her cheek, a light, comforting kiss. 'Get to bed, my dear, you've had a worrying time. You'll feel better in the morning and we'll all be laughing about it.'

He scooped up Oliver and went away without an-other word, leaving her to undress slowly, and after a sketchy wash she got thankfully into Oliver's bed, in-tent on sorting out her muddled thoughts. She was asleep within a couple of minutes.

She could have slept the clock round, but Teddy woke at around six o'clock and promptly burst into tears. She got into bed with him and cuddled him close. 'She said we didn't love Mummy any more, she said we'd forgotten her and Daddy, but we haven't, and she smacked me and Oliver tried to explain and she took him away so I ran out of the house... I went to the castle...'

'Yes, darling, I know. I guessed you would go there and that's why I came to find you, and Uncle Colin brought us both back here.'

'He's here, Uncle? May we go home?'

'As soon as we've had breakfast. Now, will you go to sleep for a little while? I'll be here; I'm going to get dressed presently and then you shall dress too.'

Teddy slept then and in a little while she got up, swathed herself in the coverlet off Oliver's bed and went in search of a bathroom. The house was quiet and she ran the bath stealthily, did the best she could with her teeth and, feeling guilty, dried herself on a splendid towel which she rather thought was there on display rather than for use. Wrapped once more in the coverlet, she stole back to the bedroom, dressed and did her face and hair and, since it was well after seven o'clock, wakened Teddy.

Oliver and Sir Colin were in the bathroom, Oliver in the bath and his uncle at the washbasin, shaving himself. Eustacia said good morning, urged Oliver to get out to substitute Teddy in the bath, then wrapped Oliver up in the towel, now very damp, and asked, 'Where did you get that razor?'

'From my bag. You're up early.'

'I've been up since before seven o'clock—I had a

bath. Isn't there another towel? This one's sopping.'
She rubbed Oliver briskly before turning her attention
to Teddy, reflecting that it was all so extraordinary,
like *Alice in Wonderland*, and yet she didn't feel that
everything was unusual, just quite normal.

She got Teddy out of the bath and rubbed him as
dry as she could and Sir Colin observed, 'Do I have
to dry myself on that towel? You'd better wring it out
first.' He let the water out of the bath and turned on
the hot tap, sitting on the side of the bath in his trousers and nothing else, quite at ease. Eustacia caught
his eye and began to laugh.

'It just isn't true,' she gurgled, 'I mean, things like
this just don't happen.' She put toothpaste on the
children's toothbrushes and stayed sitting on the side
of the bath beside Colin. 'How will you get home?'

'In the Mini, of course.'

'Four of us and the luggage?'

'Why ever not? It will be a trifle cramped, but I
don't suppose the boys will mind.' He turned off the
tap and she got off the bath, collected the boys and
marched them off to get dressed. They were in high
spirits, and presently when Sir Colin joined them,
looking as well turned out as he always did even
though there were tired lines in his handsome face,
they all trooped downstairs. Mr Kennedy came into
the hall as they reached it.

His good morning was stiff. 'Our housekeeper has
very kindly risen early and has prepared your breakfast.' He looked at the two boys. 'I'm afraid that your
grandmother is so upset by your behaviour that she is

forced to remain in bed; she is a very sensitive woman and the shock has been great.'

Eustacia had her mouth open to ask what shock; Colin's firm hand, pressing her shoulder gently, stopped her in time.

'I think we have all had a shock,' observed Sir Colin in what she privately called his consultant's voice, and just for a moment Mr Kennedy looked embarrassed. She wondered what Colin had said on the previous evening.

They went into the dining-room, which was brown like all the other rooms, and heavily furnished, sparing no expense, with dark oak. The table had been laid and they sat down to boiled eggs, rather weak tea and toast. The sour-faced woman was doubtless glad to see them go, but she wasn't going to speed them on their way with bacon and eggs.

The boys bade their grandfather a polite goodbye and he shook their small hands, observing that he hoped that the next time they met it might be in happier circumstances. 'Your grandmother is going to take some time to recover...'

Eustacia went very red in the face with rage—her wish to comment upon this was great, but she had once more encountered a glance from Colin. It was a speaking glance and she closed her mouth firmly and choked back the words she had wished to utter. It was a relief to get outside and get the boys settled in the back of the Mini while Colin saw to their luggage. Mr Kennedy stood in his doorway, making sure that they were going, she thought, and an upstairs curtain twitched. Mrs Kennedy was making sure too.

She got into the car and Colin got in beside her.

'Rather a tight fit.' he said. 'Fortunately we're all on speaking terms.' A remark which made the boys laugh their heads off, but they waved obediently to their grandfather as they drove away and Eustacia had a pang of pity for him; Mrs Kennedy wasn't the easiest of wives to live with.

'I hope I never get like that,' she said, speaking her thoughts aloud.

'You'll not get the chance,' said Colin, uncannily reading her mind. 'Have you enough room?'

She said yes happily, although his vast person had overflowed on to her. She would get cramped before long but she really didn't mind. She turned her head to look at the boys. They beamed back at her and Oliver said, 'That was a beastly breakfast—we're hungry.'

'We'll stop at the service station at Ferrybridge before we get on to the M1.' Sir Colin glanced at Eustacia. 'Comfy?'

She nodded. 'It's fun, isn't it? I shall have very hot coffee and hot buttered toast.' She sighed. 'There's such a lot to explain it's hard to know where to begin.'

'Time enough when we get home,' he said comfortably. 'Let's have a day out.'

They were on the A1 now, and she had to admire the way he handled the car, keeping up a steady pace, taking advantage of any gap in the stream of early-morning traffic. The boys kept up a constant stream of talk and she hardly noticed the miles passing until she was aware of him slowing into the service station and parking the car.

The Little Chef was half full, warm and welcoming. They sat round the table, contentedly drinking their coffee and orange juice and eating hot buttered toast, and presently Sir Colin got up. 'I'm going to telephone your grandfather,' he told Eustacia, 'and Samways and Grimstone. We'll go back to the town house this evening and go on to Turville in the morning.'

Eustacia, who would happily have spent the rest of her life in a high-rise flat with him, nodded happily.

The boys had recovered completely. 'We knew you'd come,' sighed Oliver, 'only Teddy couldn't wait...'

'That's all right, love, we quite understand,' said Eustacia, 'and you see how quickly Uncle can get to you when you need him. I should never have thought of hiring a plane.'

'That's because you're a girl,' said Oliver. 'Did you mind driving the Mini all by yourself?'

His uncle had sat down again and passed his cup for more coffee. 'I dare say she minded very much, but she was anxious to get to you. When you have to do something important you don't think about anything else.' He smiled at her. 'We shall have to think of something nice to do by way of a thank you.'

'A day at Cricket St Thomas,' said Teddy eagerly, 'you'd like that, wouldn't you, Eustacia?'

'Or Longleat with the lions,' suggested Oliver.

Sir Colin was looking at Eustacia intently. 'That

sounds splendid,' he observed, and unusually for him he hadn't heard a word the boys had said. Nor had Eustacia—she was far too busy trying to look non-chalant even while the colour flooded her face. There was something in his look which had set her heart thundering against her ribs in a most unsettling man-ner.

They packed themselves back into the Mini pres-ently and drove on.

'Since we're having a day out we might as well have lunch somewhere,' observed Sir Colin, a sugges-tion with which they all agreed enthusiastically.

They stopped in Madingley, a charming little village of thatched cottages not far from Cambridge. The restaurant was housed in an oak-panelled and beamed cottage and the food was England's best—steak and kidney pie, vegetables from the garden and apple tart and cream for a pudding. Over a large pot of coffee Eustacia said, 'That was a gorgeous meal—what a lovely day we are having.'

She had addressed the boys but she was conscious of Colin's eyes on her.

'We must do this more often,' observed Sir Colin. 'Supposing we drive over to Castle Cary and see Granny—we'll go to Turville tomorrow and go the day after, just for lunch and tea. How would you two like to have her to stay for a week? I'm going over to Holland in two weeks' time and I thought I'd take Eustacia with me. We can stay with friends and she can see something of the country while I'm lecturing.'

The boys chorused their approval and Eustacia said

primly, 'If that is an invitation, yes, I shall enjoy going to Holland.'

They were getting into the car again and Colin turned from fastening the seatbelts. 'Haso and Prudence are looking forward to seeing you again, and I promised I'd bring you with me next time I went to Holland.'

A remark which effectively quenched any ideas she might have had about him wanting the pleasure of her company.

A dignified Grimstone was waiting for them when they reached London. And for once he was smiling broadly. 'There's tea ready for you,' he told them. 'Rosie's been cooking and baking...' His elderly face creased suddenly. 'A nasty shock it was, to be sure.'

Eustacia took his hand. 'Grimstone, you have no idea how lovely it is to be home again to such a welcome. We can't wait for Rosie's tea...'

She led the excited boys up to their room, tidied them up and sent them downstairs, then went along to her own room. She looked awful, she decided, examining her face in the looking-glass—no wonder Colin hadn't had much to say to her; her face was pale with worry and lack of sleep, and her hair needed attention. She washed her face and put on make-up again and brushed her hair and then, suddenly impatient, went downstairs.

Sir Colin came in from the garden with Moses as she went into the drawing-room and thought that she had never looked so beautiful...

They ate a splendid tea with Moses, pressed against

Sir Colin's leg, gobbling up odds and ends of cake and sandwiches, and Madam Mop enjoying a saucer of milk under the table. By common consent they didn't talk about Yorkshire; Sir Colin had telephoned Mr Crump and told him what had happened with the promise that they would all return to Turville in the morning and, since the boys were tired now, Eustacia got them ready for bed and then sat them down to their supper. She was tired herself; once they had had dinner, she would go to bed. Colin was already immersed in the various letters and messages that had arrived for him; he wasn't likely to miss her.

The boys tucked up and already half asleep, she had a shower and changed into a dress and went downstairs to find that Colin had changed too. He put down the letter he was reading and fetched her a drink before sitting down by the log fire.

'There hasn't been the time or the opportunity to tell you how grateful I am to you for your part in this unfortunate incident. You must be tired and quite worn out with the worry of the whole thing. Do you feel you can tell me about it? Mr Kennedy wasn't very forthcoming yesterday evening; according to him, Teddy had been a little monster and Oliver not much better. I don't believe that, of course...'

Eustacia took a very large sip of sherry. 'They didn't have their meals with Mr and Mrs Kennedy; they had to have them in the kitchen, and each morning Mr Kennedy took them for a walk and then they went back to spend half an hour with their grandmother, who talked about their mother all the time, telling them that they must never forget that she was dead... How could she?' Eustacia polished off the sherry and set the empty glass down on the table beside her chair. Sir Colin got up and filled it again without a word and she went on. 'Of course they won't forget their mother and father and they'll go on loving them, but they can be happy too—how could she be so unkind, loading them down with her own grief? And why can't she love them? As your mother does... she's a wonderful granny.'

Eustacia drank the sherry at one go and sat back, a little bemused from the two glasses one on top of the other. Sir Colin watched her with hidden amusement. 'Indeed she is. Tell me, Eustacia, will you enjoy coming to Holland with me?'

'Oh, yes, only don't you think I should stay with the boys?'

'No. My mother and your grandfather will enjoy being in charge. I phoned her just now, and she's delighted with the idea. She is also looking forward to seeing us all tomorrow. Have the boys all they need for school next term? Do you want to bring them up to town to buy things? They're due back on Thursday next week, aren't they? I've a list on the following day—you said you wanted to see round St Biddolph's, so you can visit the wards while I'm in theatre.'

'Oh, may I?' She sat up, happy that he had remembered after all. 'And may I go into the operating theatre so that I know where you work?'

'No. You can look through the door but no more

than that. Here is Grimstone to tell us that dinner is ready.'

Very soon after their coffee she pleaded tiredness and he showed a disappointing lack of desire to keep her from her bed. She wished him goodnight in a chilly voice and cried herself to sleep.

In the morning she took herself to task—she was allowing her dreams to cloud reality and she would have to stop. She was brisk and chatty at breakfast so that Sir Colin glanced at her once or twice in a thoughtful fashion; he had never known her any more than quiet and matter-of-fact with an occasional flash of temper. But this wasn't temper, he decided, it was an act she was, for some reason best known to herself, putting on for his benefit.

He sighed, for once unsure of himself.

The visit to Castle Cary filled the next day most successfully; the boys, once they were there, had a great deal to tell their grandmother and she listened carefully before summoning Martha. 'Will you take the boys across the street and let them choose some sweets?' She handed over some money. 'And they might like to buy a comic each.'

When they had gone she settled back in her chair. 'Now let me hear the whole story,' she begged. Sir Colin told her, with Eustacia sitting quietly, her hands in her lap, saying nothing at all.

'Very unpleasant,' commented his mother finally. 'Poor children. It was splendid of you to go after them, Eustacia, and to find Teddy.'

Eustacia spoke then. 'With hindsight, I can think of

lots of ways of getting them back. It would have been just as quick to have waited for Colin to finish in the theatre; he got there almost as soon as I did.'

'Just as quick, but without heart. You knew he would follow you?'

'Oh, of course.' Eustacia smiled at Mrs Crichton and the older lady nodded and smiled too.

'Just so.'

They left soon after tea, racing smoothly back to Turville, and Eustacia allowed her mind to brood over the evening ahead. Grandfather would be there, which would make it easier to ignore the invisible barrier which had reared itself between her and Colin. She tried to think how it had happened, but she couldn't put a finger on the exact moment when she'd realised that it was there. Had she said something, she wondered, or far worse, had she allowed her feelings to show?

She was aware of it during the evening; Colin was friendly and perfectly willing to talk, but only about things which had nothing to do with them personally, and so it was until he went back to London on Monday, reminding her laconically that he would be at her disposal on Friday. 'I shall start my list at eleven o'clock—I'll come for you about half-past nine, if you can be ready by then?'

'Of course I can,' said Eustacia loftily. 'The boys have to go to school at half-past eight.'

They parted coolly, although Eustacia didn't remain cool for long; Gloria telephoned during the day, intent on seeing Colin. 'That Grimstone of his says he doesn't know where he is—I suppose he's there with you?' complained Gloria.

'No, he isn't. Probably he's operating at another hospital if he's not at St Biddolph's. Can I give him a message?'

Gloria chuckled. 'You sound too good to be true! Don't worry, I'll find him.' There was a little pause. 'I always do.'

Eustacia was ready and waiting when Colin arrived on Friday morning. She had dressed with care: a leaf-brown suit, a silk blouse the colour of clotted cream and simple but perfect gloves, shoes and handbag. She thought for a long time about a hat, and in the end she settled for a supple, small-brimmed felt, worn quite straight. It gave her dignity, or she hoped it did.

Colin wished her good morning pleasantly, took in her appearance with one swift glance, remarking that she looked just the thing, and swept her into the car. 'No time to waste,' he pointed out as he called good-bye to Mr Crump, who had come to wave them off.

'Which reminds me,' said Eustacia with icy sweetness. 'Your friend Gloria telephoned yesterday. She assured me that she would find you. I hope she did.'

'Do you really?' He sounded interested and amused. 'I must disappoint you. What did she want?'

'You,' said Eustacia waspishly.

He said nothing until he came to a lay-by, where he stopped the car and turned to look at her. 'You have allowed your imagination to cloud your good sense,' he told her calmly. 'I have taken Gloria out once or twice but no more than other women of my acquaintance—that was in my bachelor days and a perfectly normal thing to do, you must allow. I am not in love with her, nor have I ever been. Satisfied?'

She wanted to say no, but she said yes instead and they drove on, she a prey to unhappy thoughts, he apparently perfectly at ease.

As they entered the hospital he took her arm. He was a rather grave, well-dressed man, self-assured without being pompous about it; she couldn't fail to see the deferential manner with which he was greeted as they made their way to the theatre block. They went through the swing-doors and he stopped for a moment, looking down at her. 'You were in a bunched-up pinny,' he observed, 'you were very earnest and I suspect a little scared. You were beautiful, Eustacia, just as you are now.'

She gaped up at him, her eyes wide. 'Well—' she began and was interrupted by Sister's approach.

'There you are, sir,' said that lady briskly, 'with your lady wife too. Shall we have a cup of coffee before you start your list? I've got Staff Nurse Pimm to take Lady Crichton round the hospital. If you haven't finished shall she go to the consultant's room or come back here?'

'Oh, here, I think, Sister.'

She nodded. 'They've slipped in that case who wasn't fit for surgery yesterday—you might be a little later than you expect.'

'That can't be helped, can it?' he said pleasantly as they wedged themselves into Sister's office to drink Nescafé and eat rich tea biscuits and talk trivialities.

Presently a head appeared round the door to utter the words, 'Your patient's here, sir,' and Sir Colin got up.

'I'll see you presently, darling,' he said and followed Sister out and away through another door, leaving Eustacia in the care of a small, plump girl who beamed at her widely and asked where she would like to start.

The morning went swiftly; Eustacia poked her pretty nose into one ward after another, visited the canteen, the hospital kitchens, spent a long time in the children's ward, was introduced to a great many people who appeared to know all about her and was finally led back to Sister's office. 'It's only an implant,' said her guide, 'Sir Colin won't be long now. You don't mind if I go? It's been nice...' She beamed once more.

'Thank you very much, you've been wonderful, I've really enjoyed it,' said Eustacia. And she had, as she could imagine Colin at work now.

He came ten minutes later, in rubber boots and his theatre garb, his mask pulled down under his chin, a cotton cap on his head. 'Hello, been waiting long?'

'No. I had a lovely time. Have you finished?'

'Yes. Sister and my registrar will be along in a moment and we'll all drink tea. I'll need to take a look at my patients and then we'll go.' He glanced at the clock on the wall. 'I've a couple of patients to see at two o'clock—we'll have time for lunch first.'

That night, getting into bed, she reflected that it had been a lovely day. She was, she had discovered, slightly in awe of him, but she loved him too. She would have to try very hard to be the kind of wife he expected: well dressed and pleasant to all the people he worked with, a good hostess to his friends, and, above all and most important, take care of the boys. He had married her for that, hadn't he? she reminded herself.

He came to Turville for the weekend and they all went walking and spent a good deal of each day in the garden. There was a gardener but there was always a lot to do—weeds to pull and things to plant. Monday came too soon but she consoled herself with the knowledge that he would be back on Wednesday and they would be going over to Holland on the Thursday night ferry. 'And I'll drive down on Tuesday and fetch Mother,' he told her as he was getting ready to leave after breakfast. 'I'll stay here for the night.'

He bade the boys goodbye, dropped a kiss on to her cheek and drove himself off.

'You look sad,' said Teddy, and Oliver said,

'Well, of course she does, silly, Uncle Colin's gone and they like to be together like mothers and fathers do. Don't you, Eustacia?'

'Yes, oh, yes,' said Eustacia and sniffed down threatening tears.

CHAPTER NINE

EUSTACIA had plenty to occupy her after Colin left. Mrs Samways wanted advice as to which room Mrs Crichton should occupy, and there was a serious discussion as to the meals to be cooked and eaten while Eustacia and Colin were away. Then there was her packing to think of; Colin had said nothing about taking her out, and she supposed that he would be occupied the whole day and probably wouldn't be anxious to go out in the evening, but for all she knew Haso and Prudence might have quite a busy social life. She added a couple of dresses suitable for the evening and, just to be on the safe side, a black chiffon skirt and a glamorous top to go with it. That done, she turned her attention to the boys' cupboards, making sure that there was enough of everything until she got back. She strolled in the garden with her grandfather after lunch and presently fetched the boys from school. She felt restless and unhappy, and when Colin rang up later that evening she had a job not to beg him to come home, even if it was only for an hour or so. She was glad that she hadn't given way to anything so silly, for he was at his most casual, and after a minute or two she handed the phone to the boys.

The next day was better—after all, Colin would be coming home that evening. She busied herself arranging flowers, shopping in the village for Mrs Samways and attending a meeting of the church council. She felt rather at sea doing this but it was something that she could do for Colin, who wasn't always free to attend. She listened to plans for new hassocks, the church bazaar, the possibility of getting more people to sing in the choir and whether the steeple would hold out until there was money to repair it. She had plenty of good sense, and the other members of the council, all a good deal older than she, were kind and friendly. She offered to provide the material for the hassocks and went back home in time to fetch the boys from school.

Sir Colin arrived about eight o'clock with his mother, greeted Eustacia in his usual calm manner, handed Mrs Crichton over to her with the remark that they hadn't kept dinner waiting for too long, and went upstairs to say goodnight to the boys.

Eustacia led Mrs Crichton up to her room. 'I do hope you'll be comfortable,' she said, 'and it is so very kind of you to look after the boys. You will find Grandfather a great help; he plays chess with them and keeps an eye on their homework.'

'We shall manage very well, my dear,' said Mrs Crichton comfortably. 'You and Colin deserve a week together. I know he will be busy during the day but you will have your evenings free.'

'Oh, yes,' agreed Eustacia brightly. 'I dare say we shall go out quite a lot.' A remark made for the benefit of her mother-in-law. She had no idea what plans

Colin had made, and he certainly hadn't told her about them.

They went back downstairs presently and she was able to tell him about the church council. 'I promised to get the material for the hassocks,' she finished, 'I hope that was the right thing to do...'

'Oh, undoubtedly.' He turned to his mother. 'You see what an invaluable partner I have found myself!' he remarked. He spoke pleasantly, but Eustacia found herself blushing, wondering if she had sounded boastful.

Mrs Crichton gave her a quick glance and saw the blush. 'More than a partner,' she said, 'someone to love the boys and someone to come home to each evening.'

Only he doesn't, thought Eustacia, smiling brightly.

Sir Colin went back to London directly after breakfast the next morning, and after taking the boys to school Eustacia sat down with his mother and discussed the following week.

'I'll keep to your routine, my dear, as far as possible, and your grandfather will put me right if I slip up. Is Colin lecturing every day or will you be able to spend some time together?'

'I'm not sure...'

'He works too hard,' said his mother. 'You cannot imagine how delighted I was when you married, my dear, I was beginning to think that he would remain single for the rest of his days. But now he has another interest in life and later, when you have a family, he will discover that life isn't all work.'

Eustacia refilled their coffee-cups. 'For what reason did he receive his knighthood?' she asked, and missed Mrs Crichton's surprised look.

'He hates to talk about it. For outstanding work in the field of surgery. Two—three years ago now.'

'You must be very proud of him,' said Eustacia.

'Indeed I am, my dear. He is a good son and I have no doubt that he will be a good husband and father. His dear father was, and he is fond of children.'

'Yes,' said Eustacia faintly, 'he's marvellous with Oliver and Teddy.'

Sir Colin came home late that evening. He looked tired, as well he might, but he was as placid as usual, answering the boys' questions with patience before Eustacia hurried them off to bed.

'We shall miss you and Uncle,' said Teddy, 'but you are coming back, aren't you?'

'Of course, darling. And you're going to have a lovely time with Granny and Grandfather Crump. What shall we bring you back from Holland?'

They slept at once, for they had been allowed to stay up to say goodnight to their uncle, and Eustacia went back downstairs, to spend the rest of the evening taking part in the pleasant talk and stealing glances at Colin from time to time, until he looked up and held her gaze without smiling.

She saw little of him the next day; although he didn't go up to the hospital he went to his study and spent a good deal of time on the telephone and dictating letters. Eustacia strolled round the gardens with Mrs Crichton and her grandfather, to all appearances a contented young woman with no cares, while all the while she was wondering why Colin was avoiding her. He had taken the boys to school and had said that he would fetch them that afternoon and, with the excuse of the pressure of work, had shut himself in his study. It didn't augur well for their trip to Holland.

They were sailing from Harwich and left in the early evening amid a chorus of cheerful goodbyes and hand-waving. Eustacia, in a jersey outfit of taupe and look-ing her best, got into the car beside Colin and won-dered just what the next week would bring. Sir Colin, having emerged from his study the epitome of the well-dressed man, appeared as placid as usual; if he was anticipating a pleasurable few days ahead of him, there was no sign of it. He could at least pretend that he's going to enjoy himself, she reflected peevishly, and then went pink when he observed, 'I'm looking forward to this week; there should be some time be-tween lectures when we can go sightseeing.'

She mumbled something and he cast a quick look at her. 'I'm sure that Haso and Prudence will have plans for our entertainment.'

The Rolls swallowed the miles in a well-bred man-ner and they were on board with half an hour to spare. 'Too soon for bed,' Colin said. 'I'll collect you from your cabin in ten minutes and we'll have a drink be-fore we sail.'

The ship was full; they sat in the bar surrounded by a cheerful crowd of passengers which, as far as Eustacia was concerned, was all to the good. Conver-sation of an intimate nature was out of the question—

not that Sir Colin gave any sign that he had that in mind, which puzzled her, for he had said several times that they needed to have a talk together.

She went to her cabin as soon as the ship sailed and slept soundly until she was called with tea and toast just after six o'clock. She got up and dressed and left her cabin, and found Colin waiting for her.

'Would you like breakfast before we go ashore,' he asked, 'or shall we have it as we go?'

'Oh, as we go, please. Is it far?'

'About two hundred and fifty kilometres—around a hundred and ninety miles. We shall be there by lunch-time.'

They reached Kollumwoude, the village near Leeuwarden where Haso and Prudence lived, shortly before noon, having stopped on the way and eaten a delicious breakfast of rolls and butter and slices of cheese and drunk their fill of coffee. It had been a delightful drive too; Colin knew the country well and was perfectly willing to answer Eustacia's questions. The country had changed now that they were in Friesland, and she exclaimed with delight as they drove through the village and turned in through high wrought-iron gates and stopped before a three-storeyed house, its windows in neat rows across its face and with small, round towers at each end of it. The walls were covered with creeper and there were a lot of open windows, and one had the instant impression that it was someone's well-loved home.

They got out of the car and an earnest, elderly man

opened the door, to be followed at once by Prudence and, more slowly, Haso.

Their welcome was very warm. Prudence kissed Eustacia and then Colin, and Haso kissed her too before shaking Colin's hand. 'Welcome to our home,' he said and added, 'Eustacia, this is Wigge, who looks after us.'

She shook hands with him and went with Prudence into the house. It was as charming inside as it was from the outside. The hall was rather grand and the room they entered was large and lofty and splendidly furnished, but all the same it looked comfortably lived in—there was knitting cast down on a table, newspapers thrown carelessly down on the floor by a vast wing-chair and a great many flowers in lovely vases. There was a dog too, a Bouvier who lumbered to meet them and was introduced as Prince. Two very small kittens, asleep in an old upturned fur hat, completed the reassuringly cosy picture to Eustacia's eye.

'Come and see your room,' said Prudence presently. 'Lunch will be in half an hour, so there's time for a drink first.'

She led the way upstairs and into a room at the end of a corridor. 'Nice and quiet, it's at the back of the house,' said Prudence. 'Here's the bathroom,' she opened a door in the further wall, 'the dressing-room's on the other side. I'll leave you to do whatever you want to do, but don't be long.' She smiled and whisked herself away, leaving Eustacia on her own to survey the room, large and light and furnished with great comfort, with gleaming walnut and pale curtains and bedspread. The bathroom was perfection with piles of fluffy towels and bowls of soap and a white carpet underfoot, and from glass shelves there were trailing plants hanging. She paused just long enough to admire them and opened the other door. The dressing-room was a good deal smaller than the bedroom but well furnished, and Sir Colin's luggage was there. She went back to the bedroom, did her face and hair and went downstairs.

The rest of the day was taken up with an inspection of the house and garden, which was large and beautifully laid out, and in the evening there was a good deal of talk as to what they might do to amuse Eustacia.

'I don't need amusing,' she protested. 'It's lovely just being here...'

'It is nice, isn't it?' said Prudence happily. 'We'll go into Leeuwarden and spend some time shopping and the country around is worth looking at. Oh, and we must go to Sneek and Bolsward and Dokkum—'

'My love,' said Haso, 'they're only here for a week and Colin will be lecturing each day. I might even do some work myself...'

'Oh, well, I'll drive Eustacia round and perhaps we could go out one evening? There's Cremaillere in Groningen—'

'Or the Lauswolt in Beesterwaag—'

'We can dance there.'

Eustacia went to bed, convinced that no stone would be left unturned in the attempt to keep her amused during the next week. It was to be hoped that Colin would be amused too.

She saw little of him during the days which followed, although he returned in the late afternoon, when they would sit around over their drinks, talking over their day, and after dinner more often than not friends would call in, and on the second evening that they were there Prudence gave a dinner party for their closer friends and Haso's mother. Eustacia liked her at once, just as she liked his sister when Prudence took her to Groningen to meet her. Her days were full, but disappointment mounted as each day passed and Colin, kind and attentive as he usually was, made no attempt to be alone with her.

Her hopes rose when Haso announced that they would all go to Beesterwaag that evening for dinner and dancing. The hotel was some twenty miles away and they used Colin's car, the two girls sitting in the back, Prudence in russet taffeta and Eustacia in silk voile patterned in pink roses. The two men had complimented them upon their charming appearance when they had joined them in the hall, and Haso had given his wife a long, loving look which spoke volumes. Eustacia had had to be content with Colin's quiet 'charming, my dear', and when he had looked at her it was from under drooping lids which had allowed her to see nothing of his gaze.

The evening was a great success; they dined deliciously on lobster thermidor after a lavish hors-d'oeuvre, and finished their meal with fresh fruit salad and lashings of whipped cream, and since it was a party they drank champagne.

They danced too; Eustacia floated round with Colin, conscious that she looked her best. He was a good dancer and so was she, and she could have gone on forever. 'Enjoying yourself?' he asked her.

'Oh, so much, Colin. Only I wish you didn't have to be away all day.' To which he made no reply.

It was Haso, dancing with her later, who suggested that she might meet Colin for lunch in Groningen. 'Prudence can drive you there and you can come back with him later.'

He broached the subject later as they sat over their coffee, and Colin agreed placidly. 'Why not? The day after tomorrow, if you like, Eustacia, if Prudence doesn't mind driving you in.'

'A chance to do some last-minute shopping, since you'll be going the next day.'

It was when they were back home again and Prudence and Haso had gone into the garden with Prince that Eustacia found herself alone with Colin.

'You don't mind if I come to Groningen?' she asked.

'My dear girl, why should I mind?' he asked casually.

'You didn't suggest it yourself,' she told him angrily. 'We've been here for four days and you've never once wanted to—'

She paused, and he prompted, 'Wanted to what, Eustacia?'

'Be alone with me,' she muttered.

'True enough,' and at her sharp, angry breath, 'But I think that we must agree to Haso's suggestion, don't you? For the sake of appearances.'

She took a steadying breath. 'What have I done, Colin?' and then with a flash of rage, 'Oh, why did I ever come here with you, why did I ever marry you...?'

'As to that, my dear, we still have to have that talk, do we not? But somehow the right moment hasn't presented itself.'

'There is nothing to talk about,' said Eustacia icily, and when he put a hand on her arm, 'Let me go...' She darted away from him and up the staircase just as the others came back into the house.

Crying herself to sleep didn't improve her looks; Prudence took one glance at her slightly pink nose and said nothing, and after breakfast she suggested that they might drive over to Dokkum and have lunch there. 'The men won't be back until teatime and tomorrow you'll be in Groningen for most of the day.'

In the evening, when Haso and Colin came in, Eustacia was quite her usual self, rather more so than usual in fact. She wasn't a talkative girl usually, but this evening she excelled herself. When they parted for the night and Haso mentioned that she would be lunching with Colin the next day, she replied with every appearance of pleasure that she was simply delighted at the prospect.

'Well, you haven't seen much of each other,' said Prudence.

The men had gone by the time Eustacia and

Prudence got down for breakfast. They ate unhurriedly and presently got into Prudence's car and drove to Groningen. Eustacia, listening to Prudence's chatter, was thinking hard. The time had come to tell him her real feelings. She felt quite brave about it at the moment, but probably by lunchtime her courage would have oozed out of her shoes.

They had coffee at Cremaillere before Prudence walked with Eustacia to one of the two central squares in the city. 'Go down there,' she advised, pointing to a crowded, narrow street, 'keep on for a few minutes and then turn to the right. Take the first turning on the left and the hospital's about five minutes' walk away. You are sure you want to walk? I could drive you there in no time at all…'

'I'd like to walk; it's my last chance to see the city and I've heaps of time.'

'Well, yes, you have—Colin's sure to be a bit late. You know what these lectures are—someone always wants to ask questions when he's finished. Have a nice lunch together.' She took Eustacia's parcels. 'I'll take these back with me—see you later.'

Eustacia started walking. It was really the first chance she had had of talking to Colin alone for any length of time, and she intended to take full advantage of it; there was such a lot she wanted to say and it was time it was said. She wondered if she could pluck up the courage to say that she loved him and ask what they could do about it, and as she walked she began composing various speeches on the subject. She would be cool and very matter-of-fact, she decided, and match his own bland calm. She was pleased with the speeches she was making up in her head, although it wasn't likely that he would reply as she imagined, which was a drawback. All the same, she had rehearsed what she would say, and was so engrossed that she didn't turn to the right but walked briskly over the crossroads and found herself in another busy main street. Another few minutes brought her to more main roads, and this time she remembered that she had to turn right—or had Prudence said left? She stood undecided on the pavement, and since she couldn't make up her mind which way to go she stopped a passer-by and asked.

'The hospital?' said the man in English. 'Cross over and take the left-hand road, walk for five minutes and then turn right. The hospital is in that street.'

He raised his hat politely and walked on and Eustacia, very relieved, did as he had bidden. She was already ten minutes late and she hurried now; it had taken her longer than she had expected but she consoled herself with the thought that Prudence had said that Colin would be late anyway.

The street was shabby, with run-down shops between small brick houses and here and there a warehouse, and the hospital loomed large halfway down it. She went through the swing-doors with a sigh of relief and approached the man sitting behind the reception desk in the gloomy hall.

She tried out her, *'Goeden morgen'* on his rather cross face and added, 'Sir Colin Crichton?' He stared at her without speaking so she added, 'Seminar, conference?'

He nodded then, said *'Straks,'* and, seeing that she didn't understand, pointed to the clock. 'Late,' he managed.

She smiled at him and asked, 'May I wait?' and took his silence for consent, and went and sat on a hard chair against the opposite wall. She was hungry and on edge and she hoped she wouldn't have to wait too long. It was half an hour before the lifts at the end of the hall began to disgorge a number of soberly clad gentlemen, none of whom bore the least resemblance to Colin. She watched the last one disappear into the street, waited for five minutes and then got up.

The man at the desk wasn't very helpful—he shook his head repeatedly at her attempts to make him understand until finally he picked up the telephone, dialled a number and handed her the phone. 'I speak English,' said a voice. 'You wish to enquire?'

'Sir Colin Crichton—I've been waiting for him. Is he still in the hospital?'

'There is no one of that name here. He was not at the meeting held here this morning. I am sorry.' The voice ended in a smart click as the receiver was put down.

There was nothing for it but to retrace her steps, and once she got to the square she had started from she would see if Prudence was still there; she had said she had more shopping to do and Eustacia knew where the car was.

She thanked the man and made for the door. It

swung inwards as she reached it and she came to a halt against a massive chest.

'Where the hell have you been?' asked Sir Colin, and when she looked up into his face she saw that he was angry—more than angry, in a rage.

How nice it would be to be six years old again, she thought, then she could have burst into tears in the most natural way and even screamed a little...

'Here,' she said in a voice rendered wooden with suppressed feeling. 'Waiting for you.' She drew an indignant breath. 'You weren't here.'

'Of course I wasn't here, you silly little goose. You are at the wrong hospital. Although how you managed to go wrong when it was less then five minutes' walk from the square is something I fail to understand.'

'Understand?' said Eustacia pettishly. 'You don't understand anything—you're blind and wrapped up in your work and—and...'

'And?' prompted Colin, dangerously quiet.

'Oh, go away!' said Eustacia, and was instantly terrified that he might just do that.

But all he said was, 'The car's across the street. Come along.'

He shoved her into her seat with firm, gentle hands, got in beside her and drove off. 'Hungry?' he wanted to know.

'Not in the least,' said Eustacia haughtily.

'Good, in that case we might as well go back to Kollumwoude.'

And that was exactly what he did. And if he heard her insides rumbling he said nothing.

Prudence, standing at the window, saw the Rolls turn in and stop by the door. 'They're back,' she told Haso urgently. 'Something has gone wrong—just look at Eustacia's face, she can't wait to get into a dark hole and have a quiet weep. And just look at Colin...'

Haso came to stand beside her. 'Perhaps that's what they need—rather like a boil that needs to come to a head before it bursts.'

'Don't be revolting,' said Prudence and kissed him. 'What shall we do?'

'Why, nothing, my love. But we might have tea a little earlier than usual, as it is just possible that they've had no lunch.'

The blandness of Colin's face gave nothing away and Eustacia, never a talkative girl, gabbled her head off; the weather, Groningen and its delights, the splendour of its shops, the charm of the countryside all came in for an animated eulogy which continued nonstop until it was time for them to go to their rooms to change for dinner. Since it was the last evening of their brief visit there were friends and colleagues coming and Eustacia, quite exhausted with so much talking, came back from her shower and looked longingly at her bed, but the evening wouldn't last forever and she wouldn't need to talk to Colin; there would be enough guests to make that easy. She studied her two dresses and then decided on the black skirt and the top, which was a glamorous affair of cream satin exquisitely embroidered. She surveyed her person with some satisfaction when she was dressed, and went downstairs to find the men already in the drawing-room. Prudence followed her in, looking her magnificent best in a taffeta dress of hunter's green.

'That's nice,' she declared, studying Eustacia, 'and such a tiny waist.' She beamed at her. 'We're big girls, aren't we? And I'm going to get bigger…'

'I hope we shall be invited to be godparents,' said Colin.

'Well, of course you will. Haso wants a boy, I'd like twins…'

They drank a toast with a good deal of light-hearted talking and presently the first of the guests arrived.

It was after midnight when Eustacia got to bed; she had managed very well, hardly speaking to Colin during the evening but taking care that when she did she behaved like a newly married girl, very much in love with her husband. Which she was.

They left shortly after breakfast the next morning after a lingering goodbye to Prudence and Haso, and Eustacia, determined to preserve a nonchalant manner, made polite conversation all the way to Boulogne where they were to board a hovercraft. She hardly noticed that Colin answered her in monosyllables, she was so intent on keeping up a steady flow of chat. It did strike her just once or twice that when he spoke at all he sounded amused…

Their journey was uneventful, accomplished in great comfort and with a modicum of conversation. As they neared London Eustacia asked, 'Do you have to go to St Biddolph's tomorrow?'

'It depends. If you want to go to Turville you can take the Mini if I'm not free.'

She said, 'Very well, Colin,' in a meek voice; he sounded preoccupied, and if he didn't want to talk neither did she, she decided crossly.

Grimstone welcomed them with stately warmth, removed coats, luggage and Sir Colin's briefcase, ushered them into the pleasant warmth and a hectic greeting from Moses in the sitting-room and produced tea.

It was nice to be home, thought Eustacia, and was surprised to find that was how she regarded the house now. She poured tea and handed cake and Colin, with a word of apology, read the letters and messages with which Grimstone had greeted him. 'Nothing that can't be dealt with later,' he observed. 'Shall we phone Turville?'

The boys took it in turns to talk on the telephone, and then Mr Crump and Mrs Crichton detailed the week's happenings. Which all took some time, so that Eustacia had only a short time in which to tidy herself for dinner and have a drink with Colin, and even then there was no chance to talk even if she could have thought of something to say for Prudence rang up to see if they had arrived safely. Eustacia was glad of that for it gave her something to talk about while they sat at the beautifully appointed table, eating the delicious meal Rosie had cooked.

'Would you like coffee in the drawing-room?' she asked, conscious of the enquiring look Grimstone directed at her.

'Just as you like, my dear.' Colin sounded placidly uninterested, but he crossed the hall with her and sat down in his chair while she poured their coffee. They drank it in silence while she sought feverishly for something to talk about and, since her mind was blank, she poured more coffee.

'We have had very little time together,' said Sir Colin quietly, 'and, when we did, we have been at cross purposes. I think that it is time that we understood each other. Do you know why I married you, Eustacia?'

She put her cup and saucer down and looked at him thoughtfully. 'You wanted someone to look after the boys and love them and take care of them. Circumstances rather forced you into choosing me, didn't they? I don't suppose you had any intention of marrying me until it was—was thrust upon you...'

'But I had already asked you to come and live with us, had I not?'

She was a little bewildered. 'Well yes, as a kind of governess...'

'Would it surprise you if I told you that—' The telephone on the table at his elbow shrilled and he frowned as he picked it up. 'Crichton.' He spoke unhurriedly and listened patiently to whoever was at the other end. Presently he said, 'I'll be with you in ten minutes or so. No, no—not at all, you did right to call me.'

He got up and stood towering over her. 'I'm sorry, I have to go to the hospital. Fate, it seems, isn't going to allow me to tell you something I have wished to say for a long time.'

He was already at the door, but in the hall she caught up with him.

'What was it, Colin? Please tell me.'

He opened the door. 'Why not? I've been in love with you ever since I saw you that first time.'

He had gone. She stood at the open door watching the tail-lights of the Rolls disappear down the street until Grimstone, coming into the hall, saw her there and closed the door. He gave her a curious look as he did so. 'You feel all right, my lady?'

She gave him a bemused look. 'Oh, yes, thank you, Grimstone. Sir Colin has had to go to the hospital—I'm not sure how long he'll be.'

She went back to the drawing-room and sat down again with Moses and Madam Mop. 'Did you hear what he said?' she asked them in a whisper. 'That he was in love with me. But he never... I had no idea.' She drew an indignant breath. 'And fancy telling me like that just as he was going away.' The little cat got on to her lap and stared into her face. 'Yes, I know, he hadn't time to explain and I did ask him...'

She glanced at the clock—if it was just a case of examining a patient and giving advice he would be home soon. She put an arm round Moses, who had climbed up beside her, and fell into a daydream.

It was after eleven o'clock when Grimstone came into the room to tell her that he had locked up and ask, would she like him to wait up for Sir Colin?

'No, thank you, Grimstone, you go to bed. Rosie has left coffee on the Aga, I expect? I'll give Sir Colin a cup when he gets in.'

'As you wish, my lady. Shall I mend the fire?'

'No need. He won't be much longer and the room's warm. Goodnight, Grimstone.'

He gave her a grave goodnight, and went away. The house was quiet now save for the gentle ticking of the bracket clock and she sat, half asleep, waiting for the sound of the key in the door. The long-case clock in the hall chimed midnight and she got slowly to her feet. Surely Colin would be coming soon? He could have phoned, or was he regretting what he had said and deliberately staying away? She took the animals to the kitchen and settled them in their baskets and went back to the drawing-room. The fire was smouldering embers now and the room would soon be chilly. She put the fireguard before it, turned out the lights and went back into the hall, turned off all but one of the wall sconces and started up the stairs, to pause and then sit down on one of the lower treads, facing the door. If she went to bed she would only lie awake, listening for him…

The slow ticking of the clock was soothing, and after a few minutes she leaned her head against the banisters and closed her eyes.

It was half an hour later when Sir Colin let himself into his house. He stood for a moment, looking at Eustacia bundled untidily on the staircase, her head at an awkward angle, her lovely face tear-streaked, her softly curved mouth a little open. Being very much in love with her, he didn't notice the gentle snore. He closed the door, shot the bolts soundlessly, put his bag down and crossed the hall to stand looking down at her.

She woke then, stared up at him for a moment and then said, 'Would you say that again?' It wasn't what she might have said if she had been wide awake, but it was the first thought that entered her sleepy head.

He smiled slowly and the smile soothed away the tired lines of his face. He said very clearly, 'I have been in love with you ever since that first time—you wore a most unbecoming overall and I gave you a kidney dish. I didn't know it at the time, of course, I only knew that I wanted to see you again, and when we did meet I knew that I loved you, that you were part of me, my heartbeat, my very breath. It seemed that fate was to be kind to me when circumstances made it possible for us to marry, but then I began to doubt... You are so much younger than I, my darling, and somewhere in this world there must be a young man only waiting to meet you...'

Eustacia was wide awake now. 'Oh, pooh,' she said strongly. 'In the first place I don't much care for young men, and in the second place I love you too.' Quite unexpectedly two large tears rolled down her cheeks. 'I thought you didn't care tuppence for me, so I tried to be what I thought you wanted me to be.' She sniffed and he proffered a snowy handkerchief. 'We've never been alone...' she added dolefully.

'I didn't dare to be. But we are now.' He swooped down and plucked her to her feet and swept her into his arms. 'My dearest darling, we are now.' He kissed her in a slow and most satisfying manner, and then quite roughly so that she found it impossible to speak, and when she would have done, 'No, be quiet, dear heart, while I tell you how much I love you.'

'Oh, how very nice,' said Eustacia, managing to say it before he kissed her again. Then, 'I am so glad that we're married...'

She looked up into his face. His heavy lids had lifted and his blue eyes blazed down into hers. 'So am I,' he told her softly.

A Girl to Love

CHAPTER ONE

THE COTTAGE STOOD sideways on to the lane, its
wicket gate opening on to a narrow brick path between flower beds, the path ending at an old-
fashioned door with a round brass knob and a great
knocker. Its thatched roof above cob walls was
much patched, although picturesque, and doubtless
in the summer it presented a charming picture, but
just now, on a dripping November afternoon, it
looked forlorn, as forlorn as the girl opening the
gate.

She was wrapped in a rather elderly raincoat with
a scarf wound round her neck and a woolly cap
pulled well down on to a pale face, quite unremarkable save for a pair of fine dark eyes, and despite the bulky coat, she was too thin. She closed
the gate carefully, hurried up the path and let herself
into the cottage, casting off her outdoor things in
the hall and going straight into the sitting room.

It was a pleasant enough room with some nice
pieces furnishing it and a scattering of shabby armchairs. The girl switched on the light, scooped up
the sleek cat sitting in one of the chairs and with
him on her lap, sat down. The room was untidy and

across the hall the dining room table was still littered with cups and saucers and plates and the remains of cake and sandwiches consumed by friends
who had attended the funeral and returned for tea
afterwards. But that would have to wait. The girl
had too much on her mind to bother about washing
up for the moment; she'd had a shock and she
needed to go over every word Mr Banks the solic-
itor had said to her before she could face up to it.

The funeral had been well attended. Granny had
no family except herself left, but many friends, and
they had all come; it had been a busy day, and it
was only when the last of them had gone and only
Mr Banks was left that she had felt a pang of lone-
liness. At his suggestion that they should sit and
have a talk for a while she had felt better and she
had sat down opposite him, not surprised when he
had said kindly: 'Sadie, there is the will...'

She had nodded, not over interested; she had
lived with her grandmother since she was a very
small girl and although there had never been much
money she knew that the cottage would be hers.
Her grandmother's pension died with her, but there
was always a living to be earned. She had wanted
to get a job after she had left school, but her grandmother wouldn't hear of it, so although at twenty-
three she was a skilled housewife, a splendid cook
and a clever needlewoman, she wasn't trained for

anything else, and she had never thought about it much, especially during the last two years when Granny had been so crippled with arthritis that she had been forced to give up active life and depend entirely on Sadie.

Mr Banks unfolded the will and cleared his throat. Mrs Gillard had left all that she possessed to her granddaughter. But there was more to it than that; he folded the will up tidily and blew his nose, reluctant to speak. When he did, Sadie didn't believe him at first. The cottage was mortgaged up to the hilt—Granny had been living on the money for some years, for her pension hadn't gone up as wages had, and what had been a respectable income thirty years ago had dwindled to a mockery of itself... 'So I am very afraid,' said Mr Banks apologetically, 'that there is no money at all, Sadie, and the cottage will have to be sold in order to pay off the mortgage.'

She had looked at him in vague disbelief and he hastened to add: 'Your grandmother had a few pounds in some shares. I'll see that they are sold later, in the meantime I'll advance you their value.'

She had thanked him politely. 'I don't think I could bear to leave here,' she had told him, and then at his pitying look: 'But of course I must, mustn't I? I'll get some sort of job.'

Mr Banks had looked uneasy. 'Can you type? Do shorthand? I might know of someone...'

'I can't do anything like that. I can cook and sew and do the housework. I'll find something.' She had made a great effort and smiled at him. 'Don't worry, Mr Banks, I'll get a job as a housekeeper or mother's help, then I'll have a home and a job.' And before he could protest: 'I'll walk down to the village with you—you left the car at the Bull and Judge, didn't you?'

So she had seen him safely away and now she was back in the cottage which was no longer her house. She had a little time, Mr Banks had assured her, she would be given a week or two to make her plans and move out before the mortgage was fore-closed; and Mr Banks had pointed out that there was the chance that a buyer might be found for the cottage and the mortgage paid off, leaving her a little money besides.

She sat stroking the cat, searching her mind for a likely buyer, but there was no one in the village who would want it; it was a fair-sized place as cottages went, with good-sized rooms, an old-fashioned but adequate kitchen, four bedrooms and an attic as well as a bathroom, as out of date as the kitchen but still functioning, and besides there were a number of pantries and cupboards and a fair-sized garden. But it needed a new thatch and new paint, and the wallpaper had been on the walls ever since she could remember.

She got up presently and started on the washing up and when that was done, tidied the rooms, raked out the fire and took herself off to bed, with Tom the cat for company. The cottage was dreadfully empty without Granny. She hadn't got used to that yet, and her grief went deep, for she had loved the old lady dearly, but she had plenty of good sense; life had to go on and she must make the most of it. She closed her eyes on the thought, but not before a few tears had trickled from under their lids.

Nothing seemed so bad in the morning. It was a cold grey day, but once the fire was lighted and she had had her breakfast and fed Tom, she set about cleaning the cottage. She wasn't sure, but presumably someone would come to look at it. Whoever held the mortgage would want to know its value and they would send someone from a house agents.

There was no telephone in the cottage, so she would have no warning. Charlie Beard the postman came soon after breakfast, propping his bike against the old may tree by the gate and accepting a cup of tea while she looked through the handful of letters he gave her. Her heart sank at the bills—electricity, the last load of coal, the rates… When Charlie had gone she went through all the drawers in the hope of finding some money Granny might have

tucked away, and was rewarded by a few pounds
in an envelope, and these, added to what she had
in her purse, would just about pay for the coal. She
wasn't too worried about food; there were vegetables in the garden, potatoes stored in the shed at
the end of the garden; eggs could be exchanged
with cabbages any time with Mrs Coffin at the end
of the lane…and Mr Banks had said that he would
send her the money for the shares. It could be
worse, she told herself bracingly. Of course, there
were any number of vague thoughts at the back of
her head. The furniture—would she have to sell it
or would it be taken over with the cottage? And
Tom? Tom would have to go with her wherever she
went; he was too old to have another owner, although she couldn't imagine him living in any other
house but the cottage.

She finished tidying the house and went into the
garden. There were potatoes to bring in and sprouts
to pick as well as the apples stored in the outhouse.
Because it was drizzling still she put on the old mac
which had hung behind the kitchen door for she
didn't know how long, and pulled on her wellies,
and while she was out there, since she was wet
anyway, she stayed for a while tidying the flower
beds in the front garden. There was nothing much
in them now, a few chrysanthemums, very bedrag-
gled, and the rose bushes, bare now of all but a

handful of soggy leaves. Sadie pottered about until dinner time and after her meal, knowing that it would have to be done sooner or later, started to sort out her grandmother's clothes and small possessions. It was dark by the time she had finished, packing everything away tidily in an old trunk she had dragged down the narrow little stairs which led to the attic at the top of the house. And after tea, for something to do, she went from room to room to room, inspecting each of the four bedrooms carefully to make sure that they were as attractive as possible, and then downstairs to do the same in the dining room and sitting room, and lastly the kitchen, for surely she would hear something tomorrow, either from Mr Banks or from the house agents.

There was a letter from Mr Banks in the morning, but beyond the modest sum, the proceeds from the shares, which was enclosed, he had nothing to say—indeed, day followed day and nothing happened. Sadie went down to the village on the third morning to cash the money order and buy groceries and submit to the kindly questions of Mrs Beamish, the postmistress, and several other ladies in the shop. She didn't mind the questions, she had known them all her life; they weren't being curious, only sympathetic and kind, pressing her to go to tea, offering her a lift in the car next time its owner was going to Bridport, asking if she could do with half a dozen eggs. It was nice to know she had so many friends. She went back to the cottage feeling quite cheerful and after her dinner sat down and composed a letter to Mr Banks, asking him if there was any news about the cottage being sold; she was aware that selling a house took time, but almost a week had gone by and surely he would have something to tell her by now. She finished her letter and was addressing the envelope when she heard the creak of the gate and looked out to see Mr Banks coming up the path.

Mr Banks, a rather dour-looking man although kindly, greeted her so cheerfully that she immediately asked: 'Oh, have you heard something?' and then seeing that he wasn't going to answer for the moment, added quickly: 'Let me have your coat, Mr Banks—how nice to see you, only it's a wretched day for you to be out. Come and sit by the fire and I'll make tea.'

'A most miserable day, Sadie,' he agreed, 'and a cup of tea will be most welcome.'

She went into the kitchen and made the tea in a fever of impatience, then made small talk while they drank it, answering his questions politely while she longed for him to get to the point. Yes, Mr Frobisher the vicar had been to see her, and yes, she had answered almost all the letters she had received when her grandmother had died, and yes, she still had some of the money which he had sent her for the shares. 'But I paid all the bills,' she pointed out, 'so at least I don't owe anything, Mr Banks.'

'Splendid, splendid. And now I have good news for you. Through a colleague of mine I have been in touch with someone who is looking most anxiously for just such a place as this—a playwright, and I believe something to do with television. He is a widower with two children who have a governess and he lives in Highgate Village, but he is seeking somewhere very quiet where he can work uninterrupted. He will not necessarily live here, but wishes to stay from time to time for considerable periods. He wishes to inspect it tomorrow afternoon, and asks particularly that the place should be empty; that is to say, he will naturally bring the agent with him, but if you could arrange to leave the key…? About two o'clock if that's convenient. If he likes it he will purchase it at once, which means that the mortgage can be paid off immediately and since the price seems agreeable to him, there should be two or three hundred pounds for you, once everything outstanding is dealt with.'

'How nice,' said Sadie, and tried her best to sound delighted. Now that the crunch had come she was appalled at the idea of leaving not only the cottage but the village. She had lived there for twenty of her twenty-three years, and Chelcombe was her home. To earn her living she would have to go to a town, even a city, and she was going to hate it. Besides, there was Tom. She said forlornly: 'I must start looking for a job.'

Mr Banks eyed her thoughtfully. 'It might be a good idea if you put up in the village for a little while. You could go to Bridport on the bus—it goes twice a week, doesn't it? There is bound to be an employment agency there, it would be more satisfactory if you could obtain employment before you leave here.'

'I'll do that, Mr Banks. You've been awfully kind. I'm very grateful. I suppose—I suppose you don't know about the furniture?'

'No, and that at this stage can only be conjecture. If they wish to take over the house as it stands, then of course the buyer will pay for the contents, otherwise you will have to sell it, unless you can find unfurnished rooms. But if you intend going into domestic service then you could be expected to live at your place of work.' He frowned a little. 'Are you sure that there's nothing else that you can do?'

Sadie shook her head. 'I'm afraid not, but there must be plenty of housekeeping jobs, or mother's helps or something similar. In the country if I can, and with Tom, of course.'

Mr Banks heaved himself out of his chair. 'Well, my dear, I'm sure you will find just the work you are looking for. In the meanwhile, don't worry, things could have been much worse.'

With which doubtful comfort he went away.

The cottage already shone with polish and there wasn't a speck of dust to be seen. All the same, Sadie went all over it once more, making sure that it looked welcoming and cosy, and in the morning, she picked some of the chrysanthemums and eked them out with a great deal of evergreen from the hedge, and arranged a bowl here and a bowl there. She ate a hasty lunch then, made up the fire, put a guard before it, begged Tom to be a good quiet cat and not stir from his seat in the largest of the armchairs, put on her coat and headscarf, and let herself out into the bleak afternoon. She turned away from the village, for she had no wish to see whoever was coming, and walked briskly up the lane, winding its muddy way up to the crest of the hill. There was a magnificent view from the top in clear weather, but today the sad November afternoon was closing in already; in another hour it would be getting dark and even colder. She hoped that they would be gone by then; she would give them until four o'clock and then go back; if there were no lights on she would know that they had gone.

At the top of the hill she paused for breath, for

it was a steep climb and difficult going along the uneven lane, and then went on again, climbing over a stile and crossing a field to a five-barred gate with a cart track beyond it. The track was worse than the lane, but she splashed along in the muddy ruts, hardly noticing, her thoughts busy with her future. Presently she turned down a bridle path and followed it for a mile or more round the hill to come out at the top of the lane once more. By now it was almost dark; she could see the village lights twinkling below her and ten minutes downhill would bring her to the cottage. There was no light showing as she reached it. She went up the garden path quietly and tried the door. It was locked and she stooped to take the key from under the mat, where she had arranged for it to be left, and went inside.

It was warm indoors and she shed her coat and scarf and went into the sitting room to find the fire still burning nicely, and Tom still asleep. She went from room to room and found nothing had been disturbed, indeed she wondered if the man had come after all, and there was no way of finding out until the morning. She made tea and then got her supper; there was no point in planning her future until she knew what was to happen.

She knew that two days later when Charlie came whistling up the path to hand her a letter from Mr Banks. Mr Oliver Trentham wished to buy the cottage immediately. He waived a surveyor's report, raised no objection to the price and would take possession in the shortest possible time. Mr Banks added the information that after the mortgage had been paid and various fees, there would be just over three hundred pounds for her.

Sadie read it through twice and put it back in its envelope. So that was that, she wasn't sure how soon the shortest possible time would be, but she had better start packing up her own things. Mr Banks hadn't mentioned the furniture, which was annoying; she would have to write and find out and in the meantime go down to the village and see if Mrs Samways, who did bed and breakfast in the summer for those rare tourists who found their way to Chelcombe, would let her have a room until she had found herself a job. Tomorrow she would take the local bus into Bridport and see about a job.

She wrote her letter, posted it, answered Mrs Beamish's questions discreetly, and went along to see Mrs Samways. Yes, of course she could have a room and welcome, and Tom too, as long as she would be gone by Christmas. 'I've my brother Jim and his family coming over for two weeks,' she explained in her soft Dorset voice, 'and dear knows where I'm going to put 'em all.'

'Oh, I'll be gone by then,' Sadie assured her. 'Perhaps I won't want a room at all; I'm going to

Bridport tomorrow morning to see about a job. There's bound to be something.'

There wasn't. True, there were two house-keeper's jobs going, in large country houses, and not too far away, but they stipulated women over fifty and the agency lady, looking at Sadie's small thin person, and her gentle mouth, added her force-ful opinion that she simply wouldn't do.

There was a job for a lady gardener too, but there again, observed the lady with scorn, she was hardly suited, and she tut-tutted when Sadie confessed that she couldn't type or do shorthand, and hadn't got a Cordon Bleu certificate. 'What can you do?' she asked impatiently.

'Housework, and ironing and mending and just ordinary cooking—all the things a housewife does, I suppose. And I like children.'

'Well, there's nothing, dear. Come back next week and try again.' She added as Sadie stood up: 'You can always sign on, you know.'

Sadie thanked her. She would have to be des-perate to do that. Granny had belonged to a gen-eration that hadn't signed on, and she had drummed it into Sadie from an early age that it was something one didn't do unless one was on one's beam ends, and she wasn't that, not yet. She went back home and after her tea, composed an advertisement to put into the weekly local paper.

As it happened there was no need to send it. The next morning Charlie came plodding through the never-ending rain with another letter from Mr Banks. Sadie sat him down at the kitchen table and gave him a cup of tea while the letter burned a hole in her pocket.

'Bad luck about you having to leave,' observed Charlie. 'We'm all that put out. Pity it do be the wrong time of year for work, like.'

Sadie poured herself another cup and sat down opposite him. 'I hate to go, Charlie, I'm just hoping I'll find something to do not too far away.'

'Happen it's good news in your letter?'

'Well, no, Charlie, I don't think so. The cottage is sold—he'd have known that, of course—I expect it's something to do with that.'

He got up and opened the door on to the wind and the rain. 'Well, I'll be off. Be seeing you.'

She closed the door once he'd reached the gate and got on his bike to go back to the village, then she whipped the letter out and tore it open. It was brief and businesslike, but then Mr Banks was always that. The new owner of the cottage had enquired as to the possibility of finding a housekeeper for the cottage and he, Mr Banks, had lost no time in putting her name forward. She would live in and receive a salary to be agreed upon at a later date. He strongly advised her to accept the post, and

would she let him know as soon as possible if she
wished to take the job?

Sadie read the letter through several times,
picked up the placid Tom and danced round the
kitchen until she was out of breath. 'We're saved!'
she told him. 'We're going to stay here, Tom…'
She paused so suddenly that Tom let out a protest-
ing mew. 'But only if we can both stay—I must be
certain of that.' She put him down again, bundled
into her mac and wellies and hurried down to the
village.

Mrs Beamish wished her a good morning and in
the same breath: 'Charlie popped his head in,' she
observed, 'said you'd a letter from London again.'
She eyed Sadie's face with interested curiosity.
'Good news, is it, love?'

It was nice to have someone to tell. Sadie poured
the whole lot out and to the accompaniment of, 'He
be a good man, surely,' and 'Well I never did, Miss
Sadie, love,' she asked if she might use the telephone. The village had a phone box, erected by
some unimaginative person a good half a mile from
the village itself and for that reason seldom used.

Mrs Beamish not only lent the phone, she stayed
close by so that she didn't miss a word of what was
said, nodding her head at Sadie's 'Yes, Mr Banks,
no, Mr Banks,' and then, 'but Bob the thatcher
won't work in this weather: he'll have to wait until

the spring.' She looked anxiously at Mrs Beamish, who nodded her head vigorously. 'No, it doesn't leak,' said Sadie, 'it looks as though it might, but I promise you it doesn't. And what about the furniture?'

She stood listening so intently that Mrs Beamish got a little impatient and coughed, then looked put out when Sadie said finally, 'All right, Mr Banks, and thank you very much.'

There were two more customers in the shop now, both listening hard. 'What about the furniture, Sadie?' one of them asked.

'Well, he wants it, most of it, that is, but he's bringing rugs and things like that—they're to be delivered some time during next week. Mr Banks says I'll have to be at home to put things straight and get in groceries and so on.'

'So he'll be here well before Christmas?' asked Mrs Beamish, her eyes sliding over her shelves of tins and packets. He might be a good customer.

'Yes, I expect so, but I don't know if he'll be here for Christmas. I suppose it's according to whether he has to work.'

'Well, love, we're that pleased—it'll bring a bit of life to the village, having a real writer here. I suppose he'll have a car, but where is he going to put it?'

'There's room for a garage if he opens the hedge

a bit further up the lane, and he can park on that bit of rough grass just opposite the gate,' said Sadie.

Everyone nodded and Mrs Beamish said: 'You just go into the sitting room, love, while I serve Mrs Cowley and Mrs Hedger, then we'll have a nice cup of tea together—we could make out a list of groceries you might want at the same time.'

And for the next few days Sadie had no time to brood. She missed Granny more than she could say, but life had to go on and as far as she could see it was going to go on very much as before. She had run the cottage and looked after her grandmother for two or three years: instead of an old lady there would be a middle-aged man. She had a vivid picture of him in her head—rather like Mr Banks only much more smartly dressed because presumably playwrights moved in the best circles. He wouldn't want to know about the running of the cottage, only expect his meals on time and well cooked, his shirts expertly ironed, the house cleaned and the bath water hot. Well, she could do all that, and she would be doing it in her own home too.

She took the bus to Bridport and bought herself two severe nylon overalls and a pair of serviceable felt slippers so that she wouldn't disturb him round the house and experimented with her hair—something severe, she decided, so that she would look mature and sensible, but her fine mouse coloured hair refused to do as she wished; the bun she screwed it into fell apart within an hour, and she was forced to tie it back with a ribbon as she always had done.

After a week, things began to arrive from a succession of vans making their way through the mud of the lane to the gate. Rugs, silky and fine and sombre-coloured, a large desk, a magnificent armchair, a crate of pictures, fishing rods and golf clubs. Sadie unpacked everything but the pictures and stowed them away. The dining room, which she and Granny had almost never used, would be his study, she imagined. She moved out the table and chairs and the old carpet, and laid one of the splendid ones which she had unwrapped with something like awe, and when Charlie came with the letters, she got him to help her move the desk into the centre of the room. She added a straightbacked armchair from the sitting room, a small sofa table from Granny's bedroom and the bedside lamp from her own room. It wasn't quite suitable, for it had a shade painted with pink roses, but it would be better than the old-fashioned overhead light in the centre of the room. It looked nice when she had finished, and she laid a fire ready in the small grate; there was nothing like a fire to give a welcome.

She rearranged the biggest bedroom too, laying another of the rugs and moving in a more comfortable chair. The rest of the furniture was old-fashioned but pleasant enough, although the wall-paper was old-fashioned and faded here and there. The sitting room she left more or less as it was, shabby but comfortable; she had put the dining room table at one end of it and put the new arm-chair close to the fireplace and moved out a smaller table and another chair and put them in her own room. By and large she was well satisfied with her efforts.

She had had one brief letter from Mr Banks, as-suring her that all was going well; he would let her know the date of Mr Trentham's arrival as soon as possible. By then she had cleaned and polished, ti-died the shed, chopped firewood and pored over the only cookery book in the house. It was to be hoped that Mr Trentham wasn't a man to hanker after mousseline of salmon or tournedos saut; Sadie com-forted herself with the thought that if he was past his first youth, he would settle for simple fare. She made an excellent steak and kidney pudding and her pastry was feather-light.

It was two days later that she had another letter from Mr Banks, telling her that Mr Trentham pro-posed to take up residence in three days time. A cheque was enclosed—housekeeping money paid in advance so that she could stock up the larder; her salary and the remainder of the household expenses

would be paid to her at a later date. He regretted
that he was unable to say at what time of day Mr
Trentham would arrive, but she should be prepared
to serve a meal within a reasonable time of his arrival at the cottage. He added a warning that her
employer was deeply involved in a television script
and required the utmost quiet, qualifying this rather
daunting statement with the hope that Sadie's trou-
bles were now over and that she would make the
most of her good fortune.

He didn't need to warn her about being quiet,
thought Sadie rather crossly. There was no TV in
the cottage simply because Granny had never been
able to afford one; there was a radio, but she would
keep that in her own room and she wasn't a noisy
girl around the house. There was, in fact, nothing
to be noisy with. Mr Trentham could write in the
dining room with the door shut firmly upon him
and not be disturbed by a sound.

That afternoon she went down to Mrs Beamish's
shop with a list of groceries and spent a delightful
half hour stocking up necessities to the satisfaction
of herself and still more of Mrs Beamish. And the
next morning she went into Bridport and cashed her
cheque before purchasing several items Mrs Beamish didn't have, as well as visiting the butcher's and
arranging for him to call twice a week. He delivered
to Mrs Frobisher and the Manor House anyway, and

she assured him that it would be worth his while. It was sitting in the bus on the way home that she began to wonder about Christmas. It seemed unlikely that Mr Trentham would want to stay at the cottage, especially as he had children, in which case she and Tom would spend it together, but Christmas was still five weeks away and it was pointless to worry about it.

She spent the evening storing away her purchases and the next morning went to pay Mrs Beamish's bill, ask William the milkman to let her have more milk, and then tramped through the village to Mrs Pike's Farm to order logs. Together with almost everyone else in the village, she was in the habit of wooding in the autumn and she had collected a useful pile of branches and sawn them ready for burning, but with two, perhaps three fires going, there wouldn't be enough. And that done, she went home and had her tea and then sat by the fire with Tom on her lap, deciding what she would cook for Mr Trentham's first meal.

She made a steak and kidney pudding after breakfast the next morning because that couldn't spoil if he arrived late in the day, and then peeled potatoes and cleaned sprouts to go with it. For afters she decided on Queen of Puddings, and since she had time to spare she made a batch of scones and fruit cake. With everything safely in the oven she made a hasty meal of bread and cheese and coffee and flew up to her room to tidy herself. It was barely two o'clock, but he could arrive at any moment. She donned one of the new overalls, a shapeless garment which did nothing for her pretty figure, brushed her hair and tied it back, dabbed powder on her nose and put on lipstick sparingly; if she used too much she wouldn't look like a housekeeper.

The afternoon wore on into the early dark of a winter's evening. She made tea and ate a scone and had just tidied away her cup and saucer when she heard a car coming up the lane. She glanced at the clock—half past five; tea at once and supper about eight o'clock, perhaps a bit earlier, as he was probably cold and tired. She gave the fire in the sitting room a quick nervous poke and went to open the door.

Mr Trentham stepped inside and shut the door behind him. In silence he stood, staring down at her, a long lean man with thick dark hair, grey eyes and a face which any girl might dream about. He wasn't middle-aged or short, or stout; anyone less like Mr Banks Sadie had yet to meet. She stared back at him, conscious of a peculiar feeling creeping over her. She shook it off quickly and held out a hand. 'Good evening, Mr Trentham,' she said politely, 'I hope you had a good drive down. I'm Sadie Gillard, the housekeeper.'

He was smiling at her with lazy good humour, and she smiled back, relieved that he was so friendly, not at all what she had expected. Indeed, already the future was tinted with a faint rose colour. Thoughts went scudding through her head: she should have made a chocolate cake as well as the usual fruit one and got in beer. Mr Darling at the Bull and Judge would have known what to sell her...thank heaven she had made that steak and kidney pudding... She was brought down to earth by his voice, slow and deep, faintly amused.

'There seems to have been some mistake—I understood that there was to be a sensible countrywoman.' His smile widened. 'I'm afraid you won't do at all.'

CHAPTER TWO

SHE FOUGHT DOWN instant panic. 'I am a sensible countrywoman,' she told him in a calm little voice, 'your housekeeper, and I can't think why I won't do, especially as you haven't eaten a meal here or slept in a bed or had your washing and ironing done yet.'

He had his head a little on one side, watching her, no longer smiling. 'You don't understand,' he told her quite gently. 'I'm looking for a quiet, experienced woman to run this cottage with perfection and no unnecessary noise. I write for a living and I have to have peace.'

'I'm as experienced as anyone will ever be. I've lived here in this cottage for twenty years, I know every creaking board and squeaking door and how to avoid them...'

His eyes narrowed. 'Of course, stupid of me—you're Mrs Gillard's granddaughter. To turn you out of your home would be decidedly unkind.' His faint smile came again. 'At least tonight. We'll discuss it in the morning.' He turned to the door again and opened it on to the chilly evening. 'I'll get my bags.'

When he came back with the first of them Sadie asked: 'Would you like tea, sir?'

'Yes, I would, and for God's sake don't call me sir!' He disappeared into the blackness again and she went to put the kettle on and butter the scones. She had laid a tray with Granny's best china and one of her old-fashioned traycloths and she carried it into the sitting room and put it on a small table by the fire. By the time he had brought in a considerable amount of luggage and taken off his sheepskin jacket, she had made the tea and carried it in.

'What about you?' he asked as he sat down, 'or have you already had yours?'

'Yes, thank you, I have. If you want more of anything will you call? I shall be in the kitchen.' At the door she paused. 'Would you like your supper at any particular time, Mr Trentham?'

He spread her home-made jam on a scone and took a bite. 'Did you make these?' he asked.

'Yes.'

'Wild strawberry jam,' he observed to no one in particular, 'I haven't tasted it since I was a boy. You made it?'

'Yes.' She tried again. 'Your supper, Mr Trentham?'

'Oh, any time,' he told her carelessly. 'I'll unpack a few things and get my books put away. Where have you put my desk?'

'In the other room. If you wouldn't mind having your meals in here, you could use the dining room to work in.'

He nodded. 'That sounds all right. Whose cat is that, staring at me from under the table?'

'Oh, that's Tom—he's mine. I did ask about him, and you said you wouldn't mind...'

'So I did.' He buttered another scone. 'Don't let me keep you from whatever you're doing.'

She went out closing the door soundlessly. The kitchen was warm and smelt deliciously of food. She put the custardy part of the Queen of Puddings into the oven and began to whip the egg whites. Her future was tumbling about her ears, but that was no reason to present him with a badly cooked meal. When she heard him go into the hall she opened the kitchen door to tell him: 'Your bedroom is the one on the right at the top of the stairs. Would you like any more tea, Mr Trentham?'

He paused, his arms full of books. 'No, thanks. It was the best tea I've had in years. In fact I don't normally have tea, I can see that I shall have to get into the habit again. Did you make that cake too?'

'Yes.' She went past him up the stairs and switched on the light in the bedroom and pulled the curtains. It looked very pleasant in a shabby kind of way but a bit chilly, she was glad she'd put hot water bottles in the bed.

'You can come in here and help,' he called as she went downstairs, and she spent the next half hour handing him books from the two big cases he had brought with him, while he arranged them on the bookshelves she had luckily cleared. He had a powerful desk lamp too and a typewriter, and a mass of papers and folders which he told her quite sharply to leave alone. Finally he said: 'That's enough for this evening.' He gave her his lazy smile again. 'Thanks for helping.'

He went outside again presently to the car parked in the lane and came back with a case of bottles which he arranged on the floor in a corner of the sitting room, an arrangement which Sadie didn't care for at all. There was a small table in one of the empty bedrooms; she would bring it down in the morning and put the bottles on it. She collected the tea tray and started to lay supper at one end of the table, and he asked for a glass.

Granny's corner cupboard was one of the nicest pieces of furniture in the cottage. Sadie opened its door now and invited him to take what he wanted. He chose a heavy crystal tumbler and held it up to the light.

'Very nice too—old—Waterford, I believe.'

'Yes, everything there is mostly Waterford, but

there are one or two glasses made by Caspar Wistar. My grandmother had them from her grandmother. I'm not sure how they came into the family.'

'They're rare and valuable.'

She closed the cupboard door carefully. 'I don't know if you bought them with the cottage. Mr Banks is going to send me a list...'

He had picked up a bottle of whisky and was pouring it. 'No, I haven't bought them, and if you think of selling them I should get a very reliable firm to value them first.'

'Sell them?' She looked at him quite blankly. 'But I couldn't do that!'

He shrugged his wide shoulders. 'No, probably you couldn't,' he agreed goodnaturedly. 'Something smells good,' he added.

'It will be ready in ten minutes,' she told him, and went back to the kitchen.

Washing up in the old-fashioned scullery later, Sadie wondered what her chances of staying were. Undoubtedly, when they had met, Mr Trentham had made up his mind instantly that she wouldn't do, but now, since making inroads into the splendid supper she had put before him, she had seen his eyes, thoughtful and a little doubtful, resting upon her as she had cleared the table. She hadn't said a word, just taken in the coffee and put it silently on the table by the fire, then taken herself off to the kitchen, where she and Tom demolished the rest of the steak and kidney pudding and the afters before setting the kitchen to rights again. It was bedtime before she had finished. She refilled the hot water bottle, switched on the bedside light and went downstairs again to tap on the sitting room door and go in.

'There's plenty of hot water if you would like a bath,' she told him, 'and it will be warm enough by eight o'clock in the morning if you'd prefer one then.'

He looked up from the book he was reading. 'Oh, the morning, I think.'

'If you'd put the guard in front of the fire?' she suggested. 'I hope you'll sleep well, Mr Trentham.'

He smiled at her. 'No doubt of that,' he assured her. 'I've been sitting here listening for the proverbial pin to drop. I'd forgotten just how quiet it can be in the country.'

She nodded. 'Yes. Goodnight, Mr Trentham.'

'Goodnight, Sadie.'

She went up the narrow stairs, Tom plodding behind her to climb on to her bed and make himself comfortable while she had a bath and got ready for the night. She was almost asleep when she heard Mr Trentham come upstairs. He came with careful stealth, trying to be quiet, but he was a big man and probably not used to considering others all that much. He was nice, though, she thought sleepily, used to doing as he pleased, no doubt, but then according to Charlie, who read the *TV Times* and watched the box whenever he had a moment to spare, he was an important man in his own particular field. She heard his door on the other side of the landing close quietly and then silence, broken by a subdued bellow of laughter.

She was too tired to wonder about that.

She was up before seven o'clock, creeping downstairs to clear out the ashes and light the fires in both rooms as well as the boiler and then to get dressed before going down to the kitchen to cook the breakfast—porridge and eggs and bacon and toast. By the time Mr Trentham got down the table was laid and the fire was burning brightly. She wished him a sedate good morning and added: 'Tea or coffee?'

'Coffee, please. God, I haven't had a night like that in years!'

There seemed no answer to that. Sadie retired to the kitchen, made the coffee and took it in with a bowl of porridge.

'I never eat the stuff,' declared Mr Trentham, and then at the sight of her downcast face: 'Oh, all right, I'll try it.'

She had the satisfaction of seeing a bowl scraped clean when she took in the eggs and bacon. He

demolished those too before polishing off the toast
and marmalade.

'It goes without saying that you made the marmalade as well,' he observed as she cleared the table.

'Well, yes, of course. Everyone does.' She gave
him a brief smile and went back to the kitchen,
where she ate her breakfast with Tom for company
until Charlie interrupted her with a pile of letters.

'Brought a bit o' custom to the village,' he volunteered cheerfully. 'That's a posh car outside, all
right.'

Sadie gobbled up the last of her bacon, offered
a mug of tea and took the letters. Mr Trentham
wasn't in the sitting room and she could hear the
typewriter going without pause. She didn't fancy
disturbing him, not after all his remarks about peace
and quiet, but she saw no way out of it. She tapped
on the door and getting no answer, went in, laid the
post down on the edge of the desk and went out
again. She rather doubted if he had seen her.

She whisked round the cottage, not finding much
to do, for everything had been so scrubbed and polished it had had no time to get even a thin film of
dust. And then, since the typewriter was still being
pounded without pause, she went silently in with
coffee. Without looking up, Mr Trentham said:
'Open the post for me, Sadie, will you? Do it here.'

She thought of her own coffee cooling in the kitchen and picked up a paper knife on the desk. There were nine letters. Three of them were in handwriting and began Dear Oliver, and she laid them on top of the others—bills and what appeared to be business letters. Having done so she made silently for the door, to be stopped by Mr Trentham's voice.

'Where's your coffee?'

'In the kitchen.' She put a hand on the door knob.

'Fetch it and come back here, I want to have a talk with you.' He sounded so noncommittal that she guessed that he was going to tell her that she must go. And where to? she asked herself, rejoining him, her tranquil face showing nothing of the panic she was in.

'Mr Banks was quite right,' he began. 'He described you as a sensible countrywoman, and it seems to me you are. What my mother would have called an old head on young shoulders...I think we may suit each other very well, Sadie, but several adjustments must be made. We'll take our meals together—it's ridiculous that you should eat in the kitchen of your own home. You will share the sitting room as you wish, all I ask is that I should be left to myself in this room. You will refrain from lugging logs and coals into the house, I'll do that each morning or if you prefer, each night. And you're not to wear that depressing overall. We'll go to Bridport and purchase something more in keeping with your age. What is your age, by the way?'

'I'm twenty-three.'

He nodded. 'There are things to be done to the cottage. It needs a new thatch, I need a garage; a shower room would be useful. I've already arranged for a telephone to be installed, and someone should be here later today to install television.' He searched in his pockets and pulled out a cheque book. 'Here's housekeeping money until the end of the month, after that you'll be paid it on the first of each month.' He started on another cheque. 'And here's a week's salary in advance. You'll get a month's money at the same time as the housekeeping.'

He pushed the cheques towards her and she picked them up in a daze.

'All that, just for housekeeping?' she wanted to know.

'I like good food—good plain food, well cooked. I abhor things in tins and packets and frozen peas.'

'Well, there isn't a freezer,' she explained, 'and I hardly ever buy things in tins because they're too expensive.'

He smiled at her and her heart lurched. 'Splendid!' He gave her an encouraging nod and thought how beautiful her eyes were in her plain little face.

There was nothing about her to distract him from his work. 'The tradespeople call?' he wanted to know.

'Yes, and Mrs Beamish has almost all the groceries we need. I get eggs from someone in the village and I've ordered some more logs from a farm near by—they've cut down some trees and we can buy the awkward logs that won't sell easily.'

'Yes.' He sounded a little impatient and she got up, put the coffee cups on the tray.

'I'll be in the garden if you want me for anything, Mr Trentham. What would you like for lunch?'

He had picked up a sheaf of papers and was frowning over them. 'Oh, anything—we'll eat this evening.'

There was plenty of soup left over from the previous day and a mackerel pâté she had made; toast wouldn't take an instant and she could make a Welsh rarebit in no time at all. She got into her wellies and the old mac and went into the garden to cut a cabbage.

At one o'clock precisely she put her head round the door to say that lunch was about to be put on the table, and found him sitting back with a drink in his hand. He got up and followed her into the kitchen and watched while she ladled the soup and then carried the tray for her.

Beyond stating that he seldom stopped for a meal

when he was working, he had nothing to say, but Sadie noticed that every drop of soup was eaten and when she replaced that with Welsh rarebit, he ate that too—moreover, the pâté followed it. It was obvious to her that he hadn't been eating properly. Well, the housekeeping money he had given her was more than enough to buy the best of everything.

She put his coffee on the table by the fire and went away to wash up. He had insisted that she should take her meals with him, but that didn't mean that she was to bear him company at any other time. She tidied the kitchen, told him that she would be going out for an hour and would be back in good time to get his tea, and wrapped up in her old coat, walked down to the village. Mr Trentham wanted papers to be delivered each morning and they needed to be ordered. She paused outside the gate to look at the car: an Aston Martin Volante. It looked a nice car, she considered, and beautifully upholstered inside, and she remembered vaguely that it was expensive. It was a shame to keep it out in the cold and damp of November, the sooner Mr Trentham had a garage built the better.

The newspapers were ordered from Mrs Beamish and that entailed a brief gossip about the cottage's owner. Everyone in the village seemed to have seen him driving through and there was a good deal of speculation about him. Sadie was forced to admit that she knew next to nothing about him and wasn't likely to.

When she got back there was a van parked behind the car and a man on the roof fixing an aerial and another man inside installing the TV. Sadie went into the kitchen where Tom was drowsing by the stove, laid a tray for tea and made two mugs and carried them out to the men. Judging by the impatient voice coming from the dining room, Mr Trentham was being disturbed in his work and wasn't best pleased. She smoothed them down, poured them second mugs and gave them a pound from the housekeeping. When they had gone Mr Trentham summoned her into the dining room, where he was sitting at his desk; there were screwed-up balls of paper all over the floor and he looked in a bad temper. 'How can I work with all that noise?' he demanded of her.

'You arranged for the television to be brought,' she reminded him mildly. 'They've finished and gone, and since you're not working for the moment I'll make the tea.'

The ill humour left his face and he smiled at her. 'You're not at all like a housekeeper—I have one at my Highgate home and she spends her days running away from me.'

'Whatever for?' asked Sadie matter-of-factly. 'Would you like your tea on a tray here?'

'No, I would not. I'll have it with you.'

And later over his second cup of tea and third slice of cake, he observed: 'I shall get fat.'

'You can always go for a walk,' she suggested diffidently. 'The countryside is pretty and once you're out you don't notice the weather.'

'I've too much work to do.' He sounded impatient again, so she held her tongue and when he had finished, cleared away with no noise at all, and presently, in the kitchen peeling potatoes, she heard the typewriter once more.

The next morning he drove her into Bridport and much to her astonishment stalked into the biggest dress shop there and stood over her while she chose some overalls. Money, it seemed, was no object. The cheaper ones she picked out were cast aside and she was told with what she recognised as deceptive mildness to get something pretty. Taking care not to look at the price tickets, she chose three smocks in cheerful coloured linen and watched him pay for them without so much as a twitch of an eyebrow.

It was two days later when the washing machine arrived, and she had barely got over her delighted surprise at that when someone came to install the telephone with an extension in the dining room so

that Mr Trentham could use it without having to
move from his desk. It was becoming increasingly
apparent to her that his work was very important to
him; he made desultory conversation during their
meals together and he regarded her with a kind of
lazy good humour, but for the rest she was a cog
in smooth-running machinery which engineered his
comfort.

At the end of a week she knew nothing more
about him and he in his turn evinced no interest
whatever in herself. On Sunday she had been considerably surprised when he had accompanied her
to church and after the service allowed her to introduce him to Mr Frobisher, who in turn introduced
him to the Durrants from the Manor House. They
bore him off for drinks, and Mrs Durrant bestowed
a kindly nod upon Sadie as they went. She hadn't
meant to be patronising, Sadie told herself as she
went back to the cottage. She got the lunch ready
and sat down to wait. After an hour Mrs Durrant
rang up to say that Mr Trentham was staying there
for lunch, so Sadie drank her coffee and made a
scrambled egg on toast for herself, fed Tom and got
into her old coat, tied a scarf round her hair and
went for a walk.

It had turned much colder and the rain had
stopped at last. She crunched over the frosty
ground, finding plenty to think about. She had been

paid a month's salary the evening before and she intended to spend most of it on clothes. She climbed the hill briskly, her head full of tweed coats, pleated skirts, slacks and woolly jumpers. She wouldn't be able to get them all at once, of course, and after those would come shoes and undies and at least one pretty dress. She had no idea when she would wear it, but it would be nice to have it hanging in the wardrobe. Besides, there was Christmas. She hadn't been able to accept any invitations for the last two Christmases because of Granny being an invalid, but perhaps this year she would be free for at least part of the holiday. She frowned as she thought that possibly Mr Trentham would go home to his other house for Christmas and New Year too; he'd want to be with his family and he must have loads of friends in London, in which case she would be on her own.

There was a biting wind blowing when she reached the top of the hill, and she turned and walked back again in the gathering dusk. There were no lights on, the cottage was in darkness; Mr Trentham would be staying at the Manor for tea. Sadie let herself in quietly, took off her coat and went into the kitchen to put on the kettle. Mr Trentham was asleep in the comfortable shabby old chair by the stove with Tom on his knee. He opened his eyes when she switched on the light and said at once: 'Where have you been? I wanted to talk to you and you weren't here.'

'I go for a walk every afternoon,' she reminded him. 'I thought you might be staying at the Durrants' for tea. It's almost tea time, I'll get it now if you would like me to.'

He nodded. 'And can we have it here?'

She didn't show her surprise. 'Yes, of course.' She put a cloth on the table and fetched the chocolate cake she had made the day before and began to cut bread and butter, a plateful thinly sliced and arranged neatly.

'You'd better go into Bridport and buy yourself some clothes,' said Mr Trentham suddenly. 'Better still, I'll drive you to a town where there are more shops. Let's see—how about Bath?'

Sadie warmed the teapot. 'That would be heavenly, but you don't need to drive me there, Mr Trentham, I can get a bus to Taunton or Dorchester.'

'I have a fancy to go to Bath, Sadie. When did you last buy clothes?'

She blushed. 'Well, not for quite a long while, you see, Granny couldn't go out, so there wasn't any need...'

'Nor any money,' he finished blandly. 'I must buy the girls Christmas presents and I shall need your advice.'

'How old are they?'

'Five and seven years old—Anna and Julie. They have a governess, Miss Murch. Could you cope with the three of them over Christmas?'

Sadie didn't stop to think about it. 'Yes, of course. Only you'll need to buy another bed—would the little girls mind sleeping in the same room?'

'I imagine not, they share a room at Highgate. What else shall we need?'

She poured the tea and offered him the plate of bread and butter. 'That's blackcurrant jam,' she told him. 'Well, a Christmas tree and fairy lights and decorations and paper chains.' She was so absorbed that she didn't see the amusement on his face. 'A turkey and all the things that go with it—I'll be making the puddings myself, and a cake, of course, and crackers and mince pies and sausage rolls...' She glanced at him. 'The children will expect all that.'

'Will they? I was in America last Christmas; I believe Miss Murch took them to a hotel.' He smiled a little and she saw the mockery there. 'Don't look so shocked, Sadie, I suspect that you're a little out of date.'

She shook her head. 'You can't be out of date over Christmas. Even when there's not much money it can still be magic...'

He passed her the cake and took a slice himself. 'You're so sure, aren't you? Shall we give it a whirl, then? Buy what you want and leave the bills to me.'

'Yes, Mr Trentham—only you are sure, aren't you? The country is very quiet—I mean, in the town—London—there's always so much to do, I imagine, and there's nothing here. The Carol Service, and a party for the children and perhaps a few friends coming in.'

'I'm quite sure, Sadie, and it will be something quite different for the children. Now when shall we go to Bath?'

'Well, I'd like to get the washing done tomorrow...we could go on Tuesday. Do you want to buy the girls' presents then?'

'Certainly, though I have no idea what to get—I believe they have everything.'

She began to clear away the tea things. 'Do they like dolls?'

'Yes, I'm sure they do.' He sounded impatient and when he got out of the chair she said quietly: 'Supper will be about half past seven, Mr Trentham, if that suits you?'

He gave a grunting reply and a minute later she heard the typewriter. He was, she decided, a glutton for work.

It was cold and bright and frosty on Tuesday, and

leaving Tom in charge curled up by the fire, they set out directly after breakfast. Sadie had on her best coat, bought several years earlier more with an eye to its warmth and durability than its fashion. She wore her hat too, a plain felt of the same mouse brown as the coat. Mr Trentham glanced at her and then away again quickly. The women he took out were smart, exquisitely turned out and very expensive. There was only one word for Sadie and that was dowdy. He felt suddenly very sorry for her, and then, taking another quick glance at her happy young face, realised that his pity was quite wasted.

They parked the car in the multi-storey car park and walked the short distance to the centre of the city, but before Sadie was allowed to look at shop windows they had coffee in an olde-worlde coffee shop near the Abbey, and only when they had done that did they start their shopping.

Sadie had supposed that he would arrange to meet her for lunch and go off on his own, but he showed no sign of doing this, instead he led the way towards Milsom Street shopping precinct where all the better shops were. 'Blue or green,' he told her, examining the models in the windows, 'and don't buy a hat, get a beret. How much money have you?'

She didn't mind him being so dictatorial, it was like being taken out by an elder brother, she supposed. 'Well, the salary you gave me, and I've some money in the bank...'

'How much?'

'Mr Banks isn't quite sure, but at least two hundred pounds.' She looked at him enquiringly. Not a muscle of his face moved, as he said gravely:

'I should think you could safely spend half of that as well as your salary—you'll only need a little money for odds and ends, won't you?'

'Well, I must get one or two Christmas presents.'

'Probably the amount Mr Banks sends you will be more than he estimates.'

'You think so? Then I'll spend half of it.' Then her face clouded. 'Only I haven't got it yet.'

'I'll let you have a hundred pounds and you can repay me when you get it.'

She hesitated. 'You don't mind?'

'Not in the least. It would be highly inconvenient if I had to spend another day shopping.' He added with the lazy good humour she was beginning to recognise: 'So let's enjoy ourselves today.'

It took her a little while to get started; she had never had so much money to spend before in her life and she was afraid to break into the wad of notes in her purse. They went from one shop to the next, and if Mr Trentham was bored he never said so. Sadie settled finally on a green tweed coat and a matching skirt with a beret to match it and, since they hadn't cost a great deal, a sapphire blue wool dress, very simply cut. By then it was time for lunch. He took her to a restaurant called The Laden Table in George Street. It was fairly small but fashionable and Sadie wished with all her heart that she was wearing the new outfit, but she forgot that presently, made very much at her ease by Mr Trentham, who when he chose to exert himself could be an amusing companion. Besides, the food was delicious and the glass of sherry he offered her before they started their meal went to her head so that she forgot that she was by far the shabbiest woman in the room.

She spent the afternoon mostly by herself. Now that Mr Trentham had guided her away from the dreary colours which did nothing for her, he felt that he could safely leave her. 'Get a pretty blouse or two,' he suggested casually, 'and a couple of sweaters—and no brown, mind. I'll be at the coffee house at four o'clock, and mind you don't keep me waiting.'

So she spent a long time in Marks and Spencer, and came out loaded, not only with the blouses and sweaters but with a pink quilted dressing gown and slippers and a pile of undies. There was precious little money left in her purse, but she didn't care; she had all the things she had wanted most and she was content.

She got to the coffee house with a minute to spare and found him already there. She turned a radiant face to his and he took her parcels. 'I've bought everything I ever wanted,' she told him breathlessly, 'well, almost everything. It's been a lovely day.'

Over tea she asked him: 'Did you get the presents for your little girls?'

He nodded. 'I took your advice and got those workbaskets you liked. It seems a funny present for a little girl…'

'No, it's not; they like doing things, you know, and it isn't like asking for a needle and cotton from a grown-up, everything in the basket's theirs.'

'I'll take your word for it. If you've finished your tea we'd better go, Tom will be in despair.'

Sadie sat beside him in the car, enjoying the speed and his good driving. It was a cold dark evening now, but the car was warm and very comfortable, and since he didn't want to talk, she thought about her new clothes and imagined herself wearing them. Mrs Durrant would no longer be able to look down her beaky nose at her on Sundays, and at Christmas she would wear the blue dress.

At the cottage, the car unloaded and the parcels on the kitchen table, Mr Trentham said briefly: 'I'd like bacon and eggs for my supper,' and stalked away to the dining room and presently she heard the clink of bottle and glass and sighed. He drank a little too much, she considered. To counteract the whisky, she would give him cocoa with his supper.

She fed Tom, made up the fire and went to take off her things. Unwrapping the parcels would have to come later; first Mr Trentham must have his eggs and bacon.

She set the table in the sitting room and called him when she had carried their meal in. He came at once and sat down without speaking. Only when he took a drink from his cup he put it down with a thump and a furious: 'What the hell's this I'm drinking?'

'Cocoa,' said Sadie mildly. Even in such a short time, she had got used to his sudden spurts of temper and took no notice of them.

Just for a moment she thought that he was going to fling it at her across the table. Instead he burst out laughing. 'I haven't had cocoa since I was a small boy.' He stared at her for a long moment. 'Now I'm a middle-aged man. How old do you think I am, Sadie?'

She was too honest to pretend that she hadn't thought about it. 'Well, it's hard to say,' she said carefully. 'When you're pleased about something you look about thirty-five.'

'And when I'm not pleased?'

'Oh, older, of course.' She smiled at him. 'Does it matter?'

'I'm forty next birthday,' he told her briefly. 'Does that seem very old to you?'

She shook her head. 'No, it's not even middle-aged. Besides, you've got your little daughters to keep you young.'

'So I have.' He sounded bitter and she wondered why, suddenly curious to know more about him. It was strange, the two of them living in the same house and knowing nothing about each other. She reminded herself that she worked for him, her life was so utterly different from what she imagined his to be when he wasn't living at the cottage. Presumably he would finish whatever he was working on that so engrossed him, and tire of the peace and quiet and go back to London.

He went back to the dining room when he'd finished his supper, calling a careless goodnight as he went, and presently Sadie went up to bed. She tried on all the new clothes before she turned out the light. They still looked marvellous, but for some reason the first excitement at wearing them had gone. There was, after all, no one to notice them, least of all Mr Trentham.

CHAPTER THREE

SADIE SAW very little of Mr Trentham for the next two or three days. He appeared for his meals and ate them with evident enjoyment, but for the greater part of the day he was shut in the dining room with his typewriter and when he did emerge it was to put on his sheepskin jacket and go for a walk. On the fourth morning, however, he drove off in his car, saying that he wouldn't be in for lunch, but hoped to be back for tea. Which gave Sadie a chance to rush through the cottage, making as much noise as she liked, polishing furniture and hoovering floors and cleaning windows. It took her all the morning, and after a quick lunch she sat down to write a list of all the things she would need to buy for Christmas. Mr Trentham had said spare no expense, and although she very much doubted if he would keep his plan to spend Christmas at the cottage, she would have to make all the preparations just the same.

Mr Trentham didn't come back for tea; nor did he come back for dinner. Sadie waited until after nine o'clock and when he didn't come, she ate some of the casserole she had made, and put the rest on one side to be warmed up at a minute's notice. At eleven o'clock she went to bed. It was silly to worry about him; he was a splendid driver, and a man of forty should be able to look after himself. It took her quite a time to get to sleep.

He turned up at nine o'clock the next morning, after she had eaten her own breakfast and got the fires going.

'I'd like my breakfast.' He had flung open the dining room door and was halfway into the room, without saying good morning or hullo. Now he paused to say testily: 'Well, why are you looking so disapproving?'

He was coldly, bleakly angry, but Sadie wouldn't admit even to herself that she was even faintly scared. 'You went away yesterday morning, Mr Trentham, and said that you expected to be back for tea. If you'd phoned I wouldn't have cooked supper...'

He said in an amused, mocking voice which she found worse than anger: 'Since when must I keep my housekeeper informed of my comings and goings?' He added: 'I don't pay you to be nosey.'

Sadie blushed so hotly that she could feel the whole of her face burning. All the same, she stood her ground. She said with great dignity: 'I was not being nosey...' She had intended to say a good deal more but altered it to, 'I'll get your breakfast at once.'

She was a gentle girl, not given to rages, but she seethed as she cooked bacon and eggs, mushrooms and crisps of fried bread; made coffee and toast. When it was done, she tapped on the dining room door, carried the tray through to the sitting room and went upstairs to her own room, where she sat down at the little table under the window which did duty as a desk, and in a neat hand wrote out her notice, pointing out in the politest way possible that she would be prepared to go at once if he wanted her to, otherwise she would work out her remaining weeks. There was, she advised him, an excellent agency in Bridport where she felt sure he would get someone to suit him in a very short time.

She addressed an envelope, stuck it down and once downstairs, put it on his desk before going back to the kitchen. Domestic upheavals or not, meals had to be got ready, and she had a tasty minestrone soup already simmering; it had taken her quite a time to prepare, and it was as different from the tinned variety as chalk from cheese. She was grinding a touch more pepper into its delicate aroma when the door burst open and Mr Trentham came charging in waving her notice.

'What the hell do you mean by this?' he demanded savagely.

Sadie put the pepper mill down and replaced the saucepan lid. 'Well, just what I said—wasn't it clear enough? I've never written one before, so I wasn't sure…'

'And don't you ever dare to write one again,' he warned her. 'Of all the silly female nonsense, just because I happened to be mildly touchy!'

She stood in front of him, small and thin and even in her gay smock only slightly pretty, but she was quite unruffled now only though a little pale. 'I am not a silly female,' she pointed out with calm, 'and if that's what you're like when you're mildly touchy then I shan't bother with writing my notice if you have an attack of real touchiness, I shall take Tom and go.' She prevented herself just in time from adding, 'So there!'

His great roar of laughter was disconcerting. It was just as disconcerting when he said gravely: 'If I apologise, will you stay, Sadie? You really are a splendid housekeeper, and if you can ignore my ill temper and my tiresome ways, I would be grateful if you will stay. You're like a mouse around the place and your cooking is out of this world.' He smiled with such charm that she found herself smiling back. He held out a hand. 'Shake on it—I'll promise not to lose my temper unless I'm absolutely driven to it.' And when they had solemnly shaken hands: 'Something smells delicious—is it lunch?' His elegant nose flared as he sniffed.

'Only soup, and it's for lunch.' She spoke in a matter-of-fact voice. 'Would you like your coffee now?'

'Please.' He rarely said please and she blinked her long lashes. 'And I want to talk to you about Christmas.'

'I'll be ten minutes, Mr Trentham.'

But he didn't mention Christmas to start with. 'I went to a conference,' he told her. 'I'm half way through a script for a series—short stories really, linked together by one theme, love. The producer couldn't see eye to eye with me about it,' his lip curled. 'The fellow could only see love in terms of bedroom scenes, but there's more to it than that— there must be, because some people have been lucky enough to find it. I've persuaded him to change his mind, but it left me…mildly touchy.'

She gave him a thoughtful look. 'Are you very famous?'

His brows rose. 'I could be falsely modest and say no, but I'll be honest and say that for the time being at least, yes, I'm famous among my kind.'

He passed his cup for more coffee. 'And what do you think about love, Sadie?'

'Me? Well, I don't know, when I was at school

I had crushes on tennis players and film actors, but I don't think I've been in love with anyone.'

Mr Trentham nodded. 'Well, it's for people like you I'm writing this series.'

'I expect I'll enjoy it, then.'

'You're free to give me an honest criticism when you see it. And now about Christmas. I'm going to fetch the children down next week—Miss Murch will come too, of course. They'll be here for about three weeks. Will you be able to manage? I'll get extra help in if you need it.'

'Oh, but why should I? Miss Murch will be here to look after Anna and Julie, won't she? And it's as easy to cook for five as it is for two, especially when I don't have to be economical.'

'Get all you need to make a good Christmas for the children. I shall be here for Christmas Day, but I've a number of invitations; I daresay I shall be away for a good deal of the time. Most of my friends live in London and there's a good deal of merry-making planned.'

Sadie felt a pang of disappointment. 'Yes, of course,' she agreed cheerfully, 'but there'll be plenty for the girls to do. Does Miss Murch like the country?'

'I haven't the least idea.' He was suddenly bored with it all and with a muttered excuse, went back to his typewriter.

Sadie went down to the village the next morning and gave Mrs Beamish an order to make that lady's eyes sparkle. 'My word,' she exclaimed, 'wouldn't your granny have been pleased, spending all that money on extras!'

And Sadie agreed, hiding a sorrow for the old lady because she knew that her grandmother would have disliked any sign of weakness. She unpacked the groceries Mrs Beamish's schoolboy son brought up to the cottage after lunch and Mr Trentham, coming into the kitchen for a slice of cake to fill the gap between lunch and tea, demanded to know if she had all she wanted.

'No,' said Sadie, 'if you don't mind, I'll take the bus into Bridport tomorrow and get the things I can't get here. Crackers, almonds, raisins and sweets, and give an order to the butcher—they like to know in plenty of time if you want a turkey, you know.'

'No, I didn't know. It seems my education has been sadly neglected in the domestic field.' He took a second slice of cake. 'I'll drive you in.'

'I might be ages.'

'I've some shopping to do too. But why don't we go to Dorchester? Aren't there more shops there?'

'I don't suppose there are many more, but there is a Marks and Spencer.'

'Good, we'll go directly after breakfast.'

It was a raw morning when they set out, with a freezing mist shrouding the high ground at Askerswell so that Mr Trentham had to slow down to a mere forty miles an hour. Sadie could feel his impatience mounting and said soothingly: 'It clears up once we get off the dual carriageway.'

She sat back, conning her shopping list, feeling elegant in her new coat and beret. If there was time she would buy some gloves and perhaps a pair of shoes. And presents for the little girls and of course, Miss Murch. She hoped she was young and that they would get on together; it would be nice to have someone of her own age at the cottage.

They had coffee before he left her to do the shopping, saying that he had some to do for himself, and he would meet her at one o'clock exactly at the King's Arms in High East Street. There was a splendidly old-fashioned grocers close to the hotel where Sadie knew that she would be able to get all the things she needed, she could go there last of all and have time to look for presents at her leisure. Handkerchiefs for Miss Murch, she decided; expensive hand-embroidered ones, and more difficult to find, two small dolls to be dressed in clothes she would make herself.

And something for Mr Trentham. What, she wondered, would be a suitable gift from a housekeeper to her employer? She found a book and old print shop and after a good deal of browsing found a small eighteenth-century map of Dorset, nicely framed. It was rather more than she had intended to pay, but the shoes could wait until her next pay day.

But as luck would have it, she found a pair of gloves which didn't cost anything like the money she had expected to pay, and in one of the shoe shops there was a special pre-Christmas offer of leather boots at a price she could just afford. She had her well polished, worthy shoes packed and wore the new boots and positively skimmed up South Street and into High East Street. She had half an hour before she was to meet Mr Trentham; just sufficient time in which to buy the things on her list.

They had everything—dried fruits and nuts, the finest tea, the best coffee, an assortment of biscuits to make her mouth water, boxes of crackers, cheeses, things in tins she had never bought before. She only hoped there would be enough money in the wad of notes Mr Trentham had given her.

There was. She paid and then stood looking at the cardboard box which had been neatly packed with her goodies. She already had a shopping basket crammed full besides her shoes; perhaps she could leave it there and they could pick it up after lunch. She was debating the point when Mr Trentham's distinguished head was thrust through the door.

'I've brought the car round to the hotel car park,' he told her, 'if there's any shopping…' His eye fell on the overflowing box on the counter. 'Good lord, have you bought all that?'

'I daresay it looks a lot, but there's nothing there we don't actually need.' She beamed a goodbye to the elderly man who had served her with such patience and gathered up her parcels, then watched while Mr Trentham heaved the box off the counter. With it safely stowed in the boot she gave a sigh of relief. 'How very lucky that the hotel should be right next door to the grocers,' she observed, 'and such a heavenly shop—they offer you a chair, you know, and call you madam.'

'They'd better not call me madam,' said Mr Trentham tartly. He slammed down the lid of the boot and locked it. 'Lunch—I'm famished!'

They ate roast beef and everything which went with it, and he declared that it wasn't a patch on her cooking, which pleased Sadie mightily and probably accounted for the pink in her cheeks, although the claret he had given her to drink might have been the cause of that. She ate the sherry trifle with uncritical appetite while Mr Trentham contented himself with a morsel of cheese, and then they went back to the car. As they got into it she said on a breath of excitement: 'It's three weeks to Christmas!'

He gave her a lazy mocking look. 'You're nothing but a child,' he observed, and then frowned and she wondered why.

'You don't like Christmas?' she asked, unaware that the frown had nothing to do with that at all.

They were crawling up High West Street in a queue of traffic. 'It's become a commercial holiday, I seem to have lost the real Christmas years ago.'

'You'll find it again in Chelcombe,' declared Sadie. 'I think…'

'And now hush, I want to think,' he told her brusquely.

She was getting used to his sudden fits of impatience and supposed he was working out a difficult bit of script, and anyway, she had plenty to think about herself—never mind what Mr Trentham thought about Christmas, his small daughters should have the very best one Sadie could contrive for them. She got out her notebook and began to write down the ingredients for the pudding. After a while Mr Trentham demanded: 'What are you writing?'

'The pudding.'

'Oh, God,' said Mr Trentham, and put his foot down on the accelerator so that she had to give up.

They were back in the cottage well before teatime and she was a little surprised when he declared his intention of going down to the village. 'Tea at the usual time?' she wanted to know.

'Oh, have yours if I'm not back by half past four,' he almost growled at her, so that she wondered what she'd done now.

She forgot about him almost at once; all the groceries had to be unpacked and stowed away and the presents borne upstairs to be packed up in coloured paper. Later on, when she had time, she would cut out the dolls' clothes and make them up. She tidied everything away, feeling happy.

She might not have felt so happy if she had known where Mr Trentham was—at the Vicarage, in Mr Frobisher's study, talking about her.

'I have only just realised,' said Mr Trentham snappily, 'that the village might consider Sadie's situation as—er—dubious. In London the permissive society wouldn't lift so much as an eyebrow over it, but here in Chelcombe it's possible that they look askance at her sharing the cottage with me. She's my housekeeper and nothing more, of that I can assure you, but I wouldn't wish anyone to speak ill of her; she's a splendid worker and a first class cook and runs the place smoothly. That's all I asked and hoped for.'

Mr Frobisher nodded, his balding head on one side. 'I appreciate your concern, but I can assure

you that it's unnecessary. We've all known Sadie
since she was a very small girl; her grandmother,
an excellent woman, brought her up strictly and according to her own standards, which I must admit
hadn't moved with the times. Sadie is in a consequence, a little straitlaced. I feel this to be a pity
but that is merely my opinion, you understand. As
for the rest of the village, in their eyes you're a
widower with children, which sets you in a class
apart and in need of all possible assistance. That
you're a successful man cuts very little ice. You're
liked, did you know that, because you've been the
means of giving Sadie a livelihood and the blessing
of living in her own home. You need have no fears
as to Sadie's reputation, Mr Trentham, indeed she
has earned added respect because she has a trust-
worthy, well paid position.' He smiled suddenly.
'Besides, you've brought custom to the village, you
know; and I hear you're to spend Christmas here,
and your little daughters, an excuse for the local
residents to hold dinner parties and so forth.'

Mr Trentham looked surprised. 'Oh, delightful,
we shall look forward to that.' He stood up, preparing to go, but Mrs Frobisher, timing it nicely,
put her head round the door with an invitation to
stay to tea. It was dark by the time he let himself
into the cottage, to find Sadie at the kitchen table
making dumplings for the stew. They had had a

good lunch, but she had never known Mr Trentham refuse food yet. She looked up as he went into the kitchen and offered to make tea, but he refused, told her that he didn't want his supper until at least eight o'clock, and went into the dining room and began pounding the typewriter; making up for lost time, she supposed.

Sadie had never known a week fly past so fast; what with the puddings to make, the cakes to bake, the stowing of a great many bottles delivered for Mr Trentham, the preparing of the bedrooms for the children and Miss Murch, she had precious little time to herself. She took her walk each day, though, something she had done, year in, year out, and couldn't miss whatever the weather, and in between whiles, she sat sewing, fashioning clothes for the two dolls. She was a good needlewoman and found pleasure in making the finicky little garments; she had the last one done on the day before Mr Trentham was to leave for London to collect his daughters. It had meant sitting up late to do it, but now the dolls were dressed and ready, and while the little girls were staying at the cottage she would find the time to knit another outfit for each of them. She saw him off after breakfast and it was only as an afterthought that he told her that he would be back about teatime.

The cottage seemed very empty once he had

roared away down the lane, but she reminded herself that she had a lot to do and would be free to do it when and where she chose. She went first and picked some late chrysanthemums, putting a great bowl of them in the sitting room and a smaller one in Miss Murch's bedroom, and that done, she began on scones and cakes for tea; a chocolate sandwich filled with whipped cream, another fruit cake because Mr Trentham liked those best and some little iced fairy cakes. By lunchtime she had the fires going, hot water bottles in the beds and the tea table laid with one of her grandmother's old-fashioned linen and crochet cloths. There wasn't a complete tea set any more, but the cups, saucers and plates, although all different, were old and delicate and pretty. Sadie felt satisfied with her efforts as she had her lunch, and then went upstairs to change out of her smock and put on her new skirt and one of the pretty blouses. Just for once she would have to forgo her walk, but she was too excited now to mind that.

It had been a dull day, now it was already dark, with a cold wind and the hint of rain. At four o'clock she switched on the lights and took up her position in the sitting room window where she had a sideways view of the lane. She didn't have to wait very long. She was at the door when she realised that it wasn't Mr Trentham's car at all, but a taxi, and the figure coming up the path certainly wasn't him. Sadie held the door wide and Miss Murch paused on the step. She was a tall woman, slim to the point of boniness, with a good deal of jet black hair showing beneath her little fur hat. She was faultlessly made up and her coat looked expensive; she looked like a model who was past it and who had no intention of giving up. Her pale blue eyes examined Sadie's small person with cool unfriendliness, so that Sadie was left in no doubt as to what the lady thought of her, all the same she said in her pleasant soft voice: 'Miss Murch? Do come in, you must be tired and cold. There's a fire in the sitting room.' She peered over one elegant shoulder. 'Are the children with you? I thought...'

'Naturally they are. They'll stay in the car until I send for them. Mr Trentham was delayed in town, he'll be following later. What's your name?'

'Sadie Gillard.' Sadie was determined to be friendly.

'Well, Gillard, you may fetch the children and tell the driver to bring in the luggage. I've paid him and I daresay he wishes to get back to Crewkerne as quickly as possible.'

Sadie, well brought up though she had been, almost bit her tongue to stop the retort which was ready on it. Only the thought of the children sitting out there in the cold dark kept her silent. She took her old coat from behind the kitchen door and went down the path, slippery with icy rain. The driver was sitting morosely behind the wheel and behind him, sitting close together, were two small girls. They looked cold and scared, and Sadie was instantly sorry for them. She nodded to the driver and opened the door. She said softly: 'Hullo, I'm Sadie, your father's housekeeper. Will you come into the house? There's a big fire and a lovely tea waiting.'

Neither of them answered, but they got out obediently and she gave them each a hand. 'Would you mind bringing in the luggage?' she asked the driver, 'and if you can stay a few minutes I'll give you your tea—you must be cold and it's quite a drive back.'

He was already getting out of the taxi. 'I reckoned her could fetch her own stuff, but I could do with a nice cuppa since you'm offered it so kindly.'

He went round the back of the taxi, and Sadie took the small hands wordlessly offered to her and went up the path and into the cottage.

Miss Murch had taken off her coat and was sitting in front of the fire. She looked strongly disapproving and said at once: 'Anna, Julie, take off your coats and hats and sit down quietly until tea is ready. Where are the cases?'

'They'll be here in a minute.' Sadie took the

coats and smiled at the children. 'Which one is Julie and which Anna?' she asked, and held out a hand.

Their small hands were cold and they looked cold too—not cold exactly, she corrected herself, just tired and in need of a good meal. Julie was dark with big brown eyes and straight hair and Anna was dark too, only her hair was curly and her eyes were hazel. They looked at Sadie suspiciously and then at Miss Murch. It was obvious to Sadie that they didn't like that lady and they were afraid of her too. She pulled the sofa nearer the fire and invited them to sit down, then went into the hall to find the driver surrounded by cases and bags. 'I'll take them up for you, Miss...'

'Oh, would you? You're very kind. Then come into the kitchen and have that tea.'

She gave him a mug full from the pot of tea she was making, piled a plate with scones and a slice of cake, and told him to sit down and eat it. 'I'll just go in with the tea, but I'll be back presently,' she assured him.

All three were sitting just as she had left them and in an effort to lighten the situation she said cheerfully: 'Tea is ready, will you come and sit down?'

Miss Murch cast a disparaging look at the table. 'I don't allow the children to eat rich cakes,' she stated.

'These aren't rich and they're home-made; just for once perhaps you'll relax your rules?' said Sadie, and passed the scones.

'You have your meals with us, Gillard?' asked Miss Murch. She had asked for tea with no milk or sugar and was nibbling a scone with every sign of loathing.

'I do, Miss Murch. I'm called Sadie, perhaps you will be kind enough to call me that.' She spread cream and jam lavishly on to scones and offered them to the little girls. 'Excuse me for a moment and I'll see if the driver has finished his tea.'

Miss Murch looked at her with horror. 'You've left him in the kitchen? He could ransack the place!'

'Don't be silly,' said Sadie, her nice manners swept away for the moment. 'This isn't wicked London, we don't steal from each other here.'

In the kitchen she found the man ready to go. 'And thank 'ee kindly, love,' he said, and jerked his head towards the sitting room door. 'I don't envy you—nasty old lady her be.'

'Did she give you a tip?' asked Sadie.

'Cor love 'ee, no!'

She went to the tea caddy on the shelf above the stove and took out a pound note. 'Well, here you are, and I'm sure you deserve it. Mind you go back carefully.'

'Bless you, love, and a merry Christmas.' He grinned at her and went off down the path whistling, 'Good King Wenceslas,' and Sadie went back to her tea.

Anna and Julie had empty plates and were eyeing the chocolate sponge. Sadie cut generous slices and offered them without saying a word to Miss Murch, but that lady was too occupied in looking around her to notice.

'I had no idea,' she began sharply, 'that this place would be so poky and primitive—if I had, I would have refused to bring the girls here.'

'Well, if their father wants them here for the holidays, you can't do much about it, I suppose?'

'I should have protested strongly. Mr Trentham has complete confidence in me, he would have taken my advice.'

It didn't sound like Mr Trentham, somehow.

'Is this the only sitting room?' asked Miss Murch. She looked at Sadie so accusingly that Sadie only just stopped herself apologising.

'That's right. Mr Trentham uses the dining room as his study and there's a kitchen.'

Miss Murch shuddered as though kitchens were a dirty word. 'I trust that I have a room to myself?' she asked with a little sneer.

'Yes, of course. If we've all finished our tea we

can go upstairs and you can unpack. Anna, Julie, will you help me take the things into the kitchen?'

The children cast sideways glances at Miss Murch, and since she had been taken by surprise and had nothing to say, they nodded and followed Sadie. Tom was in his usual chair and the two little girls crowded round him still silent but quite animated.

'You can both talk if you want to,' said Sadie matter-of-factly, 'Tom likes company and he's very gentle.'

'It's nice here,' said Anna after a moment, 'isn't it, Julie?' They both looked at Sadie. 'We like you. May we call you Sadie?'

'Well, of course you can. Let's go and get the rest of the things, shall we? We want a tidy room in case your father comes home soon.'

'He had to go to a lunch with someone, but he said he'd leave early.'

'Then he won't be long, will he?' Sadie led the way back into the sitting room and found Miss Murch sitting by the fire again. She had turned on the TV too.

'I'm quite exhausted,' she exclaimed. 'You might take the children with you into the kitchen; we can unpack when I've had a rest.'

'They're going to help me wash up—it takes a

long time with only one, you know. But I expect you'll help me with the supper things later.'

Miss Murch smoothed the sleeve of her cashmere sweater. 'I never wash up,' she observed.

'There's always a first time,' said Sadie with a pertness she was ashamed of, but somehow Miss Murch seemed to bring out the worst in her.

They went into the kitchen and shut the door, and miraculously the little girls became just like any other little girls. They giggled and listened enchanted to all the things Sadie had planned for Christmas. She was telling them about the candlelit service she would take them to down at the village church when the kitchen door opened very quietly and Mr Trentham came in. They didn't see him at once and when they did Sadie stopped in midsentence and the two children drew sharp breaths. They looked pleased to see him, but they looked nervous, and Sadie wondered why.

She said 'Good evening, Mr Trentham,' and watched while his small daughters advanced to kiss him. He looked ill at ease and so did they; surely they weren't shy of each other? He kissed them and looked at her over their heads. 'They've been such a help,' she told him, 'they wiped the plates so carefully, and Tom's delighted to have company.'

'Where's Miss Murch?'

'Isn't she in the sitting room? She was—she's

tired and thought she would rest before they un-pack.'

He looked as though he was going to speak, but instead he turned to go out of the room. Sadie stopped him at the door. 'Would you like some tea?' she asked. 'I know it's late, but I expect supper will be a bit later, won't it?' She glanced at the children. 'Do Anna and Julie stay up?'

Two small eager faces turned towards their father. 'Why not—just this once, since they've been so good.'

He left the door open and went into the sitting room and left that door open too. Sadie heard Miss Murch, presumably taken by surprise, exclaim in a sugary voice: 'Oh, Mr Trentham, how delightful that you're so early; there are several things I feel I simply must bother you with.'

Sadie shut the kitchen door; she felt sure that one of the things would be her. She thought with regret of the Miss Murch she had imagined and wondered how she would be able to bear the real Miss Murch's company until after Christmas. Not company, exactly, she corrected herself, Miss Murch obviously didn't consider her a social equal. She went to a drawer in the kitchen table and took out a pack of cards. 'Does anyone here play Snap?' she wanted to know, and was appalled to find that they didn't.

It took them about ten minutes to master the game. They were having the time of their lives when the door opened again and both Miss Murch and Mr Trentham came in.

'Oh, my dears!' cried Miss Murch. 'You shouldn't be sitting in this kitchen—come by the nice warm fire.'

Sadie hadn't been aware that she had a nasty side to her character; she had never had occasion to show it. Now it took over with a vengeance. She said gently: 'But, Miss Murch, you asked me to keep them here in the kitchen with me so that you could have a rest. We've been quite happy.'

Miss Murch's delicately tinted face became mottled. 'We'll go and unpack.' And the children got up and went obediently after her up the stairs. Mr Trentham hadn't said a word; now he closed the door very gently.

'I wonder if I have done the right thing, having the children down here.' He spoke with a deceptive blandness which she mistrusted.

'They'll love it once they're used to it. I daresay the cottage is different from your home in London.'

'Miss Murch seems to think so. She's appalled that there's no central heating.'

'Oh dear, but I put a hot water bottle in her bed, and the children's.'

'Not mine?' She thought he was laughing at her.

'It's too early for yours,' she told him. 'What time would you like supper, Mr Trentham?'

'As soon as possible. I lunched with a friend and everything seemed to be covered in sauce—I'm not sure what I ate.'

'Well, it's steak and kidney pudding for supper with Brussels sprouts and buttered parsnips and potatoes in their jackets, and I made a trifle for pudding—I thought the little girls might like that.'

'I'll like it too. Is there any sherry in it?'

'A tablespoonful.' She looked at him guiltily. 'I took it from the dining room—you weren't here to ask. I hope you don't mind.'

'I don't mind—I should have minded if you'd given me a trifle without sherry, though.' He looked round the kitchen. 'Are you sure you can manage, Sadie?'

She gave him a surprised look. 'Of course,' she smiled suddenly, 'especially if I'm going to have help with the washing up.'

Supper was a difficult meal. The food got eaten, of course, every last crumb, although Miss Murch refused the steak and kidney and had vegetables and biscuits and cheese instead of trifle, but the little girls gobbled up their portions with heartwarming gusto and Mr Trentham, as usual, enjoyed a good second helping. He had opened a bottle of claret too, but it hadn't done much to loosen their

tongues. Miss Murch carried on a genteel monologue, name-dropping with every second breath and
constantly reminding Mr Trentham about this or
that distinguished person they had met. That he replied either not at all or with a grunt did nothing to
stop her; after a little while Sadie stopped listening
and planned the meals for the next day. The little
girls hardly spoke and then only in whispers; it puzzled Sadie that they looked at their father with such
adoring eyes and at the same time shied away from
him like frightened ponies.

Mr Trentham spooned the last of the trifle. 'It's
time you were in bed, my dears,' he said, cutting
ruthlessly into Miss Murch's account of how she
had coped with all the difficulties of the train journey that day. So they slid from their chairs and
kissed him rather shyly and then, almost without
hesitation, went and kissed Sadie too. She hugged
them with a lack of selfconsciousness, which made
Mr Trentham look thoughtfully at her. 'Goodnight,
darlings,' she said. 'Wouldn't it be fun if it snowed
tomorrow! We could make a snowman.'

Miss Murch was too ladylike to sniff, but she
registered disapproval. When she had gone, Sadie
said: 'I'm sorry, I shouldn't have said that about
snowmen—I didn't mean to encroach on Miss
Murch's ground.'

Mr Trentham leaned back in his chair and stared

at her. 'They like you,' he observed. 'Probably it's all those cakes for tea. I'm afraid Miss Murch doesn't approve of you, though.' His face was deadpan. 'They ate cake for tea and sat in the kitchen and played with Tom. I understand that cats are dirty animals.'

Sadie rose to the bait. 'What utter nonsense! Tom is cleaner than any of us—all cats are clean...' She stopped abruptly, biting her lip. 'I'm sorry, I'll keep out of their way as much as I can.'

'I think we might exempt Tom.' He got to his feet and started collecting plates.

'What are you doing?' asked Sadie, astonished.

'I suspect that my education has been neglected. I'm going to wash up!'

CHAPTER FOUR

IT WAS STILL quite dark when Sadie got up the next morning, but it had turned colder still during the night and the frost lay thick on the ground. She showered and dressed and crept downstairs, and made a cup of tea for herself before starting on the fires. She had become adept at doing this silently by now, just as she laid the table for breakfast with no sound at all before going into the kitchen to put on the porridge and put the frying pan on to heat up. By now there was a good deal of movement upstairs and presently Mr Trentham came down, poked his head round the kitchen door, demanded tea and went into the dining room; he was certainly a glutton for work. Sadie took in the tea and started on the bacon and was slicing bread when Anna and Julie came in. They wished her good morning in polite wooden little voices and then went to Tom, waiting for his breakfast.

'Would you like to put some milk in Tom's saucer?' asked Sadie. 'It's under the table there, so he can have his milk first and then a little bowl of porridge. Do you like porridge?'

They looked blank. 'It's nice,' she went on, 'we

have it every morning with lots of sugar and milk, and do you like bacon?'

They professed themselves willing to try anything and stood without making a sound while she ladled the porridge into bowls and carried the tray into the sitting room. 'Come and sit at the table,' she suggested. 'Your father will be here in a moment.'

She tapped on the door as she went past and he came out at once, kissed his children, enquired after their night and sat down to his breakfast. The porridge dealt with, Sadie fetched in bacon and eggs and the crisp fried bread that went well with it, and it was as he was serving this that he enquired where Miss Murch was.

'She said she couldn't get up until she'd had a cup of tea,' Anna gulped. 'She said Sadie was to take it up, only I forgot...'

Her father smiled at her. 'Never mind, poppet, it doesn't matter.' He got up from the table and went into the hall. 'Come down to breakfast, Miss Murch!' he bellowed. 'You'll need it—the children want to go for a walk and we've almost finished!'

Miss Murch appeared some twenty minutes later, elegant and well made up and in a cold fury. She wished Mr Trentham a chilly good morning, frowned at the children and ignored Sadie. 'Toast will do for me.' She sat down and poured herself a cup of coffee from Mr Trentham's pot.

'And when you've eaten it,' said Mr Trentham crisply, 'be good enough to come and see me in the dining room.'

He stalked out, and Sadie's heart sank; it wasn't going to be a success, this holiday. His routine which she had so carefully followed was being disorganised; worse, his very own coffee pot had been emptied by Miss Murch. She looked at the little girls and saw their forlorn faces. Living with Miss Murch couldn't be much fun for them, and she wondered if they were happy living with her in London. It was really too bad of Mr Trentham to ignore them: she wondered why. Perhaps he was so busy making a name for himself and lots of money that he had no time for them. But he already had a name for himself, and more than enough money... They were dear little girls too. She smiled at them and said: 'I saw a fox this morning, going up the hill behind the cottage.'

'What's a fox?' asked Julie, and when Sadie explained Miss Murch said crossly:

'It's all so primitive. Supposing I need to buy something, where do I go?'

'There's a shop in the village,' suggested Sadie, stubbornly friendly.

Miss Murch cast her a look of dislike. 'Not that kind of shop—I always go to Harrods.'

Unanswerable, thought Sadie, and left alone with the children after Miss Murch had crossed the hall on her high heels and tapped on the dining room door, suggested that they should all wash up. They were almost through, giggling and laughing and talking to Tom, when Miss Murch opened the door. 'You seem very anxious for the children to do the housework,' she said sourly. 'I must forbid them to come into the kitchen. You hear me, Anna, Julie? You are not to come in here with the housekeeper. Now come with me and we shall all go for a walk.'

The children looked imploringly at Sadie, but she said: 'You must do as Miss Murch asks, my dears, and you'll enjoy a walk.' She smiled brightly at them, Miss Murch included, but when they had gone the smile faded. It was going to be worse than she had imagined; Miss Murch was a petty tyrant, the children were milk and water shadows of what children should be and they didn't look happy. For the first time since she had met him, she allowed herself to be annoyed with Mr Trentham.

He came out for his coffee presently, coming into the kitchen and sitting at the table while she poured it out. 'Children gone out?' he wanted to know, and at her wordless nod: 'Why do you look like that?'

'Like what?'

'As cross as two sticks. Have you and Miss Murch been having words? She's a bit put out this morning: I daresay she finds it rather different from the house at Highgate. She'll settle down, I daresay.'

Sadie doubted that, but she wasn't going to say so, probably Miss Murch was a very good governess and he set great store by her. She stood at the sink peeling potatoes, saying nothing. It was Mr Trentham who did all the talking. His writing was going well, it seemed, he would have it finished in the next ten days. He was thinking of taking a short holiday before starting on a documentary for BBC 2. 'Somewhere warm,' he observed. 'Greece, or Corsica.' He added: 'I detest the weeks after Christmas.'

'We get snowdrops here in January,' said Sadie, and he laughed. 'Is that an inducement for me to stay here? What else?'

'Lambs—and the annual whist drive at the Vicarage, and the sales…'

'I don't think that I find any of those things very interesting.'

'No, I didn't think you would. I expect this cottage is fine for you when you're working, but in between you want to get back to your normal kind of life.'

He was watching her with a half smile. 'And what would that be, Sadie?'

'Oh, meeting interesting people—actresses and novelists and publishers—and going to the theatre and out to dinner in big restaurants and shopping at Harrods.'

'Harrods? I never go there. What should I buy there, in heaven's name? I've been going to Turnbull and Asser for years.'

Sadie had never heard of them. She said wistfully: 'There must be some gorgeous shops...'

'You've been in London, surely?'

'Oh, yes, Granny and I went with the WI about five years ago, but we didn't get further than Oxford Street.'

He said gently: 'Well, you must go again one day, but it's very noisy and crowded and you can't hear a bird sing, let alone a sparrow chirping.'

She said, almost defiantly: 'I'm happy here, but it would be nice just to see...I wouldn't want to live in London.'

'Do you know, I'm beginning to think that too.'

She waited for him to say more and was frustrated by the return of the walkers, none of whom were in a good humour. The little girls were cold, and their legs, encased in thin tights, were cold too. They were wearing all the wrong clothing—smart double-breasted cloth coats and velvet tammies:

just right for Highgate, probably, but not much use in Chelcombe. And Miss Murch had fared even worse, for she wore high-heeled suede boots, spattered with icy mud, and her coat, although elegant, just didn't suit her environment. She told the children sharply to take off their things and disappeared upstairs to her room, where she stayed, only coming down for coffee when Sadie had made hot cocoa for the little girls and given them a biscuit each. Their father, to Sadie's surprise, had stayed in the kitchen, reading the paper and drinking more coffee, and exchanging a goodnatured, desultory conversation with his daughters. He was still there when Miss Murch opened the door. 'Come out of the kitchen at once!' she ordered the children, not seeing Mr Trentham for the moment. 'And bring me my coffee in the sitting room—and mind it's hot!'

Mr Trentham looked up from his paper. 'The children may stay here as long as they wish,' he said gently, 'and there's plenty of hot coffee on the stove. Help yourself, Miss Murch.'

Which she did, with an ill grace and a nasty look at Sadie, who, busy making pastry for an apple pie, didn't notice.

'Father Christmas is coming to Bridport in two days' time,' she told the children, and cut off the edges of pastry and divided them fairly into two. 'Here, make a pie each.'

'May we—real pies?'

'Why not? I'm sure your father will enjoy them.' She handed over a pot of mincemeat. 'There are two patty pans in that drawer, you can each make a mince pie.'

Julie had begun to roll her bit of pastry. 'Will Father Christmas come here? He goes to Harrods, I saw him last year.'

'Not here, in the village. He couldn't possibly visit every little village in the country.'

'So may we go to Bridport and see him?'

'Ask your Father,' suggested Sadie, and watched the newspaper being lowered to expose a cross face.

'I'm a busy man,' he objected, 'how can I possibly get my work done if I have to traipse after Father Christmas whenever I'm asked?'

'Just once,' wheedled Sadie. 'But of course—I'd forgotten your work. Luckily there's a bus going to Bridport just before noon, would you mind if I took Julie and Anna? We could come back on the afternoon bus and be back in time to get your tea. Perhaps Miss Murch would like to come too.'

'I doubt it.' His voice was dry. He gathered up the paper and got to his feet. 'If I'm left in peace for the rest of the day, then I'll drive you in—but mind, we're coming straight back the moment you've seen Father Christmas.'

The little girls rushed at him. 'Daddy, Daddy, will you really? When shall we go?'

'We'll be at the Town Hall at twelve o'clock sharp,' said Sadie. 'You'll have plenty of time to see him and be back for lunch—hot soup and pasties. I'll have it on the table waiting to be eaten.'

'No, you won't. You started on this, you're coming too.' Mr Trentham went through the door without another word or anyone having a chance to say anything.

It grew steadily colder during the day and the next day it snowed. Miss Murch roundly refused to take the children for a walk 'They'll catch their deaths of cold,' she observed, and made herself comfortable close to the sitting room fire as she could manage, leaving the children to amuse themselves. Naturally before long they were quarrelling and bored, and with the prospect of Mr Trentham's furious face appearing round the door at any moment, Sadie left her chores, put on her old coat and her wellies and got the children's coats and shoes. Probably they would be ruined and certainly wet, but anything was better than Mr Trentham's wrath. Without saying a word to Miss Murch, she stole out of the kitchen door, the two children creeping like mice behind her, and led them to the little patch of grass where she hung the washing, now nicely blanketed in snow.

They had never made a snowman. Breathless with excitement and the pleasure of being out of doors, they slavishly followed Sadie's instructions and before long had a rather lopsided figure more or less ready. Sadie was fashioning a nose when she dropped her handful of snow and spun round at Mr Trentham's voice.

'I distinctly heard Miss Murch say that the children weren't to go outside!' he snapped. He spoke pleasantly enough, but he looked like a thundercloud.

Sadie glanced guiltily at their snow-covered shoes and the telltale splashes where a snowball had found its mark on their coats, and then she looked at the two rosy faces. 'Yes, you did, Mr Trentham, but they got bored—they're children and they need to play; just imagine, they'd never had the chance to make a snowman before. I'm sorry if you're angry, but it's done them good.'

He stood looking at her, not saying a word, although she expected to be given her notice out of hand; she was only the housekeeper, easily replaced, whereas Miss Murch was probably a paragon among governesses.

He came through the door, still staring at her in an unnerving manner, and she braced herself and then let all her pent-up breath out as Miss Murch sailed majestically out of the kitchen. She was angry, so angry that she actually pushed Mr Trentham aside. 'How dare you!' she began. 'How dare you, a mere servant, deliberately disobey my orders? I'll have you dismissed…'

'A slight misunderstanding, Miss Murch,' said Mr Trentham softly. 'I gave permission for Julie and Anna to come out here with Sadie, and may I remind you that any dismissing that might be done will be done by me?'

He went back into the house and Miss Murch, giving Sadie a dagger glance, went after him. Sadie swallowed. She was going to be sacked when it was convenient to Mr Trentham to do so, in the meantime she would have to behave as usual. She said cheerfully: 'Let's finish his face, my dears, and then we'll find an old hat and a scarf—I'm sure there's something in the shed that will do.'

So they finished their snowman, and the little girls, after a few minutes' uneasiness, forgot all about the few moments' unpleasantness and presently went back into the house, where Sadie took off their coats and shoes, and did the best she could to restore them to their pristine state. But even though she restored them she couldn't restore Miss Murch's temper. That lady refused to speak to her and during lunch carried on an animated conversation with Mr Trentham and afterwards swept the two little girls into the sitting room for a reading lesson. As for Mr Trentham, he didn't speak to Sadie at all, except to tell her that he would be out for dinner that evening. She was laying the table for their supper when he came into the room, elegant in his black tie and more aloof in his manner than he had ever been. There was no doubt about it that he was going to give her the sack. She waited for the fatal words and was very taken aback when he asked her to sew a button on his jacket. It wasn't off, only loose, but she tightened it neatly without saying a word, and when he thanked her and wished her goodnight, she said goodnight in a calm voice, although her insides were shaking. He would wait until the morning, she supposed.

She supposed wrong. Beyond greeting her at the breakfast table, he had nothing to say and the meal was eaten in a silence punctuated by Miss Murch's frequent admonishments to the children. She had been worse than awful the previous evening. Sadie, a mild girl by nature, had longed to throw something at her, but mindful of the children, she had held her tongue and listened to her companion talking at her for the length of the meal. It was a great relief when the meal had been eaten and she had been able to retire to the kitchen and wash up and presently go to bed, leaving Miss Murch sitting cosily by the fire, a book in her hand and a glass of Mr Trentham's port beside her.

But whatever had been decided about her own future, the trip to Bridport was still on. When she took in the coffee she was reminded to be ready to leave the house, and with Mr Trentham standing, as it were, with a stopwatch in his hand and making sure that everyone was on time, they all got into the car and were driven off rather faster than Sadie considered safe along the narrow country lanes, although she would never have dared to say so.

It was impossible not to be infected by the festive air which enveloped Bridport. Even Miss Murch's muttered asides about yokels and their childish pleasures couldn't spoil their fun. Sadie wormed her way well to the front of the people lining the main street and stood with a small hand in each of hers and cheered as loudly as the children round her when Father Christmas, standing in the back of an open car, drove slowly past.

Miss Murch looked the other way. Harrod's Father Christmas was to be tolerated since he was patronised by the upper crust, but this country version, even if his white whiskers were his own, didn't merit a glance. And as for Mr Trentham, he hardly noticed him; his eyes were resting thoughtfully upon Sadie's face. It could of course be the new coat and the beret, but it seemed to him that she was quite a pretty girl, not to be compared with the elegant lovely young women he knew in London—but then none of them, as far as he knew, could cook so much as an egg.

The procession was quickly over and people started making their way back home or to finish the shopping. Miss Murch took the little girls' hands and began to walk them impatiently to the car park down the street, but Mr Trentham said: 'Not so fast, Miss Murch! I think we could all do with a hot drink,' and led the way into the Greyhound Hotel behind them where they sat in its cosy, old-fashioned coffee room and the children chattered happily, so that the lack of conversation between the grown-ups hardly mattered. They included Sadie in their giggling talk, though, asking her any number of questions which she answered promptly, if not always quite truthfully, but Miss Murch would have nothing to do with such nonsense and presently began her own conversation with Mr Trentham, who answered her politely but mostly in words of one syllable which made it difficult to continue. On the whole, it was a relief when they had finished their coffee and cocoa and were ready to go home. There was a delay while the children begged to look at the shops, an idea quickly and far too sharply rejected by Miss Murch, and since Mr Trentham pointed out that he had a luncheon engagement at old Lady Benson's house just outside the village, there was nothing for it but to get into the car. Sadie had toyed with the idea of asking if she and the children could stay in Bridport for lunch and an hour's shopgazing and return on the afternoon bus, but Mr Trentham's face looked so severe that she decided against it.

Lunch was an uncomfortable meal. Miss Murch was plainly in a very bad temper and determined to take it out on everyone near her. She found fault with the little girls and went on and on about the discomforts of living in an isolated village where there was no restaurant, no cinema even, and as far as she could ascertain, no theatre within miles. And as for shops…she raised her eyes to the ceiling. 'I shall be glad when Christmas is over and we're safely back at Highgate,' she observed. 'I miss my friends.'

Sadie, determined to keep friendly at all costs, asked: 'Do the children have lots of friends? I expect they do…' She smiled at the children and wished they would smile back. They were such dears but so ungetatable.

'I am careful to choose suitable children for Julie and Anna to play with,' said Miss Murch repressively. 'I've seen no children around here.'

'Dozens of them in the village,' pointed out Sadie. 'They'll be on holiday in a day or two, there are sure to be one or two the children will like.'

'I decide with whom they shall play,' declared Miss Murch, 'and now, if you will clear this table, Julie and Anna can get out their drawing books. There's no need to go for a walk this afternoon, thank heavens.'

There was no sign of Mr Trentham, Sadie got the tea at the usual time and had cleared it away before he walked in, only to tell her that he had met the Durrants at Lady Benson's and would be dining with them.

Sadie's heart sank. The prospect of a long evening with Miss Murch for company appalled her. Later, she watched Mr Trentham leave the house once more and wished heartily that she could have crept into his coat pocket.

And it was every bit as bad as she had expected. The children were almost silent throughout supper and her own attempts to get someone to talk failed lamentably, and after the little girls had been taken up to bed she spent as long as possible in the kitchen, and after half an hour sharing the sitting room with a silent Miss Murch, she went to bed herself.

She didn't go to sleep, though; it was much later when she heard the car and Mr Trentham's firm steps up the garden path. He must have joined Miss

Murch in the sitting room, for she could hear their
voices, they were still talking when she finally fell
asleep.

She wasn't sure what woke her some hours later.
She lay in bed trying to remember what kind of a
sound it had been; that there was something she was
sure, for Tom was sitting on the end of her bed
with his ears on the alert. She got out of bed and
put on her dressing gown and slippers and leaving
the bedside light on, opened the door and crept
downstairs.

It was a bright moonlight night and very cold so
that the rooms downstairs were light enough. There
was no one in the sitting room and the dining room
door was shut, but the kitchen door was just a little
open and she opened it wider. Julie was sitting in
the old chair by the stove and Sadie slipped quickly
inside and shut the door. 'It's all right, darling, it's
only me. Don't you feel well?' She had whispered
to the child, anxious not to frighten her and still
more anxious not to rouse Miss Murch. And when
there was no answer: 'I'm going to put on the light.'

Julie was crying, her face was blotched and wet
and although the kitchen was still warm from the
day's cooking, she was wearing only a nightie and
no slippers. Sadie picked her up and sat her on her
lap. 'Tell me all about it,' she invited comfortably,
and began to rub the icy little feet.

'Daddy didn't say goodnight.'

'Well, love, he wasn't here…'

'He's never here. Miss Murch told him that she tucks us up at bedtime, but she never does—he think's she's as good as a mummy.' A fresh stream of tears rushed. 'She's horrid! I hate her, so does Anna. I wish you were our mummy, Sadie, and we could live here with you and Daddy for ever and ever.'

'But your daddy is a busy man, love, he has to work so that you can have clothes and nice things to eat.'

'Miss Murch says we can't live with him because we make too much noise. Sadie, will you ask him if we can stay here? We'll be ever so good.' Julie buried her face against Sadie's shabby red dressing gown, so it was only Sadie who saw the door open and Miss Murch standing there.

'I heard you!' she hissed. 'Turning the children against me, worming your way in! What are you after, I wonder? Getting them to like you and then setting your sights on their father, I shouldn't wonder! You're nothing but a fool—and a plain one too. Just you wait until the morning, my girl! Mr Trentham isn't going to like it when I tell him how you got the child out of bed and brought her down here in the cold and made her cry!'

'But that's not true!' cried Sadie. She was holding Julie tightly and the child had flung her arms round her neck.

'Oh, it'll sound true enough, and he listens to me.' Miss Murch smiled with a curled lip. 'I'll tell him why you did it too—in the hope that he would hear you and come downstairs and find you looking so touchingly maternal.' She tittered. 'I'll tell him that you confided in me, and I'll be so sympathetic and point out that it would be kinder to give you the sack than to let you stay on here, mooning after him.'

'Very ingenious, Miss Murch—what a pity I overheard you.' Mr Trentham, still in the beautifully tailored grey suit he had worn that evening, was standing in the hall. 'Be good enough to go to bed at once; I don't want Anna disturbed. I'll see you in the morning. Julie, I'm going to carry you up to bed, and we must be like mice so that we don't wake Anna.' His eyes studied Sadie in her dowdy dressing gown, her hair a fine curtain round her shoulders, her eyes huge in her pale face. 'Go to bed, Sadie,' he said, suddenly brisk.

Bed was cold, and Sadie picked up Tom and hugged him close. Mr Trentham had been angry, she knew the signs by now; he would give Miss Murch a good telling off in the morning and she herself would be told to go. He would be nice about it because he was fair enough to know that it hadn't

been her fault, but it was an undisputable fact that
she and Miss Murch didn't like each other, and the
children had to be considered first. He might let her
stay until after Christmas, but she doubted it. She
wasn't indispensable—after all, they had spent
other Christmases in hotels and they could again.
Such a waste, she thought unhappily; all those puddings she had been going to make, and the lovely
crackers and carefully thought out menus. She
wiped away tears with an angry hand; only little
girls cried. She went to sleep finally and woke with
a headache.

She crept downstairs at her usual time in the
morning and set about her chores. Breakfast was
almost ready and she was laying the table when
Miss Murch came down. She was elegantly dressed
as she always was and carefully made up, and she
was smiling, although her eyes were as hard as
stones.

She wished Sadie good morning and without
waiting for an answer went on in a hushed voice:
'I do apologise for the fuss I made last night. The
truth is, I sleep so badly and waking suddenly and
coming down here and finding Julie—the children
are my first concern, you know. I'm sure we can
come to some arrangement,' she went on. 'You
can't possibly be happy here. I know of several
good families who would love a housekeeper—in

London too. Think of the money you would earn and the clothes you could buy, and sooner or later you would meet some nice man and get married.' She shrugged her shoulders. 'You don't have to marry nowadays, of course, as long as you're reasonably discreet.' She came nearer to Sadie, who edged away. 'Now, surely we can come to an agreement. Suppose you give in your notice? You can tell Mr Trentham you want to spread your wings a bit, see the bright lights... He'll let you go, one housekeeper is very like another, you know. I'll give you enough money to keep you going for a few weeks...'

'You're bribing me?' said Sadie.

'Oh, no, my dear, just offered to help.'

Mr Trentham, who had come downstairs early to do some work and had been in the hall listening to this conversation, thought it time to intervene. 'I seem fated to overhear the most extraordinary conversations,' he observed irritably. 'Miss Murch, I must admire your ingenious plans, but I'm afraid they won't do. I've given the matter some thought and I've decided to send the girls to school here. They seem to me to be singularly lacking in the usual childish pleasures, perhaps a few friends of their own age will remedy that. This being so, I'm sure you'll be only too glad to return to London at once so that you can spend a civilised Christmas.

Have your breakfast and come and see me, will you? I'll give you a cheque and drive you to Crewkerne when you're ready.'

Miss Murch had the glazed look of someone who had been hit on the head. 'You can't mean that, Mr Trentham!'

'Indeed I do, Miss Murch. Sadie, bring me a cup of coffee in the dining room and go and help the children finish dressing. I'll have breakfast with them later on.'

He went into the dining room and closed the door, and Sadie, quite speechless, carried in his coffee. He didn't look up when she went in, nor did he speak. She went upstairs and brushed the little girls' hair and helped them with zips and shoelaces, and when they went down presently, Miss Murch wasn't there. From the thumpings and banging going on in her room she was packing.

Breakfast wasn't nearly as bad as she had expected. Mr Trentham talked to his little daughters although he had very little to say to her, only when they had finished he said: 'Leave these things, Sadie, and take the children down to the village, or for a walk, and don't come back for a couple of hours.'

He didn't smile at her, but she was relieved to see that he grinned at the children and bent to kiss them as he got up from the table.

It irked her very much to leave the dirty dishes, but she got the children into their hats and coats, fetched her own coat and a headscarf and started off for the village. It was lucky that there was a small amount of shopping to be done; they could spend a little time with Mrs Beamish.

The village shop might be small, but Mrs Beamish had stocked it well for Christmas. Sadie made her few purchases and then gave the children fifty pence each to spend. They had looked so surprised that she had explained: 'It's pocket money, my dears—I expect you get it every week, don't you?'

They shook their heads, and Anna asked: 'May we buy things, Sadie?'

'Of course you may. Choose what you want as long as it doesn't cost more than you've got.'

Which took quite a time, but presently, their cheeks bulging with toffee, they said goodbye to Mrs Beamish and followed Sadie down the steps and into the village street. 'Which way?' they asked.

'Let's go through the village and look at the duckpond and then we'll peep into the church; they'll be putting up the Christmas tree soon. If your father will allow it, I'll take you to the carol service.'

She had thought at first that two hours was going to be a long time to fill in, but she need not have worried. They walked all round the pond, spent quite a time in the church and then called on Mrs Coffin to get another dozen eggs, and since Mrs Coffin didn't have many visitors they stayed drinking cocoa in her stuffy sitting room while the children admired the dozens of china ornaments and then helped put the eggs carefully in Sadie's basket. It was well past the two hours Mr Trentham had decreed by the time they got back to the cottage.

The door wasn't locked and they went in cautiously. Perhaps Miss Murch hadn't gone after all, thought Sadie; Mr Trentham might have had second thoughts. He hadn't; he came out of the dining room as they stood in the hall. He said cheerfully, 'There you are. Get your things off and come into the sitting room, we're going to hold a serious discussion.'

CHAPTER FIVE

SOMEONE HAD cleared the breakfast things off the table. The children scampered to their chairs and sat looking expectantly at their father as Sadie took a seat opposite him. She had no idea what he was going to say, but she had braced herself against the news. Mr Trentham liked utter quiet while he was working, an impossibility without a governess to look after his small daughters, which meant that they would go back to Highgate or, what was more likely, there would be another governess or even an au pair coming. Well, anyone would be better than Miss Murch.

'May I have your undivided attention?' asked Mr Trentham with impatient civility, so that she went a guilty pink and stammered: 'Yes, yes, of course, Mr Trentham—so sorry...'

He didn't smile at her, but he did at the children, which she took as a good sign, nor did he sit down, but began to pace up and down the room, flinging words at them from over his shoulder.

'Miss Murch has returned to London. She will not be coming back; she found the country did not agree with her. I propose to send you, Anna, and you, Julie, to the village school for a year or so, and you will live here permanently, although it seems reasonable to suppose that we'll spend the school holidays in Highgate. When you've outgrown the school here we'll review the situation. But all this depends on Sadie.' He paused in front of her and bent a frowning gaze upon her startled face.

'Do I ask too much of you, I wonder? To run the cottage and look after Anna and Julie as well? Remember I shall still demand utter quiet while I'm working and you'll have little leisure. I shall, of course, pay you more and we must come to some arrangement whereby you have a certain amount of free time each week, and some sort of stand-in must be arranged so that you can get any help you need.'

Sadie could hardly wait for him to finish. 'Oh, I'd like that very much,' she assured him, 'that is if you think I'll do and the children want me to stay.'

He gave her a rare, kind smile. 'We all want you to stay, Sadie.'

She looked at the little girls and was reassured by their pleased faces. She would be taking on quite a job, but at least it was a worthwhile one and in her own home. 'Then thank you,' she told him, 'I'll stay.'

Mr Trentham went and sat down at the table,

facing her. 'Splendid. Now there are several things to discuss. I've already made enquiries about the school. The new term starts in the middle of January, which gives us all time to shake down and see to one or two things. Sadie, I don't think the children have the right clothes...'

'No, they haven't. Kilts and woollies and tights or trousers, anoraks and Wellington boots and lace-up shoes, warm nighties, woolly gloves...'

'You'll see to that. We'll go shopping tomorrow. Where?'

'Dorchester or Yeovil, there's a Marks and Spencer there.' She broke off to listen to Julie who wanted red boots and Anna who wanted everything green.

'You shall both choose,' she promised.

Two pairs of eyes were turned on their father. 'You'll come too, Daddy?'

'Well, I suppose I'd better, then I can pay the bills, can't I?' He turned to Sadie. 'There are several things needed. A new washing machine, a new Hoover, electric fires for the bedrooms, the shed in the garden leaks and we need another lock on the back door. The whole place wants painting, and we must have a new thatch.'

'No, not now, you can't,' observed Sadie. 'You'll need dry weather for that. But old Martin and his son in the village would do the painting as soon as the weather's right. The thatcher you'll have to book,' she added. 'It costs an awful lot of money.'

The way he said, 'Thank you for your good advice,' sent the blood into her cheeks. He had a horrid way of making her feel foolish; she wouldn't utter another word.

Mr Trentham watched the blush fade before he spoke. 'There's one other thing, Sadie. Would Tom mind if we were to have a dog?'

Joyful shrieks from the children prevented her from saying anything for a moment. 'I shouldn't think so. Would it be a puppy or a grown-up dog?'

'I thought we might go to the nearest dogs' home and see when we get there. We've never had a dog in Highgate, at least not since my marriage, and after my wife died there was no one to take a dog for walks—I was seldom home, and Miss Murch disliked them. Of course, Anna and Julie must look after him. You'll have enough to do, Sadie.'

She looked at the two excited little faces. 'I'm sure Tom can be persuaded, especially if we take care to spoil him for a bit,' and they beamed at her. The difference in the little girls was really remarkable; it was amazing what Miss Murch's absence was doing for them.

Mr Trentham broke in on her thoughts. 'Lunch?' he queried. 'I should like to get in a few hours' work...' For all the world as though they had been preventing him.

She got up from the table. 'Soup and toasted cheese,' she said, 'if you two will lay the table.'

The children had a lot to say during lunch— Christmas, the dog, their new clothes; there was no end to their chatter, and Mr Trentham laid himself out to be charming. He was tolerant of their piping voices, made jokes, discussed the presents they should buy and generally behaved as a father should. Sadie was a little astonished, but holding to the theory that one should not push one's luck, she whisked the children into the kitchen to help with the dishes and then took them off to the village. Mrs Beamish had a nice old-fashioned assortment of paper chains, the sort one had to make oneself and gum together. They spent a long time choosing them and when they got back to the cottage they crept in and sat like mice in the sitting room, absorbed in their handiwork, speaking in whispers and giggling softly. They were still happily engaged when the typewriter stopped abruptly and Mr Trentham flung open the door and shouted: 'Where's the tea, then?'

When Sadie came back with the tray from the kitchen she found him sitting with the children, making a paper chain for himself.

'I had no idea these things still existed—I used

to make them when I was a small boy, my sister Cecilia was forever telling me how badly I did them, too.'

Sadie considered that he was making rather a botch of it now, but nothing on earth would have made her say so; just to see him sitting there making paper chains was nice.

'Where's Aunt Cecilia?' asked Julie.

'At her villa in Cannes, my dear, conserving her strength for the excitements of Christmas at Kingsley Park.' He dismissed the lady with a wave of the hand, and asked, 'Crumpets for tea?'

'Yes, Mr Trentham. We'll have to have tea round this small table, if you don't mind, the chains might get muddled up if we try to move them.'

Tea was a boisterous meal with the children getting a little too excited and Mr Trentham not seeming to mind. It was Sadie who suggested that since they were all going shopping in the morning, the little girls should have their baths and get ready for bed before supper so that they could go to bed immediately after.

'A splendid idea,' observed their father. He got up and went to the dining room. At the door he said: 'I'll be out for dinner, Sadie. You two can creep in and say goodnight before you go to bed.'

Later, listening to the car roaring off much too fast down the lane, Sadie wondered where he was going. He had many friends by now, of course, and a good-looking man, famous in his own field and unencumbered by a wife, would be much in demand. She sighed as she put her solitary supper on a tray and carried it through to the sitting room. She had her daydreams like any other normal girl, but they had never worried her overmuch, but now she found herself wishing fervently that they might come true just once. Dining and dancing with a handsome man and herself in a beautiful dress, turned into a beauty overnight, queening it over everyone within sight. 'Don't be ridiculous!' Sadie told herself loudly, and started to clear away the paper chains. They were in a hopeless tangle and Mr Trentham's was only half finished. She unravelled them patiently and laid them in a large box ready to finish the next day.

Of course, very little got done the next day. Its short daylight hours were taken up with getting to Dorchester, shopping from the long list Sadie had made, eating their lunch and allowing the little girls to buy Christmas presents. Sadie found it sad that there were so few people they wanted to give presents to, but they spent a long time buying socks and a simply shocking tie for their father, and Sadie obligingly admired a very gaily patterned headscarf, which she felt sure she would be wearing after Christmas Day.

The vexed question of a present for Miss Murch was debated and settled out of hand by Mr Trentham, who decreed that a card was sufficient. 'And don't forget your Aunt Cecilia,' he reminded them. So they spent another twenty minutes or so making up their minds at the handkerchief counter and after that a further ten minutes while they took Sadie apart in turn and asked her advice as to what they should give each other. She'd already thought of that; and with an eye to Mr Trentham's desire for quiet, suggested modelling clay and a painting book and paintbox. Their father whisked them away then, looking mysterious, and she was left free to nip back to Longmans' bookshop and buy something she had seen there during the morning—a large book which with care and patience could be turned into an Edwardian town house, complete with family, servants and furniture; guaranteed to keep everyone absorbed for hours on end, she hoped.

She wondered what Mr Trentham had bought the children; probably they had all the toys they wanted in London. Sooner or later he would have to go there and bring some of them back, she supposed, for there was no question of the house at Highgate being given up—indeed, she had already faced the prospect of him wishing to go back there once his scripts were finished; he would want to go out and about and see his friends again, travel perhaps. He would sell the cottage and the little girls would be sent to a boarding school and he would be free to lead a bachelor's life until he started to write something else. And she—she had no doubt at all that when the time came, if it suited him, he would give her a splendid reference, a month's wages and forget her.

It was fortunate that she had no more time for these gloomy thoughts, for when she got to the Judge Jeffreys restaurant where she was to meet them for tea, they were already there, the children very giggly and excited, their father still, she was thankful to see, tolerantly goodnatured.

She had left a casserole in the oven and a rice pudding, creamy and stuffed with raisins, with it, so that once they were back home there was little to do save lay the table, while the children undid all the parcels and then went upstairs with their own purchases and strict instructions to Sadie not to look.

Mr Trentham had gone straight into the dining room and shut the door, and she heard the clink of glass as he poured himself a drink. Sadie, whose drinking had been limited to birthdays and Christmas and the occasional party, wouldn't have minded one herself. She was tired and after supper there would be the children to put to bed, the dishes to wash and all the new clothes to be put away, and

it would all have to be done without a sound, because he was at the typewriter again.

She gave the potatoes a vicious prod as the door
was opened by a shrewd kick from Mr Trentham's
large foot as she became aware that the typing had
ceased.

He had a bottle in one hand and a couple of
glasses which he put carefully on the table. 'I had
no idea that little girls in large doses could be so
tiring. A glass of sherry is the least I can offer you,
you must be worn to a thread.'

He filled the glasses and handed her one and
toasted her silently. She took a good sip and then
another one, savouring the fragrant dryness, 'Oh,
how very nice,' she said inadequately, and he
smiled, so that she went on, not wishing to appear
ungrateful: 'I don't know anything about sherry, or
anything else for that matter.'

He smiled again. 'No, I know. Don't drink it too
fast, it's quite heady.'

She had already discovered that. There was a
pleasant wave of lighthearted warmth washing over
her; the sips she had taken had been large ones,
there wasn't much left in the glass and she should
have refused when he filled it again. 'Don't worry,
I won't let you get tipsy,' he assured her. 'Did you
enjoy your day?'

'Very much, and so did the little girls, didn't

they? Thank you for sparing the time to take us, Mr Trentham.'

'Did you buy anything for yourself, Sadie?'

She gave him a surprised look. 'Me? Why, no, but I will later on. The sales will be at the end of December and I'll buy some more clothes then.'

'I'll drive you in to Dorchester again if you like, you can get what you want straight away.'

She shook her head and took a cautious sip of sherry. 'Thank you, but there's no need. I've got a new dress for Christmas and a blouse I've not even worn yet.'

He was watching her gravely, but she had the uneasy feeling that he was laughing at her behind the gravity. 'We might get asked out to a party.'

'Well, I shan't, though I expect you'll get any number of invitations. Lady Benson and Mrs Durrant call sometimes, or they did when Granny was alive, but we don't get asked to their houses. Sometimes I've been to Mr Frobisher's house for lunch and several times to a social evening…'

'What on earth's that?'

'Well, everyone in the village goes, and we all sit and talk and sometimes someone gives us a lecture and we have sandwiches and coffee…'

Mr Trentham's lips twitched. 'Have you ever been out to dinner with a man, Sadie?'

She considered, her memory slightly clouded by

sherry. 'Well, no, not just on my own—I used to go to the Young Farmers' annual dinner and dance, but when Granny couldn't get around any more, I stopped going.'

'And the theatre?'

'Oh, yes—I went with the WI to the Weymouth Operatic Society's production of *The Gondoliers*—it was very good. And I've been to Lyme Regis several times, there's a small theatre there—but not much else.'

Mr Trentham got up abruptly from where he had been sitting on the kitchen table. 'I'm going to London tomorrow, I shall probably not be back for a couple of days. Will you be able to manage?'

'Yes, of course.' Sadie wondered what he would say if she said no, she couldn't.

She told herself during the next couple of days that it was a good thing he wasn't in the house, because the children were able to get over their first excitement over their new clothes and run up and down stairs as much as they liked with the presents they had bought, now being packaged in gaudy paper and crooked Sellotape and laboriously labelled. And it gave her the chance to see to the puddings, make the cake and get old Martin up from the village to see to the leak in the shed; Mr Trentham would never have borne with the hammering.

All the same it was terribly quiet without Mr

Trentham roaring for his meals when he wasn't thumping his typewriter. She cleaned out the dining room, too, taking care to replace everything just where she had found it, even the piles of books and papers on the floor, and when she had finished, she sidled up the table and took a look at the sheet of paper in the typewriter. There were a few words only: *A Girl to Love*, he had written, and although she looked for the sheet that must have preceded it, she couldn't find it anywhere. Feeling guilty, she picked up her dusters and polish and went back to the kitchen, feeling as though Mr Trentham's grey eyes were on her back.

The two days became three. The little girls had finished their parcelling up and Sadie, to keep them occupied, had given them dough and told them to make mince pies. But even that had palled after a time, so they had put on their anoraks and welling-ton boots and Sadie had got into her old coat and they had gone for a long walk. Up the hill to the top and a look at the view and then down again, with the prospect of buttered toast for tea. It had got cold, cold enough to have snow, Sadie had said and she doubted very much if Mr Trentham would be home before the next day: 'So you shall have your supper,' she promised, 'and while I'm getting it, you can finish those paper chains.'

The walk had given them an appetite: 'Sausages

and chips,' said Julie, and, 'Bacon and eggs,' chipped in Anna, 'with fried bread.'

So when tea was done and they had sat for a while and watched *Blue Peter* and Sadie had shown them how to make the paper chains more elaborate, she went into the kitchen and got out the frying pan. The sausages were done to a turn and so was the bacon, and she had just started on the chips when she heard the car. The children heard it too. They flew to the door and flung it wide, letting in a stream of icy air, shrieking a welcome to their father. She heard him laughing and the door bang, and then he was in the kitchen, his dark head powdered with the snow that she had forecast.

'What a welcome!' he declared, and smiled down at Anna and Julie, hanging on to his jacket. 'You've never done that before.'

It was Anna who replied. 'Miss Murch wouldn't let us, she said that you were never to be disturbed and that you didn't like to be kissed or hugged.'

'Did she indeed?' He looked at Sadie, a pinny tucked round her small person, carefully turning her chips. 'And what do you say to that, Sadie?'

'I shouldn't think there was anything nicer than being kissed by your own children,' she said calmly.

He took off his jacket. 'Drag that into the sitting room and look in the pockets, there's something for

each of you,' and as the children rushed out: 'There
are several things just as nice,' he said softly. He
took the fork from her hand and laid it on the table
and put his arms round her. 'This, for instance,' and
he kissed her.

Sadie stood quite passive, in his arms, looking
up at him with her lovely eyes. She said in a clear
little voice: 'People do strange things at Christmas—the—the festive spirit and all that...'

He was smiling at her with the faintly mocking
kindness she found so disturbing. 'Wise Sadie, let
us by all means call it the festive spirit.' He let her
go with a casual movement. 'Whatever it is you're
having for supper smells good. Will there be
enough for me?'

'Of course. I've still got the eggs to do, the children chose what they wanted.' It was a relief to talk
about normal things. Being kissed like that had
shaken her badly—only, she told herself; because
no one had kissed her in such a fashion before;
the kisses at the Young Farmers' dance, and they
weren't all that in number, hadn't been like that at
all.

He sauntered away presently, leaving her to cook
more of everything while the children laid the table,
and over supper he entertained them with an account of the Christmas lights in Regent Street and

how lovely the shops were. But not a word as to what he had been doing or who he had been with.

Whatever it was, it must have inspired him to work harder than ever. He was downstairs before breakfast, demanding tea before banging the door on himself and his typewriter. But he came out when the bacon was sizzling in the pan and made himself amiable over breakfast, teasing the children, discussing the chances of the snow lasting, making a few commonplace remarks to Sadie about more logs, the telephone which was to be installed that very morning and the need to put some ashes outside the back door to cover the icy patches there. Looking at him stealthily, she found it hard to imagine him as he had been on the previous evening, holding her close and kissing her. He'd been glad to be home, she told herself sensibly, and resolutely shut out the picture of lovely ladies in London.

The snow started again after breakfast, and Sadie, tearing mouselike round the cottage tidying up while the little girls had another go at the paper chains, decided that a walk before lunch would be a good idea. She made the coffee, left it to keep warm on top of the stove, put a note on the kitchen table asking Mr Trentham to help himself and crept upstairs for the children's anoraks and gloves. They were leaving the cottage in the stealthiest of manners when Mr Trentham opened his door.

'Where are you all going?' he roared.

'For a walk.' Sadie didn't allow the roar to upset her; it was, after all, only a loud voice.

'I'm going with you.' He was already getting into his sheepskin jacket. 'I need inspiration as well as exercise.' He looked at Sadie, 'that's if you'll have me?'

'Well, of course we will. We thought we'd go to the top of the land and out across the field and go and see if Mrs Coffin has got any eggs.'

It was hardly a walk. They ran, and threw snowballs, and the children fell about laughing, behaving like normal children now. By the time they got to the top of the hill they had rosy cheeks and so had Sadie, and once in the field, they stopped to make a snowman, all four of them, making quite a good job of it. They were breathless as they reached Mrs Coffin's gate and it was Mr Trentham who suggested that only Sadie should go in. 'We're rather a crowd,' he pointed out.

'She'll be hurt if you don't,' Sadie pointed out. 'You're a celebrity in the village, and she'll be able to boast to all her friends that you've been to see her.'

She was right, of course. Mrs Coffin welcomed them with delight and they all trooped into her small sitting room, leaving their boots in the porch, then sat in her old-fashioned plush-covered chairs and drank the cocoa she insisted on making for them. Presently the children were allowed to go up the garden to collect the eggs from the nesting boxes while Mr Trentham entertained his hostess with London gossip. He did it very nicely and Sadie's heart warmed towards him; he was thoughtless and arbitrary and liked everything done the moment he said so, but he could be kind too.

Mrs Coffin's old eyes sparkled. As they said goodbye she said happily: 'I dunno when I've had such a day, not since the Queen Mum's birthday and Mr Frobisher lent me his black and white telly.'

Which was funny but a bit pathetic too.

Christmas came rushing at them from snowy skies—the candlelit carol service; the children's party at the Primary Church School to which Anna and Julie went, shy at first, and then joining in the games like all the other children. The carol singers, plodding up to the front door and being asked in to drink coffee and eat mince pies, the last-minute tying up of parcels and, for the first time in years, a great many Christmas cards. Mr Trentham had, it seemed, an inexhaustible number of friends and acquaintances.

And of course there were local dinner parties to which he went. Sadie was constantly washing and ironing dress shirts and offering black coffee in the morning as Mr Trentham's temper frayed at its edges.

'It's as bad as town,' he grumbled at her, on his way out for the third time in a row, 'and some of the food is atrocious.'

But Sadie was pleased when he refused several invitations for Christmas Eve. The children were in such a state of excitement that she was hard put to it to keep them occupied, and it was with a sigh of relief that she saw the three of them starting off for a walk after their lunch. It gave her a chance to make her last-minute preparations for the next day and set out the small table in the sitting room with little dishes of sweets and nuts and fruit. The chains they had hung with Mr Trentham's help a day or two earlier, and what with holly festooning the walls and Christmas candles on the mantelpiece and the tree in pride of place between the two windows, the room was more than comfortably full. The children had wanted to put the cards on every available surface too, but Sadie had persuaded them against that and instead had suggested that they should be pinned on to red paper streamers hanging down the walls of the hall. It had taken quite a time to hang them all up and she had got a little tired of the messages inside them. It seemed that Mr Trentham knew a great many girls who regarded him with the greatest possible affection. He had caught her reading some of them and had said blandly: 'Safety in numbers, Sadie. It's when there's only one left that there's danger.'

'Danger?' she had asked.

'Of falling in love, Sadie.'

They had tea round the fire when the three of them got back and an early supper with the excuse that the sooner the children went to bed the sooner the morning when their presents would come. And when they were safely in bed, Sadie set about stuffing the presents into two old pillowcases, ready for Mr Trentham to tie on to the bedrails when he went to bed.

'I had no idea what I've been missing,' he observed, obediently picking up and packing the parcels away at her direction.

'But you must have had Christmas...'

'Not this kind of Christmas, Sadie. What time do you suppose those two will wake in the morning?'

'Very early indeed; it's the one morning in the year when no one's going to tell them to go back to sleep.'

'Luckily you're an early riser,' he pointed out dryly.

Sadie remembered that well when at six o'clock the next morning two small figures stole into her room, climbed into bed one each side of her, and began to open their presents in a state of excitement all the more intense for having to be quiet. All the same, the rustling of paper and the occasional badly suppressed squeal of delight sounded very loud to Sadie. Besides, the bed was crowded, for Tom had refused to budge before his usual getting up time and there wasn't an inch to spare.

Surprisingly there was. Mr Trentham, coming in with a tea tray, took in the situation at a glance, swept the presents which littered the bed on to the floor, boomed a genial Merry Christmas at everyone and sat down on the bed too. The children screamed with delight. 'Daddy, you never brought us tea when Miss Murch was with us,' declared Julie, and: 'Is it because you like Sadie?' asked Anna.

Unlike Sadie, who had gone very red in the face, Mr Trentham remained calm. 'That's telling, but one of the reasons is the frightful din of rustling paper which had been going on for hours.' He poured tea and handed it round, and without seeming to do so, took a good look at Sadie, sitting between his daughters, her hair hanging round her shoulders, in her sensible pink winceyette nightie. Of course he knew that such garments existed, but he'd never seen one at close quarters before. There was no glamour about it, but he deduced that it would be nice and warm. He drank the tea, received his daughters' thanks for the charming little wrist watches he had given them and asked if Sadie had opened her presents yet, and when she shook her head, said: 'Well, go ahead, we all want to see what you've got.'

The headscarf came first, wrapped in a great deal of paper, and was duly admired, tried on and declared just the nicest scarf Sadie had ever seen. She kissed each child in turn and opened her other parcels—hankies from Mrs Frobisher, more hankies from Mrs Coffin, and a pair of knitted gloves from Mrs Beamish. Sadie was trying them on when Mr Trentham went out of the room and came back with a large flat box. 'Happy Christmas, Sadie,' he said, and laid it across her knees.

It was an extravagant box, tied with bright cords, and when the lid was lifted, awash with tissue paper. Sadie pushed it gently aside to reveal amber silk. She paused for a moment and looked at Mr Trentham, comfortably settled on the bed again, and he smiled and nodded his head. 'Go on, look at it.'

A crêpe-de-chine blouse and with it a matching skirt; she had never had anything like it before in her life. Its very simplicity spelt couture; its elegance was indisputable. Just looking at it made her feel beautiful.

'Oh, thank you—thank you, Mr Trentham! It's so beautiful, I can't believe it!' She held up the

blouse against herself, hardly able to believe that it
was hers. Dear kind Mr Trentham, giving her something so beautiful! She felt tears welling into her
eyes and hung her head so that her face was hidden.

'Why are you crying?' asked Julie. 'Don't you
like it? Sadie…?'

Sadie rubbed her cheeks with the back of her
hand and put the blouse back carefully. 'I'm not
crying,' she said in a wobbly voice. 'I've never had
such a lovely dress before, you see, and I'm very
happy—people cry a bit when they're very happy.'

'Oh, good,' said Julie. 'Well, kiss Daddy thank
you, then.'

It was quite obviously expected of her. She
leaned forward and kissed his cheek shyly and said,
'Thank you very much. Shall I wear it today?'

'Of course.' He looked so kind that she smiled
widely at him and asked: 'Have you opened your
presents, Mr Trentham?'

He fetched them from where they had been piled
neatly on the landing. The socks were perfect, he
declared, and the tie exactly what he wanted, he
would wear both that very day. He opened Sadie's
parcel without speaking and looked at the map for
a long moment. 'You know my tastes, Sadie,' he
said at length. 'Thank you. I shall hang it in front
of my desk so that I can look at it constantly.'

She half expected him to kiss her since he had

kissed the two little girls, but he didn't, only smiled warmly, collected up the tea tray and with the remark that he wanted his breakfast in half an hour's time, went out of the room.

That night, in her bed, tired but very content, and with the new outfit on a coathanger on the wall so that she could feast her eyes on it, Sadie went over the day minute by minute. They had all gone to church in the morning, walking there because there had been a strong frost during the night and the snow was treacherous for a car. There had been almost the entire village there, and a great deal of laughing and talking as the congregation dispersed. Sadie, greeting all the people she knew, was cheered to hear Mr Trentham refusing invitations to drinks, to supper that evening, to lunch the next day, and although he hunted he refused to join the meet at Bridport on Boxing Day morning. Instead he invited quite a number of people for drinks on Boxing Night, casually mentioning it to Sadie as they walked home.

'How many are coming?' she asked, her mind already busy with sausage rolls and vol-au-vents.

'My dear girl, how should I know? I suppose about twenty—a few more?' He had turned to look at her. 'Anna and Julie can help carry round the food,' he suggested carelessly.

Just for a moment her mind boggled at producing

a variety of bits and pieces for so many people. And the glasses would have to be got out and polished. She frowned and he said with a touch of impatience: 'What are you frowning for? No frowns, today of all days.'

So she had put her small worries out of her head and smiled for the rest of the day; and it had been a success, she considered. The turkey had been tender and Mr Trentham had carved in a masterly fashion. The puddings had been pronounced first class and they had drunk claret and then port and cracked nuts, exactly as one should at Christmas. And in the afternoon the little girls had settled to undressing and dressing their dolls and Sadie, remembering, glowed with pleasure at Mr Trentham's real surprise that she had made all the clothes herself.

They had tea quite late and soon after the children went to bed Sadie had gone back to the sitting room and sat opposite Mr Trentham until it was time to go to bed herself. He hadn't noticed her, for he was absorbed in a book so she sat like a mouse, listening to the record player. Even when she said goodnight and thanked him for a lovely day, he barely answered her, although he had got up from his chair and opened the door and wished her a good night. But what else could she expect? She was only the housekeeper, wasn't she?

She crept downstairs very early the next morning, put a clean apron over her dressing gown, and began on the pastry for the sausage rolls. It would have to be puff pastry because she had the vol-au-vents to make too. She was arranging knobs of butter on her dough for the second time when the door opened silently and Mr Trentham came in.

'What the devil do you think you're doing?' he asked sourly.

'Good morning, Mr Trentham,' said Sadie politely. 'I'm making things for this evening—I won't have time during the day. I'll make you a cup of tea in a moment, but I'm afraid I must just see to this first or it will spoil.'

For answer he filled the kettle and put it on the stove. 'Sadie, I'm sorry, I had no idea—that's what comes of living in a house where you pick up the phone and order food for a drinks party and don't give it another thought. Can you manage? Is there anything I can do to help?'

Sadie, being Sadie, took him at his word. 'Yes, please. Will you take the sausages out of the fridge and put them on that chopping board. And when you've done that make the tea.'

When he had done that: 'What next?'

'It's a bit messy, I'd better do it.'

As she had hoped he said instantly: 'I'm quite able to do whatever it is.'

'There's a sharp knife in that drawer. Cut the skin off each sausage and divide it into four.'

To her surprise he did it very neatly, looking at her with a grin when he'd finished and saying: 'You didn't think I could, did you?'

She began to shape the sausage bits into tiny rolls. 'If I make eighty?' she asked him, and stopped to drink her tea.

An hour later they were ready on the baking trays for the oven, so were the vol-au-vents, as well as cheese straws, and Mr Trentham was making another pot of tea.

'There are olives,' said Sadie out loud to herself, 'and almonds and raisins and enough cream cheese to make stuffed celery…do you suppose that will do?'

He put another mug of tea into her hand. 'Superb, Sadie—it will be a roaring success. I'll take the children for a walk this morning and give you time to see to this lot.'

On his way out of the kitchen he turned to look at her. 'My God, how I've changed!' he told her.

Far more people came than he had told her. Sadie thanked heaven that she had made another batch of everything while he and the children had been out. The cottage bulged with gentry and villagers alike, and Sadie, so elegant in her new outfit that half her friends didn't recognise her, watched her food disappear and the glasses being filled and refilled again and again. Mr Trentham was an excellent host, but beyond him filling her glass from time to time, she hardly saw him.

That the whole thing was a success was a certainty. People started to leave reluctantly long after nine o'clock and the last few didn't go until almost an hour after that. As the door closed on them, Sadie whisked the little girls upstairs, whipped off their party dresses, popped them into their nighties and tucked them up. 'Baths in the morning,' she told them as she kissed them goodnight.

The chaos downstairs was almost more than she could face—glasses and plates and crumbs and paper serviettes screwed into balls, empty bottles in corners, and Tom voicing a loud protest because he hadn't had his supper.

Sadie put on an apron, fed him and took a tray to the living room. There was no sign of Mr Trentham; probably he couldn't face the mess, and she could hardly blame him. This, she told herself wearily as she collected glasses, was what he paid her for.

He came out of the dining room a few moments later and began to pick up the empties. 'If I were to suggest leaving this until the morning you'd sling something at me, I suppose?'

'Yes, I think I should. It won't take me long. It

was a lovely party.' She yawned and he smiled at her.

'A long day, Sadie. You looked charming.'

She paused to stare at him. 'Did I—did I really? I feel quite different in this dress…'

'You've been hiding your light under a bushel for too long, Sadie.' He paused at the door. 'Leave everything in the kitchen once you've tidied this place. I'll wash up—and that's an order. Oh, and by the way, we're all going up to Highgate tomorrow afternoon, but we'll talk about that in the morning. Now off to bed with you!'

He left her standing there, her mouth open with astonishment, bereft of words.

CHAPTER SIX

SADIE HAD GONE to bed with her head in a whirl. How could Mr Trentham expect them to leave the cottage at a moment's notice like that? A silly question, she admitted to herself. He did expect it, and so they would get into the car and drive away at exactly the time he had in mind. She sat up in bed making a list of things to be done the next morning: too many for one, so she went down the list allocating tasks to the children and Mr Trentham. He would probably be annoyed, but if he wanted to go after lunch he would jolly well have to give a hand!

Having sorted things out to her satisfaction, she went to sleep. She had prudently set her alarm for half past six and by the time the others were awake she had packed for herself, tidied the house downstairs, laid the table for breakfast and washed and dressed. She told the little girls of their father's plans as she helped them dress, and by the time they sat down to breakfast they had been given their small chores to do during the morning and were agog to start. Mr Trentham, for once, came straight to the sitting room. Presumably he had finished whatever writing he was doing, or his muse wasn't awake yet. His mood seemed genial enough, so Sadie got out her list. 'If you'd be kind enough to take Tom down to Mrs Coffin just before lunch,' she suggested as she filled his cup for a second time, 'and then call at Mrs Beamish's and ask her to stop the milk and the bread—oh, and get a form from the Post Office so that the letters can be forwarded...'

'Anything else?' asked Mr Trentham with a sarcasm she could have done without. And when she shook her head, 'And what will you be doing, Sadie?'

She chose to take his question seriously. 'Pack for the girls, store the food away, cover the potato clamp—it's not earthed up enough if we get some bad frosts—turn off the water, clean the fires and lay them ready for our return, get coffee, get lunch...'

He held up a large hand. 'All right, I asked for it! What about these two?'

'They're going to dust the whole house and then put out the clothes they'll need and the toys they want to take with them. Then they'll...'

'Enough! I see that you've got the slaves fully occupied. We'll leave at half past one.'

And they did! Sadie presented herself and the two little girls at one minute to the half hour, hatted and coated and ready to leave. Tom had been taken to Mrs Coffin, all the messages had been delivered, the cases packed, lunch eaten and cleared away and the cottage as pristine as possible in the time she had had. There had been no time to ask questions; she had no idea for how long they were going and Mr Trentham hadn't seen fit to tell her. The little girls were put in the back of the car and she was told to get in beside him, then off they went.

It was hardly a good day for driving; there had been a hard frost again and the roads were treacherous, but Mr Trentham didn't appear to mind. He drove fast but with more patience than she would have credited him with, and after a little while she sat back and enjoyed herself. Only as they approached London's suburbs did she lose some of her content. Who would be at the Highgate house? Was she expected to be housekeeper there as well? Was she to be in sole charge of the children, and what would they do with themselves all day? She sat very quiet, her fine brows drawn together in a thoughtful frown.

Mr Trentham, glancing sideways at her, smiled to himself. 'I've not told you anything about my home, have I, Sadie? It's run by Mrs Woodley and her husband and there's a maid besides, Teresa. They've been with me for a long time now, and I think you'll like them. The house is quite close to Hampstead Heath and I don't think you'll find it too bad. The house is comfortable enough and Highgate is a kind of village, not quite like Chelcombe perhaps, but still, in its way, charming. The children have a few friends, not enough, I realise that now. Miss Murch was too strict in many ways—I had no idea that children could change so much. My fault, of course, I thought that if I had someone to look after them, dress and feed them, that was enough.'

Sadie was shocked. 'But they are your children,' she pointed out.

'Yes, but until they came to the cottage I saw precious little of them. My fault.' She glanced at him and saw how stern he looked; remembering something unhappy in his past perhaps, missing his dead wife. Perhaps that was why he hadn't been able to love the children. And yet, in the last week or so, he had seemed to enjoy their company. And they certainly loved him, although Sadie had been puzzled at their air of wariness when they were with him—Miss Murch probably dinning into them that they must never disturb him or take up his valuable time. 'I expect we shall find heaps to do,' she told him with an assurance which wasn't altogether genuine.

They were there by teatime and Sadie, getting out of the car in the quiet street with its row of tall houses along one pavement and an enclosed garden

on the other, was agreeably surprised. Indeed Mr
Trentham had been right; it was charming, and the
house, three-storeyed Regency with ample gardens,
could have been in any quiet country town and not
the edge of London at all. Their welcome was just
as agreeable, with Woodley, short, stout and balding, opening the door to them and beaming at her
as well as the children, and Mrs Woodley, tall and
thin with a long sharp nose, and a severe expression, wasn't severe at all, but hugged the children
with real affection and greeted Sadie warmly.

'You'll be wanting to go to your rooms,' she said
in a motherly voice which sat strangely on her severe appearance. 'The children can run upstairs and
take off their hats and coats and I'll show you
where your room is, Miss Gillard.'

'Everyone calls me Sadie. I'm the housekeeper,
you know.'

'Then Miss Sadie, if you would prefer that.' A
motherly smile which matched her voice lit up the
severity.

They went up the stairs together; a charming
staircase built in a graceful curve against one wall,
leading to a small gallery above. Here Mrs Woodley turned down a corridor leading to the back of
the house.

'I've put you next to the children,' she explained.
'They'll like to know you're close by. That Miss

Murch slept on the floor above, she said they disturbed her in the mornings.' Sadie detected tartness in the pleasant voice. 'They're looking bonny, the pair of them—Mr Trentham said they'd come on a treat. Not that he saw much of them up here, Miss Murch saw to that.'

They had come to a halt outside a closed door at the end of the passage and before Mrs Woodley opened it, Sadie asked: 'Why, they're dear children.'

Her companion nodded. 'Indeed they are, Miss Sadie, and now they'll get the chance to be real children, bless them.' She opened the door. 'This is your room. If there's anything you need, just ask me or Woodley. The children are next door just up the passage, I expect you'll all come down for tea when you're ready.'

She smiled and nodded and went away, and a moment later a small brisk little person came in with Sadie's case. 'Teresa's the name,' she said cheerfully. 'If there's anything you want me to do, just say so.'

'Why, thank you, Teresa. I forgot to ask where the bathroom is.'

Teresa crossed the room and opened a door. 'And the little girls have got one of their own.' She whisked to the door. 'Nice to have you, miss,' she said, and nipped away.

Sadie went and sat on the edge of the bed and looked around her. The room was large—enormous if she compared it with the cottage—with a small bay window overlooking the back garden, a pretty stretch of green with flower borders and one or two ornamental trees and a high brick wall shutting away the neighbours on either side. Even on a cold winter's day it was pleasant. She turned away from it and looked at the room again. It was furnished with a small brass bed and white-painted furniture and there were two velvet-covered easy chairs, as well as a dear little writing desk in the window and a shelf of books. There were delicate china ornaments here and there and a bowl of hyacinths on the dressing table. Sadie hugged herself with delight and called, 'Come in,' as someone knocked on the door.

The children, bubbling over with excitement, both talking at once. 'Isn't it super that you're next to us? Miss Murch wouldn't stay in this room, whenever Daddy went away she moved upstairs—she said we were noisy. She wouldn't let us have a light either, Sadie. May we have just a teeny one, like we do at the cottage?'

'Why, of the course, and I'm here all night, you know. What a lovely room, isn't it? Is yours as nice?'

She was led away to inspect the room next door,

even larger than hers, delightfully furnished with small beds and pretty mahogany furniture. There was a small bathroom too and a large closet half full of clothes.

'My goodness, when do you wear all these?' asked Sadie.

'Almost never. Miss Murch bought things she liked for us and sent the bills to Daddy. She used to buy things for her too.'

'Well, one day when it's wet and we can't go out, you shall show me all your pretty things and try them on. Now what about faces and hands ready for tea?'

They took her downstairs to a small sitting room to one side of the hall. There was a cheerful fire burning and comfortable chairs and a big sofa drawn up before it. The room was restful, the curtains and carpet a warm honey colour, the chairs covered in green and amber chintz. Mr Trentham was sprawled in one of the chairs, staring at the fire, but he got up as they went in and asked them to sit down, then went to the door and shouted to Mrs Woodley for tea. Woodley brought it, with Teresa coming behind with a stand of plates of bread and butter and cakes. Just like a Hollywood film, thought Sadie, pouring tea at Mr Trentham's request.

She sat quietly, joining in the talk when she was

addressed but otherwise letting the children chatter and listening to Mr Trentham's deep voice answering them. She looked round her from time to time, seeing the splendid pictures on the walls and the china ornaments lying around. No wonder Miss Murch hadn't liked the cottage after living in a house such as this one!

'You like it?' Mr Trentham's voice broke into her musing.

'Very much. It's so peaceful too, not a bit what I expected.'

'It's peaceful now—the trouble is everyone knows where I live and the house is often far too full for my liking. Your room is comfortable?'

'Oh, it's lovely, I've never had such a lovely room…' Her words sounded inadequate to her own ears, heaven knew what they sounded like to him.

He nodded. 'Good. Don't let Julie and Anna annoy you.'

'But they never do.' Her voice was drowned in their squeaky protests.

'I'm glad to hear it. I've got tickets for *Cinderella* on Saturday evening—who wants to go?'

There were screams of delight from the children and a concerted rush to embrace him. His eyes met Sadie's over their heads. 'And you, Sadie, will you come with us?'

She smiled slowly, 'I'd love to', and added like a well brought up child, 'Thank you very much.'

'It's the evening performance—I'll leave you to arrange a meal, Sadie. I've an evening date, but I'll be back in time to drive you all to the theatre—it starts at eight o'clock. We'd better allow half an hour, I suppose—so be ready by about twenty past seven, will you?'

Her pleasure was a little dimmed, for it seemed as though he were giving up his own evening's pleasure in order to go with them, and that must have been the case, for he went on: 'I shall be out quite a bit while we're here, so I'll leave you and Mrs Woodley to sort out mealtimes. Feel free to take the children out, Sadie. The Savilles at the end of the road are bound to ask them round to tea one day, of course, and you'll go with them—they've got rather a nice au pair—you'll be glad to meet someone of your own age.'

She thanked him again and added in her sensible way: 'I'll go and unpack now. Would you like me to take the little girls with me?'

Before he could answer her, Woodley opened the door. 'Mrs Langley and Miss Thornton, sir,' he announced, and stood aside to allow two ladies to come in. They were elegant creatures, wrapped in furs and bringing with them a wave of scent. They swam towards Mr Trentham with shrill cries of,

'Darling, so you're back from that dump in the country!' before they kissed him and caught his arms, one on each side of him. They were pretty women, although not so very young, and Sadie envied them from the bottom of her heart.

Mr Trentham extricated himself gently. 'Julie, Anna, come and say hullo to Mrs Langley and Miss Thornton. And this is Sadie Gillard, my house-keeper.'

Two pairs of blue eyes looked her over, although neither of the ladies bothered to speak to her, let alone nod a greeting. Mr Trentham said impatiently: 'Take the children now, will you, Sadie?' and turned to his guests. 'Well, Eileen, how's the play going? Kay, did you enjoy the Bahamas?'

Definitely not my world, Sadie decided shooing the children before her back to their rooms to unpack.

Presently Teresa came to tell her that they would be having supper at seven o'clock and would she like hers with the children or later. The master would be out.

'Oh, with the children, please, Teresa. Are there any visitors downstairs or can we come down without disturbing anyone?'

'Master's in his study. The ladies have gone, Miss Sadie. But there's a playroom just across the gallery. There's a nice fire there too.'

'We'll go there, then. Do we have supper there too?'

'No, miss, that will be downstairs in the dining room. The master likes the children to eat properly.'

The playroom was cosy with well used furniture and great cupboards filled with toys. The children were getting tired, so Sadie settled by the fire, and told them to choose a book and she would read to them.

They brought her a rather battered copy of *Grimms' Fairy Tales* and took it in turns to choose a story. Anna decided on Faithful John, which Sadie found rather bloodthirsty. She much preferred Julie's choice—the beautiful poor girl sewing by her window and the prince riding by and the girl's needle going after him—absurd and impossible, but rather sweet.

'You sounded as though you would have liked to have been the beautiful young girl, Sadie,' said Mr Trentham from the door.

She hadn't heard him come in and none of them had seen him, as they sat bunched together on the elderly sofa. He was dressed to go out, tall and good-looking and assured; he would meet interesting people, she had no doubt, lovely girls with witty tongues, and he wouldn't get impatient or frown at them, because they were plain and wore sensible clothes. A great ache swamped her chest so that she

could hardly breathe. She would have given anything in the world to have been beautiful and clever,
so that Mr Trentham would take one look at her
and cancel his evening out and stay with her. Because that was what she wanted, only she hadn't
known it until that minute. She wanted him to fall
in love with her, because she'd fallen in love with
him. She might just as well wish for the moon.

She drew rather an unsteady breath and said the
first thing that came into her head. 'It's a charming
story, Mr Trentham—but most fairy stories are.'

He smiled with a hint of mockery. 'But it doesn't
do to believe them, Sadie.' He kissed the children
goodnight and nodded to her. 'Breakfast's at half
past eight, I'll see you then.'

Presently they went down to supper. At any other
time Sadie would have enjoyed the delicious meal
eaten in such elegant surroundings, but she had no
appetite. She was still getting over the shock of dis-
covering that she loved Mr Trentham, and not just
a girlish infatuation; she loved him just as much
when he was tiresome or impatient or ill-tempered,
she knew that she would still love him when he
was an old man, stomping round the house, bawling
everyone out. She wouldn't be able to stop loving
him. Even if he married again, it would make no
difference.

Julie and Anna chattered like magpies, but towards the end of the meal they became sleepy and made no objection when Sadie whisked them upstairs and into their beds, kissed them goodnight and tucked them up.

'You won't turn out the light, will you, Sadie?' asked Julie anxiously.

'No, love—look, I'll leave this little lamp on over here, and I'm going to leave your door just a tiny bit open so that if you want me in the night all you have to do is call me.'

She went to the door in a leisurely fashion, watched by the sleepy children. 'When you get a puppy, I daresay, if you ask daddy very nicely, he might let him sleep in a basket between your beds.'

'Miss Murch said dogs and cats are dirty, she wouldn't let us stroke them...'

'They're cleaner than we are—you watch Tom washing himself next time we're at the cottage. Goodnight, darlings, I'm coming to bed myself in no time at all.'

Mrs Woodley was waiting for her in the hall. 'I wondered if you'd like to see over the house, Miss Sadie, it's nice and quiet and it'll be nice for you if you know your way around.'

It would be a good way of spending an hour before she could decently go to bed and she had no wish to be by herself, because then she would think too much. 'I'd love it,' said Sadie at once.

'You've been in the small sitting room for tea,'
began Mrs Woodley. 'This is the drawing room.
The master doesn't use it all that much, only when
he has company—it's a nice room; many's the
party he's had here too.'

It was a lovely room, high-ceilinged and with a
large bow window with window seats and elaborately draped curtains. The floor was polished wood
almost covered by a thick carpet in pale pastel colours, and the chairs and two sofas were upholstered
in the same pale colours. 'They dance here, too,'
said Mrs Woodley. 'Mr Trentham's got a lot of
friends.'

She crossed the room and opened a door in the
farther wall. It gave on to a small room, comfortably furnished, at the back of the house, with french
windows opening on to a conservatory which ran
the width of the house at the back. 'And if we walk
along here,' said Mrs Woodley, 'we come to the
music room, so-called.' This was a smallish room
with a grand piano and a pleasant arrangement of
comfortable chairs and small tables. 'And the library,' and she led the way into another small room,
lined with books, its polished floor covered with
rugs and comfortable leather armchairs.

'It's a large house,' ventured Sadie, a little out
of her depth.

'Well, a comfortable town house as houses go.

Here's Mr Trentham's study.' An austere room almost totally filled with a desk and chair and shelves
of books and papers. 'The dining room you've seen.
Now, upstairs. There's the master bedroom, not
used and hasn't been for years, the master's bedroom, guest rooms…'

Mrs Woodley led the way upstairs and opened
doors on to elegant rooms beautifully furnished and
cared for. 'Then there's your room down this passage, and the children's room, and two more guest
rooms. Upstairs there's our flat and Teresa's room
and an ironing room, as well as two more bedrooms. We won't go there this evening, I daresay
you're tired.'

Sadie said that yes, she was, and bed seemed a
good idea. 'And thank you very much, Mrs Woodley, you've all been so kind.'

She went to sleep at once, although she had
meant to stay awake for a little while and appreciate
the luxury of fine linen sheets and a quilted silk
eiderdown. It was gentle sobbing from the children's room which wakened her some hours later,
a sobbing which got louder and wilder even as she
got out of bed to listen. She didn't wait for a dressing gown or slippers but ran into the children's
room, to find Julie sitting up in bed weeping un-
controllably.

Sadie sat down on the bed and took her in her

arms. 'There, there,' she said in her gentle voice. 'It's all right, just you tell Sadie what frightened you. Did you have a dream?'

It was difficult to hear the words being sobbed out so heartrendingly.

'She said she'd shut me in the cupboard if I told Daddy, and I started to tell him at breakfast and she stopped me and made him laugh,' Julie stopped to sniff and choke, 'and she put me in the cupboard and—locked the door!'

Two small arms were flung round Sadie's neck, almost throttling her. 'Don't let her come back, Sadie, will you? It was d-dark and no one came for ages, and she smacked Anna when she tried to let me out, and we didn't have our supper...' Another bout of sobs took over and Anna woke up, got out of bed and got on to Sadie's lap. 'I had blue spots on my arms,' she said, 'but she made me wear long sleeves so that Daddy wouldn't see.'

'What didn't Daddy see?' asked Mr Trentham softly, and came to lean over the end of his daughter's bed.

Which brought another flood of tears and a long, involved account from Anna. Her father listened silently, only coming to sit on the other side of the bed and take her on his knee. When she had at last finished and Julie's sobbing had dwindled into sniffs and long sighing breaths, he said: 'My dears, this is all my fault, I should have...' he paused. 'Miss Murch seemed such a good governess, you know, it wasn't until you came to the cottage that I began to wonder. You must forgive me, it seems to me that I need someone to look after me more than you do. But Miss Murch is never coming back again, and that's a promise, so you can forget her. And now do you know what we're going to do? We're all going to have a drink of nice hot cocoa and then we'll go to bed, and tomorrow we'll think of something exciting to do.'

He put Anna down and stood up. It couldn't be all that late, thought Sadie, for he was still in his evening clothes, which reminded her that she was in her nightie, a very respectable garment, long-sleeved and high-necked but still a nightie. She said quickly: 'I'll get the cocoa. Mrs Woodley told me where it was this evening just in case I should need it.' She unwound Julie's arms from her neck. 'I won't be long.' She kissed Julie's wet cheek and padded to the door. Mr Trentham, watching her, had a look in his eyes which hadn't been there for a very long time, but she wasn't to know that. She slipped into her room, put on her dressing gown and slippers and went off to the kitchen.

The elaborate Cartel clock in the hall struck two o'clock as she pushed open the baize door which led to the kitchen and pantries. Just for a moment she allowed her thoughts to dwell on Mr Trentham's evening, but she dismissed them at once; moping over impossibilities was a waste of time. She found the milk and the cocoa and put mugs on a tray and presently took it up to the children's bedroom where she found Mr Trentham still sitting on the bed with a child on each knee. Whatever he had been saying to them had made them extremely cheerful and giggly. They drank their cocoa and got back into their beds, demanding to be kissed and tucked in, and would Sadie please keep the light on in the passage just for a little while.

'We'll leave it on all night,' promised their father, and held the door for Sadie to go through. In the passage he took the tray from her. 'I'll see to that—go back to bed and go to sleep.' He started to say something else, but sighed instead and only added a goodnight, and that in a voice suddenly austere.

Over breakfast next morning he suggested a good brisk walk across Hampstead Heath. 'I've got to go out to lunch,' he observed, 'but we've time enough if we go as soon as we've finished breakfast.'

'In a bus?' demanded the children.

'Why not? We can walk there and take a bus back.'

It was a cold clear crisp day and Highgate Village looked decidedly pleasant. Sadie would have liked to have lingered to examine the charming houses and peer into the small shops, but Mr Trentham hurried them all along until they reached the Heath where, much to her astonishment, he proceeded to run races with his small daughters and when she stood uncertainly watching, caught her by the hand and whirled her away too. And presently, breathless and glowing, they all walked on, taking paths which he must have known very well indeed, for he never hesitated until they emerged at length on the other side of the Heath and caught a bus back. They had to go on top because of the children's urgent request to do so and sat squashed together on the back seat, with everyone pointing out various landmarks to her.

It had been a lovely morning, Sadie decided, combing small heads of hair and examining hands ready for lunch, only spoilt by the fact that Mr Trentham wasn't going to be home for lunch; indeed, as they reached the hall they could hear the Aston Martin racing away, too fast as usual. She wondered who he was so impatient to meet and wished, for the hundredth time, that she knew something about his work and his friends and what he did with his time when he wasn't bashing away at his typewriter.

She sighed so profoundly that Anna asked her if she was feeling quite well.

'Never better,' declared Sadie; after all, he'd be home for tea, or at worst dinner that evening.

But although he came home during the afternoon it was to go straight to his study where the phone rang non-stop until teatime, and then, just as Sadie had looked at the clock and decided that they might all go down to the sitting room for their tea, Teresa came to say that she would bring it up to the play-room because the master had visitors.

She passed him on the stairs later, as she was going down to fetch something from the kitchen. 'I'll say goodnight to the children now,' he told her as he paused beside her, half way up. 'I've told Mrs Woodley to serve your dinner after they're in bed; I daresay you'll enjoy that better. There's a good play on television, you might like to watch it.'

Sadie thanked him quietly, wished him a pleasant evening and went on downstairs. She was beginning to regret coming to Highgate: at the cottage she had mattered, even if it was only cooking his meals and running the house; here she was of no more importance than yesterday's newspapers. No wonder he needed somewhere quiet to write, for there was very little peace for him in London, but perhaps he had got bored when he wasn't actually working…

But the next day was Saturday and they were to go to the pantomime in the evening. They all lunched together, then Sadie was dismissed kindly enough afterwards and told to go and look at the shops in the village for an hour while Mr Trentham drove the children to Hampstead to see some friends. So she helped the little girls into their coats and hats, found their gloves and made sure that their smart red shoes were clean, then sent them downstairs to their father. When they had gone, she put on her own coat and beret and set off to look around her. Almost all the shops were shut for the weekend, which was a blow, for she had some money still and longed to spend some of it. She had to content herself with a new lipstick and several pairs of tights, and then, because it was too early to go back to the house, she had a cup of coffee in a small café which despite its chic interior, looked forlorn because of its lack of customers. Saturday afternoon was, after all, a time when families were together at home, or out somewhere watching football or visiting grandparents.

She walked back presently and reached the gate just as the car drew up. She was immediately engulfed in the two children tumbling round her, talking at once so that there was no need to do more than give Mr Trentham a rather shy hello before going indoors.

They were to have supper early and since Mr Trentham was going out anyway, Sadie took the children upstairs to have their baths and put on their best dresses. They had several of these, she discovered, a little shocked at the extravagant row of expensive little dresses hanging in the cupboard. They chose sapphire blue velvet outfits finally, and then, quite ready themselves, begged to go with Sadie while she got ready herself.

There was no difficulty in choosing what she was to wear; the blue wool and the amber crêpe hung side by side in an almost empty closet, and of course it would have to be the crêpe. She had a shower and got dressed while the children sat on the side of the bed, telling her about their afternoon. 'She's a widow lady,' explained Julie, 'and she's got a little boy a bit smaller than me, and a girl we don't like. We had to play in the nursery while she and Daddy had tea. They laughed a lot.'

Just right, thought Sadie unhappily, a widow with two children; she'd be beautiful, of course, and exquisitely dressed and good with children and giving dinner parties and going to the theatre. She got into the blue crêpe and immediately felt better, because there was no doubt that it did something for her. She brushed her hair back and tied it with a matching ribbon, made up her face in a rather inexperienced fashion, and pronounced herself ready. Blow Mr Trentham and his lovely ladies! She was going to enjoy her evening.

They were ready and waiting by the time Mr Trentham came to fetch them. The little girls had been too excited to eat much and Sadie hadn't wanted to eat at all, but she had done her best because of setting a good example. Now they got into the car, Mr Trentham having duly admired their dresses and pronounced all three of them very smart indeed, and Sadie went scarlet when Anna said: 'I think Sadie looks prettier than Mrs Wilcox, Daddy, don't you?' And luckily, not waiting for an answer: 'She uses very strong scent, but Sadie smells nice.'

Fortunately, Mr Trentham made no answer other than a grunt which could have meant anything.

They had splendid seats, the middle of the front row of the dress circle, so that they missed nothing of what was going on on the stage. Sadie, quite carried away by the splendour of the theatre and the magnificence of the costumes and scenery, sat between the two children, as rapt as they were. Mr Trentham had provided a box of chocolates for them and in the interval ordered ices for them, although he went off to the bar. It wasn't until the lights went up for the last time that Sadie had a chance to say how heavenly it had been. He was helping Julie into her coat and looked across at her, doing the same for Anna. 'I'm glad you enjoyed it, Sadie,' he said quietly. 'I found it heavenly too.'

It was getting on for eleven o'clock by the time

they got back. Sadie whisked the children upstairs and into bed in no time at all, and was leaving the room when Mr Trentham came in. He said good-night to the sleepy little girls and followed Sadie out into the passage.

'Are you hungry?' he asked her.

She was, although she hesitated to say so, not that it mattered, because he didn't give her a chance to reply. 'We'll go somewhere and have supper. Teresa's watching the late night film, so the children will be all right. Where's your coat? Fetch it and we'll go now.'

Sadie hadn't uttered a word and now she saw that it would be useless to anyway. She got her coat and followed him downstairs and out to the car and sat without a word as they drove away. 'A pleasant evening,' he observed blandly. 'Let's see if we can make it still pleasanter.'

CHAPTER SEVEN

THEY WERE driving back the way they had come, back towards London's heart. After a few moments Sadie ventured: 'Isn't it a bit late for supper?'

Mr Trentham had been waiting for that. 'This isn't Chelcombe, Sadie, there are plenty of places open until the small hours.' And when she didn't answer! 'You're not tired?'

Of course she was tired, but she had no intention of saying so. She said primly: 'Since I've been at the Highgate house, I've not done anything to make me tired.'

'Good. We're going to Kettners. Have you heard of it?' and when she shook her head, 'They take their last orders at one o'clock in the morning.'

'How awful for the people in the kitchen,' said Sadie, and Mr Trentham laughed with the faint mockery she disliked so much.

'You and I see the world through different eyes, Sadie. If it comforts you at all, they get very good money. I hope it won't spoil your appetite.'

'No, I don't think so, I'm really quite hungry.'

She was glad of the amber crêpe as he ushered her into Kettner's restaurant. It was almost full and they had to walk through a crowded room to reach their table. Sadie walked to it behind the head waiter, her head held high, her plain little face serene, very anxious not to let Mr Trentham down.

The supper he had suggested wasn't quite what she had envisaged. The menu was extensive and written in French. She worked out one or two items with inward shudders at the prices and then said in her quiet way: 'Would you mind choosing for me, Mr Trentham?'

He ordered smoked Scotch salmon with brown bread and butter and lemon wedges, for them both, and then crêpes de volaille Florentine for her and a steak for himself. And when they had demolished the salmon and the crêpes arrived said with relief: 'Oh, it's pancakes with a chicken filling and spinach and cheese sauce.'

Mr Trentham agreed gravely and wished that the chef could have heard her. The pudding she chose for herself: Mont Blanc, a purée of chestnuts with whipped cream which she consumed with childish relish under Mr Trentham's amused gaze while he toyed with a little Stilton.

He had laid himself out putting her at her ease, talking about nothing in particular and making no effort to persuade her to drink more than one glass of the excellent hock he had chosen for her. She had been a little surprised to find that he was drinking a red wine while hers was white, but she had sense enough to know that the choice of wines was quite outside her province, nor had she any intention of asking him; she could get a book and read it up for herself.

Coffee was brought and over it Mr Trentham began to talk about more personal matters, and Sadie, nicely relaxed by the hock, was only too eager to listen.

'Sunday tomorrow,' said Mr Trentham. 'What about church?'

'Well, yes, I'd like to go if it's convenient.'

'We'll all go to St Paul's, the evening service.' He smiled at her.

'I'd like that very much, but are you sure…'

'Quite sure, Sadie. I thought that in the morning we might drive out to Pine Ridge Dogs' Home, to see if we can find a puppy for the children. They'll keep it for us until we go back to the cottage.'

'The children will love that. Couldn't we bring it back with us?'

'Well, I suppose so, you'll have extra work…'

'But I haven't any work,' she pointed out. 'I haven't done a thing since we came to Highgate.'

'You've looked after the children.' He put down his coffee cup. 'I feel guilty about them, Sadie. I thought that if they had a first class governess and everything they wanted, that that would be sufficient. I suppose that I wanted to forget the past and they were part of it. And now I begin to see what I've missed...'

She said, anxious to comfort him: 'You mustn't feel guilty, Mr Trentham. Miss Murch was clever, only the children knew what she was really like and she threatened them when they tried to tell you. You heard them the other night.'

'I should have listened to them, not dismissed the matter lightly as though it was just a childish fantasy. I'm not much use as a father, I'm afraid.'

She said bracingly: 'You will be if you practise hard enough!' She went pink. 'I'm sorry, I had no right to say that.'

He put down his coffee cup. 'You're almost too good to be true,' he observed, 'and much too good for me, Sadie.' His tone held mockery and the pink became red.

She said gruffly: 'I'm not good at all...'

He drank the brandy the waiter had brought him and lifted his hand for more, then continued just as though she hadn't spoken: 'A kind of nanny-cum-mother confessor. If I confess to you you won't tell anyone, will you?'

'Of course not, but I don't think you should talk like this to me, Mr Trentham—I'm only your housekeeper.'

'Ah, yes, but that's the crux of the matter. You're

not only my housekeeper, Sadie—and don't look at me in that enquiring manner, because I have no intention of explaining to you—not yet, anyhow.'

He leaned back in his chair for all the world as though he intended to sit there until breakfast time, and when she couldn't help giving a quick look at the clock on the further wall of the restaurant: 'Don't worry, they won't bring me the bill until I ask for it.'

It was half past one in the morning and she wanted to go to bed, but she guessed that even if she suggested that they should go home, Mr Trentham would ignore her. He wanted to talk and she would have to let him, for obviously he regarded her as someone in whom he could safely confide. She should be thankful for that, she reminded herself, even though he thought of her as a nanny. She poured herself another cup of coffee, black this time to keep her awake, and sat back quietly, her hands quiet in her lap.

'You don't wear any jewellery,' observed Mr Trentham, surprisingly.

'I haven't any.'

'I've never met anyone quite like you before,' he smiled briefly. 'The women I know spend a fortune on clothes and expect diamonds on their birthdays. I doubt if any of them would know how to stop a child crying and they certainly wouldn't get up in

the night just for a few childish sobs.' Just for a
moment mockery twisted his firm mouth. 'They
wouldn't wear flannel nighties either.'

'Winceyette,' said Sadie in a clear voice.

'Is that what it's called? I don't think that my
wife—Stella—would have known what it was. She
had her things made to order by Janet Reger.' And
at Sadie's questioning look: 'A very expensive de-
signer of women's undies.' He lifted a finger and a
waiter brought more coffee and Sadie poured a cup
for them both. 'She liked only the best of everything. She didn't want children, but it was the done
thing to have a son. I suppose that's why she didn't
love Anna or Julie—oh, she was fond of them for
half an hour a day, clean and sweet-smelling and
with Nanny waiting to take them away the moment
time was up.' He broke off. 'Do you hate me for
telling you this?'

'No,' said Sadie. She was sitting motionless, but
her feelings showed plain on her face. 'Only I don't
quite understand...did you love the children...?'

Mr Trentham considered the matter at some
length, going off into a brown study from which he
emerged to say thoughtfully: 'I saw very little of
them: my work took me away from home a good
deal. Stella and I no longer loved each other and I
think that prevented me loving Julie and Anna. The

love was there, but it was somehow smothered. I doubt if you would understand that.'

'Why not? I'm not a halfwit.' She spoke so severely that he laughed.

'Do you know that I have a very poor opinion of women?' he asked her.

'Yes, you've made it plain from time to time. Mr Trentham, I think we should end this conversation, you're going to feel awful about it in the morning.'

'I haven't finished, and I never do things by halves.' He went on almost casually: 'Stella had a succession of boy-friends, you know. I did my best to understand at first—after all, I was away for weeks on end and she was young and very pretty and bored. Making a home and bringing up children were two things she couldn't stomach. In the end she left me—us. Anna was four and Julie was two and a half.' He drank the rest of his coffee. 'Woodley and Mrs Woodley and Teresa were wonderful; they coped until Miss Murch came along, and she seemed the answer to everything. Stella was killed soon after she left me—in a power boat joy-riding off the California coast. I find it difficult to lie to you, Sadie, so I won't tell you that I minded. I was sorry, in the way that anyone would be sorry to hear of the death of someone young and pretty, but that was all. Only a very few of my closer friends knew that she'd left me for good, and to escape the sympathy I didn't need I chose work that would keep me away from England for weeks, sometimes months. It was a mistake, I know that now. I should have stayed at home, but—I'm not making excuses—I didn't think that the children loved me.' He added in a suddenly harsh voice: 'Well, what have you to say to that?'

Sadie said calmly, 'The children adore you, and you've discovered what fun they are and love them too. I think that's the most important thing you've told me. I'm truly sorry about your wife—you've been lonely for years, haven't you? I know you've had your work and you're famous and I expect you've got quite a lot of money, but none of these are all that important, are they?' She stopped frowning. 'I expect I sound like a prig, but I don't mean to. Mr Trentham, I think you must marry again.' It cost her a lot to say that cheerfully. 'The children were talking about the lady you took them to have tea with—they seemed to think you might…'

His laugh was genuinely amused. 'Oh, my dear little Sadie, you mustn't believe all you hear. Pamela's the last woman on earth I would marry. No, I've ideas of my own.'

'I'm sorry—it's none of my business, but you did ask me…'

'So I did. What are we going to do about this in the morning?'

'I think it might be best if we forgot everything we've said, Mr Trentham.' She glanced at the clock: it was well after two now and one of the waiters was stifling a yawn, which made her want to yawn too. 'And thank you for bringing me out to supper; the food was lovely and it's a heavenly restaurant.'

'And the company, Sadie?' he was half smiling.

'There's been nothing wrong with your company, Mr Trentham.' She looked at him with her pretty dark eyes. 'You have been very kind giving me such a splendid treat.'

He lifted a hand and the waiter came with the bill, and presently they were in the car again, going back to Highgate. Neither of them said anything. Sadie wondered if Mr Trentham was regretting his evening. She hoped not. For her part, she would remember it for always; at least he liked her enough to talk to her as a person; she had always suspected that for most of the time he had thought of her as someone in the background who produced bacon and eggs when he wanted his breakfast and ironed his shirts.

The house was quiet as they went in, with only one lamp burning on the console table in the hall. Sadie went straight to the staircase with a quiet, 'Goodnight, Mr Trentham,' and was already half way up when he stopped her. She turned at the sound of her name and he came to the foot of the stairs and stood looking up at her. But after a moment he muttered: 'No, not now—go to bed,' and turned away and went into his study.

He was already at the breakfast table, deep in the Sunday papers, when she went down to breakfast with the children. He wished them all good morning, cautioned them to be ready by ten o'clock to go out and resumed his reading, but when the children had eaten most of their breakfast he put the papers down. 'Sadie and I decided last night that we might all go and choose a dog this morning,' he announced, and in the ensuing excitement, any awkwardness Sadie had been feeling went by the board.

It was a grey day but dry, and once at Pine Ridge, they spent an hour or so inspecting every dog there was. In the end they all agreed on Gladstone, no longer a puppy, who had been found wandering and half starved by the side of a motorway. He was rather on the large side and though mostly black labrador, his appearance hinted at a variety of ancestors. But he was liked by them all and, as Mr Trentham pointed out, would be less trouble for them to train than a puppy. He paid the sum asked of him, added a donation of a generous size and shepherded his party back to the car, with the little girls both holding Gladstone's lead.

In the car, driving back, he caught Sadie's eye as she turned round to look at the two children with the dog between them, on the back seat.

'I seem to have been missing a lot,' he said quietly, 'although probably I shall go berserk if that animal disturbs me while I'm working.'

She saw happily that he didn't mean a word of it.

Gladstone, after an initial inspection of his new home with the little girls as guides, settled down with a commendable aplomb, accepting the old travelling rug Mrs Woodley produced as his own, eating his meals tidily in the kitchen and returning to his rug after tea when he discovered that his new family were going out. 'And he'll still be here when we get back,' Sadie pointed out matter-of-factly when the children argued that they wanted to stay at home with him, 'but you don't often get the chance of going to church with your father.'

'And you?' asked Julie anxiously.

'And me,' Sadie smiled, and bent to kiss her.

The Cathedral was surprisingly full, and Sadie, used to the small church with its enthusiastic untrained choir, was a bit overawed. But the singing was sheer heaven and at the end of Evensong she got up and started to go reluctantly. While they were at Highgate she would contrive to come at least once more. They went out into the cold dark evening and bundled into the car and drove back through the almost empty streets to Gladstone, waiting patiently for them on his rug.

There was a slight contretemps when it was time for the children to go to bed. They wanted Gladstone to go to bed too, although Sadie pointed out that it was a little early for him: 'Besides, he'll have to go out for a quick walk later on.'

'But if he's with us, he'll look after us,' said Anna anxiously.

Sadie looked at Mr Trentham, pouring himself a drink and, she suspected, on his way to his study. They were his children and Gladstone was his dog; let him decide.

'Let's compromise. Let him stay downstairs until I've taken him for his walk, then he shall come upstairs and sleep in your room. That's a promise.'

And this they accepted without demur. Sadie saw them to bed, tucked them up and kissed them and hesitated about going downstairs again. Suppose Mr Trentham wanted to unburden himself again? Suppose, which was worse, he regretted the previous evening? On the other hand, if she didn't go down exactly as she always did, he might think that she had attached more importance to their talk than he would wish. She went downstairs, very slowly.

There was no sign of him. She went to the small sitting room and got out the knitting she had start-

ed—gloves for the children—and it was all of half
an hour before Woodley, coming to make sure that
the fire was burning well, informed her that Mr
Trentham had gone out. 'Some party or other,
miss—the master is much in demand socially.' He
sounded faintly disapproving.

'I expect so,' said Sadie in a disinterested way.
'And there's no need to make the fire up for me,
Woodley, I think I'll go to bed; it's been quite a
full day.' She looked at the dozing Gladstone. 'I'll
take him round the square and settle him with the
children as their father promised. I'd better leave a
note, hadn't I?'

Woodley agreed gravely. 'A nice quiet dog, Miss
Sadie, and very good for the children. There's paper
and pen in the little desk under the window.'

She wrote her note, got her coat and attached
Gladstone to his lead. It was a clear frosty night
now and she marched briskly up one side and down
the other side with the obedient Gladstone trotting
beside her. Back inside, Woodley was waiting to
open the door and wordlessly proffered a towel for
the dog's paws. Sadie, taking it gratefully, pondered
the fact that it took no time at all to get into the
habit of being waited on, and with pleasantness too.
In a week or two she'd be back at the cottage, peeling potatoes and scrubbing the sink.

It was the very next day, when Mr Trentham appeared suddenly in the middle of lunch, he informed them that he was going away for a brief holiday. 'A week—ten days, I'm not sure. The Greek Islands, I think. I've some thinking to do.' He glanced briefly at Sadie. 'You'll be all right? No point in leaving an address—I'll probaby ring you anyway.'

Sadie nodded just as she had done on the other occasions when he had asked her the same question.

'Are you going by yourself, Daddy?' asked Anna, and when he said yes, Sadie felt a surge of relief. It didn't last long, though; probably he was joining someone on some idyllic island where they would laze in the sun all day and dance half the night...

Mr Trentham asked curtly: 'You don't look very happy about it, Sadie?'

She came back to reality with a bump. She said primly: 'On the contrary, Mr Trentham, I'm perfectly happy, thank you.'

'May we have a party, a teeny-weeny one, while you're away, Daddy?' asked Julie. She smiled enchantingly at him and he smiled back.

'I don't see why not, if Sadie doesn't mind.' He lifted an eyebrow at Sadie, who said promptly:

'What a lovely idea—we'll write the invitations today and ask Mrs Woodley to make some cakes.'

'And have games and make a noise?' asked Julie hopefully.

'Well, as it's a party I daresay we shall do that too,' said Sadie. 'When shall we have it?'

The discussion became lively and Sadie, peeping at Mr Trentham, thought that he looked a little forlorn. She wanted to comfort him, tell him that they would miss him, and did he really have to go? but she squashed all that. After all, he was able to make his own decisions and do exactly what he liked, and if he chose to go away and leave his children while he wallowed on some magical beach that was his own business. She said cheerfully: 'Well, let's go and make that list and then go and see Mrs Woodley. Perhaps she'll let us go shopping for her.'

It was Julie who asked: 'When are you going away, Daddy?'

'This afternoon, love.'

'Oh, then we'll say goodbye now, shall we? We're going to be busy.'

By the time they had got back from the shops with Mrs Woodley's list of jellies and almonds and icing sugar and extra eggs, he had gone. It was silly to feel sorry for him, Sadie told herself. If she could see him now, boarding a plane with a host of friends, exchanging clever small talk with not a care in the world, she would see how wasted her feelings for him were and what a waste of time it was loving him, only surely that was never a waste. She sighed deeply and then, because it was no good crying for the moon, she fetched the invitations she had written at the children's dictation, put Gladstone's lead on, and went along to the post.

The party was for three days' time and since the children hadn't many friends and they all lived close by, there was no reason for any of them to refuse. Sadie, in the kitchen helping Mrs Woodley decorate the trifles, was glad to have something to do; she was missing Mr Trentham very much indeed; it was like walking round with an empty space inside you, and no amount of common sense could make it feel any different. Presently she went along to help the little girls into their party dresses and then got into her blue dress; the first little guests would be arriving at any minute.

The party was a success, although it wasn't the sort of party Sadie would have had for her own children. She didn't consider that the row of nannies sitting round the drawing room wall made any contribution to its success, nor did she think that the children had enough friends—indeed, she wasn't at all sure that they were real friends, and they certainly didn't enjoy themselves like the children at the Christmas party at Chelcombe. All the same, the little girls were delighted with the whole affair, talking about it endlessly while they had their supper and she got them ready for bed.

'That silly Lucy Price,' said Anna, 'she kept saying that she didn't feel well, she sicked up her trifle and her nanny was furious!' She added smugly: 'I'm always well, aren't I, Sadie?'

But she didn't want her breakfast in the morning and when Sadie took her temperature, it was over a hundred. 'I don't feel well,' said poor Anna, and burst into tears against Sadie's comforting shoulder.

Sadie put her back to bed, gave Julie her painting book and paints in the playroom and went to consult with Mrs Woodley. 'There was a little girl who was ill at the party, Anna mentioned it last night—Lucy Price. I wondered if I telephoned to see if she's started something. And it would be kind, if it's not an awful nuisance, if someone could take Gladstone for a quick walk?'

Woodley obliged with his usual dignity and Sadie went off to phone. Lucy had 'flu, said Nanny at the other end, and they'd had the doctor and Sadie had better get him too. There was a lot of 'flu about, went on the voice, as though that helped the matter.

Sadie phoned the doctor, consulted with Mrs Woodley again and when that gentleman came accompanied him upstairs to Anna's bed. Doctor Rogers was tall and thin and inclined to be pompous, and he quite evidently didn't think much of Sadie. 'The housekeeper, are you?' he commented, 'Well, I suppose you can cope with some simple nursing. The child's poorly, but she'll pick up once the antibiotic starts working. Keep her in bed and give her a light diet.' He looked at her curiously. 'Where is Mr Trentham?'

'Abroad.'

'Ah, well, there's no need to bother him at the moment.' He bade her a rather distant good day and went downstairs where Woodley was waiting to let him out.

He had said that the antibiotics would take a little time to work, and in the meantime Anna got worse. Sadie thanked heaven for the kind Woodleys, and Teresa took over Julie and Gladstone and left her free to nurse the child, who became more restless as the day wore on and by nightfall had a high fever. Julie was moved to another bedroom close by with Gladstone for company and Sadie prepared for a long night. Round about four o'clock in the morning, Anna fell asleep, and Sadie, still sitting in the chair she had drawn up near the bed, went to sleep too.

She woke when Anna did, gave her a drink, washed her hot face and hands and put her into a clean nightie, then gave her another drink and her medicine. Her temperature was lower, perhaps the antibiotic was already doing its good work.

But as the day wore on, Sadie saw that although Anna was a little better, she was by no means on the mend yet. There would be another bad night, possibly two. She had had her meals on a tray in the playroom and Julie had eaten in the kitchen with the Woodleys and Teresa in the hope that she wouldn't get 'flu as well. Sadie, trying to make Anna comfortable for the night, wished with all her heart that Mr Trentham would phone. He didn't, of course. She spent another almost sleepless night again, although in the morning it was obvious that Anna was better.

With a child's resilience she demanded food, and when she wasn't eating she was sleeping. Sadie thanked heaven silently and caught up with her own sleep as best she could, taking catnaps whenever Anna did. Julie was still being looked after by the Woodleys, and it was during the afternoon that Woodley came upstairs to see Sadie. He had just been out with Gladstone and came to tell her that Mrs Woodley wasn't quite happy about Julie. She was looking hot and flushed and was off her food.

Sadie pushed back the hair she had been longing to wash for two days now. 'Oh, Woodley, has she got 'flu now, do you suppose? I'll get Doctor Rogers again...'

He came within the hour, pronounced in a pompous what-can-you expect voice that Julie had 'flu, handed over another lot of antibiotics, assured Sadie that Anna was progressing nicely, and took himself off.

He had looked at Sadie's tired white face as she accompanied him down to the hall, and thought what a very plain girl she was. Which was true enough. She hardly looked her best with the prospect of another broken night which depressed her very much.

She had put Julie to bed in her own shared room with Anna and once she had settled her, she fetched Teresa to sit with the two of them while she showered and got into her nightie and dressing gown, had a hurried meal and took over again. Julie was querulous and Sadie had a nasty feeling that she was going to be a bad patient. And she was right. The child refused to lie down, to drink the barley water she was offered, to stop crying... Sadie, fortified by the hot coffee and sandwiches Mrs Woodley had provided, read one story after another, the words dancing hazily before her heavy eyes, her tongue tying itself into knots. The one blessing was that Anna, with all the resilience of youth, was sleeping peacefully.

About two o'clock, Julie at last fell asleep, and Sadie seized the chance to go to the kitchen and fetch more cold drinks. One light had been left on in the hall; she crept down in the dimness, jug in hand, and was half way across the hall when a sound at the front door made her stop dead.

It was a very small sound, but at that hour of the night it scared her stiff. She gripped the jug tightly in both hands and watched the door.

It opened and Mr Trentham walked in.

CHAPTER EIGHT

THE WAVE OF relief and delight which swept over Sadie at the sight of him took all the colour, and that wasn't much, from her face and made her dizzy. It was instantly replaced by quite irrational fury.

'Where have you been?' she hissed at him. 'You're never home when you're wanted!'

Mr Trentham had shut the door and was leaning against it, watching her. His brows rose and he half smiled. 'Well, well,' he said gently, 'what a welcome home! You sound like a loving wife and you look...' he stopped and stared hard at her. 'You look frightful. What's happened?'

To be told she was looking frightful, however true it was, was the last straw on the camel's back; two large tears rolled down Sadie's cheeks. But crying got you nowhere; she wiped them away with the back of her hand, steadied her voice and said: 'Julie and Anna have got 'flu. Anna's getting better, but Julie is feverish and not very well.'

Mr Trentham crossed the hall in a couple of long strides, took the jug from her and put a large hand on her shoulder. 'Oh, my poor little Sadie! You've had no sleep, no rest, probably no food—you're exhausted!'

'No, just tired. Mrs Woodley has been marvellous, so has Teresa, and Woodley has been looking after Gladstone...I must get some more lemonade, the children get thirsty. Do you want anything to eat or drink, Mr Trentham?'

'No, and if I did you certainly wouldn't be allowed to get it. Fetch the lemonade; I'll come up with you.'

He threw off his coat and put his case down in the hall and when she came back, walked upstairs with her to the children's room. They were sleeping still, but Julie was restless and flushed.

Mr Trentham put the jug down on a table. 'Now tell me exactly what has to be done,' he commanded in a quiet voice, 'and then you'll go to bed. And no arguing, please. If you don't go quietly I shall pick you up and carry you there.'

He meant it. Sadie said: 'Very well, thank you, but I should like to get up about seven o'clock so that I can see to them both.' And when he nodded: 'This is what you have to do...' It wasn't much; giving drinks, shaking pillows, bathing a too warm little face and hands, soothing...

He nodded. 'OK—off you go,' and she went thankfully to bed, too tired to feel unhappy because he thought she looked frightful.

She slept soundly until her alarm clock woke her, and when she went to the children's room it was to find Anna sleeping quietly and Julie curled up in her father's arms. They were both asleep too. Sadie silently made the bed, went to the kitchen where she found Teresa making tea, filled the lemonade jug once more, and bore it, together with tea for two, back to the children's room. Anna stirred as she went in and Sadie took her temperature, gave her a drink and went to run her bath, thankful that at least one child was normal again. She wrapped Anna in her dressing gown and sat her on a chair while she made the bed, and then, since the other two showed no sign of waking, bathed her and popped her back into bed. The tea would be cooling by now; she poured herself a cup and sat down on the edge of Julie's bed to drink it, but only for a moment. Mr Trentham opened his eyes, yawned hugely and asked in a carrying whisper: 'Tea?'

He looked worn out, with a night's growth of beard and bags under his eyes and his hair going in all directions; Sadie had never loved him so much. She poured his tea and took it to him and he cradled Julie carefully in one arm to take it. 'You've slept?' he asked.

'Very well, thank you, Mr Trentham. Anna's much better, almost well in fact, and I fancy that when Julie wakes she'll be feeling more herself.'

She heard her voice, very prim, very cool, exactly opposite to what she was feeling.

'Still angry with me, Sadie?' he asked lazily.

'No, Mr Trentham. I—I—was tired. I'm sorry if I was rude.'

'And yet, when you saw me, you looked...over the moon.' He held out his cup for more tea. 'I wonder why?'

She said stiffly: 'Naturally I was glad to see someone.'

'I'm disappointed. I hoped you were glad to see me.' He drank his tea, and as Julie stirred: 'Will you see to her now? Anna's asleep.'

'She's been awake, I gave her a bath and popped her back in bed.'

He put the half-asleep Julie in her arms. 'Do I see you at breakfast?' he wanted to know.

'It rather depends on how Julie is.'

He nodded and got up and Sadie asked hesitantly: 'Did you have a good holiday?'

With his hand on the door handle he turned to look at her. 'No,' he said, 'I did not. The sensible thoughts I should have had were very completely obscured by daydreams.' His fine mouth turned down at its corners. 'At my age too! I even found myself quoting poetry. You know Robert Herrick?' and before she could nod a little uncertainly, 'He wrote ''How love came in, I do not know''—well,

I don't know either. My peaceful, hardworking life has been shattered, and I find that I have no interest in anything.'

Anna had wakened up and was sitting up in bed, listening. 'Why don't you stop working, Daddy, and go out every evening with a pretty lady? I s'pect she'd be interesting.'

He smiled at her but he looked longest at Sadie. 'That might be an idea. Who shall I start with?'

'Sadie, of course.'

Sadie bent over the tray and no one could see her face. 'No, love, that wouldn't do; I'm not pretty and I'm not a lady. I'm sure you can think of someone else.'

'You're not a bit pretty, but your eyes smile,' said Anna, 'but I see what you mean. There's Miss Thornton and Mrs Wilcox, though she's rather old.'

'But very handsome,' suggested her father softly, his eyes still on Sadie. 'I think I must take your advice, Anna.' He smiled slowly. 'What do you think, Sadie?'

'Since you didn't enjoy your holiday, Mr Trentham, I should think it might be a good idea to—renew your friendships.' She made herself look at him then, presenting him with a politely interested face which gave away nothing of her feelings.

He said blandly: 'I shall take your very sound advice, Sadie. That is if you promise not to meet me on the stairs every night and demand to know where I've been.' And when she prudently held her tongue: 'Would you like help with the children? Shouldn't Doctor Rogers come again?'

'I can manage very well, thank you, but I would like the doctor to come and advise me how long they should remain indoors.'

He nodded. 'I'll arrange that. Anna seems quite well again.' He grinned at the child as he spoke. 'And Julie is on the mend, I hope.'

Thank heaven they had recovered so quickly, thought Sadie, although they weren't out of the wood yet. There would be a few days' convalescence and both children would be peevish and bored. She foresaw endless games of Ludo and Scrabble and herself hoarse from reading Hans Andersen's fairy tales. But they were dear children and she was fond of them, and once they could go out again she would plan one or two outings. She took Julie's temperature, wondering when they would be going back to the cottage. No one had mentioned it, but of course. The children wouldn't be going to school for another ten days and she was quite prepared for Mr Trentham's habit of waiting until the last minute before telling her anything.

Julie's fever was much less and she showed some interest in her breakfast. Sadie washed her and sat her up in bed, bade Anna keep an eye on her and

went away to have her bath and dress. She was on
the point of going down to the kitchen to get their
trays when Teresa appeared.

'Morning, Miss Sadie,' she beamed at the little
girls. 'Better, aren't they—isn't that nice now? The
master says you're to go to breakfast and I'll bring
up the trays.'

'But, Teresa, I don't suppose you've had your
breakfast yet...'

'Yes, I have, miss. I'll stay with these two while
they eat.'

'Well, thank you, Teresa, you're kind. I shan't
be long.'

'You eat a good breakfast, miss. You had a bad
night, so I'm told—you should have called us.'

'I expect I should have, only Mr Trentham came
home as I was going to the kitchen. He was kind
enough to stay with the children and I had a good
sleep.'

Mr Trentham was already at the table when Sadie
reached the dining room. He got up and pulled out
a chair for her, wished her good morning, asked
Woodley to bring some fresh toast and excused
himself for continuing to read his post. His manner
was pleasant, but he sounded absentminded.

Sadie ate her breakfast in silence and as quickly
as she was able; she quite appreciated that Mr Trentham had a large post to read, but surely he could

have spared a word or two? As it was every swallow and every crunching bite into her toast sounded
like thunder in the awful quiet. She could have
eaten more, for although she was a small girl and
still too thin, she had a healthy appetite, but she got
up from the table as soon as she decently could,
murmured her excuses and made for the door. She
had taken two steps when Mr Trentham raised his
head.

'Why are you whispering?' he wanted to know.

She stood still, half turned towards him. 'I'm not.
You didn't look as though you wanted to be disturbed.'

'I am already disturbed, Sadie.' A remark which
meant nothing to her. 'Will you sit down again for
five minutes?' he added, to her great surprise.
'Please.'

She sat composedly and looked at him. No one
would have guessed that he had spent the night in
a chair with a small girl on his knees. He looked
well rested, well groomed and wore the smilingly
bland expression which she never quite knew how
to take.

'As soon as the children are quite better, I think
a day at my sister's might be a good idea—you'll
come too, of course. She lives at Maidenhead. And
a day at the Tower, perhaps? Don't look so astonished, Sadie, it's the done thing to take your young

there. They love dungeons and suchlike horrors at their age.' He paused to think. 'I wonder if they've been on a bus tour of London? We might do that as well. When does school start at Chelcombe?'

'I'm not quite sure, but I believe it's about the sixteenth.'

'Good—what with escorting the three of you during the day and wining and dining the pretty ladies thrust upon me so ruthlessly by my daughter, I imagine I shall have no time for daydreams. Do you have daydreams, Sadie?'

She said quietly: 'Oh, yes, Mr Trentham, I should think most people do.'

'And what are yours, I wonder? To marry a millionaire and live happily ever after.'

She said even more quietly: 'Just to live happily ever after.'

'Money doesn't appeal to you?' He was laughing at her.

'Of course it does, but it's not much use…I mean, what would be the use of marrying a millionaire if you didn't love him?'

'What—you'd rather have a flask of wine, a loaf of bread and thou, than an unlimited dress allowance?'

'Well, of course I would.' She was suddenly impatient with him. 'Was there anything else you wanted to talk about, Mr Trentham?'

He sighed. 'A great many things, Sadie, but not now. I'll bring Doctor Rogers up when he comes.'

She escaped with something like relief.

Anna was sitting up in bed, demanding to get up, and Julie was well enough to listen to the story Sadie was reading by the time Doctor Rogers arrived. Anna was pronounced well, although she was to stay in the house for another day, and Julie, with a normal temperature now, could get up on the following day provided she had no more fever. The two men went away and Sadie helped Anna dress; before she had finished Mr Trentham was back again. 'I'll have Anna with me,' he offered, and frowned a little at Sadie's surprise. 'She can do a jigsaw or draw in the study while I write some letters.' He added tetchily: 'You have no need to look like that, Sadie, I'm quite capable of looking after my daughter.'

He had gone, with Anna prancing along beside him, before she could utter a word.

And Anna stayed with him for the rest of the day. It wasn't until her bedtime that she finally came upstairs, full of the things she had done and what she would do on the next day and the jigsaw she had almost managed to finish. Sadie got her ready for bed, fetched Julie's supper and presently, with both little girls asleep, went downstairs herself.

Just in time to see Mr Trentham getting into his

coat in the hall. He was wearing a dinner jacket and when he saw her, he called out: 'I think I've earned an evening out, don't you, Sadie?'

She was tired and dispirited, but she answered him cheerfully. 'Indeed you have, Mr Trentham; I hope she's a very pretty lady.'

He crossed the hall to her and to her great surprise, bent down and kissed her. 'I'm out of practice,' he told her airily. 'That's by way of a rehearsal.'

She stood quite still until he had gone out of the house, then she went to her supper. Mrs Woodley had cooked a delicious meal, but Sadie didn't really notice what she was eating. She felt as though her heart was breaking—but that, of course, was nonsense. Hearts didn't break, they might crack a little, but cracks could be mended.

She didn't see Mr Trentham at all during the following day. She heard his voice in the hall as she helped the little girls get dressed, but there was no sign of him at breakfast; away all day, Woodley told her, and only back in the evening for an hour to change his clothes for some dinner or other. So the three of them repaired to the playroom and passed the day happily enough, on the little girls' part at any rate, in painting and making plasticine models and playing with Gladstone. After lunch, Sadie, longing for a breath of air, got Teresa to sit with the children while she put on her coat and took the dog for a walk. It was another grey cold day, but it was dry, and she stepped out briskly with Gladstone striding out beside her. She walked for half an hour and then turned for home, feeling better, telling herself that self-pity would get her nowhere. She arrived back at the house with glowing cheeks, took Gladstone down to the kitchen for his tea, and went back to the playroom.

She heard Mr Trentham come in presently just as the three of them, greatly hindered by Gladstone, were finishing a jigsaw. They were on the floor before the fire and Sadie didn't get up as the children ran to meet their father. Instead she busied herself collecting up the pieces and putting them back in their box. She had said good evening pleasantly, but that was all. He looked tired again and in no mood for small talk, and she was surprised when he asked: 'Do you think the children are well enough to go to Maidenhead tomorrow?'

There were screams of delight. 'Yes, I think so. If I wrap them up warmly and they don't get tired— I mean, a long day…'

'It won't be a long day, you forget, I have to be home to change for the pretty lady.' He gave her a mocking smile and when Julie asked: 'Is she very pretty, Daddy?' answered: 'Absolutely stunning, love.'

'Prettier than the one you're going out with this evening?'

'Oh, definitely.'

'It's not Mrs Langley? She laughs so loud.'

'No, it's Miss Thornton, she hardly laughs at all, but she's on a diet, so I expect that makes her sad.'

'What sort of a diet?'

'Lettuce leaves and yogurt to keep her a lovely shape.' He swung the child up in the air, kissed her soundly, did the same for Anna, bade a casual goodnight to Sadie and went away. He came back almost at once.

'We'll go directly after breakfast,' he said, and went out again.

It was a lovely morning, frosty and cold sunshine and a pale blue sky. The little girls, well wrapped up with Gladstone panting happily across their feet, were packed into the back of the car, Sadie, in her tweed coat and the blue wool dress, was told briskly to get in beside Mr Trentham and they were off. The rush hour was almost over and the mid-morning traffic was only just starting. Mr Trentham drove south to Hammersmith, got on to the M4 and raced along it to Maidenhead, turning off through Bray before he reached the town. Lady Crawley lived on the other side of the village in a large, rambling house set in a small park. It looked comfortable and lived in, a supposition borne out by the opening of a side door and the emergence of three children and two large dogs, followed by their mother, walking with unhurried dignity.

Mr Trentham had got out, opened the door and allowed his children and Gladstone to meet the on-coming pack, and then gone round to Sadie's side and ushered her out too. His sister had reached them by now, smiling and sailing through children and dogs with unruffled calm.

She embraced her brother and turned to Sadie, who was feeling shy, and put a friendly arm through hers. 'Nice to see you,' she told her. 'You must be feeling like chewed string! 'Flu's ghastly at the best of times, combine it with small children and it's beyond words. Come on in and have coffee. The children will be all right for a bit. Nanny's coming down in a moment; she'll see that they get their cocoa and look after them until lunch.'

She slipped an arm in her brother's and the three of them walked into the house, using the side door. It opened on to a stone-floored passage, full of clob-ber; wellingtons, fishing rods, old tennis shoes and racquets, a cricket bat or two, raincoats hung on pegs, dog leads, and where it opened into a small carpeted lobby, a basket with a cat and kittens.

'Tabitha's been at it again, I see,' said Mr Tren-tham idly as they all paused to admire the little creatures. 'I'll have one of them—Mrs Woodley fancies a cat about the house. We'd better have two, then they'll be company for each other.' They went on through a door on the other side of the lobby and came into a square hall, panelled and rather dark, and so into a pleasant room, handsomely furnished but rather untidy. Lady Crawley swept a pile of magazines off a chair and invited Sadie to sit down.

'Take her coat,' she commanded her brother, 'and put it in the hall and ask Maria to bring the coffee, will you?' She sat down herself near Sadie. 'My husband's at his office this morning, but he'll be back after lunch. I'd like him to meet you,' and then: 'What do you think of Oliver?'

Sadie hadn't expected that. She went very red and repeated: 'Oliver?' in a parrotlike voice. 'Mr Trentham…he's—well, he's…'

'Difficult, bossy, moody, bad-tempered—I know, but he's quite a darling really.' She eyed Sadie, who felt like something under a microscope. 'You've discovered all that for yourself.' It was a statement, not a question, and Sadie said with a touch of defiance: 'Yes, I have.'

Her companion had no intention of letting the matter rest there; luckily Mr Trentham and the coffee arrived and his sister said at once: 'Come and tell me about your holiday. Was it a success?'

'If you mean did I achieve peace and quiet—no,

it was an utter failure; on the other hand, I had my mind made up for me.'

She smiled at him. 'You'll try your luck?'

He nodded and went on pleasantly: 'Nanny's fetched the children inside—the dogs too. They've gone up to the nursery, she's got her hands full.'

Sadie put down her coffee cup. 'Perhaps I could help...' she began.

Mr Trentham said sternly: 'Certainly not! It's your day off, more or less, I must owe you a week of them at least. Besides, this is a heavensent opportunity to discuss the party.'

Sadie just managed not to ask: 'What party?' and was glad that she hadn't when he went on: 'I'll make it informal, I think, don't you? Buffet supper—dancing—I owe a great many evenings out, so I'll ask them all and get them dealt with at the same time. There'll be about fifty, I should think. You'll come, my dear?'

'Of course. Are we to dress up?'

He shrugged. 'I can't imagine any of the girls turning up in woollen dresses!' His eyes fell on Sadie, who had gone scarlet and he said at once: 'Sadie dear, I had no intention—forgive me, you look charming in that dress. I mean no unkindness to you, of all people.' He crossed to her chair and picked up her hand and kissed it gently. 'You look

nice in a sack,' he finished, and smiled at her so
that her heart turned over.

His sister regarded them with smiling eyes. 'Sadie should wear taffeta.' She frowned in thought.
'Something rich—I know, a dark green. Don't
whatever you do, buy something demure and grey.'
And seeing Sadie's mouth opening to protest: 'And
don't tell me you aren't going to get a dress—of
course you are. There's a very good boutique in
Highgate Village, they're bound to have something.
Oliver, see that she goes there.'

'I will.' He had gone back to his chair, and Sadie,
her cheeks cooling, asked, 'When is the party to
be?'

He grinned at her. 'Well, I've several more pretty
ladies—five days from now? I'll do some phoning
this evening.'

'Pretty ladies?' asked his sister.

'Ah yes, my daughters and Sadie seem to think
that I might take more interest in things if I were
to go out more often with pretty ladies. I've got
through three so far.'

'And not, I hope, raised their hopes,' said his
sister severely.

The children joined them for lunch. They were
nicely behaved but chatty, so that conversation between the grown-ups was scanty, and after lunch
they all put on hats and coats and went outside to

inspect some trees that had just been planted, the three dogs trailing them. Presently they were joined by the master of the house, who kissed the children, his wife and Sadie, shook hands with his brother-in-law and asked if it was time for tea. They went back to the house then, and Sadie found herself walking with him, completely at ease because he was so friendly.

They had tea and muffins out of a silver dish round the sitting-room fire, the children, tired now, sitting crosslegged on the carpet before the fire. It was all very domestic and cosy. It was Anna who said: 'I wish we could do this every day, Daddy—we've never done it at home, have we?'

'No, darling, and I can't think why not. We must make a habit of it.'

They went back to Highgate then, driving against a stream of homegoing cars up the M4 and weaving a slow way through crowded streets.

As soon as they were indoors Mr Trentham, who had hardly spoken on their way back, went to his study and shut the door, and Sadie took the two children upstairs, tidied them for their supper and went along to the playroom, where they had a fast and furious game of Old Maid before they went down to the dining room.

There was no sign of Mr Trentham, but he appeared briefly as they sat at table, kissed his little daughters goodnight and then kissed Sadie too, in an absent minded manner, which made her distraite for the rest of the evening.

He wasn't at breakfast the next morning, Woodley mentioned discreetly that he had gone up to the BBC headquarters to discuss a script. 'Quite a business it is too, miss,' he confided, 'all these people sitting round a table, all having their say—something in the Middle East, I fancy, though Mr Trentham did tell me that he rather fancied doing one of these fashionable spy stories.'

'He must be very clever and know lots of people.'

'Indeed he does. I understand he's to give a party shortly, miss—you'll be able to meet some of them, I daresay. Actors and actresses and suchlike.' Woodley sniffed in a genteel fashion. 'Not really the master's type, if I may say so, Miss Sadie.'

'I expect they're very clever and amusing, Woodley. We're going to take Gladstone for a walk—can we do any shopping for Mrs Woodley?'

'I'll ask her. Anna and Julie like the shops—they were never allowed to do the shopping when Miss Murch was here. Such happy little things they are now, begging your pardon, miss.'

Sadie thought that was a compliment and beamed at him. 'I'm glad you think so, Woodley.'

It must have been almost eleven o'clock that evening before she saw Mr Trentham. She would have been in her room long since, but there had been a film on the TV she had wanted to see and she had stayed up. She was coming out of the sitting room when he came into the house.

'Still up, Sadie?' he wanted to know. 'Checking up on me?'

'Certainly not, Mr Trentham, I've been watching a film.' She crossed the hall to the stairs. 'I think Woodley has gone to bed,' she observed. 'Can I get you anything?'

'No, thanks, I'm surfeited with nut cutlets and bean shoots. Don't ever fall in love with a vegetarian, Sadie. Is there a fire in the sitting room still? Good, I shall sit by it and drink myself insensible.'

'Why?' asked Sadie.

'That's about the only way in which to expurge the last few hours.'

'You're upset. Wasn't she pretty enough?'

'Are you being pert?' he asked her, and then laughed. Sadie left the stairs and went towards him. She had guessed right, he had already had enough to drink; she had read somewhere that one could mop up too much alcohol by eating something. 'I shall make you a sandwich,' she told him, 'and bring you a cup of coffee.'

There was cold beef in the fridge, she made an outsize sandwich, heated the coffee and carried them back to the sitting room. Mr Trentham was lying on the sofa with his eyes closed. He opened them as she reached the sofa. 'Even if I hadn't been caught, hook, line and sinker long ago, I am now,' he told her. 'You are above rubies, Sadie.'

Sadie didn't answer. She put down the tray on a small table by the sofa, removed the whisky decanter to a distance and poked up the fire. Then she wished him goodnight and went upstairs to bed.

He was at breakfast when they got down the next morning, wished them a perfectly normal good morning, submitted to his daughters' hugs and once they had started on their porridge, suggested that they might all go to the Tower. 'Always provided that you eat all your breakfast and that Sadie will come with us.'

Breakfast had never been eaten so quickly, and since Sadie, in answer to his questioning look, had said that of course she'd love to go too, there was nothing to stop them leaving directly after breakfast. In the car Mr Trentham said: 'By the way, everyone's coming to the party. You'd better go and buy that dress tomorrow or my dear sister will take me to task. Do you know which shop it is?'

'Yes, I think so, your sister gave me the name.'

And after that he had no more to say until he had parked the car and they had been admitted. 'Let's get a Yeoman Warder to ourselves,' he suggested, and took Sadie's arm. 'And mind and listen to all that he has to say so that you can answer the children's questions later on.'

It was difficult to give her full attention with her arm tucked so comfortably in his. The Tower had been finished in the eleventh century, built by William the First and his son, used as a fortress and then encircled by two walls. They were led from one grim apartment to another, and the grimmer they were the more the children enjoyed it, asking bloodthirsty questions about the unfortunate people who had been imprisoned in them, looking at the names carved into the stone walls. Sadie found it all very sad, and was glad when they went to see the Crown Jewels. They were so magnificent that they didn't look real, but she gazed with the same rapt attention as the children. Mr Trentham, who had let go her arm, stood a little apart, watching her and smiling a little.

It was time for lunch by the time they were out in the modern world again. Mr Trentham took them back to the car and drove them to Mark Lane to the Viceroy Restaurant, where they ate a delicious meal, handsomely served, and discussed at great length all they had seen that morning. And Sadie found herself joining in with as much enthusiasm as the children, quite forgetting to be suspicious of Mr Trentham's smile—indeed, she smiled back at him so warmly that his bland good humour almost slipped; only his eyes gleamed each time he looked at her.

They got back home during the afternoon and since the children were still excited, Sadie suggested tea in the playroom, a short walk with Gladstone and to bed a little earlier than usual after their supper. Of Mr Trentham there was no sign. He had disappeared as he so often did, leaving no trace. Once the children were tucked up and asleep she went down for her own meal and then went to bed. It had been a lovely day as far as it went. She sighed and slept.

The next day, leaving the children with Teresa, she went to the boutique. She had money enough, for she had little enough to buy for herself. Now, with every penny she had in her purse, she walked into the shop, encouraged by the quite reasonable prices on the price tags in the window.

Lady Crawley had said green taffeta, and she went slowly along the rails firmly rejecting the sensible browns and greys hanging there. 'It has got to be green,' she told the pleasant woman in the shop, 'and taffeta…'

The woman looked doubtful. 'I might have something in the stockroom—our sale isn't till next week, but I could let you have it at sale price. You're a size ten, aren't you?'

She bustled away and came back with a dress over her arm. It wasn't taffeta, but it was a glowing green organza over a silk slip with a wide V neck and short tight sleeves. Sadie tried it on, staring at the image in the mirror; she looked quite different and she wasn't very happy about the neckline; it seemed a bit low, although the woman assured her that it was modest enough. But the rest was quite perfect. Sadie bought it, and since the woman had taken several pounds off its price, there was enough money to buy slippers.

She was lucky again, for the sales were still on. She browsed from one shoe shop to the next, making up her mind, and finally settled for bronze sandals because they would go very nicely with the amber crêpe too.

Back at the house, she had a dress rehearsal with the two little girls, Teresa and Mrs Woodley an admiring audience. They pronounced her purchases quite perfect and were sworn to secrecy not to say a word to anyone, something they found very difficult when they went downstairs to have tea with their father. They were almost bursting with their secrets, and only Sadie's warning glances stopped them from giving him hints.

'I'm to be surprised, I suppose. May I not have the smallest hint, Sadie?'

'Well, it's not a sack,' said Sadie, and went pink under his amused eyes.

He took himself out of the house the next day; the drawing room was being got ready for the dancing and Mrs Woodley was busy in the kitchen making canapés for the party, although she had told Sadie that there would be a van coming from Fortnum and Mason with party food. 'And Mr Trentham likes my sausage rolls,' she confided. 'I always make a good batch of those, he hasn't much patience with those fiddly bits and pieces.'

Sadie, anxious to help, had volunteered to do the flowers, and she and the children spent a happy morning arranging daffodils and hyacinths and narcissi and pots of cyclamen and even lilac. The florist's bill would be astronomical, and from what she had seen carried into the kitchen, so would the food bill. She didn't know much about drinks; probably that bill would be as much as the other two together.

They'd had a picnic lunch in order to leave Mrs Woodley free to make her canapés. They had tea round the fire in the sitting room and then, because the children were restless, she put on Gladstone's lead and took all three of them for a brisk walk round the square. By the time they got back it was to supper, baths and bed. She tucked them up, kissed them both, left Gladstone in charge and went along to get ready for the evening. There was still no sign of Mr Trentham and it was getting on for half past seven.

She had promised to do a last-minute round to make sure that everything was as it should be; she bathed and changed into the new dress, did her face, put her hair up in a neat chignon, and went downstairs.

They were fated to meet in the hall. Mr Trentham let himself in as she was halfway to the drawing room, and Sadie didn't stop. She said:

'Good evening, Mr Trentham, you'll have to hurry.'

He stood looking at her. 'This is hardly a hurrying moment,' he said softly.

'Stand still, Sadie. I want to look at you.'

CHAPTER NINE

SADIE FOUND HERSELF quite breathless. 'Your sister said green,' she said, 'and I said I'd just take a quick look round.'

He ignored this. 'I want to talk to you, Sadie.'

'Mr Trentham, you can't, you really must go and change.'

He tossed his coat on to a chair. 'I've waited so long, I can wait a little longer,' he observed, and then as he reached the stairs and prepared to go up them, 'You look beautiful, Sadie, I want you to remember that during the evening.' Half way up he turned. 'Are the children in bed?'

'Yes, but not asleep.'

'I'll go and see them before I change.'

There was no time to think about what he'd said. Sadie flew round the house, checking this and that, going to the kitchen to make sure that Mrs Woodley had everything ready and if there was anything she could do.

'Bless your heart, miss, no, everything is just fine. You look a treat for sore eyes, that you do—such a pretty dress too. You run along and enjoy yourself; they'll be arriving any minute now.'

Sadie retreated to the small sitting room. She might be in a pretty dress and a guest of Mr Trentham, but she was also his housekeeper. She would wait until almost everyone had arrived and then she would go into the drawing room.

She stayed there for almost half an hour, and not until the house was humming with voices did she cross the hall and slip into the drawing room, to be immediately pounced upon by Mr Trentham. 'Where on earth have you been? Come and meet a few people...'

She was passed from group to group, carefully noting names and faces, noting too the beautiful clothes and the jewels the women wore, and after a time she wished that Mr Trentham would let her slip away to a quiet corner instead of keeping her by his side; the men were kind enough, but the women looked at her with unfriendly eyes and called her darling when they didn't mean it.

But presently Mr Trentham was called away and she slipped away too. With any luck, she would be able to escape; but not just yet, it seemed. Someone had put the record player on and people were already dancing; a young man with a rather stupid face put out a hand and stopped her.

'Let's dance,' he said, and whisked her off to the centre of the room. Sadie had never had much chance to dance, but she was light on her feet and quick to learn. Mr Trentham, coming back into the room, saw her apparently enjoying herself and turned away with a small frown. A minute later he was dancing with Mrs Langley.

Judging from the noise, the party was a great success. By suppertime everyone was talking at the top of his or her voice; the record player was blaring and Woodley and Teresa were having their trays of drinks emptied as fast as they could fill them. Sadie, dancing with a short stout man who talked about nothing else but the films he produced, was beginning to get a headache. The man droned on and on and she sought feverishly for a good reason for leaving him. The children... She broke in on his account of a recent film he had made and told him very politely, in a voice full of regret, that she must really go and see if the children were all right.

'Take your duties seriously, don't you?' he asked slyly.

She missed the slyness. 'That's what I'm paid for,' she told him, and slipped away.

She shut the drawing-room door after her and sighed with relief. The sigh turned to a gasp as it was opened at once behind her and Mr Trentham joined her. 'And where are you off to?' he wanted to know.

'Just off to make sure the children are asleep.'

'You're not enjoying yourself, are you?'

She tempered her honesty with a white lie. 'Well, I'm not used to this—this kind of evening.'

'Not even in the line of duty?'

She said anxiously: 'I'm letting you down? I'm sorry, but you must know by now that I'm not witty or clever.' She added with a hint of bitterness: 'I'm not even a pretty lady.'

He took her hands. 'That isn't what I meant. You'll find it hard to believe, but I don't like this kind of an evening either. But it's part of my work; knowing everyone—that's what I meant—in the line of duty.'

Sadie stared up at him, puzzled. 'You mean because I work for you?'

He shook his head. 'I'd quite forgotten that. No, I hoped…' The door opened behind them and the short stout man came out.

'Children by any other name,' he said to Sadie, and dug her in the ribs, winking at her. 'You're a sly puss, aren't you, girlie?'

Mr Trentham's hand tightened on her arm. 'You're barking up the wrong tree, Sam. I'm sure you didn't mean a word of that.' His voice sent shivers down her spine and, from the look of him, down Sam's as well.

'No offence, just my fun—splendid young lady—my apologies.' He looked at Mr Trentham.

'Wanted to see you, old fellow, about that contract—it'll only take a couple of minutes of your time.'

'Very well—Sadie, come down again when you've seen to the children.'

She nodded and went upstairs. When she was out of sight, Mr Trentham turned his attention to his companion. 'My future plans are a bit uncertain,' he observed coolly. 'What have you in mind?'

The children weren't asleep. Indeed, they had never been more wide awake. They sat up in bed and demanded to know what dresses the ladies were wearing, what Sadie had eaten, had she danced, was Daddy enjoying himself?

She answered their questions patiently and finally, because they wouldn't settle, let them put on their dressing gowns and slippers and creep along to the gallery with her and peep down through its wrought iron railings.

There were several people in the hall now, going to or coming from the dining room and the smaller sitting room where the food was laid out.

'There's Miss Thornton in that pink dress,' whispered Anna, nipping Sadie's arm. 'She looks horrid—I do hope Daddy doesn't want to marry her.'

Sadie agreed with silent fervour.

'And there's Mrs Langley and Mrs Trevor talk-

ing to that fat man. There's no sign of Daddy—
where is he?'

'With his guests,' whispered Sadie, and hoped
with all her heart that he was. She had given the
matter some careful thought and had come to the
conclusion that although he made light of his lovely
lady friends, he really was thinking of getting married to one of them; little things he had let fall…it
didn't bear thinking about.

'Bed, darlings,' she whispered, and they all crept
back and she tucked them up once more, giggling,
but sleepy now. She sat down in a chair, glad of a
few minutes' quiet, not wanting to go back downstairs but knowing that she would because Oliver
had asked her to. And she mustn't think of him as
Oliver; he must be Mr Trentham, now and always.
Always? She went and peered at her face in the
dressing table mirror. There was, she had to admit,
absolutely nothing to attract a man in it.

Sadie made sure that the children were really
asleep and went to the half open door, then paused.
Two women were standing with their backs to her,
gossiping, not attempting to lower their voices. It
took her a couple of seconds to realise that they
were discussing her and Mr Trentham.

'One wonders what he sees in her.' It was the
younger of the two women who spoke, and Sadie

dimly remembered meeting her earlier in the evening.

'But you know what a clever devil he is—she was only the housekeeper to start with, now she's tied up with the kids. He's charmed her into it, and that couldn't have been difficult; she's no beauty. I suppose she makes a change.'

They laughed together and the other, older woman said: 'Plain bread and butter between the cake, dear!'

'Plain's the word, darling. And I bet you that dress she's wearing is one he bought for her.' She laughed again, a spiteful sound. 'I wonder he shows her off in the way he does.'

'He's no fool; I heard that they're after him to write that documentary about the Middle East—you know the one I mean—very convenient for him, he's got her so enslaved with those kids of his that she'll stay to look after them until he feels like coming home again, then probably he'll hint at wedding bells just around the corner.'

'Not for her, though—Reggie told me in the strictest confidence that Oliver's planning to get married. This stupid creature from God knows where looks just the kind to love him for ever and give in to his every whim while he nips off with his bride.'

'Wonder who she is?'

'I've no idea—none of us have—haven't we all been trying to marry him for the last few years, and as far as I know, we've none of us succeeded in getting behind that suave charm.'

They began to stroll towards the stairs. 'All the same, I'd be willing to give it a whirl—marrying him. I often think we don't know him at all.'

The older woman's answer was lost as they went downstairs, leaving Sadie, very quiet, very white, standing by the door. She felt sick and near to tears, remembering every word of their conversation. Was that what Mr Trentham's friends thought of her? That she was a silly country girl, dazzled by his face and wealth, allowing him to pull the wool over her eyes until he found it convenient to sack her? And did he think of her in the same way? Did he laugh at her secretly? She couldn't believe that. She put her small determined chin up and went downstairs, and her heart lifted when he came across the room to meet her.

'Children all right?' he wanted to know. 'Sadie, I'm thinking of signing a contract for a script about the Middle East. This isn't the time or the place to discuss it, but they want some sort of an answer by the morning.'

So it was true; he was making use of her, because she knew now that he must have some idea of her feelings and was turning them to his own advantage. She didn't want to believe it of him, but there didn't seem any other answer, and here in the din and bustle of the party, she couldn't think straight. She didn't quite meet his eyes. 'What about the children?'

'They're going to Cecilia for a day or two, they can stay longer—you could go with them, it will give you a break. We'll have to get them down to the cottage in time for school, of course.' He smiled at her and her heart rocked against her ribs. 'There's a great deal of planning to do—that will have to come presently.'

There was no need for her reply as they were joined by the short fat man. He tapped Sadie on the shoulder. 'Well, girlie, it all depends on you, you know. What's it to be, yes or no?'

Mr Trentham interposed coldly: 'She's hardly had time to make up her mind. I suggest we leave it until the morning.' He looked at Sadie's sober white face and gave a puzzled frown. 'We'll talk about this later.' And when the man had gone away: 'What's happened, Sadie? Has someone said something to upset you?'

She choked on a lie, and shook her head instead. Just in that last minute or two she had discovered that she couldn't go on. She loved him and she had grown fond of the children, but there was no happiness for her in a future where he was married to someone else and she was the housekeeper, nanny, dwindling into her thirties, her forties. She would have to cut loose quickly, go right away. He could find another governess as well as someone to run the cottage, go to his Middle East job and marry this girl; for there was a girl, of that she was sure.

She was hardly aware of the rest of the evening. Presently people began to leave until the very last had gone through the doors and Woodley was locking up. It was late, but while her courage was high, she must settle the matter. And Mr Trentham made it easy for her, strolling out of the drawing room, his hands in his pockets, smiling.

'Thank God that's over! Shall we have a drink before we go to bed? And talk…'

'Nothing to drink, thank you, but I should like to talk.'

He came to a halt, the puzzled frown back again. 'Yes?'

'I should like to leave, Mr Trentham. I should like to go back to the cottage…'

He interrupted her. 'Homesick? Well, I'm afraid I'm tied up for a couple of days, but I'll drive you down as soon after that as possible.'

'You don't understand. I mean I want to leave— you and the children…'

His eyes narrowed. 'My dear girl, have you lost your wits or had too much sherry?'

Sadie shook her head. 'No. I'll go by train to-morrow, please. I'll pack my things there and go…'

'Where to?'

She looked away. 'I'll think of something.'

'And what about Tom?'

'I wondered if you would mind very much if he stayed at the cottage? The children love him and it's his home.'

'Yours too, Sadie.' His voice was very gentle.

She heaved a deep sigh. 'I've quite made up my mind—if you don't object, Mr Trentham.'

'Of course I object, and I want to know your reasons.'

'I'd rather not explain.'

'Then don't. I've no wish to force your confidence.' His voice was harsh. 'Presumably you have your excuses ready for the children—I thought you were fond of them, but I've been mistaken, as indeed I've been mistaken about other things. Make whatever arrangements you think fit—you may as well go tomorrow, I'll take the children to my sister's.'

He opened his study door and went inside without another word.

Sadie stood looking at the closed door. She only needed to take a few steps and open it and tell him about the gossiping women and ask him… What? If he loved her? That would be ridiculous. Whom he intended to marry? What was to become of her? Had he been jollying her along all these weeks for his own ends? She found that she couldn't do it. Presently she went upstairs and undressed, got her case from the closet and packed her things. The sooner she went now the better. There were the children to tell, of course, and that would be ghastly. She lay in bed rehearsing what she was going to say, and what she would say to Oliver, too. Presently, from sheer misery, she slept.

The little girls were blissfully unobservant of her white face and pink-tipped nose in the morning. They received her news with noisy regret, but since they believed she was only going for a few days while they visited their aunt, they cheered up quickly enough. Over the breakfast table Anna wanted to know if she couldn't go with them for a few days and then go to the cottage. 'You could, you know, Sadie,' she begged.

'Well, love, I thought it would be a good idea if I just popped down to the cottage and made sure that Tom was all right and get it a bit ready for your return, and there's a basket to get for Gladstone and some things to buy…'

It was a successful red herring, and presently they all went upstairs to pack the children's clothes, and Sadie, more than thankful that Mr Trentham hadn't been at breakfast, arranged their things.

But he was there in the hall when Teresa came to say that the children were to go down to their father, and since it would have invited questions from the children if she hadn't gone too, Sadie went with them. They shed a few tears as she kissed them goodbye, but cheered up quickly enough when she pointed out the grand time they were going to have at their Aunt's. And as for Mr Trentham, he preserved a bland countenance which betrayed none of his feelings, bidding her a polite goodbye as they left. She went back to her room and had a good cry, then washed her face, finished her packing and went to say goodbye to the Woodleys and Teresa. Mr Trentham had said that he wouldn't be back for lunch, but she dared not take the risk of seeing him again, so she got Woodley to get her a taxi and went to get her outdoor things.

It was then that she saw the envelope on her dressing room table, and she tore it open, hoping wildly that he had written to her. There was a month's salary inside, nothing more. It was a good thing that she hadn't the time to have another good cry—as it was, she was hard put to it not to do so as she left, for the Woodleys and Teresa seemed sad to see her go.

It was a long tiring journey, but she was lucky enough to catch the last afternoon bus to Chelcombe. It was dark as she began the walk up the lane to the cottage, and in the cold and the gloom as she went up the path, it looked far from welcoming. Moreover, she had forgotten all about food, and now, after nothing to eat all day, she was hungry.

She unlocked the door and went inside, switching on all the lights as she went through the house. There was tea, of course, and sugar and some tinned milk and some tins of soup. She made a meal of sorts, dragged her case upstairs, undressed, and armed with several hot water bottles, went to bed. She would have all the next day to sort things out, air the cottage and lay the fires ready for the children's return.

She hadn't expected to go to sleep, but she was so tired and unhappy that she could no longer think straight. Sleep overcame her before she had put two coherent thoughts together.

It was pitch dark and very cold when she woke up and she knew at once that something had woken her. She sat up in bed, the bedclothes up to her chin, and listened. The noise came again, very faint, a gentle scraping. Someone trying to open a window? She got out of bed, bundled on her dressing gown and slippers and opened her door. The noise had stopped; she crept down the landing to the head of the stairs and started cautiously down them. She was almost at the bottom when the light was put on, freezing her with fear so that her shriek was whispered.

Mr Trentham stood just inside the door, his sheepskin coat open over his dinner jacket. He looked tired, very tired, cross and at the same time satisfied about something.

'Aren't you going to ask me where I've been? You accused me once of never being home when I was wanted, but somehow I think I was right in thinking that I am wanted, Sadie. It is, of course, quite ridiculous that I should be forced to get up from a friend's dinner table, get into the car and come racing down here just to prove my point.'

Sadie came slowly down the rest of the stairs and stood in front of him.

'I don't understand—they said...'

'Ah, they—at the party, no doubt, dropping poisonous gossip into each other's ears for the lack of anything better to do. And you believed them? I'm surprised at you, Sadie—darling Sadie.'

She was so anxious to explain that the words came tumbling out without much sense. 'Well, you see, I wouldn't have, only when you said you'd been offered this job in the Middle East, and they said...'

He tossed his jacket into a corner and pulled her close. 'My darling girl, I don't want to hear what they said. They don't exist in our world; you should never believe all you hear.'

'I tried not to, but they said you were going to get married, and—oh, Oliver, I couldn't bear that…'

'Well, you'll have to learn to, sweetheart, because you're the girl I'm marrying and if you hadn't been so busy being a housekeeper and mothering the children, you'd have seen that for yourself.'

'Oh, Oliver!'

He kissed her then, long and soundly, but presently she lifted her head.

'The children, and Gladstone and Tom…'

'The children and Gladstone will stay at Cecilia's until we're married. Tom will come here, of course, just as soon as we return here.'

'But the job in the Middle East?'

'I've said I can't do it for six months at least—family commitments.'

'Oh, but that little fat man…'

'Quiet,' said Oliver, and fell to kissing her again.

Ring in
a Teacup

CHAPTER ONE

THE SUN, already warmer than it should have been for nine o'clock on an August morning, poured through the high, uncurtained windows of the lecture hall at St Norbert's Hospital, highlighting the rows of uniformed figures, sitting according to status, their differently coloured uniform dresses making a cheerful splash of colour against the drab paintwork, their white caps constantly bobbing to and fro as they enjoyed a good gossip before their lecture began—all but the two front rows; the night nurses sat there, silently resentful of having to attend a lecture when they should have been on their way to hot baths, unending cups of tea, yesterday's paper kindly saved by a patient, and finally, blissful bed.

And in the middle of the front row sat student nurse Lucy Prendergast, a small slip of a girl, with mousy hair, pleasing though not pretty features and enormous green eyes, her one claim to beauty. But as she happened to be fast asleep, their devastating glory wasn't in evidence, indeed she looked downright plain; a night of non-stop work on Children's had done nothing to improve her looks.

She would probably have gone on sleeping, sitting

bolt upright on her hard chair, if her neighbours hadn't dug her in the ribs and begged her to stir herself as a small procession of Senior Sister Tutor, her two assistants and a clerk to make notes, trod firmly across the platform and seated themselves and a moment later, nicely timed, the lecturer, whose profound utterances the night nurses had been kept from their beds to hear, came in.

There was an immediate hush and then a gentle sigh from the rows of upturned faces; it had been taken for granted that he would be elderly, pompous, bald, and mumbling, but he was none of these things—he was very tall, extremely broad, and possessed of the kind of good looks so often written about and so seldom seen; moreover he was exquisitely dressed and when he replied to their concerted 'good morning, sir,' his voice was deep, slow and made all the more interesting by reason of its slight foreign accent.

His audience, settling in their seats, sat back to drink in every word and take a good look at him at the same time—all except Nurse Prendergast, who hadn't even bothered to open her eyes properly. True, she had risen to her feet when everyone else did, because her good friends on either side of her had dragged her to them, but seated again she dropped off at once and continued to sleep peacefully throughout the lecture, unheeding of the deep voice just above her head, explaining all the finer points of angiitis obliterans and its treatment, and her friends, sharing the quite erroneous idea that the occupants of the first two rows were quite safe from the eyes of the lecturer on the platform, for they believed that he always looked above their heads into the body of the hall, allowed her to sleep on. Everything would have been just fine if he hadn't started asking questions, picking members of his audience at random. When he asked: 'And the result of these tests would be…' his eyes, roaming along the rows of attentive faces before him, came to rest upon Lucy's gently nodding head.

A ferocious gleam came into his eyes; she could have been looking down into her lap, but he was willing to bet with himself that she wasn't.

'The nurse in the centre of the first row,' he added softly.

Lucy, dug savagely in the ribs by her nervous friends, opened her eyes wide and looked straight at him. She was bemused by sleep and had no idea what he had said or what she was supposed to say herself. She stared up at the handsome, bland face above her; she had never seen eyes glitter, but the cold blue ones boring into hers were glittering all right. A wash of bright pink crept slowly over her tired face, but it was a flush of temper rather than a blush of shame; she was peevish from lack of sleep and her resentment was stronger than anything else just at that moment. She said in a clear, controlled voice: 'I didn't hear what you were saying, sir—I was asleep.'

His expression didn't alter, although she had the feeling that he was laughing silently. She added politely, 'I'm sorry, sir,' and sighed with relief as his gaze swept over her head to be caught and held by the eager efforts of a girl Lucy couldn't stand at any price—Martha Inskip, the know-all of her set; always ready with the right answers to Sister Tutor's questions, always the one to get the highest marks in written papers, and yet quite incapable of making a patient comfortable in bed— The lecturer said almost wearily: 'Yes, Nurse?' and then listened impassively to her perfect answer to the question Lucy had so regrettably not heard.

He asked more questions after that, but never once did he glance at Lucy, wide awake now and brooding unhappily about Sister Tutor's reactions. Reactions which reared their ugly heads as the lecture came to a close with the formal leavetaking of the lecturer as he stalked off the platform with Sister Tutor and her attendants trailing him. Her severe back was barely out of sight before the orderly lines of nurses broke up into groups and began to make their way back to their various destinations. Lucy was well down the corridor leading to the maze of passages which would take her to the Nurses' Home when a breathless nurse caught up with her. 'Sister Tutor wants you,' she said urgently, 'in the ante-room.'

Lucy didn't say a word; she had been pushing her luck and now there was nothing to do about it; she hadn't really believed that she would get off scot free. She crossed the lecture hall and went through the door by the platform into the little room used by the lecturers. There were only two people in it, Sister Tutor and the lecturer, and the former said at once in a voice which held disapproval: 'I will leave you to apologise to Doctor der Linssen, Nurse Prendergast,' and sailed out of the room.

The doctor stood where he was, looking at her. Presently he asked: 'Your name is Prendergast?' and when she nodded: 'A peculiar name.' Which so incensed her that she said snappily: 'I did say I was sorry.'

'Oh, yes, indeed. Rest assured that it was not I who insisted on you returning.'

He looked irritable and tired. She said kindly: 'I expect your pride's hurt, but it doesn't need to be; everyone thought you were smashing, and I would have gone to sleep even if you'd been Michael Caine or Kojak.'

A kind of spasm shook the doctor's patrician features, but he said merely: 'You are on night duty, Miss—er—Prendergast.' It wasn't a question.

'Yes. The children's ward—always so busy and just unspeakable last night, and then I had a huge breakfast and it's fatal to sit down afterwards,' and when he made no reply added in a motherly way: 'I expect you're quite nice at home with your wife and children.'

'I have not as yet either wife or children.' He sounded outraged. 'You speak as though you were a securely married mother of a large family. Are you married, Miss Prendergast?'

'Me? no—I'd be Mrs if I were, and who'd want to marry me? But I've got brothers and sisters, and we had such fun when we were children.'

His voice was icy. 'You lack respect, young lady, and you are impertinent. You should not be nursing, you should be one of those interfering females who go around telling other people how to lead their lives and assuring them that happiness is just around the corner.'

She tried not to blush, but she couldn't stop herself; she was engulfed in a red glow, but she looked him in the eye. 'I don't blame you for getting your own back,' she added a sir this time. 'Now we're equal, aren't we?'

She didn't wait to be dismissed but flew through the door as though she had the devil at her heels, back the way she had come, almost bursting with rage and dislike of him; it took several cups of tea and half an hour in a very hot bath reading the *Daily Mirror* before she was sufficiently calmed down to go to bed and sleep at last.

Lucy forgot the whole regrettable business in no time at all; she was rushed off her feet on duty and

when she was free she slept soundly like the healthy
girl she was, and if, just once or twice, she remembered the good-looking lecturer, she pushed him to
the back of her mind; she was no daydreamer—besides, he hadn't liked her.

She had expected a lecture from Sister Tutor, but
no word had been said; probably, thought Lucy, she
considered that she had been sufficiently rebuked for
her behaviour.

She went home for her nights off at the end of the
following week, a quite long journey which she
could only afford once a month. The small village
outside Beaminster, which wasn't much more than a
village itself, was buried in the Dorset hills; it meant
going by train to Crewkerne where she was met by
her father, Rector of Dedminster and the hamlets of
Lodcombe and Twistover, in the shaky old Ford used
by every member of the family if they happened to
be at home.

Her father met her at the station, an elderly man
with mild blue eyes who had passed on his very ordinary features to her; except for the green eyes, of
course, and no one in the family knew where they
had come from. He led her out to the car, and after
a good deal of poking around coaxed it to start, but
once they were bowling sedately towards Beaminster, he embarked on a gentle dissertation about the
parish, the delightful weather and the various odds

and ends of news about her mother and brothers and sisters.

Lucy listened with pleasure; he was so restful after the rush and hurry of hospital life, and he was so kind. She had a fleeting memory of the lecturer, who hadn't been kind at all, and then shook her head angrily to get rid of his image, with its handsome features and pale hair.

The Rectory was a large rambling place, very inconvenient; all passages and odd stairs and small rooms leading from the enormous kitchen, which in an earlier time must have housed a horde of servants. Lucy darted through the back door and found her mother at the kitchen table, hulling strawberries—a beautiful woman still, even with five grown-up children, four of whom had inherited her striking good looks, leaving Lucy to be the plain one in the family, although as her mother pointed out often enough, no one else had emerald green eyes.

Lucy perched on the table and gobbled up strawberries while she answered her mother's questions; they were usually the same, only couched in carefully disguised ways: had Lucy met any nice young men? had she been out? and if by some small chance she had, the young man had to be described down to the last coat button, even though Lucy pointed out that in most cases he was already engaged or had merely asked her out in order to pave the way to an introduction to one of her friends. She had little to tell this time; she was going to save the lecturer for later.

'Lovely to be home,' she observed contentedly. 'Who's here?'

'Kitty and Jerry and Paul, dear. Emma's got her hands full with the twins—they've got the measles.'

Emma was the eldest and married, and both her brothers were engaged, while Kitty was the very new wife of a BOAC pilot, on a visit while he went on a course.

'Good,' said Lucy. 'What's for dinner?'

Her parent gave her a loving look; Lucy, so small and slim, had the appetite of a large horse and never put on an ounce.

'Roast beef, darling, and it's almost ready.'

It was over Mrs Prendergast's splendidly cooked meal that Lucy told them all about her unfortunate lapse during the lecture.

'Was he good-looking?' Kitty wanted to know.

'Oh, very, and very large too—not just tall but wide as well; he towered, if you know what I mean, and cold blue eyes that looked through me and the sort of hair that could be either very fair or grey.' She paused to consider. 'Oh, and he had one of those deep, rather gritty voices.'

Her mother, portioning out trifle, gave her a quick glance. 'But you didn't like him, love?'

Lucy, strictly brought up as behoved a parson's

daughter, answered truthfully and without embar-
rassment.

'Well, actually, I did—he was smashing. Now if
it had been Kitty or Emma…they'd have known
what to do, and anyway, he wouldn't have minded
them; they're both so pretty.' She sighed. 'But he
didn't like me, and why should he, for heaven's
sake? Snoring through his rolling periods!'

'Looks are not everything, Lucilla,' observed her
father mildly, who hadn't really been listening and
had only caught the bit about being pretty. 'Perhaps
a suitable regret for your rudeness in falling asleep,
nicely phrased, would have earned his good opinion.'

Lucy said 'Yes, Father,' meekly, privately of the
opinion that it wouldn't have made a scrap of difference if she had gone down on her knees to the
wretched man. It was her mother who remarked
gently: 'Yes, dear, but you must remember that Lucy
has always been an honest child; she spoke her mind
and I can't blame her. She should never have had to
attend his lecture in the first place.'

'Then she wouldn't have seen this magnificent
specimen of manhood,' said Jerry, reaching for the
cheese.

'Not sweet on him, are you, Sis?' asked Paul slyly,
and Lucy being Lucy took his question seriously.

'Oh, no—chalk and cheese, you know. I expect he
eats his lunch at Claridges when he's not giving

learned advice to someone or other and making pots of money with private patients.'

'You're being flippant, my dear.' Her father smiled at her.

'Yes, Father. I'm sure he's a very clever man and probably quite nice to the people he likes—anyway, I shan't see him again, shall I?' She spoke cheerfully, conscious of a vague regret. She had, after all, only seen one facet of the man, all the others might be something quite different.

She spent her nights off doing all the things she liked doing most; gardening, picking fruit and flowers, driving her father round his sprawling parishes and tootling round the lanes on small errands for her mother, and not lonely at all, for although the boys were away all day, working for a local farmer during the long vacation, Kitty was home and in the evenings after tea they all gathered in the garden to play croquet or just sit and talk. The days went too quickly, and although she returned to the hospital cheerfully enough it was a sobering thought that when she next returned in a month's time, it would be September and autumn.

Once a month wasn't enough, she decided as she climbed the plain, uncarpeted stairs in the Nurses' Home, but really she couldn't afford more and her parents had enough on their plate while the boys were at university. In less than a year she would qualify and get a job nearer home and spend all her days off there. She unpacked her case and went in search of any of her friends who might be around. Angela from Women's Surgical was in the kitchenette making tea; they shared the pot and gossiped comfortably until it was time to change into uniform and go on duty for the night.

The nights passed rapidly. Children's was always full, as fast as one cot was emptied and its small occupant sent triumphantly home, another small creature took its place. Broken bones, hernias, intussusceptions, minor burns, she tended them all with unending patience and a gentleness which turned her small plain face to beauty.

It was two weeks later, when she was on nights off again, that Lucy saw Mr der Linssen. This time she was standing at a zebra crossing in Knightsbridge, having spent her morning with her small nose pressed to the fashionable shop windows there, and among the cars which pulled up was a Panther 4.2 convertible with him in the driving seat. There was a girl beside him; exactly right for the car, too, elegant and dark and haughty. Mr der Linssen, waiting for the tiresome pedestrians to cross the street, allowed his gaze to rest on Lucy, but as no muscle of his face altered, she concluded that he hadn't recognised her. A not unremarkable thing; she was hardly outstanding in the crowd struggling to the opposite pavement—mousy hair and last year's summer dress hardly added up to the spectacular.

But the next time they met was quite another kettle of fish. Lucy had crossed the busy street outside the hospital to purchase fish and chips for such of the night nurses who had been out that morning and now found themselves too famished to go to their beds without something to eat. True, they hadn't been far, only to the Royal College of Surgeons to view its somewhat gruesome exhibits, under Sister Tutor's eagle eye, but they had walked there and back, very neat in their uniforms and caps, and now their appetites had been sharpened, and Lucy, judged to be the most appropriate of them to fetch the food because she was the only one who didn't put her hair into rollers before she went to bed, had nipped smartly across between the buses and cars and vans, purchased mouthwatering pieces of cod in batter and a large parcel of chips, and was on the point of nipping back again when a small boy darted past her and ran into the street, looking neither left nor right as he went.

There were cars and buses coming both ways and a taxi so close that only a miracle would stop it. Lucy plunged after him with no very clear idea as to what she was going to do. She was aware of the taxi right on top of her, the squealing of brakes as the oncoming cars skidded to a halt, then she had plucked the boy from under the taxi's wheels, lurched away and with him and the fish and chips clasped to her bosom, tripped over, caught by the taxi's bumper.

She wasn't knocked out; she could hear the boy yelling from somewhere underneath her and there was a fishy smell from her parcels as they squashed flat under her weight. The next moment she was being helped to her feet.

'Well, well,' observed Mr der Linssen mildly, 'you again.' He added quite unnecessarily: 'You smell of fish.'

She looked at him in a woolly fashion and then at the willing helpers lifting the boy up carefully. He was screaming his head off and Mr der Linssen said: 'Hang on, I'll just take a look.'

It gave her a moment to pull herself together, something which she badly needed to do—a nice burst of tears, which would have done her a lot of good, had to be squashed. She stood up straight, a deplorable figure, smeared with pieces of fish and mangled chips, her uniform filthy and torn and her cap crooked. The Panther, she saw at once, was right beside the taxi, and the same girl was sitting in it. Doctor der Linssen, with the boy in his arms, was speaking to her now. The girl hardly glanced at the boy, only nodded in a rather bored way and then looked at Lucy with a mocking little smile, but that didn't matter, because she was surrounded by people now, patting her on the shoulder, telling her that she was a brave girl and asking if she were hurt; she had no chance to answer any of them because Mr der Linssen, with the boy still bawling in his arms, marched her into Casualty without further ado, said in an authoritative way: 'I don't think this boy's hurt, but he'll need a good going over,' laid him on an examination couch and turned his attention to Lucy. 'You had a nasty thump from that bumper—where was it exactly?' and when she didn't answer at once: 'There's no need to be mealy-mouthed about it— your behind, I take it—better get undressed and get someone to look at it...'

'I wasn't being mealy-mouthed,' said Lucy pettishly, 'I was trying to decide exactly which spot hurt most.'

He smiled in what she considered to be an unpleasant manner. 'Undress anyway, and I'll get someone along to see to it. It was only a glancing blow, but you're such a scrap of a thing you're probably badly bruised.' To her utter astonishment he added: 'For whom were the fish and chips? If you'll let me know I'll see that they get a fresh supply— you've got most of what you bought smeared over you.'

She said quite humbly: 'Thank you, that would be kind. They were for the night nurses on the surgical wards...eight cod pieces and fifty pence worth of chips. They're waiting for them before they go to bed—over in the Home.' She added: 'I'm sorry I haven't any more money with me—I'll leave it in an envelope at the Lodge for you, sir.'

He only smiled, pushed her gently into one of the

bays and pulled the curtains and turned to speak to Casualty Sister. Lucy couldn't hear what he was saying and she didn't care. The couch looked very inviting and she was suddenly so sleepy that even her aching back didn't matter. She took off her uniform and her shoes and stretched herself out on its hard leather surface, muffled to the eyes with the cosy red blanket lying at its foot. She was asleep within minutes.

She woke reluctantly to Casualty Sister's voice, begging her to rouse herself. 'Bed for you, Nurse Prendergast,' said that lady cheerfully, 'and someone will have another look at you tomorrow and decide if you're fit for duty then. Bad bruising and a few abrasions, but nothing else. Mr der Linssen examined you with Mr Trevett; you couldn't have had better men.' She added kindly: 'There's a porter waiting with a chair, he'll take you over to the home—Home Sister's waiting to help you into a nice hot bath and give you something to eat—after that you can sleep your head off.'

'Yes, Sister. Why did Mr der Linssen need to examine me?'

Sister was helping her to her reluctant feet. 'Well, dear, he was here—and since he'd been on the spot, as it were, he felt it his duty...by the way, I was to tell you that the food was delivered, whatever that means, and the police have taken eye-witness accounts and they'll come and see you later.' She smiled hugely. 'Little heroine, aren't you?'

'Is the boy all right, Sister?'

'He's in Children's, under observation, but nothing much wrong with him, I gather. And now if you're ready, Nurse.'

Lucy was off for two days and despite the stiffness and bruising, she hadn't enjoyed herself so much for some time. The Principal Nursing Officer paid her a stately visit, praised her for her quick action in saving the boy and added that the hospital was proud of her, and Lucy, sitting gingerly on a sore spot, listened meekly; she much preferred Home Sister's visits, for that lady was a cosy middle-aged woman who had had children of her own and knew about tempting appetites and sending in pots of tea when Lucy's numerous friends called in to see her. Indeed, her room was the focal point of a good deal of noise and laughter and a good deal of joking, too, about Mr der Linssen's unexpected appearance.

He had disappeared again, of course. Lucy was visited by Mr Trevett, but there was no sign of his colleague, nor was he mentioned; and a good thing too, she thought. On neither of the occasions upon which they had met had she exactly shone. She dismissed him from her mind because, as she told herself sensibly, there was no point in doing anything else.

She was forcibly reminded of him later that day

when Home Sister came in with a great sheaf of summer flowers, beautifully ribboned. She handed it to Lucy with a comfortable: 'Well, Nurse, whatever you may think about consultants, here's one who appreciates you.'

She smiled nicely without mockery or envy. It was super, thought Lucy, that the hospital still believed in the old- fashioned Home Sister and hadn't had her displaced by some official, who, not being a nurse, had no personal interest in her charges.

There was a card with the flowers. The message upon it was austere: 'To Miss Prendergast with kind regards, Fraam der Linssen.'

Lucy studied it carefully. It was a kind gesture even if rather on the cold side. And what a very peculiar name!

It was decided that instead of going on night duty the next day, Lucy should have her nights off with the addition of two days' sick leave. She didn't feel in the least sick, but she was still sore, and parts of her person were all colours of the rainbow and Authority having decreed it, who was she to dispute their ruling?

Her family welcomed her warmly, but beyond commending her for conduct which he, good man that he was, took for granted, her father had little to say about her rescue of the little boy. Her brothers teased her affectionately, but it was her mother who said: 'Your father is so proud of you, darling, and so are the boys, but you know what boys are.' They smiled at each other. 'I'm proud of you too—you're such a small creature and you could have been mown down.' Mrs Prendergast smiled again, rather mistily. 'That nice man who stopped and took you both into the hospital wrote me a letter—I've got it here; I thought you might like to see it—a Dutch name, too. I suppose he was just passing…'

'He's the lecturer—you remember, Mother? When I fell asleep.'

Her mother giggled. 'Darling—I didn't know, do tell me all about it.'

Lucy did, and now that it was all over and done with she laughed just as much as her mother over the fish and chips.

'But what a nice man to get you another lot—he sounds a poppet.'

Lucy said that probably he was, although she didn't believe that Mr der Linssen was quite the type one would describe as a poppet. Poppets were plump and cosy and good-natured, and he was none of these. She read his letter, sitting on the kitchen table eating the bits of pastry left over from the pie her mother was making, and had to admit that it was a very nice one, although she didn't believe the bit where he wrote that he admired her for bravery. He hadn't admired her in the least, on the contrary he had complained that she smelt of fish…but the flowers had been lovely even if he'd been doing the polite thing; probably his secretary had bought them. She folded the letter up carefully. 'He sent me some flowers,' she told her mother, 'but I expect he only did it because he thought he should.'

Her mother put the pie in the oven. 'I expect so, too, darling,' she said carefully casual.

Lucy was still sitting there, swinging her rather nice legs, when her father came in to join them. 'Never let it be said,' he observed earnestly, 'that virtue has no reward. You remember my friend Theodul de Groot? I've just received a telephone call from him; he's in London attending some medical seminar or other, and asks particularly after you, Lucy. Indeed he wished to know if you have any holiday due and if so would you like to pay him a visit. Mies liked you when you met seven—eight? years ago and you're of a similar age. I daresay she's lonely now that her mother is dead. Do you have any holiday, my dear?'

'Yes,' said Lucy very fast, 'two weeks due and I'm to take them at the end of next week—that's when I come off night duty.'

'Splendid—he'll be in London for a few days yet, but he's anxious to come and see us. I'm sure he will be willing to stay until you're free and take you back with him.'

'You would like to go, love?' asked her mother.

'Oh, rather—it'll be super! I loved it when I went

before, but that's ages ago—I was at school. Does Doctor de Groot still practise?'

'Oh, yes. He has a large practice in Amsterdam still, mostly poor patients, I believe, but he has a splendid reputation in the city and numbers a great many prominent men among his friends.'

'And Mies? I haven't heard from her for ages.'

'She helps her father—receptionist and so on, I gather. But I'm sure she'll have plenty of free time to spend with you.'

'Wouldn't it be strange if you met that lecturer while you were there?' Mrs Prendergast's tone was artless.

'Well, I shan't. I should think he lived in London, wouldn't you?' Lucy ran her finger round the remains of custard in a dish and licked it carefully. 'I wonder what clothes I should take?'

The rest of her nights off were spent in pleasurable planning and she went back happily enough to finish her night duty, her bruises now an unpleasant yellow. The four nights went quickly enough now that she had something to look forward to, even though they were busier than ever, what with a clutch of very ill babies to be dealt with hourly and watched over with care, and two toddlers who kept the night hours as noisy as the day with their cries of rage because they wanted to go home.

Lucy had just finished the ten o'clock feeds on her last night, and was trying to soothe a very small, very angry baby, when Mr Henderson, the Surgical Registrar, came into the ward, and with him Mr der Linssen. At the sight of them the baby yelled even louder, as red in the face and as peppery as an ill-tempered colonel, so that Lucy, holding him with one hand over her shoulder while she straightened the cot with the other, looked round to see what was putting the infant into an even worse rage.

'Mr der Linssen wants a word with you, Nurse Prendergast,' said the Registrar importantly, and she frowned at him; he was a short, pompous man who always made the babies cry, not because he was unkind to them but because he disliked having them sick up on his coat and sometimes worse than that, and they must have known it. 'Put him back in the cot, Nurse.'

She had no intention of doing anything of the sort, but Mr der Linssen stretched out a long arm and took the infant from her, settling him against one great shoulder, where, to her great annoyance, it stopped bawling at once, hiccoughed loudly and went to sleep, its head tucked against the superfine wool of his jacket. Lucy, annoyed that the baby should put her in a bad light, hoped fervently that it would dribble all over him.

'Babies like me,' observed Mr der Linssen smugly, and then: 'I hear from Mr Trevett that you are going to your home tomorrow. I have to drive to Bristol—I'll give you a lift.'

She eyed him frostily. 'How kind, but I'm going by train.' She added: 'Beaminster's rather out of your way.'

'A part of England I have always wished to see,' he assured her airily. 'Will ten o'clock suit you?' He smiled most engagingly. 'You may sleep the whole way if you wish.'

In other words, she thought ungraciously, he couldn't care less whether I'm there or not, and then went pink as he went on: 'I should much prefer you to stay awake, but never let it be said that I'm an unreasonable man.'

He handed the baby back and it instantly started screaming its head off again. 'Ten o'clock?' he repeated. It wasn't a question, just a statement of fact.

Lucy was already tired and to tell the truth the prospect of a long train journey on top of a busy night wasn't all that enthralling. 'Oh, very well,' she said ungraciously, and had a moment's amusement at the Registrar's face.

Mr der Linssen's handsome features didn't alter. He nodded calmly and went away.

CHAPTER TWO

LUCY SAT stiffly in the comfort of the Panther as Mr der Linssen cut a swathe through the London traffic and drove due west. It seemed that he was as good at driving a car as he was at soothing a baby and just as patient; through the number of hold-ups they were caught up in he sat quietly, neither tapping an impatient tattoo with his long, well manicured fingers, nor muttering under his breath; in fact, beyond wishing her a cheerful good morning when she had presented herself, punctual but inimical, at the hospital entrance, he hadn't spoken. She was wondering about that when he observed suddenly: 'Still feeling cross? No need; I am at times ill-tempered, arrogant and inconsiderate, but I do not bear malice and nor— as I suspect you are thinking—am I heaping coals of fire upon your mousy head because you dropped off during one of my lectures…It was a good lecture too.'

And how did she answer that? thought Lucy, and need he have reminded her that her hair was mousy? She almost exploded when he added kindly: 'Even if it is mousy it is always clean and shining. Don't ever give it one of those rinses—my young sister did and ended up with bright red streaks in all the wrong places.'

'Have you got a sister?' she was surprised into asking.

'Lord, yes, and years younger than I am. You sound surprised.'

He was working his way towards the M3 and she looked out at the river as they crossed Putney Bridge and swept on towards Richmond. She said slowly, not wishing to offend him even though she didn't think she liked him at all: 'Well, I am, a bit... I mean when one gets—gets older one talks about a wife and children...'

'But I have neither, as I have already told you. You mean perhaps that I am middle-aged. Well, I suppose I am; nudging forty is hardly youth.'

'The prime of life,' said Lucy. 'I'm twenty-three, but women get older much quicker than men do.'

He drove gently through the suburbs. 'That I cannot believe, what with hairdressers and beauty parlours and an endless succession of new clothes.'

Probably he had girl-friends who enjoyed these aids to youth and beauty, reflected Lucy; it wasn't much use telling him that student nurses did their own hair, sleeping in rollers which kept them awake half the night in the pursuit of beauty, and as for boutiques and up-to-the-minute clothes, they either made their own or shopped at Marks & Spencer or C. & A.

She said politely: 'I expect you're right' and then made a banal remark about the weather and presently, when they reached the motorway and were doing a steady seventy, she closed her eyes and went to sleep.

She woke up just before midday to find that they were already on the outskirts of Sherborne and to her disjointed apologies he rejoined casually: 'You needed a nap. We'll have coffee—is there anywhere quiet and easy to park?'

She directed him to an old timbered building opposite the Abbey where they drank coffee and ate old-fashioned currant buns, and nicely refreshed with her sleep and the food, Lucy told him about the little town. 'We don't come here often,' she observed. 'Crewkerne is nearer, and anyway we can always go into Beaminster.'

'And that is a country town?' he asked idly.

'Well, it's a large village, I suppose.'

He smiled. 'Then let us go and inspect this village, shall we? Unless you could eat another bun?'

She assured him that she had had enough and feeling quite friendly towards him, she climbed back into the car and as he turned back into the main street to take the road to Crewkerne she apologised again, only to have the little glow of friendliness doused by his casual: 'You are making too much of a brief doze, Lucy. I did tell you that you could sleep all the way if you wished to.' He made it worse by adding:

'I'm only giving you a lift, you know, you don't have to feel bound to entertain me.'

A remark which annoyed her so much that she had to bite her tongue to stop it from uttering the pert retort which instantly came to her mind. She wouldn't speak to him, she decided, and then had to when he asked: 'Just where do I turn off?'

They arrived at the Rectory shortly before two o'clock and she invited him, rather frostily, to meet her family, not for a moment supposing that he would wish to do so, so she was surprised when he said readily enough that he would be delighted.

She led the way up the short drive and opened the door wider; it was already ajar, for her father believed that he should always be available at any time. There was a delicious smell coming from the kitchen and when Lucy called: 'Mother?' her parent called: 'Home already, darling? Come in here—I'm dishing up.'

'Just a minute,' said Lucy to her companion, and left him standing in the hall while she joined her mother. It was astonishing what a lot she could explain in a few seconds; she left Mrs Prendergast in no doubt as to what she was to say to her visitor. 'And tell Father,' whispered Lucy urgently, 'he's not to know that I'm going to Holland.' She added in an artificially high voice: 'Do come and meet Mr der Linssen, Mother, he's been so kind…'

The subject of their conversation was standing

where she had left him, looking amused, but he greeted Mrs Prendergast charmingly and then made small talk with Lucy in the sitting room while her mother went in search of the Rector. That gentleman, duly primed by his wife, kissed his youngest daughter with affection, looking faintly puzzled and then turned his attention to his guest. 'A drink?' he suggested hospitably, 'and of course you will stay to lunch.'

Mr der Linssen shot a sidelong glance at Lucy's face and his eyes gleamed with amusement at its expression. 'There is nothing I should have liked better,' he said pleasantly, 'but I have an appointment and dare not stay.' He shot a look under his lids at Lucy as he spoke and saw relief on her face.

Her mother saw it too: 'Then another time, Mr der Linssen—we should be so glad to give you lunch and the other children would love to meet you.'

'You have a large family, Mrs Prendergast?'

She beamed at him. 'Five—Lucy's the youngest.'

The rector chuckled. 'And the plainest, poor child—she takes after me.'

Lucy went bright pink. Really, her father was a darling but said all the wrong things sometimes, and it gave Mr der Linssen the chance to look amused again. She gave him a glassy stare while he shook hands with her parents and wished him an austere goodbye and added thanks cold enough to freeze his bones. Not that he appeared to notice; his goodbye to her was casual and friendly, he even wished her a pleasant holiday.

She didn't go to the door to see him off and when her mother came indoors she tried to look nonchalant under that lady's searching look. 'Darling,' said her mother, 'did you have to be quite so terse with the poor man? Such a nice smile too. He must have been famished.'

Lucy's mousy brows drew together in a frown. 'Oh, lord—I didn't think—we did stop in Sherborne for coffee and buns, though.'

'My dear,' observed her mother gently, 'he is a very large man, I hardly feel that coffee and buns would fill him up.' She swept her daughter into the kitchen and began to dish up dinner. 'And why isn't he to know that you're going to Holland?' she enquired mildly.

Lucy, dishing up roast potatoes, felt herself blushing again and scowled. 'Well, if I'd told him, he might have thought…that is, it would have looked as though… Oh, dear, that sounds conceited, but I don't mean it to be, Mother.'

'You don't want to be beholden to him, darling,' suggested her mother helpfully.

Lucy sighed, relieved that her mother understood. 'Yes, that's it.' She took a potato out of the dish and nibbled at it. 'Is it just the three of us?'

'Yes, love—the others will come in this evening, I hope—the boys just for the night to see your godfather. Kitty's visiting Agnes'—Agnes was a bosom friend in Yeovil—'but she'll be back for supper and Emma will come over for an hour while Will minds the twins.'

'Oh, good—then I'll have time to pack after dinner.'

She hadn't many clothes and those that she had weren't very exciting; she went through her wardrobe with a dissatisfied frown, casting aside so much that she was forced to do it all over again otherwise she would have had nothing to take with her. In the end she settled for a jersey dress and jacket, a swimsuit in case it was warm enough to swim, a tweed skirt she really rather hated because she had had it for a couple of years now, slacks and a variety of shirts and sweaters. It was September now and it could turn chilly and she would look a fool in thin clothes. She had two evening dresses, neither of them of the kind to turn a man's head, even for a moment. It was a pity that both her sisters were tall shapely girls. She rummaged round some more and came upon a cotton skirt, very full and rose-patterned; it might do for an evening, if they were to go out, and there was a silk blouse somewhere—she had almost thrown it away because she was so heartily sick of it, but it would do at a pinch, she supposed. She packed without much pleasure and when her mother put her head round the door to see how she was getting on, assured her that she had plenty of clothes;

she was only going for a fortnight, anyway. She added her raincoat and a handful of headscarves and went to look at her shoes. Not much there, she reflected; her good black patent and the matching handbag, some worthy walking shoes which she might need and some rather fetching strapped shoes which would do very well for the evenings. She added a dressing gown, undies and slippers to the pile on the bed and then, because she could hear a car driving up to the Rectory, decided to pack them later with her other things; that would be her father's friend, Doctor de Groot.

She had forgotten how nice he was; elderly and stooping a little with twinkling blue eyes and a marked accent. Her holiday was going to be fun after all; she sat in the midst of her family and beamed at everyone.

They set off the next morning, and it didn't take Lucy long to discover that the journey wasn't going to be a dull one. Doctor de Groot, once in the driver's seat of his Mercedes, turned from a mild, elderly man with a rather pedantic manner into a speed fiend, who swore—luckily in his own language—at every little hold-up, every traffic light against him and any car which dared to overtake him. By the time they reached Dover, she had reason to be glad that she was by nature a calm girl, otherwise she might have been having hysterics. They had to wait in the queue for the Hovercraft too, a circumstance which caused her companion to drum on the wheel, mutter a good deal and generally fidget around, so that it was a relief when they went on board. Once there and out of his car, he reverted to the mild elderly gentleman again, which was a mercy, for they hadn't stopped on the journey and his solicitous attention was very welcome. Lucy retired to the ladies' and did her hair and her face, then returned to her seat to find that he had ordered coffee and sandwiches. It took quite a lot of self-control not to wolf them and then help herself to his as well.

They seemed to be in Calais in no time at all and Lucy, fortified with the sandwiches, strapped herself into her seat and hoped for the best. Not a very good best, actually, for Doctor de Groot was, if anything, slightly more maniacal on his own side of the Channel, and now, of course, they were driving on the other side of the road. They were to go along the coast, he explained, and cross over into Holland at the border town of Sluis, a journey of almost two hundred and thirty miles all told. 'We shall be home for supper,' he told her. 'We don't need to stop for tea, do we?'

It seemed a long way, but at the speed they were going she reflected that it wouldn't take all that long. Doctor de Groot blandly ignored the speed signs and tore along the straight roads at a steady eighty miles an hour, only slowing for towns and villages. He had had to go more slowly in France and Belgium, of course, for there weren't many empty stretches of road, but once in Holland, on the motorway, he put his foot down and kept it there.

It seemed no time at all before they were in the outskirts of Amsterdam, but all the same Lucy was glad to see the staid blocks of flats on either side of them. She was tired and hungry and at the back of her mind was a longing to be at home in her mother's kitchen, getting the supper. But she forgot that almost as soon as she had thought it; the flats might look rather dull from the outside, but their lighted windows with the curtains undrawn gave glimpses of cosy interiors. She wondered what it would be like to live like that, boxed up in a big city with no fields at the back door, no garden even. Hateful, and yet in the older part of the city there were lovely steepled houses, old and narrow with important front doors which opened on to hidden splendours which the passer-by never saw. To live in one of those, she conceded, would be a delight.

She caught glimpses of them now as they neared the heart of the city and crossed the circular *grachten* encircling it, each one looking like a Dutch old master. She craned her neck to see them better but remembered to recognise the turning her companion must take to his own home, which delighted him. 'So you remember a little of our city, Lucy?' he asked, well pleased. 'It is beautiful, is it not? You shall explore...'

'Oh, lovely,' declared Lucy, and really meant it. The hair-raising trip from Calais, worse if possible than the drive to Dover from her home, was worth every heart-stopping moment. She could forget it, anyway; she would be going back by boat at the end of her visit and probably Doctor de Groot would be too busy to drive her around. Perhaps Mies had a car...

They were nearing the end of their journey now, the Churchilllaan where Doctor de Groot had a flat, and as it came into view she could see that it hadn't changed at all. It was on the ground floor, surrounded by green lawns and an ornamental canal with ducks on it and flowering shrubs, but no garden of its own. The doctor drew up untidily before the entrance, helped her out and pressed the button which would allow the occupants of the flat to open the front door. 'I have a key,' he explained, 'but Mies likes to know when I am home.'

The entrance was rather impressive, with panelled walls and rather peculiar murals, a staircase wound itself up the side of one wall and there were two lifts facing the door, but the doctor's front door was one of two leading from the foyer and Mies, warned of their coming, was already there.

Mies, unlike her surroundings, had changed quite a lot. Lucy hadn't see her for almost eight years and now, a year younger than she, at twenty-two Mies was quite something—ash-blonde hair, cut short and curling, big blue eyes and a stunning figure. Lucy, not an envious girl by nature, flung herself at her friend with a yelp of delight. 'You're gorgeous!' she declared. 'Who'd have thought it eight years ago— you're a raving beauty, Mies!'

Mies looked pleased. 'You think, yes?' She returned Lucy's hug and then stood back to study her.

'No need,' observed Lucy a little wryly. 'I've not changed, you see.'

Mies made a little face. 'Perhaps not, but your figure is O.K. and your eyes are *extraordinaire*.'

'Green,' said Lucy flatly as she followed the doctor and Mies into the flat.

'You have the same room,' said Mies, 'so that you feel you are at home.' She smiled warmly as she led the way across the wide hall and down a short passage. The flat was a large one, its rooms lofty and well furnished. As far as Lucy could remember, it hadn't changed in the least. She unpacked in her pretty little bedroom and went along to the dining room for supper, a meal they ate without haste, catching up on news and reminding each other of all the things they had done when she had stayed there before.

'I work,' explained Mies, 'for Papa, but now I take a holiday and we go out, Lucy. I have not a car…' she shot a vexed look at her father as she spoke, 'but there are bicycles. You can still use a *fiets*?'

'Oh, rather, though I daresay I'll be scared to death in Amsterdam.'

The doctor glanced up. 'I think that maybe I will take a few hours off and we will take you for a little trip, Lucy. Into the country, perhaps?'

'Sounds smashing,' agreed Lucy happily, 'but just pottering suits me, you know.'

'We will also potter,' declared Mies seriously, 'and you will speak English to me, Lucy, for I am now with rust.' She shrugged her shoulders. 'I speak only a very little and I forget.'

'You'll remember every word in a couple of days,' observed Lucy comfortably. 'I wish I could speak Dutch even half as well.'

Mies poured their after supper coffee. 'Truly? Then we will also speak Dutch and you will learn quickly.'

They spent the rest of the evening telling each other what they did and whether they liked it or not while the doctor retired to his study to read his post. 'I shall marry,' declared Mies, 'it is nice to work for Papa but not for too long, I think. I have many friends but no one that I wish to marry.' She paused. 'At least I think so.'

Lucy thought how nice it must be; so pretty that one could pick and choose instead of just waiting and hoping that one day some man would come along and want to marry one. True, she was only twenty-three, but the years went fast and there were any number of pretty girls growing up all the time. Probably she would have to settle for someone who had been crossed in love and wanted to make a second choice, or a widower with troublesome children, looking for a sensible woman to mind them; probably no one would ask her at all. A sudden and quite surprising memory flashed through her head of Mr der Linssen and with it a kind of nameless wish that he could have fallen for her—even for a day or two, she conceded; it would have done her ego no end of good.

'You dream?' enquired Mies.

Lucy shook her head. 'What sort of a man are you going to marry?' she asked.

The subject kept them happily talking until bedtime.

Lucy spent the next two days renewing her acquaintance with Amsterdam; the actual city hadn't changed, she discovered, only the Kalverstraat was full of modern shops now, crowding out the small, expensive ones she remembered, but de Bijenkorf was still there and so was Vroom and Dreesman, and C. & A. The pair of them wandered happily from shop to shop, buying nothing at all and drinking coffee in one of the small coffee bars which were all over the place. They spent a long time in Krause en Vogelzang too, looking at wildly expensive undies and clothes which Mies had made up her mind she would have if she got married. 'Papa gives me a salary,' she explained, 'but it isn't much,' she mentioned a sum which was almost twice Lucy's salary—'but when I decide to marry then he will give me all the money I want. I shall have beautiful clothes and the finest linen for my house.' She smiled brilliantly at Lucy. 'And you, your papa will do that for you also?'

'Oh, rather,' agreed Lucy promptly, telling herself that it wasn't really a fib; he would if he had the money. Mies was an only child and it was a little hard for her to understand that not everyone lived in the comfort she had had all her life.

'You shall come to the wedding,' said Mies, tucking an arm into Lucy's, 'and there you will meet a very suitable husband.' She gave the arm a tug. 'Let us drink more coffee before we return home.'

It was during dinner that Doctor de Groot suggested that Lucy might like to see the clinic he had set up in a street off the Haarlemmerdijk. 'Not my own, of course,' he explained, 'but I have the widest support from the Health Service and work closely with the hospital authorities.'

'Every day?' asked Lucy.

'On four days a week, afternoon and evenings. I have my own surgery each morning—you remember it, close by?'

'That's where I work,' interrupted Mies. 'Papa doesn't like me to go to the clinic, only to visit. I shall come with you tomorrow. Shall we go with you, Papa, or take a taxi?'

'Supposing you come in the afternoon? I shall be home for lunch and I can drive you both there, then you can take a taxi home when you are ready.'

The weather had changed in the morning, the bright autumn sunshine had been nudged away by a nippy little wind and billowing clouds. The two girls spent the morning going through Mies' wardrobe while the daily maid did the housework and made the beds and presently brought them coffee.

She prepared most of their lunch too; Lucy, used to giving a hand round the house, felt guilty at doing nothing at all, but Mies, when consulted, had looked quite surprised. 'But of course you do nothing,' she exclaimed, 'Anneke is paid for her work and would not like to be helped, but if you wish we will arrange the table.'

The doctor was a little late for lunch so that they had to hurry over it rather. Lucy, getting into her raincoat and changing her light shoes for her sensible ones, paused only long enough to dab powder on her unpretentious nose, snatch up her shoulder bag, and run back into the hall where he was waiting. They had to wait for Mies, who wasn't the hurrying sort so that he became a little impatient and Lucy hoped that he wouldn't try and make up time driving through the city, but perhaps he was careful in Amsterdam.

He wasn't; he drove like a demented Jehu, spilling out Dutch oaths through clenched teeth and taking hair's-breadth risks between trams and buses, but as Mies sat without turning a hair, Lucy concluded that she must do the same. She had never been so pleased to see anything as their destination when he finally scraped to a halt in a narrow street, lined with grey warehouses and old-fashioned blocks of flats. The clinic was old-fashioned enough too on the outside, but once through its door and down the long narrow passage it was transformed into something very modern indeed; a waiting room on the left; a brightly painted apartment with plenty of chairs, coffee machine, papers and magazines on several well-placed tables and a cheerful elderly woman sitting behind a desk in one corner, introduced by the doctor as Mevrouw Valker. And back in the passage again, the end door revealed another wide passage with several doors leading from it; consulting rooms, treatment rooms, an X-ray department, cloakrooms and a small changing room for the staff.

'Very nice,' declared Lucy, poking her inquisitive nose round every door. 'Do you specialise or is it general?'

'I suppose one might say general, although we deal largely with Reynaud's disease and thromboangiitis obliterans—inflammation of the blood vessels—a distressing condition, probably you have never encountered it, Lucy.'

She said, quite truthfully that no, she hadn't, and forbore to mention that she had slept through a masterly lecture upon it, and because she still found the memory of it disquieting, changed the subject quickly. The first patients began to arrive presently and she and Mies retired to an empty consulting room, so that Mies could explain exactly how the clinic was run. 'Of course, Papa receives an honorarium, but it is not very much, you understand, and there are many doctors who come here also to give advice and help him too and they receive nothing at all, for they do not wish it—the experience is great.' She added in a burst of honesty: 'Papa is very clever, but not as clever as some of the doctors and surgeons who come here to see the patients.'

'Do they pay?' Lucy wanted to know.

'There are those who do; those who cannot are treated free. It—how do you say?—evens up.'

Lucy was peering in the well equipped cupboards. 'You don't work here?'

'No—it is not a very nice part of the city and Papa does not like me to walk here alone. When we wish to go we shall telephone for a taxi.'

Lucy, who had traipsed some pretty grotty streets round St Norbert's, suggested that as there would be two of them they would be safe enough, but Mies wasn't going to agree, she could see that, so she contented herself with asking if there was any more to see.

'I think that you have seen all,' said Mies, and turned round as her father put his head round the door. 'Tell Mevrouw Valker to keep the boy van Berends back—she can send the patient after him.' He spoke in English, for he was far too polite to speak Dutch in front of Lucy, and Mies said at once: 'Certainly, Papa. I'll go now.'

The two girls went into the passage together and Mies disappeared into the waiting room, leaving Lucy to dawdle towards the entrance for lack of anything better to do. She was almost at the door when it opened.

'Well, well, the parson's daughter!' exclaimed Mr der Linssen as he shut it behind him.

'Well, you've no reason to make it sound as though I were exhibit A at an old-tyme exhibition,' snapped Lucy, her temper fired by the faint mockery with which he was regarding her.

He gave a shout of laughter. 'And you haven't lost that tongue of yours either,' he commented. 'Always ready with an answer, aren't you?'

He took off his car coat and hung it any old how on a peg on the wall. 'How did you get here?'

Very much on her dignity she told him. 'And how did you get here?' she asked in a chilly little voice.

He frowned her down. 'I hardly think…' he began, and then broke off to exclaim: 'Mies—more beautiful than ever! Why haven't I seen you lately?'

Mies had come out of the waiting room and now,

with every appearance of delight, had skipped down the passage to fling herself at him. 'Fraam, how nice to see you! You are always so busy…and here is my good friend Lucy Prendergast.'

He bent and kissed her lovely face. 'Yes, we've met in England.' He turned round and kissed Lucy too in an absent-minded manner. 'I've just one check to make. Wait and I'll give you a lift back.'

He had gone while Lucy was still getting her breath back.

Mies took her arm and led her back to the room they had been in. 'Now that is splendid, that you know Fraam. Is he not handsome? And he is also rich and not yet married, even though he has all the girls to choose from.' She giggled. 'I think that I shall marry him; I am a little in love with him, you know, although he is old, and he is devoted to me. Would we not make a nice pair?'

Lucy eyed her friend. 'Yes, as a matter of fact, you would, and you're a doctor's daughter, too, you know what to expect if you marry him.'

'That is true, but you must understand that he is not a house doctor, he is consultant surgeon with many hospitals and travels to other countries. He has a practice of course in the best part of Amsterdam, but he works in many of the clinics also. He has a large house, too.'

'It sounds just right,' observed Lucy. 'You wouldn't want to marry a poor man, would you?'

Mies looked horrified. 'Oh, no, I could not. And you, Lucy? You would also wish to marry a man with money?'

She was saved from answering by the entrance of a young man. He was tall and thin and studious-looking, with fair hair, steady blue eyes and a ready smile. He spoke to Mies in Dutch and she answered him in what Lucy considered to be a very off-hand way before switching to English.

'This is Willem de Vries, Lucy—he is a doctor also and works at the Grotehof Ziekenhuis. He comes here to work with Papa.' She added carelessly: 'I have known him for ever.'

Willem looked shy and Lucy made haste to say how glad she was to meet him and added a few rather inane remarks because the atmosphere seemed a little strained. 'Did you go to school together?' she asked chattily, and just as he was on the point of replying, Mies said quickly: 'Yes, we did. Willem, should you not be working?'

He nodded and then asked hesitantly: 'We'll see each other soon?' and had to be content with her brief, 'I expect so. You can take us to a *bioscoop* one evening if you want to.'

After he had gone there was a short silence while Lucy tried to think of something casual to say, but it was Mies who spoke first. 'Willem is a dull person. I have known him all my life, and besides, he does not kiss and laugh like Fraam.'

'I thought he looked rather a dear. How old is he?'

'Twenty-six. Fraam is going to be forty soon.'

'Poor old Fraam,' said Lucy naughtily, and then caught her breath when he said from the door behind her:

'Your concern for my advanced age does you credit, Miss Prendergast.'

She turned round and looked at him; of course she would be Miss Prendergast from now on because she had had the nerve to call him Fraam, a liberty he would repay four-fold, she had no doubt. She said with an airiness she didn't quite feel: 'Hullo. Listeners never hear any good of themselves,' and added: 'Mr der Linssen.'

His smile was frosty. 'But you are quite right, Miss Prendergast. It is a pity that we do not all have the gift of dropping off when we do not wish to listen, though.'

Her green eyes sparked temper. 'What a very unfair thing to say—you know quite well that I'd been up all night!'

Mies was staring at them both in turn. 'Don't you like each other?' she asked in an interested way.

'That remains to be seen,' observed Mr der Linssen, and he smiled in what Lucy considered to be a nasty fashion. 'Our acquaintance is so far of the very slightest.'

'Oh, well,' declared Mies a little pettishly, 'you will have to become friends, for it is most disagreeable when two people meet and do not speak.' Her tone changed to charming beguilement. 'Fraam, do you go to the hospital dance next Saturday? Would you not like to take me?' She added quickly: 'Willem can take Lucy.'

Lucy, watching his handsome, bland features, waited for him to say 'Poor Willem,' but he didn't, only laughed and said: 'Of course I would like to take you, *schat*, but I have already promised to take Eloise. Besides, surely Willem had already asked you?'

Mies hunched a shoulder. 'Oh, him. Of course he has asked me, but he cannot always have what he wants. And now I must find someone for Lucy.'

They both looked at her thoughtfully, just as though, she fumed silently, I had a wart on my nose or cross-eyes. Out loud she said in a cool voice: 'Oh, is there to be a dance? Well, don't bother about me, Mies, I don't particularly want to go—I'm not all that keen on dancing.'

And that was a wicked lie, if ever there was one; she loved it, what was more, she was very good at it too; once on the dance floor she became a graceful creature, never putting a foot wrong, her almost plain face pink and animated, her green eyes flashing with pleasure. She need not have spoken. Mies said firmly: 'But of course you will come, it is the greatest pleasure, and if you cannot dance then there are always people who do not wish to do so. Professors...'

Mr der Linssen allowed a small sound to escape his lips. 'There are some most interesting professors,' he agreed gravely, 'and now if you two are ready, shall I drive you back?'

'Which car have you?' demanded Mies.

'The Panther.'

She nodded in a satisfied manner. 'Fraam has three cars,' she explained to Lucy, 'the Panther, and a Rolls-Royce Camargue, which I prefer, and also a silly little car, a Mini, handy for town but not very comfortable. Oh, and I forget that he has a Range Rover somewhere in England.'

'I have a bicycle too,' supplied Mr der Linssen, 'and I use it sometimes.' He glanced at Lucy, goggling at such a superfluity of cars. 'It helps to keep old age at bay,' he told her as he opened the door.

Lucy sat in the back as he drove them home, listening to Mies chattering away, no longer needing to speak English, and from the amused chuckles uttered by her companion, they were enjoying themselves. Let them, brooded Lucy, and when they reached the flat, she thanked him in a severe voice for the lift and stood silently while Mies giggled and chattered for another five minutes. Presently, though, he said in English: 'I must go—I have work to do. No, I will not come in for a drink. What would Eloise say if she knew that I was spending so much time with you?' He kissed her on her cheek and looked across at Lucy who had taken a step backwards. She wished she hadn't when she saw the mocking amusement on his face. 'Good night, Miss Prendergast.'

She mumbled in reply and then had to explain to Mies why he kept calling her Miss Prendergast. 'You see, I'm only a student nurse and he's a consultant and so it's not quite the thing to call him Fraam, and now he's put out because I did and that's his way of letting me know that I've been too—too familiar.'

Mies shrieked with laughter. 'Lucy, you are so sweet and so *oudewetse*—old-fashioned, you say?' She tucked an arm under Lucy's. 'Let us have coffee and discuss the dance.'

'I really meant it—that I'd rather not go. Anyway, I don't think I've anything to wear.'

Mies didn't believe her and together they inspected the two dresses Lucy had brought with her. 'They are most *deftig*,' said Mies politely. 'You shall wear this one.' She spread out the green jersey dress Lucy had held up for her inspection. It was very plain, but the colour went well with her eyes and its cut was so simple that it hardly mattered that it was two years old. 'And if you do not dance,' went on Mies, unconsciously cruel, 'no one will notice what you're wearing. I will be sure and introduce you to a great many people who will like to talk to you.'

It sounded as though it was going to be an awful evening, but there would be no difficulty in avoiding Mr der Linssen; there would be a great crush of people, and besides, he would be wholly taken up with his Eloise.

Lucy, in bed, allowed her thoughts to dwell on the enchanting prospect of turning beautiful overnight, and clad in something quite stunning in silk chiffon, taking the entire company at the dance by storm. She would take the hateful Fraam by storm too and when he wanted to dance with her she would turn her back, or perhaps an icy stare would be better?

She slid from her ridiculous daydreaming into sleep.

CHAPTER THREE

LUCY DRESSED very carefully for the dance, and the result, she considered, when she surveyed herself in the looking glass, wasn't too bad. Her mousy hair she had brushed until it shone and then piled in a topknot of sausage curls on the top of her head. It had taken a long time to do, but she was clever at dressing hair although she could seldom be bothered to do it. Her face she had done the best she could with and excitement had given her a pretty colour, so that her eyes seemed more brilliant than ever. And as for the dress, it would do. The colour was pretty and the silk jersey fell in graceful folds, but it was one of thousands like it, and another woman would take it for what it was, something off the peg from a large store; all the same, it would pass in a crowd. She fastened the old-fashioned silver locket on its heavy chain and clasped the thick silver bracelet her father had given her when she was twenty-one, caught up the silver kid purse which matched her sandals and went along to Mies' room to fetch the cloak she was to borrow.

Mies looked like the front cover of *Vogue*; her dress, blue and pleated finely, certainly had never seen anything as ordinary as a peg; it swirled around her, its neckline daringly low, its full skirt sweeping the floor. She whirled round for Lucy to see and asked: 'I look good, yes?' She was so pleased with her own appearance that she had time only to comment: 'You look nice, Lucy,' before plunging into the important matter of deciding which shoes she should wear. Lucy, arranging Mies' brown velvet cape round her shoulders, fought a rising envy, feeling ashamed of it; if it wasn't for Mies and her father she wouldn't be going to a big dance where, she assured herself, she had every intention of enjoying herself.

They were a little late getting there and the entrance hall of the hospital was full of people on their way to leave their wraps, stopping to greet friends as they went. Doctor de Groot took them both by the arm and made his way through the crowd and said with the air of a man determined to do his duty that he would stay just where he was while they got rid of their cloaks and when they rejoined him, he offered them each an arm and told them gallantly, if not truthfully in Lucy's case, that they were the two prettiest girls there.

The dance was being held in the lecture hall and a rather noisy band was already on the decorated platform while the hall itself, transformed for the occasion by quantities of flowers and streamers, was comfortably filled with dancers. Mies was pounced upon by Willem the moment they entered, leaving Doctor de Groot to dance with Lucy. He was a poor dancer and she spent most of her time avoiding his feet, and as he was waltzing to a rather spirited rumba, she was hard put to it to fit her steps to his; it hardly augured a jolly evening, she reflected, and then reminded herself that at least she was on the floor and not trying to look unconcerned propped up against a wall.

The band blared itself to a halt and she found herself standing beside Doctor de Groot, and staring at Mr der Linssen who still had an arm round a willowy girl with improbable golden hair worn in a fashionable frizz and wearing a gown with a plunging neckline which Lucy privately considered quite unsuitable to her bony chest. The sight of it made her feel dowdy; her own dress was cut, she had been quick to see, with a much too modest neckline. If she had had a pair of scissors handy, she felt reckless enough to slice the front of it to match the other dresses around her; at least she wasn't bony even if she was small and slim.

She exchanged polite good evenings and was relieved when Mies joined them with the devoted Willem in tow, to kiss Mr der Linssen and shriek something at his companion who shrieked back. She then turned to Lucy to exclaim: 'Is it not the greatest fun? You have danced with Papa? Now I will find you

someone to talk to,' she included everyone: 'Lucy
does not wish to dance…'

It was Willem who ignored that; as the band struck
up once more he smiled at her: 'But with me, once,
please?'

It was one of the latest pop tunes; Lucy gave a
little nod and followed Willem on to the almost
empty floor; perhaps she wouldn't have any more
partners for the rest of the evening, but at least she
was going to enjoy this. She dipped and twirled and
pivoted in her silver sandals, oblivious of the astonished stares from the little group she had just left. It
was Mies who said in an amazed voice: 'But she said
that she didn't like to dance!'

'She is a mouse of a girl and dowdy,' observed
the tall girl, 'but one must say that she can dance.'

Mr der Linssen turned to look at her. 'Is she
dowdy?' he asked in an interested voice. 'She seems
to me to be quite nicely dressed.'

The two girls looked at him pityingly. 'Fraam, can
you not see that it is a dress of two years ago at least
which she wears?'

'I can't say that I do.' He sounded bored. 'Shall
we join in?'

Lucy had no lack of partners after that. Willem,
for all his shyness, had a great many friends; she
waltzed and foxtrotted and quickstepped and went to
supper with Willem and a party of young men and
girls, and if their table was a good deal noisier than

any of the others the looks they got were mostly of frank envy, for they were enjoying themselves with a wholeheartedness which was completely unselfconscious.

And after supper, as she was repairing the curly topknot and powdering her nose with Mies, that young lady remarked: 'You dance so well, Lucy, I am surprised, but I am also glad that you enjoy yourself,' she added with unconscious wisdom: 'You see, it has nothing to do with your dress.'

Lucy beamed at her. 'Oh, my dear, if I were wearing a dress like yours I'd be well away—just as you are.'

'But I am not away, I am here.'

'Ah, yes—well, it's a way of saying you're a thundering success.'

'Thundering?'

'Enormous,' explained Lucy patiently. 'Doesn't Willem dance well?'

Mies shrugged. 'Perhaps—I have danced with him so often that I no longer notice.' Her eyes brightened. 'But Fraam—now, he can dance too.'

'Who's the beanpole he's with…the thin girl?'

'That is his current girl-friend. He has many friends but never a close one—that is, girls, you understand.'

They started down the corridor which would take them back to the dance. 'Well, he seems pretty close with you, love,' declared Lucy comfortably.

'I worked on it,' confided her friend, 'but you see I have known him for a long time, just like Willem, and he doesn't—doesn't see me, if you know what I mean.'

'I know just what you mean,' said Lucy.

But apparently Mr der Linssen had seen her, for a little later he cut a polite swathe through the group of young people with whom Lucy was standing, said, equally politely: 'Our dance, I believe, Lucy,' and swung her on to the floor before she could utter whatever she might have uttered if she had had the chance.

After a few surprised moments she said to the pearl stud in his shirt front: 'I suppose you're dancing with me because it's the polite thing to do.'

'I seldom do the polite thing, Miss Prendergast. I wanted to dance with you—you are by far the best dancer here, you know, and I shall be sadly out of fashion if I can't say that I have danced at least once with you.'

For some reason she felt like bursting into tears. After a moment she said in a tight little voice: 'Well, now you have, and I'd like to stop dancing with you, if you don't mind. You're—you're mocking me and in a minute you will have spoilt my evening.'

They were passing one of the doors leading to a corridor outside and he had danced her through it before she could say anything more. 'I'm not mocking you,' he said quietly, 'and if it sounded like it, then I'm sorry. Perhaps we don't always see quite eye to eye, Lucy, but you're not the kind of girl to be mocked, by me or anyone. I'll tell you something else since we're—er—letting our hair down. You look very nice. Oh, I know that your dress isn't the newest fashion, but it's a good deal more becoming than some that are here tonight.' He added: 'I am so afraid that something will slip,' so that she laughed without meaning to. And: 'That's better,' he observed. 'Shall we finish our dance?'

Which they did and as he danced just as well as she did, Lucy enjoyed every minute of it, but at the end he took her back to Doctor de Groot and she didn't speak to him again. She saw him continuously, dancing most of the time with the tall beauty and several times with Mies, but he didn't look at her even, and when eventually the affair finished and they came face to face in the entrance, his good night was said without a smile and carelessly as though she had been a chance partner whom he had managed to remember.

On Monday Doctor de Groot's receptionist, whom Mies helped for the greater part of each day, was ill so that Mies had to go to work, which left Lucy on her own. Not that she minded; she had presents to buy before she went home at the end of the week, and besides, she wanted to roam through the city, taking her own time and going where she fancied.

It was raining on Monday, so she did her shopping, going up Kalverstraat and Leidsestraat doing more looking than buying and enjoying every moment of it. She had a snack lunch at one of the cafés she and Mies had already visited and then, quite uncaring of the heavy rain, wandered off down Nieuwe Spiegelstraat to gaze into the antique dealers' windows there. She got back very wet but entirely satisfied with her day and since Mies would have to work for at least one more day, she planned another outing as she got ready for bed that night.

This time she ignored the shops and main streets and went off down any small street which took her eye, and there were many of them; most of them bisected by a narrow canal bordered by trees and a narrow cobbled road, the lovely houses reflected in the water. She became quite lost presently, but since she had the whole day before her, that didn't worry her, the sun was shining and the sky was a lovely clear blue even though the wind had a chilly nip in it.

It was while she was leaning over a small arched bridge, admiring the patrician houses on either side of the water, that somebody came to a halt beside her. Willem, smiling his nice smile and wishing her a polite good day.

'Well,' said Lucy, 'fancy seeing you here—not that I'm not glad to see you—I'm hopelessly lost.'

'Lost?' he sounded surprised. 'But I thought…' he hesitated and then went on shyly: 'I thought you might be visiting Mr der Linssen, he lives in that large double-fronted house in the centre there.'

He nodded towards a dignified town house with an important front door, wide windows, and a wrought iron railing guarding the double steps leading up to its imposing entrance.

Lucy looked her fill. 'My, my—it looks just like him, too.'

Willem gave her a reproachful look. 'It is a magnificent house.'

'And I'm sure he's a magnificent man and a splendid surgeon,' said Lucy hastily. 'I just meant it looked grand and—well, aloof, if you see what I mean.'

Willem saw, all the same he embarked on a short eulogy about Mr der Linssen. Obviously he was an admirer, fired by a strong urge to follow in his footsteps. Lucy listened with half an ear while she studied the house and wondered what it was like inside. Austere? Dark panelling and red leather? Swedish modern? She would never know. She sighed and Willem said instantly: 'I am free until three o'clock. Would you perhaps have a small lunch with me?'

'Oh, nice—I was just wondering where I should go next. Are we a long way away from the main streets?'

He shook his head. 'No, not if we take short cuts.' He waited patiently while she took another long, lingering look—too lingering, for before she turned away the front door opened and Mr der Linssen came out of his house. He looked, she had to admit, very handsome and very stylish; his tailor's bill must be enormous. She turned away, but not quickly enough; he had seen them, although beyond giving them a hard stare he gave no sign of doing so. Probably he thought she was snooping, just to see where he lived. She went a little pink and marched away so quickly that Willem, for all his long legs, had to hurry to keep up with her.

'You're going the wrong way,' he told her mildly. 'We could have stayed and spoken to Mr der Linssen.'

'Why? He didn't look as though he wanted to know us,' and when she saw the shocked look on his face: 'I'm sorry, but that's what I think—he…at least, I think he doesn't like me.'

Willem gave her a puzzled look. 'Why not? He's nice to everyone, unless he has good reason to be otherwise.'

'Oh, well, we can't all like each other, can we?' She smiled at him. 'Let's have that lunch, shall we?'

They ate toasted sandwiches and drank coffee in a little coffee shop just off the Kalverstraat and presently the talk turned to Mies. It was Willem who brought her into the conversation and Lucy followed his lead because it was quite obvious to her that he wanted to talk about her.

'She's so pretty,' said Willem, 'but she's known

me for years and I'm just a friend.' He looked stricken. 'She doesn't even see me sometimes.'

'Just because you are a friend,' explained Lucy. 'Now if something were to happen—if you fell for another girl perhaps, or lost your temper with Mies— I mean really lose it, Willem, or weren't available when she wanted you, then she would look at you.'

He looked surprised. 'Oh, would she? But I haven't got a bad temper; I just can't feel angry with her, and if she asked me to do something for her I'd never be able to refuse...'

'Then you're going to fall for a girl,' said Lucy. 'How about me?'

Willem's mild eyes popped. 'But I haven't...'

'Don't be silly, of course you haven't, but can't you pretend just a bit? Just enough to make her notice?'

'Well, do you think it would work? And wouldn't you mind?'

'Lord, no,' she spoke cheerfully, aware of an unhappy feeling somewhere deep inside her. 'It might work—only I'm only here for five more days, you know. You'll have to start right away.' She paused to think. 'I'll just mention that I've spent the afternoon with you and this evening you can ring me up...'

'What about?'

'Oh, anything, just so long as you do it—recite a

poem or something. Then I'll say that you're taking me out tomorrow.'

'But I can't—I'm on duty.'

She sighed. 'Willem, you have to—to play-act a bit, never mind if you're on duty—so what? Mies won't know, will she? If you're off in the evening you can come round and take me out for a drink; ask her too and then pay attention to me, if you see what I mean.'

Willem was a dear but not very quick-witted. 'Yes, but then Mies will think…'

'Just what you want her to think—treat her like an old, old friend.'

'She is an old…' He caught Lucy's exasperated eye. 'Oh, well, yes, I see what you mean. All right.'

They parted presently, Willem to his duty in the hospital, Lucy to return to the flat, brooding over what she would say and hoping that it would work. And she supposed that she would have to apologise to Mr der Linssen when she had the chance.

That chance came long before she expected it. The flat was empty when she got to it, Mies was still at the surgery with her father and the housekeeper was out shopping so that when the door bell rang Lucy, armed with the list of likely callers which Mies had thoughtfully drawn up for her, went to answer it. It could be clothes back from the cleaners, the man to see to the fridge, the piano tuner… She opened the door, confident that she was quite able to deal with

all or any one of them. Only it wasn't anyone on her
list; it was Mr der Linssen standing there, looking
rather nice until he saw who she was and his face
iced over. She wished that his blue eyes weren't so
hard as she wished him a rather faint good afternoon
and added in a small voice: 'I'm afraid there's no
one else here but me.'

He looked over her shoulder at nothing in particular. 'In that case perhaps I may come in and leave
a note for Doctor de Groot.' He spoke so politely
that she almost smiled at him and then turned it off
just in time as he observed: 'Don't let me keep you
from whatever you are doing.'

'I'm not doing anything—I've only just got
back...' It seemed the right moment to explain the
afternoon's little episode. 'You must have thought
me very rude this afternoon, staring at your house
like that, only I didn't know it was yours. I'd got
lost and then Willem came along and explained
where I was and told me where you lived. I could
see that you were annoyed.'

'Indeed?' He had paused in his writing of the note
to look at her and his eyebrows asked such an obvious question that she felt bound to go on.

'Well, yes—you didn't take any notice of us at all,
did you? It was just as though you didn't see me.'

'Your powers of observation are excellent, Miss
Prendergast. You were quite right, I do my utmost
not to see you, although since we seem to bump into

each other far too frequently, I find it becomes increasingly difficult.' He handed her the note. 'Perhaps you will give this to Doctor de Groot when he returns.'

She took it in a nerveless hand and said something she hadn't meant to say at all. 'Are you going to marry that girl—the beautiful one you danced with?'

He looked so thunderous that she took a step backwards. 'If I do, it will be entirely your fault,' he flung at her, and made for the door.

Anyone else would have left it prudently there, but not Lucy. She asked: 'Why do you say that? If you dislike me as much as all that I can't see that it makes any difference whom you marry.' She added kindly: 'There's no need to get so worked up about it, I'm sure you can marry just whom you like and I should think she would do very nicely…' A sudden thought caused her to pause. 'Perhaps you're in love with Mies? Of course, I never thought of that—she likes you very much, you know, but Willem gets in her way, but that's all right because he's rather taken to me, so if you had any ideas about keeping away from her because of him, you don't need to…'

He was at the door and she couldn't see his face. 'What a remarkable imagination you have! Have you nothing better to do with your time?'

'I'm on holiday,' she pointed out. 'You look very put out, if you could spare the time to go home and take a couple of aspirin and lie down for half an hour...' Her words were drowned in his shout of laughter as he went out and banged the door after him.

An ill-tempered man, she reflected as she went along to the kitchen to put the kettle on, and really she should dislike him, but she didn't. She hadn't forgotten how gentle he had been with the small boy outside St Norbert's and in an offhand sort of way, he'd been gentle with her too. She wondered what he would look like if he smiled and his blue eyes lost their icy stare. She would never know, of course. Whenever she met him she said or did something to annoy him. Somehow the thought depressed her, and even the pot of strong tea she made herself did little to cheer her up.

Mies came in presently, rather cross and tired, which was perhaps why she only shrugged her shoulders when Lucy told her about her meeting with Willem. And when he telephoned later and Lucy told her that he had asked her out for the following evening, all she said was: 'Nothing could be better; there is a film I wish to see and I shall ask Fraam to take me.' She had a lot to say about Fraam that evening, although none of it, when Lucy thought about it later, amounted to anything at all, and she harped on her feelings about him; she would marry him at once, she had declared rather dramatically, and when Lucy had asked prosaically if he had asked her yet, had said peevishly that he would do so at any time. It seemed strange to Lucy that he wasn't aware of Mies' feelings, but perhaps Mies was concealing them—clever of her, for Mr der Linssen didn't strike her as the kind of man who wanted a girl to fall into his lap like an apple off a tree. She supposed they would make a very happy couple, although at the back of her mind was the unvoiced opinion that Mies was too young for him—not in years, that didn't matter, but in her outlook on life, and it was going to be hard on poor Willem. Lucy curled up in a ball and closed her eyes. Her last sleepy thought was of the lovely old house where Mr der Linssen lived; she would dearly love to see inside it.

And so she did, but hardly in the manner in which she would have wished. It was a house which asked for elegance; well groomed hair, a nicely made-up face, good shoes and as smart an outfit as one could muster, so it was irritating at the least to discover herself inside its great door in slacks, a raincoat which was well-worn to say the least of it, and a headscarf sopping with rain.

She had popped out directly after breakfast to buy the fruit which Mies had forgotten to order the day before, and as the greengrocer's shop was in a nearby main street, she took a short cut—a narrow dim *steeg* bounded by high brick walls, with here and there a narrow door, tight closed. It was really no more than an alley and infrequently used, but now, as she turned into it, she had seen a group of boys bending over something on the ground. They had looked round at the sound of her footsteps and then got to their feet and raced off, their very backs so eloquent of wrongdoing that she had broken into a run, for they had left something lying there... A cat, a miserable scrawny tabby cat with a cord tightly drawn round its elderly neck. She had dropped to her knees on the wet, filthy cobbles and tried frantically to loosen the knot. She needed a knife or scissors and she had neither; she picked the beast up and ran again, this time towards the busy street she could see at the end of the *steeg*. It was only as she emerged on to it that she paused momentarily—a shop or a passer-by, someone with a pocket knife... The pavement seemed full of women and the nearest shop was yards away. Lucy was on the point of making for it when she heard her name called. At the kerb was a Mini and in it Mr der Linssen, holding the door open. She had scrambled in and demanded a knife with what breath she had left and he, with a brief glance which took in the situation, had drawn away from the kerb back into the stream of traffic. 'I can't stop here—there are lights ahead—it's only a few yards, let's pray they're red.'

They were. He had whipped out a pocket knife and carefully cut the cord and was ready to drive on as the queue of cars started up again. Lucy looked at the cat; it looked in a poor way and she said frantically: 'Oh, please, take me to a vet...'

'We'll take him home, it's close by.' Mr der Linssen had sounded kind and assured. 'If he's survived so far, he's still got a chance. Let him stay quiet in the meantime, he needs to get some air into his lungs.'

And when they had reached his house, he took the cat from her and ushered her in through the door and into a long narrow hall with panelled walls and an elaborate plaster ceiling and silky carpets on its black and white paved floor, only she hadn't really noticed them then, she had been so anxious about the cat. She hadn't noticed either that she was dripping all over his lovely carpets, her hair sleeked to her head and her scarf awash on top of it. She had been dimly aware that a stout middle-aged man had appeared silently and helped her off with her raincoat and taken the deplorable scarf with a gentle smile and had hurried to open a door, one of several leading from the hall. A large light room because of its high windows, furnished with a great desk with a severe chair behind it and several more comfortable ones scattered around. There were shelves of books too and a thick carpet under her feet as she hurried along behind Mr der Linssen.

He had settled the cat carefully on a small table and bent to examine it while she stood by, hardly daring to look. Presently he had unbent himself. 'Starved,' he had observed, 'woefully neglected and one or two tender spots, but no broken bones or cuts and as far as I can tell, the cord didn't have time to do too much damage.'

And Lucy, to her shame, had allowed two tears to spill over and run down her cheeks. She went hot with mortification when she remembered that, although he had pretended not to see them, turning away to ring the bell and when the same stout man appeared soft-footed, giving some instructions in his own language. Only then had he turned round again so that she had had the time to wipe the tears away. 'Rest and food,' he observed cheerfully, 'and in a few days' time he'll be on his feet again. What are we going to call him?'

'You mean you'll keep him? Give him a home?'

'Why not? My housekeeper has a cat, they'll be company for each other and Daisy won't mind.'

'Daisy?' She had been aware of a strange feeling at his words; could Daisy be the lovely girl who had been at the dance?

'My golden Labrador. Ah, here is Jaap with the milk.'

The cat's nose twitched and it put out a very small amount of tongue, but that was all; lapping seemed beyond it. Lucy had dipped a finger in the creamy warmth and offered it and after a minute the tongue had appeared again and this time it licked her finger eagerly, even if slowly. It had taken quite a time to get the milk into the cat and by then it had been tired with the effort. Mr der Linssen, sitting on the side of his desk, watching, had simply said: 'Good, two-hourly feeds for a day or so, I think,' and had nodded in a satisfied manner when Jaap appeared with a box, cosily lined with an old blanket. Lucy had watched the little animal carefully laid in it and borne away and in answer to her questioning look, Mr der Linssen had said: 'To the kitchen—it's warm there and there are plenty of people to keep an eye on it. I'll find time to see a friend of mine who's a vet and ask him to give the beast a going over.'

He had come to stand in front of her and there seemed a great deal of him. 'Thank you very much, I'm so grateful.' She looked down at her sensible shoes, muddied and wet. The damage she must have done to those carpets!

'Well,' said Mr der Linssen easily, 'I think we've earned a cup of coffee, don't you?'

Lucy looked at him, noticing now that he was in slacks and a sweater and needed a shave. 'You've been at the hospital. Oh, you must be tired. I—I won't have any coffee, thank you, I was going shopping for Mies.' The name reminded her of their previous conversation and she flushed uncomfortably. But he had chosen to forget, it seemed, for he had spoken pleasantly.

'Only since four o'clock. I'm wide awake but famished. Do keep me company while I have my breakfast, in any case your raincoat won't be dry yet.'

So she had gone with him to a charming little

room at the back of the house. It overlooked a small paved yard surrounded with roses and even in the light of the grey morning outside, it was cosy; mahogany shining with polishing and a rich brocaded wall hanging, ruby red, almost obscured by the paintings hung upon it. He had sat her down at a circular table and poured coffee for her, just as though he hadn't heard her refusing it. And she was glad enough to drink it, it gave her something to do while he made his breakfast, talking the while of this and that and nothing in particular. Presently, when he had finished, she said rather shyly that she should go and he had agreed at once. Remembering that she felt a little hurt, but stupidly so, she told herself. There was no reason why he should wish for her company; he had been helpful and kind and courteous, but probably he had had just about enough of her by then. But he had taken her to see the cat before she went; sleeping quietly before the Aga in the enormous, magnificently equipped kitchen in the basement, and then he had excused himself because he had patients to see and Jaap had shown her out with a courtesy which had restored her self-esteem.

She had thought about the whole episode quite a lot during the day. The house, what she had seen of it, was every bit as lovely as she had imagined it would be and considering that Mr der Linssen had no time for her, he had been rather a dear. She hoped that she would hear about the cat—perhaps Mies could find out for her. She ate her solitary lunch and then wrote a letter, forgetting that she would more than likely be home before it got there, but she couldn't settle to anything. She supposed that seeing the house had excited her; she had been so curious about it…

Mies came home presently with the news that the receptionist would be back in the morning so that she would be free once more, and they fell to planning the day. 'And we'll get Willem to take us to the *bioscoop*,' declared Mies, and then said a little crossly: 'Oh, well, isn't he taking you this evening? I forgot. Not that I care, I see too much of him, he is always under my feet.'

So Lucy felt a little guilty as she and Willem, who was free after all, walked down Churchilllaan to the nearest bus stop. Mies might not love Willem, but she had got used to him being around; he had been her slave, more or less, for years, and anyway, she had said that she wanted to marry Fraam. It was all rather muddled, thought Lucy, waiting beside Willem to cross the street. There wasn't much traffic about, for the weather was still wet and chilly; she watched the cars idly. Mr der Linssen's Panther de Ville or the Rolls for that matter, or failing those, his Mini would be preferable to a bus ride. The Rolls slid past as she thought it, with him at the wheel and Mies beside him. Mies didn't see her, but he did. His smile was cool and she looked away quickly to see if Willem had seen them too. He hadn't, and a good thing too, she decided. Bad enough for her evening to be spoilt, although she wasn't quite clear as to why it should be. There was certainly no reason for Willem to have his evening spoilt too.

CHAPTER FOUR

AT BREAKFAST the next morning Mies monopolised the conversation. She had, quite by accident, she explained airily, met Fraam when she went out to post letters and he had taken her to the hospital to pick up some notes he had wanted before bringing her home. It was only after a lengthy description of this that she asked nonchalantly if Lucy had enjoyed herself.

Lucy answered cautiously. It was a little difficult; she had promised to help Willem to capture Mies' attention and she fancied that Mies wasn't best pleased that he had taken her out, but on the other hand if Mies was really in love with Mr der Linssen and he with her, surely they should be allowed to stay that way? And in that case what about Willem?

'Willem is nice to go out with,' she observed, aware that it was a silly remark. 'I expect you go out with him quite a lot.'

Mies shrugged. 'When there is no one else.'

'He wondered,' persisted Lucy, 'if we might all go out this evening—just for a drink somewhere.'

She was a little surprised at Mies' ready agreement. 'Only it must be dinner too,' she insisted. 'We will go to 't Binnenhofje, the three of us—Papa has an engagement and will not be home; it will be convenient to go out.'

'It sounds lovely,' agreed Lucy, 'but didn't you tell me it was wildly expensive? I mean, Willem…'

'Do not worry about Willem, he has plenty of money, his family are not poor. I will telephone him and tell him to book a table for eight o'clock.'

'I don't think I've anything to wear,' said Lucy worriedly.

'The patterned skirt and the pink blouse,' Mies decided for her, 'and I—I shall wear my grey crêpe.' She got up as she spoke. 'I shall telephone now.'

And she came back presently with the news that Willem would be delighted to take them out and would call for them in good time. 'And now what shall we do with our day?' enquired Mies. 'You have bought presents already? Then we go down to the hospital; there is something I have to deliver for Papa—a specimen.'

Lucy didn't mind what she did; she enjoyed each day as it came, although she did make the tentative suggestion that they might go to the clinic just once more before she went home.

'But why?' asked Mies. 'You have seen it.'

'Yes, but I found it very interesting.'

'Well, there is no time,' said Mies positively. 'Today is Friday and on Saturday you go home. Why do you want to go?'

'I said—it's interesting, but it doesn't matter, Mies. I've had a simply super time, you've been a dear—you must come and stay with us…'

'If I am still unmarried,' said Mies demurely. 'And now we go out. We can take a bus and walk the rest of the way.'

Lucy agreed readily although at the back of her mind was the vague idea that she wanted to see Mr der Linssen just once more before she left Amsterdam. She wasn't sure why, perhaps to make sure that he was as taken with Mies as she was—apparently—with him. But now it seemed unlikely that she would see him again, not to speak to, that was. Possibly she would attend another of his lectures in the future and watch him standing on the lecture hall platform, holding forth learnedly about something or other. Pray heaven she wouldn't be on night duty.

It was another wet day; she put on her raincoat and the sensible shoes, wondering about the cat. She could of course telephone Mr der Linssen's house and find out. She tied a scarf under her determined little chin and joined Mies in the hall.

The bus was packed and they had to stand all the way so that the short walk at the end of it was welcome even though it was wet. The hospital looked gloomy as they approached it and it wasn't much better inside. Lucy, told to stay in the entrance hall while Mies went along to the Path. Lab., wandered round its sombre walls. Mies was being a long time;

Lucy had gone round the vast echoing place several times, perhaps she had some other errand or had met someone. Willem, or Mr der Linssen? And had it been arranged beforehand? she wondered. She paused to stare up at a plaque on the wall. She couldn't understand a word of it, but probably it extolled the talents and virtues of some dead and gone medical man.

Advancing footsteps and voices made her turn round in time to see Mr der Linssen coming down the central staircase, hedged about by a number of people, rather like a planet with attendant satellites. He passed her within a foot or so, giving her a distant nod as he went and then stopped, spoke to the man beside him and came back to her, leaving the others to go on. He wasted no time in unnecessary greetings but: 'You return to England tomorrow, do you not?'

She nodded, studying him; he looked different in his long white coat; she liked him better in slacks and a sweater...'How's the cat?' she asked.

'Making a good recovery. He has the appetite of a wolf but a remarkably placid disposition.'

'He's no trouble?' she asked anxiously. 'You really are going to keep him?'

He frowned. 'I told you that I would give him a home. Have you any reason to doubt my word?'

Very touchy. Lucy made a vigorous denial, then sought to lighten the conversation. 'Mies is here— she went to the Path. Lab.'

Mr der Linssen nodded carelessly. 'She comes frequently with specimens from her father's clinic.' He seemed to have nothing to say and Lucy wondered just why he had stopped to speak to her. She tried again. 'I expect you're very busy…'

'Offering me a chance to escape, Miss Prendergast?' His voice was silky. 'But you would agree with me that not to say goodbye to you would be lacking in good manners?'

This wasn't a conversation, she thought crossly, it was questions and answers, and how on earth did she answer that? She said carefully: 'Well, I'm glad you stopped to say goodbye, and considering, it was kind of you to do so.'

'Considering what?'

She looked up at him and glimpsed an expression on his face she had never seen before. It had gone before she could decide what it was, to be replaced by a polite blandness. And that told her nothing at all.

She said in a serious voice: 'You said once that you tried not to see me but somehow we keep meeting—it's silly really, because we don't even live in the same country. I was surprised to see you at the clinic—I never thought…but I've tried to keep out of your way.'

'Have you indeed? I wonder…' His bleep interrupted him and she heard his annoyed mutter. She was taken completely by surprise when he bent and

kissed her fiercely before striding away to the porter's lodge across the hall and picking up the telephone there. He was racing up the staircase without
so much as a glance in her direction, and all within
seconds. Lucy was still wondering why he had kissed
her when Mies arrived.

'Was I a long time?' She looked smug. 'I met
Fraam.'

Lucy, accompanying her out of the hospital entrance, forbore from saying that she had met him too.
For the last time, she reminded herself.

She wondered, as she dressed that evening, if their
dinner party was going to be a success; three wasn't
an ideal number, Mies could surely have found another man. Lucy, determined to do justice to the occasion even if she was going to be the odd one out,
took time to roll her hair into elaborate curls again.
And it was worth the effort, for the hair-do added
importance to her pink blouse and patterned skirt.
Not that it mattered, since there would be no one to
see. She wondered too how Willem would behave;
was he going to carry on pretending that he was gone
on her or would he devote himself to Mies?

She took a last look at herself in the looking glass
and went along to borrow the brown cloak again, for
she had nothing else.

Mies looked lovely, but then she always did. The
grey crêpe was soft and clinging and feminine and,
unlike the gown she had worn to the dance, demure.

Lucy, admiring it, thought that it might please Willem mightily.

It did. When he arrived at the flat he could hardly take his eyes off Mies, and he certainly didn't notice her marked coldness towards him. And if he's going to drool all over her all the evening, he'll never get anywhere, thought Lucy crossly, and then told herself that she was silly to bother, she wouldn't see them again for a long time, and by then they would either have married or have forgotten each other.

't Binnenhofje was a smart place. Lucy immediately knew herself to be a trifle old-fashioned in her dress the moment they were inside its door. The younger women were wearing rather way-out dresses and the older ones were elegantly turned out in the kind of simple dress which cost a great deal of money. True, there were one or two tourists there, easily recognisable in their uncrushable manmade fibres, but all the same, she felt like a maiden aunt. She corrected herself; like the parson's daughter. Which naturally put her in mind of Mr der Linssen and she had leisure enough to think about him, for Willem and Mies were deep in a conversation of their own for the moment. But presently they remembered that she was there, excused themselves laughingly on the plea that they had been reminiscing, and began a light hearted chatter which lasted them through the starters and the Sole Picasso.

It was while Lucy was deciding between crêpes

Suzette and Dame Blanche that she happened to look
up and see Mr der Linssen sitting at a table on the
other side of the restaurant. He had a stunning redhead with him this time, but he wasn't looking at
her, he was staring at Lucy who was so surprised
that she dropped the menu and ordered a vanilla ice
cream—something, she told herself silently, she
could have had at home any time and wasn't really
a treat at all. She took care not to look at him again,
something she found extraordinarily difficult because
she wanted to so badly, but it wasn't for a little while
that she realised that Mies knew that he was there,
which would account for her animated conversation
and her gorgeous smile, as well as the casual way
her gaze swept round the place every minute or so.
He hadn't been staring at her at all, Lucy concluded,
but at Mies; they had both known the other was to
be there.

They must be terribly in love. She frowned. In that
case why hadn't they dined together? The redhead
couldn't be anyone very important in his life if he
was so smitten with Mies, and poor Willem could
have taken her out without Mies planning this dinner
and no one would have been any the wiser, and much
happier. For Willem had seen him now; Lucy could
see him thinking all the things she herself had just
mulled over, because he looked puzzled and worried
and then put out. He made it worse by asking Mies
if she knew that Fraam was sitting nearby and when

she said Oh, yes, of course, wanted to know if she
had known before they had arrived at the restaurant.

Mies gave him one of her angelic smiles. 'Willem,
that's why I wanted to come.'

Lucy plunged into what she could see was fast
becoming a ticklish situation.

'I thought it was a farewell dinner party for me,'
she said lightly, and was instantly deflated by Mies'
'Oh, Lucy, that was a good reason for coming, do
you not see?'

She swallowed her hurt pride. 'Then why not have
just dined with Mr der Linssen? Willem and I would
have been quite happy in a snack bar.'

Mies said huffily: 'He already had a date, I found
that out, but now he can see me, can he not, and that
is better than nothing.'

Willem had remained silent, but now he began to
speak. It was unfortunate for Lucy that he did so in
his own language, but whatever he was saying he
was saying in anger—nicely controlled, but still anger. Something which so surprised Mies that she just
sat and listened to him, her lovely mouth slightly
open, her eyes round. What was more, she didn't
answer back at all. Lucy, her coffee cooling before
her, sat back and watched them both and was glad
to see that Mies was actually paying attention to Willem, even looking at him with admiration. When he
had at last finished she said something softly in quite
a different voice from the one she usually used when

she spoke to him, and then smiled. Lucy was pleased to see that he didn't smile back, only went on looking stern and angry and somehow a lot older than he was, then turned to her and said with great dignity: 'I am sorry, Lucy, that we have spoilt your last evening here. You were quite right, you and I would have had a pleasant evening together. Mies has behaved disgracefully. I have told her that she is spoilt and has had her way far too long; it is time that she grew up, and I for one do not wish to have anything to do with her until she has done so.'

It seemed a little severe. Lucy gave him a rather beseeching look which somehow she managed not to change to one of understanding when the eyelid nearest her winked. Willem, it seemed, was a man of parts.

Mies, of course, hadn't seen the wink. She said softly still: 'Oh, Willem, you're joking,' and then when he didn't reply: 'You are, aren't you?'

He gave her a long steady look across the table. 'You and I will have a talk, Mies, but not now. We are giving Lucy a farewell dinner party, are we not?'

And Mies, to Lucy's surprise, agreed meekly. They finished the meal in an atmosphere of enjoyment, even if they all had to work rather hard at it, and when they left presently, Mies did no more than nod across at Fraam as did Willem. Lucy didn't look at him until the very last moment and then only for a few seconds. He smiled so faintly that she wasn't sure if he had or not. They went home in a taxi, on the surface in good spirits. It wasn't until Lucy was in bed and on the edge of sleep that she began to wonder who was in love with whom; whichever way she looked at it, she hadn't helped much. True, Willem had pressed her hand and thanked her when she had wished him goodbye, but she wasn't quite sure why, and as for Mies, she was her usual gay self, only she didn't mention Fraam at all. Lucy wasn't sure if that was a good sign or not.

She was to return on the night ferry to Harwich and go from there straight to St Norbert's where she was due on duty the following morning, which meant that she still had the whole day in Amsterdam. Packing was something which could be done in half an hour—indeed, she had it almost finished by the time she went to breakfast. Doctor de Groot bade her goodbye at the table, for he had a day's work before him and was going on to a meeting in the evening, so that he wouldn't get home until she had left, but Mies was free and the two of them planned a last look at the shops with coffee at one of the cafés or in the Bijenkorf and after lunch at the flat, one last canal trip through the city. True, Lucy had taken the trip twice already, but she found it fascinating and as she pointed out to Mies, it would fill in the afternoon very nicely and the weather was too good to waste it in a cinema.

The canal boat was only half full and they sat as

far away from the guide as they could, so that Mies could point out the now familiar highlights of the trip to Lucy. 'Oh, I'd like to live here,' breathed Lucy, craning her neck to see the last of the smallest house in the city.

Mies turned to look at her. 'Well, all you have to do is to marry someone who lives here,' she observed.

'I don't know anyone…'

'That is not so; you know Willem and you know Fraam.'

'But Willem never looks at anyone but you, Mies, and Mr der Linssen…' Lucy sighed, 'well, take a look at me, and then think of all those lovely girls I've seen him with.' She added firmly: 'Besides, he's not my type.'

Mies hadn't been listening. 'Willem doesn't look at other girls?' she wanted to know.

'You know he doesn't. He talked about you all the time when we were out.'

'But he is angry with me. Perhaps I shall never see him again.' Mies sounded worried.

'Oh, pooh, of course you will, but I think he'll read you a lecture when he does.'

'Read a lecture?'

Lucy explained. 'And you'd better listen,' she declared, 'unless you're really in love with Mr de Linssen or he's in love with you.'

Mies looked a little shy. 'It would be such a triumph,' she confided. 'He would be a prize which would make me the envy of all.'

'You make him sound like an outsize fish—you ought to make up your mind, Mies.'

Her friend turned thoughtful blue eyes on to her. 'You wish Fraam for yourself, perhaps, or Willem?'

'Good lord, no!' Lucy was genuinely shocked. Willem was a dear, but the only feelings she had for him were motherly, and as for Mr der Linssen…she stopped to think about that; certainly not motherly. She decided not to pursue the matter further.

It had been decided that it would be better for her to catch an earlier train to the Hoek. The boat train was invariably full and it was far better to get on board before it arrived. The two girls had tea out and then went back for Lucy to finish the last of her packing before having a light supper. Lucy felt a vague sadness when it was time to leave; she had had a lovely holiday, she declared to Mies, who had gone to the station to see her off. 'And you must come and see us.' She kissed Mies warmly, 'and I hope you…' She tried again: 'I hope that whatever you decide, you'll be very happy. Let me know.'

She hung out of the window, waving for as long as she could see Mies on the fast receding platform. The station wasn't exactly beautiful, but it was clean and airy and had an atmosphere of bustle and faint excitement and in the gathering dusk of a fine September evening, it looked romantic too—anything could happen, she thought vaguely as she turned away and sat down—only not to her, of course. Anything romantic, that was.

She occupied her journey staring from the window, watching the lights in the villages and towns as the dusk deepened, conscious that she would have liked to have got out at each stopping place and got on a train for Amsterdam. She fell to wondering what would happen if she followed her inclination instead of obeying circumstances; Mies would be surprised but nice about it and so would her father, but she suspected that it would fall very flat the second time round. She would have to go off on her own—she became rather carried away here—get a job and somewhere to live. Her sensible head told her that there were things like money, work permits and an ability to speak the language standing in the way of her fantasy, and it would be more sensible to concentrate upon her future in England.

Less than a year now and she would take her Finals. She tried to imagine herself as a staff nurse, even as a ward Sister, but failed singularly in her efforts to get enthusiastic about it. She went back to peering through the dusk at the placid countryside. But now it wasn't placid any more; the train was running through the busy Europort, its chimneys and refineries mercifully hidden by the evening dark, and then it had slid to a quiet halt in the Hoek station. The train wasn't very full. Lucy waited until most of the passengers had got out and then got down on to the platform and turned round to haul out her case. Her hand was actually about to touch it when Mr der Linssen's calm voice said, 'Allow me,' from somewhere behind her, causing her to shoot round like a top out of control and go smack into his trendy waistcoat. 'Well,' said Lucy, 'I never did!' She retreated a few inches and looked up at him. 'I mean—you here and whispering at me like that—I nearly took off!'

She gave him a questioning look and he said at once: 'Doctor de Groot couldn't get away to see you off. I hope you don't mind me standing in for him?'

She was surprised but nicely so. 'That's awfully sweet of him to think of it, and nice of you. Did you happen to be coming this way?'

'Er—yes, in a manner of speaking.' He spoke with a soothing casualness which made it all seem very off-hand and relieved her of any feelings of guilt that she might be wasting a perfectly good evening for him.

'Have you got your ticket?' He had conjured up a porter and handed over her case. 'There's time for a cup of coffee—it will give everyone else a chance to go on board. The boat train isn't due in for some time yet.'

A cup of coffee would be nice, thought Lucy, it must have been the thought of that which made her feel suddenly quite cheerful. They walked through to the restaurant, full of travellers, heavy with smoke and smelling of well-cooked food. There weren't any empty tables; they sat down at one in the window, opposite a stout middle-aged pair who smiled at them and wished them good evening and then resumed their conversation over bowls of soup.

'Hungry?' asked Mr der Linssen, and when she hesitated: 'I am. Let's have soup before the coffee.'

'I did have a kind of supper before I left,' explained Lucy, 'but the soup smells delicious.'

She smiled across at the woman opposite her, who beamed back at her and spoke in Dutch. Mr der Linssen answered for her, falling into an easy conversation in which only a word or two made sense to her, and when he shook his head and laughed a little she asked a little impatiently: 'Why do you laugh? What are you talking about?'

The soup had come, he handed her pepper and salt and offered her a roll before he answered. 'The lady thought that we were man and wife, but don't worry, I put her right at once.'

'I'm not worried,' Lucy said tartly, 'why should I worry about something so absurd? This soup is quite heavenly.'

Her companion's eyes gleamed momentarily. 'We make good soup in Holland,' he offered with the air of a man making conversation. 'My mother is a splendid cook and makes the most mouth-watering soups.'

'Your mother?' Lucy swallowed a spoonful and burnt her tongue. 'I didn't know you had a mother.'

He considered this, his head a little on one side. 'I don't remember you ever asking me,' he pointed out placidly. 'I have a large family, as large as yours. I hope that you will give my regards to your parents when you see them. Do you go home?'

She spooned the last of her soup. 'No, I'm due back on duty at two o'clock tomorrow. I'll go home as soon as I get days off, though.'

'And you take your Finals soon?' he asked idly.

'Next summer.' Their coffee had come and she handed him a cup.

'Ah—then I presume you will embark on a career?'

'Well, I haven't much choice,' said Lucy matter-of-factly. 'I expect I shall like it once I'm in a—a rut.'

'You have no wish to get out of a rut? To marry?' He added: 'To—er—play the field?'

What a silly question, she told herself silently. She turned her green eyes on him. 'Me? You're joking, of course.' She went on kindly: 'I expect you're so used to taking out beautiful girls…they're the ones who play the field, though I'm not quite sure what that means…that you don't know much about girls like me. Parsons' daughters,' as if that explained completely.

Apparently it did. He sat back in his chair, very

much at his ease. 'You know, you're quite right. What an interesting little chat we are having.' He glanced at the paper-thin gold watch on his wrist.

'Unfortunately I think you should go on board; the boat train is due in ten minutes or so.'

Lucy got up at once. Her companion might have found their chat interesting, but she had not, although she didn't quite know why. She thanked him politely for her soup and coffee, reiterated her hope that he hadn't wasted too much of his evening on her, and went to the ticket barrier.

Mr der Linssen stayed right with her. As she got out her ticket he said: 'I could of course give you a meaningless social peck on your cheek. I prefer to shake hands.'

She was conscious of deep disappointment; a peck on the cheek from someone like Fraam would have done a great deal more for her self-esteem than a handshake. She stuck out a capable little hand and felt his firm cool fingers engulf it. 'I've had a very pleasant holiday,' she told him, for lack of anything more interesting to say.

He let her hand go. 'The finish of a chapter,' he observed blandly, 'but not, I fancy, the end of the book. Run along now, Lucy.'

The porter was ahead with her case, so she went through the barrier and didn't look back. A long time ago, when she had been a shy teenager, spending her first evening at a village dance with the doctor's son, he and a friend had taken her home at the end of the evening. They had said goodbye at the gate and she had turned round half way down the short drive to the Rectory to wave, and surprised the pair of them laughing at her. She had never turned round since— not that she had had much chance; she didn't go out all that much. Perhaps Mr der Linssen was looking at her in that same hateful mocking way; she longed to know, but she wasn't going to take any chances.

On board she was ushered into a stateroom with an adjoining shower, a narrow bed and all the comforts of a first class hotel.

'There's a mistake,' she told the steward. 'I'm sure Doctor de Groot didn't book this cabin for me.'

He gave her an impassive look and fingered the large tip in his pocket. 'This is the cabin booked for you, miss.' He added in a comfortable tone: 'The ship's half empty, I daresay that's why.' He nodded to the dressing table. 'There's flowers for you, miss.'

A bouquet, not too large to carry, of mixed autumn blooms, beautifully arranged. The card with it was typed and bore the message: 'Happy memories, Lucy.' It wasn't signed; Mies must have sent it, bless her. Lucy sniffed at the roses and mignonette and Nerine Crispa tucked in between the chrysanthemums and dahlias and carnations; they would make a splendid show in her room at the hospital. She felt a return of the vague longing to rush back to Amsterdam, but ignored it; it was a natural disappointment because her holiday was over, she told herself as she unpacked what she would need for the night before going up on deck to watch the ship's departure.

St Norbert's looked depressingly familiar as the taxi drew up outside its grimy red brick walls and her room, even when the flowers had been arranged in a collection of borrowed vases, looked like a furnished box. She unpacked quickly, had a bath and in her dressing gown went along to the pantry to see if any of her friends were off duty. Beryl, from Men's Medical, was there, so was Chris, on day duty on Children's. They hailed her with pleasure, invited her to share the pot of tea they had made, and adjourned to her room for a nice gossip until it was time to don uniform and go to lunch.

The meal, after the good living in Doctor de Groot's flat, seemed unimaginative; Lucy pushed a lettuce leaf, half a tomato and a slice of underdone beef round her plate, consumed the milk pudding which followed it, and took herself through a maze of passages to the Principal Nursing Officer's office.

Women's Surgical was to be her lot; day duty for three months and would she report herself to Sister Ellis at once, please. The Principal Nursing Officer, a majestic personality with a severe exterior and a heart of gold, pointed out that as several of the nurses on that ward had fallen sick with a throat bug, Lucy's return was providential and she must expect to do extra work from time to time. Time which would, it was pointed out to her, be made up as soon as possible.

Lucy said 'Yes, Miss Trent,' and 'No, Miss Trent,' and hoped that life wasn't going to be too hard; Sister Ellis was an elderly despot, old-fashioned, thorough and given to reminiscing about her own training days when, it seemed, she worked for a pittance, had a day off a month, worked a fifty-six-hour week and enjoyed every minute of it. She never tired of telling the student nurses about it, always adding the rider that she had no idea what girls of today were coming to. No one had ever dared tell her.

Women's Surgical was on the top floor, a large, old-fashioned ward with out-of-date sluice rooms, side wards tucked away in awkward corners and bathrooms large enough to take half a dozen baths in place of the old-fashioned pedestal affairs set in the very centre of their bleak white tiles. Lucy climbed the stairs slowly because she still had a few minutes to spare, and pushed open the swing doors which led to a kind of ante-room from which led short passages to Sister's office, the kitchen, the linen cupboard and a small dressings room. Straight in front of her were more swing doors leading to the ward; she could hear voices, curtains being pulled and the clatter of bedpans coming from behind them. Just nicely in time for the B.P. round, she thought sourly as she tapped on Sister's door. Amsterdam seemed a long way away.

CHAPTER FIVE

LUCY, a hard worker, found her capacity being stretched to its limits; even with Sister Ellis's splendid and uncomplaining example, her days were gruelling. One of the staff nurses went off sick on the day following her arrival on the ward and she found herself doing the work of two. Something, as Sister Ellis assured her, she was perfectly capable of doing, and indeed that was true, only it left Lucy too tired to think two thoughts together by the end of the day. But she had her reward; after a week the nurses began to trickle back from sick leave and two days later, she was given her days off with an extra one added on to make up for the extra hours she had worked. Sister Ellis had given her an evening off too so that she packed her overnight bag during her dinner hour, raced off the ward at five o'clock, tore into her clothes, and leaving Chris to clear up the mess, made for Waterloo Station, determined not to miss a moment of her freedom.

Her mother met her at Crewkerne because her father had a Parish Council Meeting and Lucy prudently offered to drive home. Mrs Prendergast had learned to drive a car of necessity, not because she particularly wanted to and she treated the Ford as an arch-enemy, only waiting to do something mean when she was driving it; consequently she gripped the wheel as though she had been glued to it, braked every few yards, ill-treated the clutch and never went faster than forty miles per hour. Fortunately her family had nerves of steel and patient dispositions; all the same, they ganged up to prevent her driving whenever possible. Lucy took the wheel now, and since her mother wanted to talk, didn't hurry overmuch, answering her parent's questions with all the detail that lady liked to have. 'And that nice man who brought you home,' enquired Mrs Prendergast, 'did you see him?'

'Oh, yes,' admitted Lucy cheerfully, 'several times. He lives in Amsterdam and knows Doctor de Groot quite well—he and Mies are very thick.'

She didn't see her mother's face fall. 'She must be a good deal younger than he is…'

'Mies is a year younger than I am, Mother. There's someone else after her, though, such a nice young man, Willem de Vries. They grew up together.'

'He'll find it difficult,' observed Mrs Prendergast.

Lucy said 'Um,' in a non-committal manner. She had changed her mind about Willem, he was a dark horse. True, someone like Fraam der Linssen could make rings round him if he had a mind to, but surely if he had wanted Mies he would have made sure of her ages ago.

'What are you thinking about?' asked her mother suddenly.

'Mies,' said Lucy promptly. 'She's so lovely, Mother, you have no idea. She has gorgeous clothes too...'

'You didn't have the right dress for that dance,' observed Mrs Prendergast far too quickly.

Lucy took the car gently through Beaminster and out into the narrow country road leading to home. 'It was perfectly all right,' she declared. 'You wouldn't have liked the dresses most of the girls wore—nothing on under the bodice—I mean, they were cut so low there just wasn't room.'

Her mother made a shocked sound. 'Don't tell your father, darling.'

Lucy giggled. 'Of course not, but it's quite the thing, you know—I didn't see any of the men minding.'

Her mother shot her a sideways look. 'I don't suppose they minded at all.' She frowned. 'All the same, you must get a new dress before the winter, darling.'

Lucy nodded. 'O.K., but I'll wait until I'm invited, Mother dear, otherwise it's just a waste of money. And there's a lot of life in that green dress yet.'

'There's a lot of life in the old tweed coat I wear when I feed the chickens,' declared her mother briskly, 'but that's no reason to wear it to church.'

'I'll buy a new dress,' promised Lucy, and pulled up tidily at the front door of the Rectory.

The stone-flagged hall smelled of wax polish and lavender mixed with something mouthwatering from the kitchen. Lucy sighed with deep content as she went in. It smelled of home, and hard on the thought was another one; that Fraam der Linssen's house smelled of home too, despite its grandeur. A wave of something like homesickness caught at her throat and she told herself that she was being ridiculous; one wasn't homesick for a house one had seen only once, and that fleetingly. It was because she was tired, she supposed as she followed her mother into the kitchen and then back into the dining room with her supper on a tray.

She spent a good deal of her days off talking, relating the day by day happenings of her holiday in Amsterdam. Her parents hadn't been there for many years and it was difficult for them to understand that it had changed. 'Though the *grachten* are just the same,' she consoled them. 'Some of the houses are used as offices, but they look just the same from the outside.'

'And where does that nice man live?' asked her mother guilelessly.

'Mr der Linssen? He's got a mansion in a dear little side street with a canal running down the centre. I went inside one day—just into a sitting room, with a cat I found—he's given it a home.'

It sounded rather bald put like that and she could see her mother framing a string of questions which she forestalled with: 'Doctor de Groot's clinic is pretty super—he works frightfully hard, a lot of the medical men give him a hand there.'

'Mr der Linssen?' asked Mrs Prendergast.

Lucy gave a soundless sigh. Her mother had the tenacity of a bulldog, she would end up by extracting every detail about him. 'He goes there, too. I didn't see much of him, though, although he's so friendly with Mies.' She drew a breath. 'He avoided me as much as he could; he was always polite, of course, but he told me that he—he tried not to see me.'

This forthright speech didn't have the desired effect. Her mother paused in her knitting to look at nothing. 'Now why should he say that?' she asked no one in particular. But she didn't mention him again for the whole of the three days in which Lucy was home, and nor, for that matter, did anyone else, a fact which she found decidedly frustrating. After all, she had seen quite a lot of him while she had been in Amsterdam, but she found bringing him into the conversation very difficult. She decided to forget about him and busied herself around the house with her mother, or drove her father through the quiet lanes when he went visiting. They were delightfully empty now; the summer visitors, and they weren't many, had gone and the local inhabitants had returned to their rural activities, and with autumn advancing the village social life was waking up. Handicrafts, knit-ins, whist drives were very much the order of the day. Lucy obediently put in an appearance at a knit-in, hating every moment of it, for she couldn't knit well and the conversation tended to centre round little Tom's adenoids, old Mrs Drew's rheumatism and the mysterious ailment which had attacked Farmer Will's pigs. After a little while she found her thoughts wandering. That they should wander to Mr der Linssen was natural enough, she told herself; he had been part and parcel of her holiday, and that was still fresh in her head.

She went back to St Norbert's refreshed and ready for work. And that was a good thing, for there was plenty of it. There had been no empty beds when she had gone off duty three days earlier; now, although four patients had been discharged and their beds filled, there was a row of beds down the centre of the ward as well. Five in fact, occupied by ladies of various ages and all a little ill at ease, situated as they were in full view of everyone around them. Of course they wouldn't stay there long, as soon as their turn came for the operating theatre they would exchange beds with someone convalescent enough to spend the day out of bed and retire to the centre of the ward at bedtime. But in the meantime they sat up against their pillows trying to look as though they always slept in the middle of a room anyway, with a constant stream of people brushing past them on either side. Lucy, racing methodically to and fro, found time to feel truly sorry for them and at the risk of not getting done, paused to have a quick word with them in turn. They were all rather sweet, she decided; the old lady in the first bed was really only there because there was nowhere else to put her; she was a terminal case which stood a small chance of recovery if she were operated upon and none at all if she wasn't. There were those who might argue that she was taking up valuable space when it was needed so urgently for those who had a better chance and were younger, and that she was of the same opinion was obvious from her apologetic air and anxiety to please. Lucy, doing her best to dispel that look, gave the old dear a second helping of supper and a pile of magazines to look at. The girl in the bed behind her was young and pretty and terrified. She had a troublesome appendix, to be whipped out during a quiescent period, and no amount of reassuring both from the other patients and the nurses could convince her that she would survive the operation.

'You'll be sitting in a chair this time tomorrow,' Lucy promised her, 'or almost. Here's Mr Trevett to look at you, he's a poppet and he's got two daughters about the same age as you.'

She attended the consultant while he made a brief examination, exchanged the time of day with his houseman, saw them to the door and returned to go round the ward, checking the post-operative cases and then reporting to Sister in her office. Today had been busy, she reflected sleepily as she went off duty;

tomorrow would be even worse, with six cases for theatre and she didn't know how many more for X-ray. She yawned widely, accepted the mug of tea someone had ready and plunged, inevitably, into hospital talk.

The day began badly. There had been a bad accident in during the early hours of the morning and the main theatre in consequence would start the list late; the six apprehensive ladies would have to wait. It was a pity that Maureen, the girl with the appendix, coaxed to calm by the day staff when they arrived on duty, and the first to go to theatre, should be delayed for more than an hour, for by the end of that time, even though sedated, she was in a fine state of nerves. Lucy, walking beside the trolley at last, holding a hand which gripped hers far too tightly, couldn't help wishing the day done.

The old lady went last and by then the morning had slipped into early afternoon, with everyone going full pelt and getting a little short-tempered what with curtailed dinner, two accident admissions and the routine of the ward to be fitted in. The part-time nurses came and went and Lucy, off at five o'clock, saw little chance of getting away until long after that hour; the old lady had proved a tricky case and didn't return from theatre until well past four o'clock, and then only because Intensive Care were so full they were unable to keep her. Sister Ellis, bustling about with her sleeves rolled up, exhorting her staff to even harder work, took an experienced look at the tired old face, still barely conscious, and appointed Lucy to special her in the corner bed which had been vacated for her.

It was after seven before she was relieved, although she hadn't noticed the time; her patient was a challenge and she had taken it up with all the skill she possessed. The operation had been successful and would ensure at least a few more years of life, but a successful operation wasn't much good unless the after-care was of the best. Indeed, Lucy would have stayed even longer if it had been necessary, for she was sure that the old lady would recover, but she handed over, said goodnight to Sister Ellis and went wearily off duty. She was almost at the Nurses' Home when she remembered the letter in her pocket she meant to post to her mother. Sighing a little, she retraced her steps and went out of the hospital entrance; there was a letter box on the corner of the street which would be cleared that evening. She had slipped the letter in and was turning to go back when she saw the Panther de Ville, going slowly with Fraam der Linssen at the wheel and for a wonder, no one beside him. He didn't see her, nor did he go into the hospital entrance. She watched the elegant car out of sight, conscious that she had wished that he had seen her. Probably he wouldn't have stopped, she told herself robustly, and marched back to her supper and a reviving pot of tea in the company of such of her friends who were off duty. That she dreamt about Fraam der Linssen all night was pure coincidence, she told herself in the morning.

The old lady was better. Lucy, bustling round with charts and checking drips, was delighted to see that, and Maureen, helped from her bed and made comfortable in a chair, admitted with a grin that there hadn't been anything to get into a panic about, after all. And the other ladies were coming along nicely too; yesterday's hard work had been worth it.

Lucy had a lecture in the afternoon, one of Sister Tutor's stern discourses about ward management delivered in such a way that they were all left with the impression that their futures were totally bound to hospital life for ever and ever. Lucy, going back on duty, felt quite depressed.

It was a couple of days later when a notice on the board bade all third year nurses, all staff nurses and as many ward Sisters as could be spared to attend a lecture to be given by Mr der Linssen. It was to be at two o'clock on the following day and Lucy, who was off duty for that afternoon, decided immediately that she wouldn't go, only to be told by Sister Ellis that her off duty had been changed so that she might attend the lecture. 'Because you've worked very hard, Nurse Prendergast,' said Sister Ellis kindly, 'and deserve some reward. Mr der Linssen is an exceedingly interesting man.'

Lucy agreed, although privately she considered

him interesting for other things than lecturing. She would sit well back, she decided; there would be a large number of third year student nurses and they would take up a good many rows—the back one would be at least half way up the hall.

Her friends had kept a seat for her in an already full hall and she settled herself into it. Just in time; punctually to the minute Sister Tutor's procession advanced across the platform, followed briskly by Fraam who advanced to his desk, acknowledged the upward surge of young ladies rising to their feet and then quite deliberately looked along the rows. He found Lucy easily enough, he stared at her for a long moment and without looking any further, began his lecture—this time about Parkinson's disease and its relief through the operation of thalamotomy, to be undertaken with mathematical precision, he observed severely, and went on to describe the technique of making a lesion in the ventro-lateral nucleus of the thalamus. Lucy, making busy notes like everyone else, listened to his deep, calm voice and missed a good deal so that she had to copy feverishly from her neighbours.

At the end, she filed out with the rest of the nurses, not looking at the platform where several of the Sisters had intercepted Mr der Linssen as he was about to leave, in order to ask questions. He must have answered them with despatch because he and Sister Tutor were coming towards her down the narrow passage used as a short cut back to the main hospital and there was no way of avoiding them unless she turned tail and walked away from them. She wished now that she had gone the long way round with the others, but the lecture had run late and she was already overdue; Sister Ellis would be wanting to go to her tea and so would Staff. Not sure whether to look straight ahead or look at them as they passed, she compromised by darting a sideways glance. Sister Tutor gave a brisk nod and went on saying whatever it was she was engaged in; Mr der Linssen gave her a cool unsmiling look which left her wondering if she were invisible. By the time she had reached the ward she was quite cross about it; after all, they had seen quite a lot of each other not so long ago, enough to warrant a nod, surely. Her small, almost plain face wore such an expression for the rest of the day that several patients asked her if she felt ill and Sister Ellis, more forthright, wanted to know if she were in a fit of the sulks, because if so, her ward wasn't the place in which to have them. Lucy said she was sorry meekly enough and pinned a smile on to her nicely curved but wide mouth until she went off duty, when she allowed it to be replaced by a scowl.

The scowl was still there when she reached her room and because she wasn't in the mood to drink tea with her numerous friends, she declared that she would have a bath and go to bed early. She was indeed in her dressing gown when the warden, a thin, ill-tempered woman, came grumbling up the stairs. 'It's for you, Nurse Prendergast. Eight o'clock and I should be off duty, heaven knows I've had a busy day.' A gross exaggeration if ever there was one; she had come on duty at one o'clock, but Lucy let that pass. 'There's someone to see you—at the front entrance of the home. You'd better dress yourself and go down.'

'Who is it?'

The warden shrugged. 'How should I know? Didn't give a name, said he knew your parents.'

The vague idea that it might have been Fraam died almost before it was born; it sounded like someone from the village, probably with a parcel—her mother had on occasion sent cakes and such like bulky articles by parishioners going to London for one reason or another.

'I'll go down,' said Lucy. 'Thanks.'

She dressed again, this time in slacks and a sweater because her uniform had already been cast into the laundry bin. She didn't bother over-much with her hair but tied it back with a bit of ribbon, barely looking in the looking glass as she did so, thrust her feet into her duty shoes and went downstairs.

The Home was quiet but for the steady hum of voices from behind its many closed doors. There was a very comfortable sitting room on the ground floor, but everyone much preferred sitting cosily, packed tight in someone's bedroom, gossiping and drinking pots of tea until bed time. Lucy crossed the rather dark, tiled hall and opened the heavy front door and found Fraam der Linssen on the other side of it.

She was aware that her heart was beating a good deal too fast and she had to wait a second or two before she could say in a steady voice: 'Good evening, Mr der Linssen. You wanted to see me?'

'Naturally I wished to see you, Lucy. I have messages from Mies and a scarf which you left behind and have been asked to deliver to you.' And when she just stood there: 'Am I allowed to come inside? It is now October, you know, and chilly.'

She opened the door a little wider. 'Oh, yes—of course. There's a room where we may receive visitors.'

He looked around at the rather bleak little room into which she ushered him. 'Designed to damp down the strongest feelings,' he observed blandly. 'I wonder how many young men survive a visit here?'

She answered him seriously. 'Well, if they're really keen, it doesn't seem to matter,' she told him, and wondered why he smiled. She glanced round herself at the upright steel chairs and the table with the pot plant. 'It is rather unfriendly, I suppose. I've only been here once before.'

'Was he—er—put off?' asked Mr der Linssen in an interested voice.

'It was my godmother on a visit from Scotland,' she explained 'Is Mies well?'

She had sat herself on one of the awful chairs but he, after a thoughtful look, decided to stand, towering over her. She thought how alien he looked in the anonymity of the visitors' room. She would, she supposed, always associate him with the lovely old house in Amsterdam.

He took his time answering her. At length: 'She is very well and sends her love. I took her out a few days ago, she looked very beautiful and turned all heads.'

Lucy nodded. 'She's one of the loveliest girls I've ever seen.' She stared across at him. 'Don't you think so?'

'Indeed I do. She made me promise to take you out for a meal while I was over here. Will you come now?'

She looked at him with horror. 'Now? Like this? You're joking!'

'You look all right to me, but change into something else if you wish to.' He glanced at his watch. 'Is ten minutes enough? We'll go somewhere quiet.'

Where he won't feel ashamed of me, thought Lucy, and was on the point of refusing when he repeated: 'I promised. I like to keep my promises.'

She got to her feet. 'Ten minutes,' she told him, and went back to her room. They were going somewhere quiet, he had said. She decided what to wear while she took a lightning shower. The tweed coat, an expensive garment she had bought years ago and which refused to wear out, and the Marks & Spencer velvet skirt with a shirt blouse. She pinned her hair with more regard to neatness than style, spent a few minutes on her face and sped downstairs. At any rate, she wouldn't disgrace a steak bar or a Golden Egg.

Mr der Linssen had other plans. He helped her neatly into the Panther and drove gently through the evening traffic, chatting about this and that. It wasn't until she saw that they were going down the Brompton Road that she stirred uneasily in her comfortable seat. 'Knightsbridge?' she queried doubtfully. 'I'm not dressed…'

'The Brompton Grill.' His voice reassured her, and she was still further reassured when they reached the restaurant and she saw that many of the tables were occupied by people dressed like themselves. Not, she decided, casting a sideways glance at her companion, that she was wearing anything to equal Mr der Linssen's beautifully cut suit. She forgot all that presently; the sherry he ordered for her sharpened her appetite, for she had skipped supper, and she agreed happily to caviar and toast for starters, Poussin en Cocotte to follow and a lemon syllabub to round off these delicacies, while her companion enjoyed a carpet-bag steak followed by the cheese board. And all the while her host carried on a gentle conversation about nothing at all.

But over coffee he suddenly asked briskly: 'And how are you getting on, Lucy? Your Finals are not so far off, are they? Have you any plans?'

She eyed him over the table and shook her head.

'Perhaps you plan to get married?' He sounded casual.

'Me? No.'

'I rather thought that Willem fancied you.'

She poured them each more coffee. 'Did Mies tell you that?'

He gave her a little mocking smile. 'My dear Lucy, I have eyes in my head and I might remind you that I've been around for quite a while.'

It was difficult to know what to say, so she decided not to say anything but asked instead: 'Are you and Mies going to get married?'

He dropped the lids over his eyes so that she couldn't see their expression. His face was so bland that she said quickly: 'No, don't answer, I can see that you aren't going to anyway...'

'You haven't answered me, either, Lucy.'

She frowned and he went on: 'It's difficult to lie when you're an honest person, isn't it?'

She threw him a startled look. 'Yes. You were very rude after the lecture. I don't understand you at all, Mr der Linssen. Here you are taking me out to dinner and yet you looked right through me only an hour ago.' She went pink as she spoke, remembering that he had once said that he tried not to see her.

He studied her face before he spoke. 'I wonder what Sister Tutor would have said if I had—er—greeted you with any degree of familiarity? I thought it best to keep to our roles of nurse and lecturer, and as for taking you out to dinner, did I not tell you that Mies made me promise to do so?'

Indignation almost choked her, but she managed an: 'Of course, stupid of me to have forgotten.' She put down her coffee cup. 'Would you please take me back now? It was a delicious dinner, thank you. You'll be able to tell Mies that you did exactly as she asked.'

He looked surprised. 'Now what on earth?…ah, I see, I put that very badly, did I not?'

Her eyes glowed green. 'No—you're like me, you find it difficult to tell lies. I should have hated it if you'd said how much you'd enjoyed meeting me again.'

He didn't answer her, only lifted a finger for the bill, paid it, helped her into her coat and accompanied her out to the car. Driving back he asked quite humbly: 'You won't believe me if I told you that I have enjoyed every moment of this evening?'

'No, I won't.' That sounded a little bald, so she added kindly: 'There's no need, you know. I think it was nice of you to take me out just because Mies wanted you to.' They were turning into the hospital forecourt. 'Will you give her my love, please? It was a lovely holiday—and Willem—will you give him…' she hesitated, 'my regards?'

He got out to open her door and she held out a hand. 'I hope you have a good journey back,' she observed politely, and then a little rush because she had only just remembered: 'How is the cat?'

'In splendid shape—you wouldn't recognise him, he has become so portly.'

'You were very kind to him.' She tugged at her hand which he was still absentmindedly holding, but he didn't let it go.

'Kinder than I have been to you, Lucilla.'

She tugged again and this time he let her hand go. 'You've been very kind,' she repeated, longing for poise and an ability to turn a clever sentence. 'I must go.'

He caught her so close that the squeak of surprise she let out was buried in his waistcoat. 'I almost forgot,' his hand came up and lifted her chin gently: 'I had to give you this from Mies.'

She had never been kissed like that before. When he released her she stood staring at him blankly until he turned her round, opened the door and popped her through it. Even when he had shut it gently behind her she went on standing there until the warden, muttering to herself, came out of her little flat by the office to ask what Lucy thought she was doing. 'Gone midnight,' stated the lady. 'I don't know what you girls are coming to, coming in at all hours—no wonder you never pass your exams!'

Lucy turned to look at her, not having heard a word. 'It was a lovely evening,' she said, and added: 'But of course, he didn't mean the last bit.' She smiled at the warden, tutting and muttering by her door. 'Have you ever been kissed, Miss Peek?'

She didn't wait for that lady's outraged answer, but wandered off up the stairs and into her room where she undressed, got her clean uniform ready for the morning and went along to lie in far too hot a bath while she tried to sort out her thoughts. But she was tired and they refused to be sorted; she gave up in the end and went to bed to fall at once into a dreamless sleep, so deep that she missed the night nurse's rap on her door and only had time to swallow a cup of tea and half of Chris's toast on her way to the ward.

As the day advanced her common sense reasserted itself. Fraam der Linssen had gone again and probably she wouldn't see him any more, and he had done just what Mies had asked him to do, hadn't he? Perhaps he had pretended that he was kissing Mies. Lucy let out a great sigh and Maureen, having her neat little wound re-sprayed, giggled. 'What's up?' she wanted to know. 'You look as though you'd had your purse stolen.'

Lucy laughed. 'That would be no great loss; it's two weeks to pay day.'

If secretly she had hoped to see Fraam again, she was to be disappointed; he had disappeared as suddenly as he had arrived and although she wrote to Mies later in that week, she took care not to ask about him, only made a lighthearted reference to his visit and that very brief. She didn't mention his visit when she went home, though; her mother, like all mothers, would read romance into a dinner *à deux*; there was plenty to talk about anyway, for on that particular trip home her brothers and sisters were all there too. They all teased her a great deal, of course, but being the youngest girl she came in for a little spoiling too. The weather had turned uncommonly cold too; they went for long walks, breathing the frosty air and the smell of bonfires and windfall apples rotting in the orchards, and in the evening they sat round a fire, roasting chestnuts and cracking the cobnuts they had picked on their walks. The days had never gone by so quickly. Lucy went back to St Norbert's with the greatest reluctance, only cheered by the thought that she would be returning in three weeks' time; she had five days holiday still to come and Sister Ellis, always fair to her nurses, had promised that she should add them to her days off so that she would have a whole week at home. She would have to do some studying, of course, but most of the day would be hers in which to potter round the Rectory, drive into Beaminster for the shopping and help her father with the more distant of his parish visits.

These simple pleasures were something to look forward to; she reminded herself of them each day as she did the dressings, urged unwilling patients to get out of their beds when they didn't want to, and urged those who wanted to and weren't in a fit state to do so to remain in bed for yet another day. The old lady was back too; she had been discharged to a convalescent home, but her condition had worsened and she was in her old bed in the corner by Sister's office, and this time there would be no going to the convalescent home or anywhere else. The nurses quietly spoilt her—extra cups of tea, the best books when the library lady came round, a bottle of Lucozade on the locker because she had faith in its strengthening properties, and a constant stream of cheerful talk from whoever was passing her bed. She appreciated it all, making little jokes and never complaining, and during the last few days, when she was drowsy from the drugs to ease her, she would manage to stay awake long enough to whisper some small word of thanks. She died very quietly the day before Lucy was due to go on holiday, holding her hand while Lucy talked calmly about this and that until there was no need to talk any more. Sometimes, thought Lucy, going off duty, nursing was more than she could bear, and yet perhaps that had been the best way. The old lady had had no family and no friends, she might have gone on living in a lonely bedsitter with no one to mind what happened to her. Lucy, a tender-hearted girl, had a good weep in the bath and then, a little red-eyed, packed ready for her holiday.

CHAPTER SIX

THE OLDER MEMBERS of her father's parish had told
Lucy that it would be a severe winter, and she had
no reason to doubt their words as she left St Norbert's very early the next morning. The bus was
crowded and cold and the sky hung, an ugly grey,
over the first rush of earlier commuters. Lucy, going
the other way, found Waterloo surprisingly empty
once the streams of passengers coming to work had
ended their race out of the station. She had ten
minutes before the train left; breakfastless, she
bought herself a plastic beaker of tea, which, while
tasting of nothing, warmed her up. She had just
enough time to buy some chocolate before the train
left; she munched it up, tucked her small person into
the corner seat in the almost empty carriage, and
went to sleep.

The guard woke her as the train drew in to Crewkerne and she skipped on to the platform, refreshed
and ravenous, to find her father deep in conversation
with the doctor from Beaminster, on his way to London. She was greeted fondly by her parent and with
a friendly pat on the back from the doctor who had
known her from her childhood. Both gentlemen then

finished their conversation at some length while Lucy stood between them, her head full of pots of tea, home-made cakes and the cheese straws her mother always kept on the top shelf of the cupboard. She promised herself that she would eat the lot—if only she could get to them.

In the car at last her father observed apologetically: 'Doctor Banks and I were discussing Shirley Stevens—young Ted's wife, you know. She's expecting her first child very shortly and he's trying to get her into hospital a few days earlier. They're very isolated and even in good weather the lane is no place for an ambulance.'

'There's the district nurse,' offered Lucy helpfully.

'Yes, dear, but she has her days off, you know, and when she's on duty she has an enormous area to cover—she might not be available.'

'Where does Doctor Banks hope to get a bed?'

'Wherever there's one in his area. He's gone to London to some meeting or other. He'll try Yeovil on the way back; Crewkerne say they can't take her before the booked date.'

'Poor Shirley,' said Lucy, 'let's hope he's lucky at Yeovil—there's Bridport, of course.'

'Fully booked.' He turned the car into the Rectory drive. 'Here we are. I daresay you're hungry, Lucilla.'

She said 'Yes, Father,' with admirable restraint and rushed into the kitchen. Her mother was there, preparing vegetables, so were the cheese straws. Lucy, with her mouth full, sat on the kitchen table, stuffing her delicate frame while she answered her mother's questions about the journey, her need for a good meal and whether she had been busy at the hospital. But her usual catechism was lacking, and Lucy, who had been looking forward to tell all about her dinner with Fraam der Linssen, felt quite let down.

But not for long; over a late breakfast the three of them discussed her week's holiday and there was more than enough to fill it; a whist drive at the Village Hall, the W.R.V.S. meeting and how providential that Lucy should be home because the speaker was ill and she could act as substitute. 'First Aid,' murmured her mother helpfully, 'or something, dear, it's only for half an hour, I'm sure you'll be splendid.'

'Me? Mother, I've forgotten it all.' A statement which called forth amused smiles from her parents as they passed on to the delights of country dancing on Thursday evenings.

It was lovely to be home again, free to do exactly as she pleased and yet following the simple routine of the Rectory because she had been born and brought up to it. There was no hardship in getting up early in the morning when she could go straight out into the country for a walk if she was so inclined, something she combined with errands for her father in the other parishes, the distribution of the parish magazine and visits to the ladies who took it in turns to do the flowers in the little Norman church. The week slid away, each day faster than the last; the First Aid lecture was pronounced a rattling success, she won the booby prize at the whist drive and spent an energetic evening dancing the Lancers and Sir Roger de Coverley and the Barn Dance, partnered by a local farm hand, who proved himself a dab hand at all of them. She woke the next morning to the realisation that it was her last but one day. On Sunday she would have to go back and, worse, in six weeks' time she was due for a move. Women's Surgical had been busy, but she had been happy working there. Ten to one, she told herself, tearing into slacks and a sweater, I'll be sent to that awful Men's Medical. But she forgot all that; it was a cold day with lowering skies again and everyone in the village forecast snow; just the weather for a walk, she decided, and armed with sandwiches, set off for an outlying farm where there was an old lady, bedridden now, but still someone to be reckoned with. She liked her weekly visit from the Rector, but today Lucy was to fill his place; there was urgent business at the other end of the wide-flung parish and he couldn't be in two places at once.

She enjoyed the walk. The ground was hard with frost and there was no wind at all, although as she gained higher ground she heard it sighing and howling somewhere behind the hills. And the sky had darkened although it was barely noon. She hurried a little, her anorak pulled cosily close round her glowing face, her slacks stuffed into wellingtons. She would eat her sandwiches with the old lady and make tea for them both, since the men would all be out until two o'clock or later; they would be getting the cattle in, she guessed, against the threatening weather.

The farmhouse was large and in a bad state of repair. But it was still warm inside and the furniture was solid and comfortable. Old Mrs Leach was in her usual spot, by the fire in the roomy kitchen, sitting in a Windsor chair, her rheumaticky knees covered by a patchwork rug. She greeted Lucy brusquely and after complaining that it was the Rector she liked to see, not some chit of a girl, allowed Lucy to make tea and ate some of her sandwiches. The small meal mellowed her a little; she treated Lucy to a lengthy complaint about non-laying chickens, straying sheep and the difficulties of making ends meet. Lucy listened politely. She had heard it before, several times, and beyond a murmur now and again, said nothing. Mrs Leach was very old and got confused; she had never accepted the fact that her grandson who now ran the farm was making it pay very well, but persisted in her fancy that they were all on the edge of disaster. She dropped off presently and Lucy cleared away their meal and washed up, then put a tray of tea ready. The grandson's wife would be back from Beaminster shortly and the old lady liked a cup of tea. She sat down again then and waited for Mrs Leach to wake up before bidding her goodbye and starting off home again.

She wasn't surprised to see that it was snowing, and worse, that the wind had risen. The countryside, already thinly blanketed in white, looked quite different and although it was warmer now, the wind, blowing in gusts and gathering strength with each one, was icy. Lucy was glad to see the village presently and gave a sigh of content as she gained the warmth of the kitchen where she took off her wet things and went to find her parents, the thought of tea uppermost in her mind.

It was already dusk when Lucy went into the kitchen to get tea; an unnaturally early dusk by reason of the snow, whirling in all directions before a fierce wind. They hadn't had a blizzard for years, she remembered, and hoped there wasn't going to be one now. The howl of the wind answered her thought and when she went to peer through the window she had the uneasy feeling that the weather was going to worsen. She carried in the tea tray and put it on the lamp table by her mother's chair, then went to find her father. His study was at the end of a long draughty passage and the wind sounded even louder.

He looked up as she went in, observing mildly:

'Bad weather, I'm afraid, Lucy. If this snow persists there will be a good many people cut off, I'm afraid.'

They had their tea by the fire, in the cosy, shabby sitting room, while Lucy made a list of parishioners who might need help if the weather got really bad. She finished the list over her last cup of tea, handed it to her father and went off to the kitchen again with the tray, saying cheerfully as she went: 'I don't suppose it will be needed…there aren't any emergencies around, are there?'

She was wrong, of course; she was drying the last of the delicate fluted china which had belonged to her grandmother when there was an urgent banging on the kitchen door, and when she opened it Ted Stevens, one of the farm hands at Lockett's Farm, rushed in, bringing with him a good deal of snow and wind.

'Trouble?' asked Lucy. 'Sit down and get your breath.' She poured a cup of tea from the pot she hadn't yet emptied and handed it to him, and when he had gulped a mouthful:

'I'd say, Miss Lucy—the wife's expecting and the baby's started. I thought as 'ow I'd telephone from 'ere, but nothin' will get through—the snow's already drifting down the lane and the road's not much better.'

'And Nurse Atkins is in Yeovil—it's her day off.' Lucy started for the door. 'I'll see what Father says, Ted—finish your tea; I won't be a minute.'

She was back in a very short time, her parents with her. 'Lucy will get to your wife,' declared the Rector. 'She knows her way—you stay here, Ted, and I'll telephone and see what's to be done—you'll have to act as guide when the ambulance or whatever can be sent arrives.' He turned to Lucy, already struggling into her wellingtons. 'And you'll stay with Shirley until someone gets through to you, my dear…and wrap yourself up well.'

Mrs Prendergast hadn't said a word. She was stuffing a haversack with the things she thought might be useful to Lucy and then went to fetch an old anorak into which she zipped her daughter with strict instructions to take care. 'And I'll get the spare room bed made up just in case it's needed.' She added worriedly: 'I wish one of your brothers were home.'

They exchanged glances. Lucy, very well aware that her mother disliked the idea of her going out into the blizzard on her own, grinned cheerfully. 'Don't worry, Mother, it's not far and I know the way like the back of my hand.'

An over-optimistic view, as it turned out, for once outside in the tearing wind and the soft, feathery snow, she knew that she could get lost very easily in no time at all. And once she had started valiantly on her way, she knew too that it was going to be a lot further than she had supposed. True, in fine weather it was barely twenty minutes' walk, now it was going to take a good deal longer. But thoughts of poor Shirley, left on her own and probably in quite a state by now, spurred her on. She followed the country road, fortunately hedged, and came at last to the turning which led to the Stevens' cottage. It wasn't so easy here; several times she found herself going off its barely discernible track, but at length she saw the glimmer of a light ahead. It was plain sailing after that, if she discounted sprawling flat on her face a couple of times and almost losing a boot in a hidden ditch. She stopped to fetch her breath at the cottage door and then opened it, calling to Shirley as she went in.

The wind and snow swept in with her so that once in the tiny lobby she had to exert all her strength to get the door closed again. 'Just in time,' she told herself as she shook the snow off herself, and repeated that, only silently, when she opened the living room door and saw Shirley.

Her patient was a large, buxom girl, rendered even more so by the bulky woollen garments she was wearing. Her hair, quite a nice blonde, was hanging round her puffy, red-eyed face and the moment she set eyes on Lucy she burst into noisy sobs.

'I'm dying,' she shrieked, 'and there's no one here!'

'Me—I'm here,' Lucy assured her, and wished with all her heart that she wasn't. 'I'll make a cup of tea and while we're drinking it you can tell me how things are.'

She walked through the cluttered little room to the kitchen and put on the kettle, then went back again to ask one or two pertinent questions.

The answers weren't entirely satisfactory, but she didn't say so; only suggested in a placid voice that Shirley might like to get undressed. 'I'll help you,' went on Lucy, 'and then if you would lie on the bed—how sensible to have had it brought downstairs—we'll work out just how long you've been in labour and that might just give us the idea as to how much longer the baby will be.'

Having delivered this heartening speech she made the tea, assisted the girl to get out of her clothes and into a nightgown and dressing gown and turned back the bedcovers. And it had to be admitted that in bed, with her hair combed and her poor tear-stained face mopped, Shirley looked more able to cope with whatever lay before her. They drank their tea with a good many interruptions while she clutched at Lucy's hand and declared that she would die.

'No, you won't, love,' said Lucy soothingly, busy calculating silently. It didn't make sense; from what she could remember of her three months on the maternity ward, Shirley should be a lot further on than she was. She cleared away the tea things and assuming her most professional manner, examined her patient; there wasn't a great deal to go by, but unless she was very much at fault, the baby was going to be a breech. She had seen only one such birth and she wasn't sure if she would know what to do. She suppressed a perfectly natural urge to rush out of the cottage into the appalling weather outside, assured Shirley that everything was fine, and set about laying out the few quite inadequate bits and pieces she had brought with her, telling herself as she did so that things could have been worse; that at any moment now help could arrive. She gave a sigh at the thought and then gulped it down when someone outside gave the door knocker a resounding thump.

'We're in the sitting room,' she shouted. 'How quick you've been…' she looked over her shoulder as she spoke and let out a great breath, then: 'I didn't expect you!'

'I can see that,' agreed Fraam affably. He towered in the narrow doorway, covered in snow, which he began to shake off in a careless fashion before he divested himself of the rucksack on his back. 'And leave the questions until later, dear girl. Sufficient to say that I happened to be hereabouts and it seemed a good idea for me to—er—act as advance guard.'

He looked very much the consultant now, in a beautifully cut tweed suit and a silk shirt. It was a pity, Lucy thought wildly, that he had had to stuff his exquisitely cut trousers into wellingtons; she was on the point of mentioning it when he asked blandly: 'This is the lady…?'

She made haste to introduce him and then listened to him putting Shirley at her ease; he did it beautifully, extracting information effortlessly while he gently examined her. When he had finished he said: 'Well, I'm not your regular doctor, Mrs Stevens, but I don't think he would object if I gave you something to help the pains; you may even get a little sleep. It will be an hour or two yet and unless an ambulance can get through very shortly you will have to have the baby here. You will be quite safe. Nurse Prendergast is excellent and I won't leave you at all.'

'You're foreign.' There was a spark of interest in Shirley's eyes.

'Er—yes, but I do work over here quite a bit.' His smile was so kind and reassuring that she smiled back quite cheerfully. 'And now will you take this? It will help you considerably.'

Shirley tossed off the contents of the small glass he was holding out and Lucy tucked her in cosily while Fraam made up the fire and then went to shrug on his coat once more. 'I'll fetch in more wood,' he said.

'He's a bit of all right, Miss Lucy,' whispered Shirley, 'even if he is foreign.' She managed a grin. 'Between the two of you it'll be O.K., won't it?'

'Of course,' said Lucy stoutly. 'You're going to have a little doze, just as the doctor said, and everything's going to be fine.' And as Shirley grimaced and groaned, 'Here, let me rub your back.'

She had Shirley nicely settled by the time Fraam got back. He stacked the wood carefully, had another look at his patient and said casually: 'We're going to leave you for a few minutes, Mrs Stevens—just to discuss the routine, you know. Will you mind if we go into the kitchen and almost close the door? No awful secrets, you understand.' He sounded so relaxed that Shirley agreed without a murmur and Lucy, obedient to his nod, slid past him into the tiny kitchen, shivering a little at its chill, made even chillier by the wind tearing at its door and window.

She said in an urgent whisper: 'It's a breech, isn't it? I don't know a great deal about it, but it looked…'

'You are perfectly right, Lucy—it is a breech, at least the first one is.'

Her eyes grew round and so did her mouth. 'Oh, no!' she exclaimed in a whispered squeak. 'You must be mistaken,' and then at his bland look: 'Well, no—I'm sorry, of course you aren't.'

He inclined his head gravely. 'Good of you to say so, Lucilla.'

'And don't call me that,' she whispered fiercely.

His formidable eyebrows arched. 'Why not? Is it not your name?'

'You know it is—only—only you make it sound different…'

'I mean to—it's a pretty name.' He leaned forward and kissed her, brief and hard, on her astonished mouth and went on, just as though he hadn't done it: 'Of course the ambulance hasn't a chance of getting through—I suggested to your father that he tried to contact the army and get hold of something with caterpillar tracks; they might get her doctor through—if they can't then you will have to be my right hand, dear girl.'

She gazed at him in horror. 'Oh, I don't fancy that—I don't think…'

'You won't need to,' he pointed out blandly, 'I'll tell you what to do as we go along. Mrs Stevens should doze for another hour or so, on and off. Make a cup of tea like a good girl, will you, for once we start I don't expect we'll have time for anything. I'll get the things out of my case—there's some brandy there too. I thought Mrs Stevens might be glad of it when everything's over.'

He went back into the sitting room and bent over the bag he had brought with him while Lucy made tea again. He joined her presently, accepted the mug she offered him and whispered on a chuckle: 'I like the odds and ends you brought with you—practical even though not quite adequate.'

She gave him a cross look. 'Well, I wasn't to know it was going to be twins and a breech.'

He spooned sugar lavishly. 'True, Lucy. You didn't add any food to your collection, I suppose?'

'A tin of milk—for the baby, you know,' she pointed out kindly, 'and there's some chocolate in my anorak—it's quite old, I think…'

'We'll save it until we're starving, then.'

She poured tea for them both. 'How did you get here?'

He chose to misunderstand her. 'Through the snow—your father gave me the direction.'

'Yes, of course,' she said impatiently, 'but how did you get here—to the village, I mean?'

'Ah, yes—well; there was something I wanted to ask you to do for me, but this is hardly the time. We can have a nice little chat later on.'

She let that pass. 'Yes, but did you come by car?'

He looked surprised. 'How else? Doctor de Groot sent his love, by the way.'

She re-filled the teapot; it wouldn't do to waste the tea and he had said that there might not be time…'You've seen him recently?'

'Yes—he's ill again.' He added infuriatingly: 'But no more about that; let us go over the task lying ahead of us.' He handed her his mug. 'Now as I see it…' He began to instruct her as to what she might expect and she listened meekly, inwardly furious because he was being deliberately tiresome.

He made her repeat all he had told her, which she did in a waspish little voice which caused a very pronounced gleam in his eyes. All the same, she had cause to be thankful towards him later on; Shirley continued to doze on and off for the next hour or so, but presently she wakened and the serious business of the evening, as Fraam matter-of-factly put it, began. Lucy, well primed as to what she must do, none the less had the time to see how well Fraam managed. Shirley wasn't an easy patient, expending a great deal of useful energy on crying and railing at her two companions, but he showed no sign of annoyance, treating her with a kindly patience which finally had its reward as Shirley calmed down after he had repeatedly assured her that she wasn't going to die, that the baby would be born very shortly and that she would feel herself in excellent spirits in no time at all.

The first baby was a breech, a small, vigorously screaming boy whom Lucy received into a warmed blanket. 'A boy,' Fraam told his patient, 'a perfect baby, Mrs Stevens. You shall hold him in just a minute or two, we'll have the other baby first.'

He had chosen the exact moment in which to tell her. Shirley, delighted with herself and no longer frightened, took the news well and except for exclaiming that they couldn't afford two babies, she made no fuss, and Fraam, bending over her, reassured her with a comfortable assurance that she would undoubtedly get help. 'You'll get the child allowance, won't you, and I'm sure your husband's employer will be generous.'

Lucy wasn't too sure about that; Farmer Lockett wasn't a generous man; it looked as though her father would need to come to the rescue, as he so often did. She heard Fraam say comfortably: 'Well, we must see what can be done, mustn't we?' and felt annoy-

ance because it was easy for him to talk like that; he
would be miles away as soon as he decently could
and would forget the whole thing. But in the meantime at least, he behaved with exemplary calm, making tea while Lucy made the excited mother comfortable and when they had all had a cup, suggesting
in a voice which expected no opposition that Shirley
should have a nice sleep for an hour while they kept
an eye on the babies.

There was only one cot; Lucy found herself sharing the heat of the fire with Fraam, each of them
cradling a very small sleeping creature, cocooned in
blanket. Fraam, wedged into an armchair much too
small for him, had the infant tucked under one arm
and his eyes closed. How like him, thought Lucy
crossly and rather unfairly, to go to sleep and leave
her with two little babies and a mother who at any
moment might spring a load of complications...

'I'm not asleep,' Mr der Linssen assured her, still
with his eyes closed. 'Both infants are in good shape
and I expect no complications from their mother. I
will warn you if I feel sleepy, I have shut my eyes
merely as a precaution.'

He didn't say against what, but Lucy remembering
his remark—a long while ago now—that he tried not
to see her, went a bright pink and went even pinker
when he opened one eye to study her. 'You look very
warm,' he observed, 'but I think that you will have
to bear it.' His glance fell on the small bundle she

was holding so carefully. 'I'll have another look at them later on. If all goes well, you can have them both while I get in more wood and forage round a bit. Once Mum's awake it will ease the situation.'

The eye closed and Lucy was left to her own thoughts. Why was he here? He had said that he had something to ask her and that Doctor de Groot was ill again, but surely a letter would have done as well? Or perhaps he was on holiday? Was it something to do with Mies? Her thoughts chased themselves round and round inside her tired head and were snapped as if on a thread when the old-fashioned wall clock let out a tremendous one.

She turned her head to make sure she had heard aright and whispered: 'Isn't anyone coming?'

'Well, hardly.' He had opened both eyes again and smiled at her kindly. 'They'll have to wait for morning, you know.' They sat listening to the howl of the wind encircling the little house and he added comfortably: 'We're fine here for the moment. Close your eyes, Lucy, I'll catch the baby if you drop it.'

She gave him an indignant glance and he smiled again. 'You'll have chores later on,' he insisted gently, 'and you'll be in no fit state to do them.'

It made sense; she shut her eyes meekly, secretly determined to stay awake. The clock was striking four when she opened them and Mr der Linssen was sitting exactly as he had been, only now he had a little baby tucked under each arm. Miraculously they were still asleep.

'Oh, I'm sorry,' began Lucy, to be stopped by his: 'Feel wide-awake enough to take these two and keep an eye on Mum? She hasn't stirred, but she will very soon. I'll have a look round.'

He handed her the tiny pair and stretched hugely and went soft-footed into the hall for his jacket. Lucy felt the rush of air as he let himself out and then heard no more above the sound of the wind. He would, she judged, have some difficulty in reaching the woodshed. She looked across at Shirley, who was showing signs of waking; she would want some attention and a cup of tea, but how to do that with her arms full of babies? She was still pondering her problem when Mr der Linssen came back. She could hear him in the hall, getting out of his jacket and taking off his boots, and presently he came on his enormous socked feet into the room.

He grinned across at her. 'There's a goat,' he informed her softly, 'and chickens. I've dug a path through the drift behind the cottage and brought down enough coal and wood to keep us going for the rest of the day.'

'Where are they?' asked Lucy urgently.

'In the shed almost at the end of the garden. Can you milk a goat, Lucy?'

She said matter-of-factly: 'Well, of course I can.

I'll go and see to the poor thing as soon as possible, but Shirley's beginning to rouse.'

He came and took the infants from her. 'Good, I'll sit here—there's nowhere else I can go with these two—while you cope with her. Let me know if there's anything worrying you, but if everything's as it should be she can have them while you see to the livestock and I get the tea.'

Shirley, now that she was the proud mother of twins, had assumed an assurance which was rather touching. Between them, she and Lucy managed very well, ignoring Mr der Linssen's impersonal broad back which had, of necessity, to be there too. Washed, combed and comfortable, Shirley sat up against her pillows and delightedly took possession of her family.

Mr der Linssen, taking her pulse and temperature, congratulated her on their beauty and size while he listened to Lucy's gentle slam of the door.

'The goat,' he explained to his patient, 'and the chickens. Lucy's gone to see to them.'

Shirley nodded. 'Oh, I'd forgotten them—there's Shep and Tibby, too…'

'Dog and cat? I didn't see any sign of them. I expect they're sheltering somewhere, if they don't turn up I'll go and look for them. Now I'm going to make some tea and then we can decide on our breakfast.' He added comfortably: 'I daresay someone will be along soon, now.'

He sounded so sure and certain that Shirley only nodded; she had her twins and she was content.

Outside Lucy found things rather worse than she had imagined. The wind was as fierce as ever and the snow, still falling, had piled against the side and back of the little house. The path Mr der Linssen had dug was already covered over and she seized the shovel he had prudently left by the door; she might need it.

The goat was housed alongside the woodshed and the chickens next door. She found fodder for the goat and feed for the chickens, then found a bucket and milked the beast before going in search of the eggs. There were quite a few, so at least they wouldn't starve. She piled them into an old basket, set fresh water and prepared to go back to the house. She was shutting the hen house door when a faint sound made her look down; a small cat had emerged from under the hen house floor and was eyeing her.

'Come on indoors, then,' invited Lucy, and started down the path, rather weighed down with eggs and milk and shovel. The little beast darted ahead, looking back to see if she were following, and then sat down outside the door beside a sheepdog, waiting patiently to be let in. He looked cold and hungry, but he obviously belonged; Lucy opened the door and the three of them went in together.

Mr der Linssen welcomed them with a cheerful: 'Ah, there you are. Shirley was wondering what had happened to Shep and Tibby. I'll feed them, shall I? There's tea in the pot, Lucy.'

'Shep went after Ted,' explained Shirley, 'he's that fond of him.' A faint anxiety creased her placid face. 'I wonder where my Ted is?'

Mr der Linssen answered from the kitchen where he was feeding the animals.

'I imagine he's in the village waiting to guide an ambulance here,' he observed placidly. 'There's a good deal of snow about and they might not be able to find their way.'

Lucy drank her tea feeling peeved; no one had mentioned the goat or the chickens. She took her cup out to the kitchen and filled the kettle; the twins would need attention in a little while and she wanted some cool boiled water. She was joined almost at once by Mr der Linssen, who closed the door gently behind him before he spoke. 'Not too good outside, is it?' His eyes lighted on the eggs and milk. 'I see that you've been your usual practical self—you must show me some time.' He poured the milk into a saucepan and put it on to boil.

'What are we going to do?' asked Lucy. She felt cross and grubby and longed above all things for five minutes at her own dressing table.

'Breakfast, my dear. Porridge, I think, don't you?' He was at his most urbane, his head in a cupboard. 'Eggs, bread and butter,' his voice came from inside, 'tea, we have them all here.'

She gave his back an exasperated look. 'I didn't mean breakfast…'

He straightened up and closed the cupboard door. 'Wait, dear girl, wait. So far Shirley is quite satisfactory and the babies are warm and content. We'll take a look at them and get them to feed—if they do, that will take us over the next few hours.'

'But supposing they don't? We might be here for the rest of the day.'

He nodded his head with a calm which made her grind her small even teeth. 'I should think it quite likely, although there is a good chance that a helicopter will get here sometime before dark.'

She felt better. 'You think so? I'm on duty tomorrow.'

He spooned tea into the pot while she stirred the porridge. 'The trains will be delayed and I doubt if anything much could get through the roads.'

'You mean I'll not be able to get back?' She wasn't quite sure if she felt pleased about it or not.

'Do you mind?' He sounded amused.

Lucy didn't answer that. 'The porridge is ready,' she remarked rather more sharply than she had meant to. 'Are you hungry?'

He was busy with plates and spoons. 'Famished. Lunch yesterday was my last meal.'

'Oh, Fraam!' she had spoken without thinking, her voice warm with concern. 'I'll cook you three eggs…' She remembered then that she had called him Fraam and added hastily, 'Mr der Linssen.'

'I don't know about him, but Fraam could eat three quite easily, thank you. Have we more than this bread?'

'There's half a loaf in the bread bin…much more than we shall need.'

He looked as though he were going to speak, but instead he spooned the porridge into three bowls, put them on a tray and carried it into the living room.

Breakfast was a cheerful meal, the infants tucked up and still sleeping while the three of them fell upon the food, and when they had finished and Mr der Linssen had gone into the kitchen to do the washing up, Lucy dealt with her three patients.

It was light now, as light as it would be while the snow continued. She tidied the little room, made up the fire, fed Shep and Tibby again, found a place for them to settle before the hearth and then, leaving Mr der Linssen to keep an eye on everyone, went upstairs to the tiny bedroom and did what she could to tidy her person. Even when she had washed her hands and face in the old-fashioned basin and combed her hair, she didn't think she looked much better, but at least she felt rather more so. Her face was clean and her hair reasonably tidy; not that that mattered; when she went downstairs Mr der Linssen glanced at her with a casual, unseeing look which made her wish most heartily that she hadn't bothered.

But he pulled up a chair to the fire, put the cat on her lap and told her to go to sleep in a kind enough voice. 'I'll rouse you the moment anything happens,' he promised.

She hadn't meant to close her eyes, but she was weary by now. She didn't hear the helicopter, nor did she stir until the cat was taken gently from her lap and she was shaken just as gently awake.

'They're here,' he told her quietly. 'I'll go out to them. Get Shirley wrapped up, will you?'

She already had everything necessary packed in a case, and was nicely ready when Mr der Linssen came back with the pilot, carrying a light stretcher between them, as well as a portable incubator. The twins were small, they would fit into it very nicely. Lucy left the men to get Shirley on to the stretcher and turned her attention to the infants; and that done to her satisfaction, put on her anorak.

'Don't bother with that,' Mr der Linssen's voice held quiet authority. 'I'll come back for the infants.'

She stared at him. 'But aren't we going too?'

'No. Ted's waiting at the Rectory, they'll pick him up and take him on to Yeovil with Shirley and he'll hope for a lift back or get on to a snow plough if there's one coming this way. He wants to get back as quickly as he can—we'll go as soon as he arrives.'

She had no answer to this but bade Shirley a warm goodbye and went back to the incubator. Mr der Linssen was back again inside five minutes and took that away too with a brief: 'They're rather pushed for room, but they'll manage.' He had gone again before she could answer.

She stood in the room, untidy again, listening to the helicopter's engines slowly swallowed up in the noise of the wind, feeling let down and lonely. How awful it would be if Fraam had gone too and left her alone. She shivered at the very idea, knowing it to be absurd but still vaguely unhappy. Shep's whine disturbed her thoughts and she got up to let him out.

There was nothing to see outside and only the wind blowing, although the snow had stopped now. She shut the door and went back to the mess in the room behind her, telling herself to stop getting into a fuss about nothing; there was plenty of work to get on with and if one worked hard enough one didn't think so much. She picked up a broom and started on the great cakes of snow in the little hall. 'The wretch!' she cried pettishly. 'He needs a good thump—if he were here…'

CHAPTER SEVEN

'BUT I AM HERE,' Fraam's cheerful voice assured her as he opened the door and then stood aside as she swept the snow outside. 'Although from your cross face, I don't think I'll ask why you were wanting me.' He took the broom from her. 'The snow has stopped and the wind is lessening, but I'm afraid the lane is completely blocked—it will need a snow-plough.' He gave her a long, deliberate look. 'Now hop into bed, Lucy. I'll make up the fire and then I'm going outside to clear a path round the house.'

She was glad to obey him without arguing, for she was peevish for want of sleep. She got on to the bed without a word and was already half asleep as he tucked the quilt round her.

She awoke to the domestic sound of something sizzling on the stove and saw that the table had been laid and pulled close to the bright fire. She tidied the bed, poked at her hair before the looking glass and went to peer into the kitchen.

Mr der Linssen was frying eggs, and beans were bubbling in a saucepan. He looked completely at home and somehow very domestic. His casual: 'Slept well?' was reassuringly matter-of-fact and calm, as though he made a habit of cooking scratch meals in snowbound cottages.

Lucy, good-humoured again, thanked him politely and asked if there was any news.

'None.' He turned the eggs expertly. 'The telly doesn't work and there's no battery for the radio.' He turned to smile at her. 'Just you and me, Lucilla. Two eggs?'

They ate their meal cosily before the fire and half way through it Lucy remembered to ask if he had cleared the path.

He nodded. 'Oh yes, and I've widened the one to the shed.'

'Then I can milk the goat and see to the chickens.' She poured more tea for them both. 'Do you suppose we'll get away before dark?'

He leaned back and the chair creaked alarmingly under him. 'Perhaps.' He sounded casual about it. 'I would suggest attempting it on foot, but we can't leave the animals, and I don't like to leave you here alone.'

Lucy went a little pink. 'You don't have to worry about me. I would be perfectly all right.'

'Certainly—all the same I have no intention of leaving you.' He finished his tea and went on: 'I should imagine they will get a snowplough through to us and bring Stevens with it; he'll stay and we'll go back.'

'That sounds too good to be true,' observed Lucy, and started to clear the table.

But it wasn't. She was cooking a hot mash for the chickens and explaining just what she was doing to Fraam at the same time when they heard the drone of a snowplough, although it was half an hour before it reached the cottage with Ted Stevens on it just as Mr der Linssen had prophesied, and over cups of tea Ted told them that Shirley and the twins were safely in hospital and that he would stay at the cottage, going down to the Rectory each day to get news of them. He was profuse in his thanks although a little in awe of Mr der Linssen's elegance and great size, even in his stockinged feet and rolled-up sleeves. He wrung their hands, thanked them once again, pressed a dozen eggs on Lucy and walked with them to the snowplough, with old Tom Parsons, who had driven it there, striding ahead. It was a bit of a squeeze; three of them in the cab and Lucy, perched between the two men, was glad of Fraam's arm holding her steady. It was a bumpy, sometimes slow ride and cold, but she felt content and happy. She wasn't sure why.

They were expected at the Rectory; the kitchen door was opened the moment they began to make their way up the kitchen garden path and Mrs Prendergast welcomed them with a spate of questions as she urged them to take off their jackets and go straight into the kitchen where they found a table laden with home-made bread, soup, great pats of butter, pots of pickles, cold meat and a large fruit cake.

'I didn't know when you'd be back,' she explained, 'so I thought a little of everything would do. Never mind about washing and tidying yourselves; you'll need a good meal first.' She beamed at them. 'I've a pan of bubble and squeak all ready and bacon and fried bread, and tea or coffee…' but here she was interrupted by her husband, who had come hurrying in with a bottle of whisky under one arm and glasses in his hand. 'To keep out the cold,' he explained, putting them down carefully before embracing his daughter and greeting Mr der Linssen warmly. 'We are very anxious to hear your news,' he observed, 'we were a little worried at first,' he glanced across at his guest. 'Indeed, before you came, we were very worried about our little Lucilla. We were relieved to hear from the helicopter pilot that you were both in good spirits and safe and sound.'

He poured whisky and then went down the cellar steps to fetch up a bottle of port for the ladies.

'You don't mind if I sit down to table like this?' asked Mr der Linssen.

'Heavens, no—food first and baths afterwards. You'll stay the night, of course—we've put your Range Rover in the barn, by the way.'

Mr der Linssen swallowed his whisky with pleasure. 'You're very kind, Mrs Prendergast.' His glance slid to Lucy, sitting on the table swinging her legs, sipping port. 'I should like that very much.' And when Lucy glanced up at his words, he smiled at her. She wasn't sure if it was the port or his smile which was warming her.

They made a splendid meal, for after the soup Mrs Prendergast set on the table there was the bubble and squeak and everything which went with it as well as the cake and a large pot of tea. She sat at the foot of the table smiling at them both and when she judged they had eaten their fill, she urged: 'Now do tell us all about it—your father has his sermon to finish and supper will be late.'

So Lucy began, but when she got to the bit where Mr der Linssen had arrived, he took over from her, very smoothly, making much of what she had done to help him, until she exclaimed: 'Oh, you're exaggerating!'

'No—how would I have managed without you? You forget the goat and the chickens—why, before today I had never heard of hot mash.'

They all laughed, and he added: 'And of course the babies—I'm not very experienced with infants.'

Mrs Prendergast made an unbelieving sound. 'And you a doctor—I simply don't believe you!'

'A surgeon, Mrs Prendergast,' he corrected her gently, 'and I haven't delivered a baby since my student days.'

Lucy, nicely full of delicious food, was losing interest in the conversation. Mr der Linssen's deep voice came and went out of a mist of sleepiness. It was very soothing; she closed her eyes.

She was dimly aware of being picked up and carried upstairs, two powerful arms holding her snugly. She wanted to tell Fraam to put her down, but it was too much bother. She tucked her untidy head into his shoulder and slipped back into sleep.

'Worn out,' observed her mother, briskly turning back the bedclothes. 'We'll leave her to sleep for a while.'

Mr der Linssen laid Lucy gently on her bed, bent down and deliberately kissed her sleeping face, then waited while Mrs Prendergast tucked her in. 'The darling's absolutely out cold.'

'The darling's absolutely darling,' remarked Mr der Linssen at his most suave.

Mrs Prendergast bent over her daughter with the deepest satisfaction. Her dear plain little Lucy was loved after all, and by such a satisfactory man. She beamed at him as they left the room.

It was quite dark when Lucy woke up and when she looked at the clock she discovered that it was almost ten o'clock. She got up and opened her door; lights were on downstairs and she could hear voices. Fraam would be gone, she supposed, the Range Rover would be able to follow the tracks of the snowplough and there was no reason why he should stay, even though her mother had invited him to do so. She had a shower, got into a nightie and dressing gown and wandered downstairs, wondering about him. He would have been on his way somewhere or other; she hadn't asked and now she worried about it; he hadn't had much sleep...

For a man who hadn't slept, he looked remarkably fresh, sitting opposite her father in the sitting room, with her mother between them, knitting. She stopped in the doorway, muttering her surprise as the two men got to their feet and her mother turned to look at her. It was Mr der Linssen who came to meet her and take her arm. His 'Hullo, Lucy,' was cheerfully casual as he pushed her gently on to the sofa beside her parent.

'You ought to be in bed,' said Lucy, 'you've had almost no sleep.'

He smiled but said nothing and went and sat down again, and Mrs Prendergast asked sharply: 'No sleep?'

'I had a good nap while Lucy cleared up my mess,' he assured her.

'All the same, you must be tired—I should have thought... Finish the row for me, Lucy, I'll get supper. Toasted cheese?' she suggested, 'and there are jacket potatoes in the Aga,' and when everyone nodded happily, she swept out of the room with: 'You men will want beer, I suppose. Lucy, you'd better have cocoa.'

Lucy said 'Yes, Mother,' meekly and went on

knitting, suddenly conscious of Fraam's eyes on her. It disconcerted her so much that she dropped a stitch and decided to go and help her mother.

The kitchen was warm and comfortable in a rather shabby fashion; Lucy could remember the two chairs each side of the Aga and the huge scrubbed table since she was a very little girl. She set the table now and called the men to their supper and watching Mr der Linssen tucking into the simple food with obvious pleasure, wondered if he found it all very strange after his own lovely house. It seemed not; he washed up with her father to the manner born and then went back to sit by the fire while she and her mother went upstairs to bed, sitting back in his chair as though he had done it every day of his life. She kissed her father goodnight, smiled a little shyly at their guest and got into her bed, vaguely content that he should be there in her home, looking so at ease. She would have liked to have pondered this more deeply, but she went to sleep.

There would be no leaving on the following day, that was plain enough to Lucy when she got up in the morning. True, the snow had stopped, but there had been a frost during the night and there was still enough wind to make the clearing of the drifts a difficult matter. The telephone wasn't working and the snowplough had gone off to the main road again and the country road it had cleared was covered once more. Save for the impersonal voice on the radio telling them what bad weather they were having, Dedminster, Lodcombe and Twistover were cut off from the rest of the world. Lucy didn't mind; in fact, when she stopped to think about it, she was rather pleased. And Mr der Linssen seemed to have no objections either. He ate a huge breakfast and then volunteered to shovel snow. Lucy, helping her mother round the house, found herself impatient to join him, but it wasn't until they had had their morning coffee that she felt free to do so. He was clearing the short drive to the gate and beyond a casual 'Hullo' he hardly paused in his work as she settled down to work beside him. It was hard work, too hard for talking, and besides, she only nibbled at the easy bits while he kept straight on however deep the snow, but it was pleasant to work in company.

But presently she remembered something and paused to lean on her spade and ask: 'Why did you want to ask me something?'

Fraam heaved a shovelful of snow to one side before he too paused.

'Ah, yes—Doctor de Groot asked me to find you while I was over here. He is ill, I told you that— perhaps you don't know that he has Reynaud's Disease? In its early stages—he wants me to operate, he also wants you to nurse him. Mies is no good at nursing and after the first day or so he refuses to stay in hospital—his idea is for you to look after him at the flat.'

Lucy stood looking at him. 'But I'm not a qualified nurse and I don't know much about Reynaud's Disease or its treatment.' She went red under his amused look, reminding her plainly that if she had stayed awake during that lecture of his, she might not be so ignorant, but he didn't say that, only: 'I'll prime you well; there's not much to it. But can you get leave?' He added casually: 'I daresay that if I made a point of asking for you, your Nursing Officer might consent.'

She looked doubtful. 'Miss Trent? She might. I've got two weeks still, though I'm not supposed to have them until after the New Year…'

'You wouldn't mind giving up your holiday?'

'I wasn't going anywhere, only here, at home.'

He nodded. 'So if it could be arranged, you would agree? I intend operating soon—a week, ten days, that gives him a chance to enjoy Christmas. He'll need a few weeks' convalescence, he plans to spend it with Willem's people in Limburg.'

'Willem? Oh, does that mean that he and Mies… I mean, are they going to get married? I thought— that is, she told me she was going to marry you.'

He gave a great bellow of laughter. 'My dear girl, I've known Mies since she was in her cradle. Whenever she falls out with Willem and there's no other admirer handy, she pretends she's in love with me— it fills the gap until she's got Willem on his knees again. Only this time he stayed on his feet and she was so surprised that she's agreed to marry him.'

Lucy breathed a great sigh of relief. 'Oh, I am glad!'

He stared hard at her. 'Are you? He appeared to be taken with you while you were in Amsterdam.'

'That wasn't real; you see, he thought—at least, I thought that if he took me out once or twice Mies might mind, but then I wasn't sure because you might have been in love with her…'

'My God, a splendid tangle your mind must be in! It takes a woman to get in such a muddle.'

Lucy picked up her shovel and attacked the snow with terrific vigour. 'Nothing of the sort,' she observed haughtily. 'Men don't understand.'

'And never will. Now, are you going to nurse Doctor de Groot?'

'If he really wants me to and if Miss Trent will let me have another holiday, yes, I will.'

He was shovelling again, but he paused long enough to say: 'Not much of a holiday, I'm afraid.'

'I've had my holiday,' said Lucy soberly.

He stopped shovelling to look at her, studying her slowly, his head a little on one side. 'Are you rationed to one a year?' he wanted to know.

'Of course not!' she had fired up immediately and then went on with incurable honesty: 'Well, actually, I do only have one a year—I mean, to go away.'

'To dance in a green dress—such a pretty dress, too.'

Her pink cheeks went a shade pinker. 'You don't need to be polite,' she assured him rather severely. 'I've had that dress for three years and it's quite out of fashion.'

'But it suits you, Lucy.'

Because I'm the parson's daughter, she thought wryly, and wished suddenly and violently that she was a rich man's daughter instead, with all the clothes she could possibly wish for and a lovely face to go with them so that Fraam would fall in love with her... She attacked the snow with increased vigour to cover the rush of emotion which flooded her. Of course that was what she had wanted—that he should fall in love with her, because she was in love with him, hopelessly and irrevocably, only it wasn't until this very minute that she had known it.

'You look peculiar,' observed Fraam. 'Is anything the matter?'

Lucy shook her head and didn't speak, for heaven knows what she might have said if she had allowed her tongue to voice her thoughts. She would die of shame if he were ever to discover her feelings; he would be so nice about it, she felt that instinctively— kind and gentle and underneath it all faintly amused. She would be nonchalant and frightfully casual, as though he were someone she had just met and didn't really mind if she never saw again. And indeed for the rest of that day and the day after that too, she was so casual and so nonchalant that Mr der Linssen looked at her even more than usual, his eyes gleaming with something which might have been laughter, although she never noticed that. Mrs Prendergast did, of course, and allowed herself the luxury of wishful thinking…

Fraam drove Lucy back on the following day, the Range Rover making light work of the still snow-bound roads, and because he had seemed so sure that Miss Trent would grant her a further two weeks holiday, she had packed a bag ready to go to Holland, explaining to her mother while she had done it.

Her mother had expressed the opinion that it was a splendid thing that she could repay her father's old friend by nursing him. 'Just as long as you're home for Christmas, darling,' she observed comfortably, and Lucy had agreed happily; Christmas was weeks away.

She had been decidedly put out when they arrived at St Norbert's that afternoon, for Fraam had carried her bag inside for her, said rather vaguely that he would be seeing her, and driven off. And what about Doctor de Groot? she asked herself crossly as she went up the stairs to her room. Had he thought better of having her as a nurse? Had Fraam changed his mind or his plans and forgotten to tell her? Was she to go meekly back to the ward and wait until wanted? She wouldn't do it, she told herself roundly as she unpacked her case, pushing the extra things she had brought with her in anticipation of another stay in Holland into an empty drawer.

And nobody said anything to her when she reported for duty, relieved to find that she was still on Women's Surgical. The ward was busy, not quite as hectic as it had been, but still a never-ending round of jobs to be done and she plunged into them thankfully, resolutely refusing to think about Fraam, which wasn't too difficult while she was busy; it was when she was off duty, doggedly studying for her Finals, that she found it hard not to pause in her reading and think about him instead, and worst of all, of course, was bedtime when, once the light was out, there was nothing at all to distract her thoughts.

It was during the evening of the fifth day that a junior nurse came down the ward to where Lucy was readjusting Mrs Furze's dressing and told her that Sister wanted her in the office.

Lucy paused, forceps poised over the gauze pad. 'Two ticks,' she objected, 'I can't leave Mrs Furze half done. Is it desperate?'

'I don't know—Sister poked her head round her door and told me to find you.'

Lucy began to heave her patient up the bed. 'Well, will you tell her I'm on my way?'

Her junior scurried off and she finished making Mrs Furze comfortable, collected her bits and pieces on to a tray and bore them off to the dressings room.

She was quick about it, only a few minutes elapsed before, her tray tidily disposed of and her hands scrubbed spotless, she tapped on Sister's door and went in.

Sister Ellis was sitting at her desk, looking impatient. Fraam was standing by the narrow window, looking as though he had all day in which to do nothing.

'And what,' Sister Ellis wanted to know awfully, 'kept you so long, Nurse Prendergast? Not only have you kept me waiting, but Mr der Linssen, with no time to spare, has been kept waiting also.'

Lucy's mild features assumed a stubborn look; she was overjoyed to see Fraam, but the joy was a little swamped at the moment by the knowledge that she wasn't looking her best. She was tired, her hair was ruffled and her nose shone. Not that these would make a mite of difference to his attitude towards her, so that it was ridiculous of her to mind, anyway. She said meekly: 'I'm sorry, Sister, but I couldn't leave Mrs Furze at once…'

Sister Ellis snorted. 'In my young days…' she began, and then thought better of it. 'Mr der Linssen wishes to speak to you,' she finished. She settled back in her chair as she spoke, intent on missing nothing.

Fraam took his cue smoothly, with a pleasant smile for Sister Ellis and a gentle 'Hullo, Lucy,' in a voice which sounded as though he were really glad to see her again and quite melted her peevishness. He went on to explain that he had spoken both to Miss Trent and Sister Ellis and both ladies had been so kind as to make it possible for Lucy to take the remainder of her annual holiday. 'Seventeen days,' he commented, 'which should give Doctor de Groot ample time to get over the worst. You are still agreeable, I take it?' he wanted to know.

Lucy tucked away a strand of mousy hair. 'Yes, of course. When am I to go?'

'Tomorrow evening, if you are willing. I shall be operating early on the morning of the following day and would be obliged if you would take up your duties then.' He looked at Sister Ellis. 'If I may, I will have the tickets sent here tomorrow morning. I shall be returning to Amsterdam this evening, but I will arrange for someone to meet you at Schiphol and bring you to the hospital.'

Sister Ellis nodded graciously; Mr der Linssen was behaving exactly as she considered a distinguished surgeon should, no familiarity towards her nurse— true, he had called her Lucy, but the strict professional discipline had altered considerably over the years—and a gracious acknowledgement of her own help in the matter. Lucy Prendergast was a good little nurse, one day she would make an excellent ward Sister. She said now, ready to improve the occasion: 'You will learn a good deal, I hope, Nurse; other methods are always worth studying, and any knowl-

edge you acquire will doubtless come in useful when
you sit your Finals.'

Lucy said: 'Yes, Sister,' and stole a look at Fraam.
She wondered why he looked as though he was
laughing to himself. Really he seemed quite a
stranger standing there so elegant and cool, it was
hard to imagine him shovelling snow and making tea.
She found his eyes upon her and knew that he was
thinking the same thing, and looked away quickly.

'If Mr der Linssen has given you all the instruc-
tions he wishes, you may go, Nurse. Send Night
Nurse in to me in five minutes and then go off duty.
Goodnight.'

'Goodnight, Sister. Goodnight, Mr der Linssen.'
She didn't quite look at him this time.

She had expected to see him again, she had to
admit to herself later; she had gone off duty, eaten
her supper and repaired to her room, accompanied
by a number of her friends, to undertake the business
of packing, and all the while she had her ears cocked
for the telephone, only it had remained silent and she
had gone to bed feeling curiously unhappy. There
had been no reason why Fraam should have tried to
see her again; the whole arrangement was a businesslike undertaking, planned to please Doctor de
Groot—and what, she asked herself miserably, could
be more proof, if proof she needed, that Fraam
wasn't even faintly interested in her? She tossed and
turned for a good bit of the night and went on duty

in the morning looking so wan that Sister Ellis wanted to know if she felt well enough to travel that evening.

She went off duty at one o'clock and obedient to the instructions she had received with her ticket, took herself to the airport and boarded a flight to Schiphol. It was a miserably cold evening and it suited her mood exactly.

It was cold at Schiphol too and she shivered as she followed the routine of getting herself and her luggage into the outside world again. There hadn't been many people on the flight and the queue before her thinned as they reached the main hall. She wondered who would meet her; someone from the hospital presumably, but how would she recognise him or her? She put her case down and it was picked up again at once by Fraam.

'A good flight, I hope?' he wanted to know. 'I thought it better if I fetched you myself, in that way we can save a lot of time; I can give you the facts of the case as we go.'

'Good evening,' said Lucy on a caught breath, 'and yes, thank you, the flight was very comfortable.' And after that brief exchange they didn't speak again as he led her to the car park. He had the Mini this time and what with her case and him she found it rather cramped. She sat squashed beside him while he drove into Amsterdam, listening carefully to his impersonal voice taking her through the case, and because she had expected that he would take her straight to the hospital, she was taken aback when he stopped the car and when she peered out, discovered that they were outside his house. 'Oh,' said Lucy blankly, 'I thought…'

'Supper first.' Fraam was already out of the car and at the same time the door of his house opened and Jaap's portly figure stood waiting for them, framed in the soft shaded lights of the hall.

Lucy got out then, because Fraam was holding the car door open for her and besides, it was cold. He took her arm across the narrow brick pavement and ushered her up the steps and into the warmth beyond to where Jaap was waiting, holding the door wide, smiling discreetly at them both. And there was some-one else in the hall; an elderly very stout woman, with pepper-and-salt hair dressed severely, and wear-ing an equally severe black dress, neatly collared and cuffed with white.

'This is Bantje,' explained Fraam, 'Jaap's wife, she will take you upstairs. I'll be in the drawing room when you're ready.'

Lucy went up the lovely carved staircase behind Bantje, trying to see everything at once; the portraits on the wall beside it, the great chandelier hanging above her head, the great bowls of flowers…and once in the gallery above, her green eyes darted all over the place, anxious not to miss any of the beauty around her. She hadn't much time, though, for the housekeeper crossed the gallery and opened an elaborately carved door and smiled at her to enter. The room was large by Lucy's standards, and lofty, with a handsome plaster ceiling and panelled walls. The furniture was a pleasant mixture of William and Mary and early Georgian, embellished with marquetry, against a background of dim chintzes and soft pinks. Left alone, she did her hair, washed her face in the pink-tiled bathroom adjoining, and then spent five minutes looking around her. Even if she never saw it again, she wanted to remember every detail. Satisfied at last, she did her face in a rather perfunctory fashion and went downstairs. Fraam was in the hall, sitting in one of the huge armchairs, but he got up when he saw her and took her arm as she hesitated on the bottom step.

'It's a little late,' she observed. 'Oughtn't I to go to the hospital? Don't they expect me?'

'Of course they expect you. I told them that I would take you there not later than midnight.'

High-handed. She had her mouth open to say so and then closed it again as they went into a very large, very magnificent room; dark oak and crimson was her first impression and she had no chance to get a second one because she saw that there were people already in it: a handsome elderly couple standing before the enormous hooded fireplace, a young man so like Fraam that she knew at once that he was his brother, and a pretty girl who could only be his wife. Her first feeling was one of annoyance that he hadn't warned her; she was, to begin with, quite unsuitably dressed; a nicely cut tweed skirt and a shirt blouse with a knitted sweater on top of it were suitable enough for travelling but hardly what she would have chosen for an evening out. She eyed the other ladies' long skirts as she was introduced; Fraam's mother and of course his father, his brother and as she had guessed his wife, all of whom welcomed her charmingly.

'My family, or at least part of it, happened to be in Amsterdam,' observed Fraam coolly, 'and now how about a drink?'

Lucy could scarcely refuse, so she asked for a sherry and prayed that it wouldn't have too strong an effect on her empty insides, but when it came she found to her relief that it was a small glass and only half full; perhaps that was the way they drank it in Holland. She sipped cautiously, answering her companions' pleasant questions and was relieved when Jaap opened the door and announced that supper was ready.

A rather different supper from the one her mother had produced for them in the Rectory's kitchen not so long ago; pâté and toast, a delicious dish of sole cooked with unlikely things like bananas and ginger and pineapple followed by small wafer-thin pancakes, filled with ice cream and covered with a brandy sauce. A potent dish, Lucy decided, and was

glad that she had had only one glass of the white
wine she had been offered.

They had their coffee in the drawing room, which,
after the restrained simplicity of the Regency dining
room, seemed more magnificent than ever. Lucy,
feeling a little unreal, sat on an enormous button-
backed sofa and talked to Fraam's father; a nice old
man, she decided, who must have been as good-
looking as his son and still was handsome enough.
She felt at ease with him, just as, surprisingly, she
had felt at ease with his mother, a rather formidable
lady with a high-bridged nose and silver hair who
nonetheless had a charming smile and a way of making her feel as though she had known every one in
the room all her life. She had talked to Leo, Fraam's
brother, too, and his wife Jacoba, and as she got up
to leave presently she was aware of deep envy for
the girl Fraam would eventually marry; not only
would the lucky creature have him for a husband,
she would have his family too, to welcome her with
warmth into their circle and make her one of them.

She sighed without knowing it and Mevrouw der
Linssen said at once: 'You are tired, my dear, and
no wonder. Fraam shall take you to the hospital at
once—we have been most selfish keeping you from
your bed.' And she had kissed Lucy good night. So,
for that matter, had every one else, except Fraam of
course. He had driven her back quickly, handed her
over to one of the night Sisters, wished her good

night, expressed the hope that she would remember all that he had told her, and gone away again. She had felt a little lost, standing there at the entrance of the Nurses' Home, but she was sleepy too; she accompanied the night Sister up the stairs to a pleasant little room on the first floor, listened with half an ear to instructions about uniform, to whom she must report, and where to go for breakfast, and went thankfully to bed. She had plenty to think about, but it would have to wait until the morning.

And when the morning came, she had no time. A pretty girl who introduced herself as Zuster Thijn and begged to be called Ans fetched her at breakfast time, sat her down at a table with a dozen others, supplied her with coffee and bread and butter and cheese, introduced her widely and then hurried her along to the Directrice's office.

That lady reminded Lucy forcibly of Miss Trent; kind, severe and confident that everyone would do exactly as she wished them to. She outlined Lucy's duties in a crisp, very correct English, struck a bell on her desk with a decisive hand and when a younger and only slightly less severe assistant appeared, consigned Lucy into her care.

She would never find her way, thought Lucy, skipping along to keep up with her companion's confident strides. The hospital was old, added to, modernised and generally made over and she considered that unless one had been fortunate enough to grow up with the alterations, one needed a map. They gained the Private Wing at last, and she was handed over to the *Hoofdzuster*, a placid-looking woman somewhere in her forties, with kind eyes and a ready smile and a command of the English language which while not amounting to much, was fluent enough.

'Doctor de Groot is in a side room,' she explained, 'he will go to the *operatiezaal* in an hour, so you will please renew your acquaintance with him, give him his injection and accompany him, there to remain until Mr der Linssen has completed the operation. It has been explained to you what is to be done?' She nodded her head. 'So you will know what is expected of you, you will remain with him for the rest of this day and you will be relieved by a night nurse. You will receive free time on another day. You understand me?'

'Yes, thank you, Sister. I understand that Doctor de Groot is to go home within a few days.'

'That is so. Now I take you to your patient.'

Lucy had expected to see Mies there, which was silly, for visiting would hardly be allowed before the operation. Doctor de Groot was propped up in bed looking ill but quite cheerful and talking with some vigour to Fraam, who was leaning over the end of his bed, listening. They both looked at Lucy as she went in, said something to the *Hoofdzuster*, who smiled and went away, and then stared at Lucy once more. She bore their scrutiny for a few moments and then wished them a rather tart good morning.

Her patient grinned at her. 'Hello, Lucy, I'm very glad to see you, my dear. I can't think of anyone I would rather have to look after me. My little Mies is no good as a nurse, not this sort of nursing at any rate. We're going home in three days' time—I've Fraam's promise on that. And now,' he added testily, 'what about giving me my pre-med?'

Fraam nodded at Lucy, not in greeting, she was quick to see, but as a sign that she could draw up the necessary drug in the syringe lying ready in its little dish. She did so without speaking, gave it to him to check, administered it neatly and gave Doctor de Groot a motherly little pat.

'We'll have a nice chat when you're feeling like it,' she promised.

He stared up at her. 'I'm the worst patient in the world!'

'And I'm the severest nurse,' she assured him. 'Now close your eyes, my dear, and let yourself doze—I'll be here.'

She went to get rid of the syringe and then to look at the charts and papers laid out ready for her once the operation was over. Fraam was still there, indeed he hadn't moved an inch, but he wasn't Fraam now, he was the surgeon who was going to perform the operation and she was the nurse in charge of his case.

'Was there anything more that I should know about?' she asked him calmly.

'Not a thing,' he assured her, 'at present. I daresay I'll have a few more instructions when you're back here.' He moved then, going soft-footed to the door. 'I'll see you later.'

An hour later Lucy, swathed in a cotton gown and with her hair tidied away beneath a mob cap which did nothing for her at all, stood by Doctor de Groot's unconscious form, ready to hand the anaesthetist anything he might require. Mr der Linssen was there, naturally, with his assistant, a houseman or two, theatre Sister and a team of nurses, and it all looked exactly the same as the operating theatre at St Norbert's, only of course they were all speaking Dutch. Not that much was said; Mr der Linssen liked to work in peace and quiet; bar the odd remark concerning some interesting phase during the operation, and a quiet-voiced request for this or that instrument, he worked silently, completely absorbed in his task; the division of the sympathetic chain of cervical nerves so that his colleague's right arm might become normal again, free from pain and the threat of gangrene quashed once and for all.

He worked fast, but not too fast, and despite his silence the people around him were relaxed. Bless him, thought Lucy lovingly, he deserves all the pretty girls he dates and his lovely house and his nice family; thoughts which really made no sense at all.

He straightened his long back at last, nodded to his assistant and left the theatre and in due time Doctor de Groot was borne back to his bed. He had already opened his eyes and muttered something and gone directly back to sleep again. Lucy, arranging all the paraphernalia necessary to his recovery, was too intent on her task to notice Mr der Linssen in the doorway watching her. When she did see him she concluded that he had only just arrived and informed him at once about his patient's pulse and general condition. 'His hand is warm and there's a good wrist pulse,' she went on. 'Do you want half-hour observations?' After the shortest of pauses, she added 'sir.'

His manner was remote and courteous, they could have been strangers. 'Please. I want to know if you are uneasy about anything—anything at all. Zuster Slinga will be in from time to time.'

He went to bend over his patient and then without saying anything else or even looking at her, went away.

He returned, of course, several times, to study her careful charts, check Doctor de Groot's pulse and scribble fresh instructions. Lucy, who had been cherishing all the dreams of a girl in love, however hopelessly, did what she had to do with meticulous care and calm and when, later in the day, she had a few minutes to herself, she tucked the dreams firmly away; they didn't go well with the job she was doing. You're a fool, she told herself as she sipped a wel-

come cup of coffee, and fools get nowhere—stick to
your job, Lucy my girl, and leave daydreaming to
someone with the time for it.

An excellent maxim which she obeyed for at least
the rest of that day.

CHAPTER EIGHT

IT BECAME APPARENT to Lucy within the next day or so that they could have managed very well without her. Certainly Doctor de Groot was a very bad patient, ignoring everything that was said to him, ordering his own diet in a high-handed fashion, and using shocking language when his will was crossed. Lucy took it all in good part, coaxed him in and out of bed, obediently held mirrors at the correct angle so that he could inspect the ten neat stitches Mr der Linssen had inserted alongside his spine, and rationed his visitors with an eagle eye to the length of their visits. Mies came each day, of course, prettier than ever and usually with Willem in tow. She had a ring now, a diamond solitaire which sparkled and shone on her graceful hand. Lucy admired it sincerely and tried not to feel envy at Willem's air of complacent satisfaction. It would have been better if she had had more to do, for once Doctor de Groot had recovered from the operation there was little actual nursing to be done. The wing was well staffed, a nurse could have been spared to look after him easily enough. She puzzled over it and on the third day, when Fraam came to pay his evening visit, she broached the subject, following him outside into the corridor as he left the room. But to her queries he made only the vaguest of answers, saying finally: 'Well, Doctor de Groot likes you, Lucy, you are contributing to his recovery—besides, I'm allowing him home the day after tomorrow.' He gave her a questioning look. 'You're happy? They're kind to you? You get your off duty?'

'Oh yes, thank you, everyone's super. I'm glad Doctor de Groot is doing so well. I didn't know that he was ill, he never mentioned it.'

Fraam smiled. 'No. But he began to lose the use of his fingers and it was noticed...'

'By you?' Lucy smiled with a warmth to light up her ordinary face. 'Can he do a bit more when he's home? He's sometimes a bit difficult—I mean, wanting to go back to work...'

'Out of the question for a little while, but we must think up something—someone from the clinic could call round each day and give him particulars of the cases...I'll see about that.' His eyes searched hers. 'You're to have a day off once he's settled in—I'll get a nurse to relieve you.'

'I'm all right, thank you. I wouldn't know what to do with a whole day to myself.'

'No? We'll see.' He turned abruptly and strode away from her and she went back to her patient, sitting up in bed and grumbling because someone had forgotten to send some books he had particularly asked for.

The move back to Doctor de Groot's flat was made with the greatest of ease; the patient was getting his own way so he was his normal pleasant self, a gentle elderly man with a joke for everyone. Lucy prayed that his mood would last as she installed him in his own room and equipped the dressing room leading from it with the necessities she might require. And it did, but only until that evening, when Doctor de Groot exploded into rage because no one had been to see him. 'Probably the clinic is in a complete state of chaos,' he barked at Lucy. 'Why has no one kept me informed? Why hasn't Fraam been to see me?'

As though in answer to his question the telephone rang and Lucy hurried to answer it. Fraam's voice was quiet and calm. 'Lucy? Can you get Doctor de Groot to the telephone? I'm tied up at the hospital, but at least I can give him some details about the clinic. Is he anxious about it?'

'Yes,' said Lucy baldly. 'I'll get him.'

She gave her patient an arm across the room, pushed a chair under him and went out of the room and returned ten minutes later to find him quite cheerful again. 'Willem is coming round in the morning,' he told her. 'He's down at the clinic now, so he will have the very latest reports. Fraam won't be over for a time.' He cast Lucy a quick look and she schooled her features into polite interest. 'Plenty of work at the hospital,' he explained, 'and his social life is rather full at the moment.'

'Indeed?' Lucy wondered which girl it was this time—perhaps it was the right one; she was bound to turn up sooner or later. She sighed soundlessly and said brightly: 'Mies will be back tomorrow, won't she?' Mies was staying with Willem's family for a couple of days.

Three days went by. On each of them Fraam telephoned for a report on his patient and Willem, when he called, examined him before he sat down to recount the happenings at the clinic. It was quite late on the third evening, while Mies and Willem were at the *bioscoop*, that the front door bell sounded and Lucy went to answer it. 'Hullo,' said Fraam, 'rather late for a visit, I'm afraid, but I've managed to fit it in.'

Between what? Lucy asked herself silently. He was in a dinner jacket, so presumably he was either on the way to or from some social function.

She wished him good evening in a rather colourless voice and led the way to her patient's room. Doctor de Groot was sitting by the fire, a table loaded with books and papers at his elbow. He thrust these aside as his visitor went in and welcomed him with real pleasure, to plunge at once into a series of questions, brushing aside Fraam's enquiries as to his own health. He did pause once to ask Lucy to make them some coffee and when she had done so and poured it out for them both, suggested that she might go to bed. 'We'll be talking for some time and I'm quite able to get myself into bed later on.'

It was Fraam who answered him. 'I'm going to take those stitches out—they're due out in the morning, and an hour or two sooner won't matter. Then Lucy can get you settled in bed and if you still want to talk, we can carry on from there. I can't come tomorrow—I'm operating in the morning and I've a date after that.'

'If you say so,' grumbled Doctor de Groot. 'I shall go down to the clinic tomorrow.'

'No, you won't. I'm free, more or less, on the day after, though; we'll all three go, but don't imagine you're going to do any work. Willem can take over for a week or two. And Lucy must have a free day—after you've convinced yourself that the clinic is still standing, I shall hand you over to Mies for the rest of the day—Lucy needs a change.'

Lucy stood listening to him, not all that pleased that he was arranging everything without a word to her. Supposing she didn't want a day off? No one had consulted her about it—besides, in another week she would be going home again. She would have liked to have told him so, but he forestalled her by asking her where her own coffee cup was and when she said she didn't want any, suggested that she should make ready for the removal of the stitches.

Everything she needed was in the dressing room.

She laid scissors and forceps and a sterile towel and swabs ready and waited there quietly while the two men drank their coffee. When they joined her presently Fraam asked, half laughing, 'Don't you like us any more, Lucy?'

She didn't answer but took his jacket when he took it off and then offered him a clean towel with which to dry his hands. The stitches took no time at all; Fraam whisked them out, laid them neatly on a bit of gauze so that Doctor de Groot might check them for himself, sprayed the neat incision and washed his hands again. 'Shall we finish our talk?' he wanted to know.

'Certainly. Lucy, go to bed.'

She eyed him calmly. 'I can't—not until Mies comes in, she's mislaid her key so I'll have to open the door.'

'I'll do that.' Fraam sounded a little impatient. 'I'll see that Doctor de Groot gets into his bed, too. Goodnight, Lucy.'

She wished them both goodnight in a quiet voice which betrayed none of the annoyance she felt.

And the next morning Doctor de Groot told her happily that Fraam would be calling for them the following morning and could she be ready by ten o'clock. 'A brief visit to the clinic,' he explained airily, 'and then you are to have the rest of the day to yourself. Mies will come for me in a taxi.'

'When?'

'Oh, don't worry, you will be able to see me safely into it before you go off.'

'But Doctor de Groot, I'm not sure that I want to have a day off—I've no plans.'

He waved a vague hand. 'Plans? What does a young thing like you want with plans? All Amsterdam before you and you want plans! Go out and enjoy yourself—have you any money, my dear?'

'Yes, thank you, enough for a meal and that sort of thing.'

'Ah, good. If it's not too cold outside, we'll walk to the corner and back, shall we?'

She had both of them ready by ten o'clock, Doctor de Groot well muffled against the chilly wind and herself buttoned into her winter coat. She was wearing a sensible pair of shoes too; if she was to spend the day walking around the city, she had better have comfortable feet. 'What time shall I come back?' she asked.

'Any time you like, Lucy—take a key and let yourself in.'

She had a clear mental picture of herself filling in the evening hours with a cinema and then eating a *broodje* as slowly as possible. She hadn't enough money to go to a restaurant and she wasn't sure that she wanted to even if she had.

Fraam was punctual, driving the Rolls so that the doctor should have a comfortable ride. Mies had gone on ahead, for she had continued to work while her father was ill, but she would leave early that day in order to go back home with him. She had been a little mysterious when she had told Lucy the evening before, but Lucy hadn't asked questions; it would be something to do with Willem, she supposed.

The clinic was crowded with patients. Fraam, leading the way down the passage to Doctor de Groot's room, sat him in his chair and said: 'You may have half an hour.'

'My dear Fraam, what can I do in that short time?'

'Nothing much, that's why I said half an hour. Longer tomorrow, perhaps. Now, what do you want to do first? See Willem—Jo's here, too, and so is Doctor Fiske.'

'Willem and Fiske, then. What about you?'

'I'll see a couple of patients while I'm here.' Fraam's eyes slid to Lucy, standing between them. 'Will you wait for half an hour, Lucy? Perhaps with Mies.'

She couldn't really see why she had to wait. There were plenty of people to see the doctor back to his house; on the other hand, there would be less day to get through… She nodded and went to find Mies and give her a hand with the patients' files.

It seemed less than half an hour when Fraam put his head round the door: 'Mies, your father's ready to leave.' He had his own coat on again, too, so presumably he was driving them back after all. Lucy got up too and went to the door with Mies, to find a taxi there and Doctor de Groot already in it. He called cheerfully to her as Mies got in and she smiled and waved and then turned away to start walking into the city. Mies had said it wasn't a very nice part for a girl to walk alone, but she wasn't worried about that.

Fraam's hand on her arm stopped her before she had gone ten yards.

'Wrong way,' he observed blandly, 'the car's over here.'

'I should like to walk,' she told him, 'thank you all the same.'

'So you shall, but I can't leave the car here, I'll take it home and we can start walking from there.'

'We?' she asked weakly.

'I told you that I had a day off.'

'Yes—but…'

'Well, we're going to spend it together.'

It didn't make sense. 'It's very kind of you,' she began, 'but there's no need. I mean, I don't suppose you get many days off and it's a pity to waste one.'

'Why should I be wasting it?' He sounded amused, standing there on the pavement, looking down at her.

'Well,' she began once more, 'with me, you know.'

There was no one about, the bleak street was empty of everything but the wind, the shabby buildings around them presented blind fronts. Fraam bent down and kissed her very gently. 'For a parson's daughter,' he said in a gentle voice to melt her very bones, 'you talk a great deal of nonsense.' He took her arm and stuffed her just as gently into the Rolls and got in beside her. 'I'm going to marry you,' he told her. 'You can think about it on the way to the house.'

Of course she thought about it, but not coherently. Thoughts tumbled and jostled themselves round her head and none of them made sense. They were half-way there before she ventured without looking at him: 'Why?'

'We'll come to that later.'

'Yes, but—but I thought—there's a girl called Eloise…' She paused to think. 'And that lovely girl who was in the car when the little boy ran across the road…'

'For the life of me I can't remember her name. She was just a girl, Lucy, like quite a few others. Eloise too.' He allowed the Rolls to sigh to a dignified halt before his house and turned to look at her. 'Do you mind?'

'No, not in the least.' A whopping great lie; she minded very much, she was, she discovered, fiercely jealous of each and every one of them.

'No? I'm disappointed, I hoped that you would mind very much.' He didn't sound in the least disappointed.

Jaap had the door open and his dignified smile held a welcome. 'Coffee is in the small sitting room,' he informed them, and led the way across the hall to throw open a door. Lucy, following him, thought that Fraam must be one of the few people left in the world whose servants treated him as though he were something to be cherished.

The room was small and extremely comfortably furnished with deep velvet-covered chairs and sofas in a rich plum colour. The walls were white and hung with paintings—lovely flower paintings, delicately done. There was a fire burning in the small marble fireplace and as they went in a stout, fresh-faced girl brought in the coffee tray.

'Take off that coat,' suggested Fraam, 'and sit over here by the fire.' He had flung his own coat down as they had entered the hall and she put hers tidily over the back of a chair and sat down, wishing she was wearing something smarter than the tweed skirt and woolly sweater she had considered good enough for her day out.

She was feeling awkward too, although it was obvious that Fraam was perfectly at ease. He gave her her coffee and began to discuss what they should do with their day, but only to put her at her ease, for presently he said: 'Supposing we don't do any sight-seeing and go to my mother's for lunch?'

She choked a little on her coffee. 'Your mother? But does she…where does she live?' She tried to sound cool while all the while all she wanted to do was to fling down her delicate coffee cup and beg him to explain—there must be some reason why he wanted to marry her, he couldn't love her, and surely she wasn't the kind of girl with whom a man got infatuated? Perhaps she was a change from all the lovely creatures she had seen him with?

She heard him laugh softly. 'You're not listening and I can read every thought in your face, Lucy. Mother lives in Wassenaar. If you like, we'll have lunch with her and my father and then go for a walk—there's miles of beach—it's empty at this time of year.' He got up to fill her coffee cup. 'You don't believe me, do you? Perhaps when we've had our walk, you will.'

They set out half an hour later, Fraam chatting easily about nothing that mattered and Lucy almost silent, a dozen questions on her tongue and not daring to utter one of them.

Fraam's parents had a house by the sea, with the golf course behind the house and the wide sands only a few hundred yards away. The house was large and Edwardian in style, with a great many small windows and balconies and a roof which arched itself over them like eyebrows. It was encircled by a large garden, very neat and bare now that winter was upon them, but behind the flower beds there were a great many trees, sheltering it from the stares of anyone on the road. Lucy, who still hadn't found her tongue, crossed the well raked gravel beside Fraam and when he opened the door beneath a heavy arch, went past him into a square lobby. They were met here by a bustling elderly woman who opened the inner door for them, made some laughing rejoinder to Fraam's greeting and then smiled at Lucy. 'This is Ton—she housekeeps for my mother. If you like to go with her you can leave your coat.'

He spoke in a friendly way, but there was nothing warmer in his manner than that; Lucy, following Ton across the hall to a small cloakroom, began to wonder if she had dreamt their conversation. She still looked bewildered when she returned to where he was waiting for her in the hall, but it hadn't been a dream; he bent and kissed her hard before taking her arm and ushering her down a short passage and into a room at the side of the house. It was high-ceilinged, as most Dutch houses are, with a heavily embossed hanging on the walls, a richly coloured carpet covering most of the parquet floor and some quite beautiful William and Mary furniture.

Fraam's parents were there, standing at one of the big windows looking out over the garden, but they turned as they went in and came forward to greet them, looking not in the least surprised. And although nothing was said either then or during the lunch they presently ate, she couldn't fail to see that she was regarded as part of the family, so that presently, walking briskly along the hard sand with Fraam, she was emboldened to ask: 'Do your parents know—about—well, about you asking me to marry you?'

He had tucked a hand under her arm, steadying her against the wind. 'Oh, yes—I mentioned it some time ago.'

She turned her head to look at him. 'Some time ago? But you never said...' She trailed off into silence, and watched him smile.

'No. I had to wait for the right moment, didn't I?' He stopped and turned her round to face him. 'And perhaps this is the right moment for you to give me your answer.'

He hadn't said that he loved her, had he? But he wanted to marry her. She would make him a good wife; she was sure of that because she loved him. She put up a hand to tuck in a strand of hair the wind had whipped loose.

'Yes, I'll marry you, Fraam. I'm—I'm still surprised about it, but I'm quite sure.'

'Why are you sure, dear girl?'

She met his steady gaze without affectation. 'I love you, Fraam; I didn't know until that day we were shovelling snow...'

'I know, Lucy.' His voice was very gentle.

She looked at him, startled. 'Oh, did you? How?'

He had pulled her close. 'I'm a mind-reader, especially when it comes to you.' He kissed her slowly. 'We'll marry soon, Lucy—there's no reason why we shouldn't, is there?'

She rubbed her cheek against the thick wool of his coat. 'Yes, there is. I have to give a month's notice.'

'I'll settle that,' he told her carelessly. 'You won't need to go back to St Norbert's.'

'Oh, but I must—I mean, it will all have to be explained.' She frowned a little. 'I can't just walk out.'

'We'll sort that out later on.' Fraam started to walk again, his arm round her shoulders. 'We'll telephone your mother and father when we go back.'

'They'll be surprised.'

He said on a laugh: 'Your mother won't.' And then: 'You'll be able to leave Doctor de Groot in a couple of days and come to my house until we can go back to England—I've several cases coming up, I'm afraid…'

'Oh, but I can't do that!'

She felt his hand tighten on her shoulder. 'You haven't met my young sister yet, have you? She's coming to pay me a visit—you'll enjoy getting to know her.'

'Oh,' said Lucy again, 'well, yes, I shall.' The wind was in their faces now and the seashore looked bleak and grey under the wintry sky—the bad weather had come early, there had been no mild days for quite a while. She was cold even in her winter coat but so happy that she hardly felt it. None of it seemed real, of course; just a lovely dream which could shatter and become her mundane life once more with no Fraam in it. 'I can't think why...' she began, and caught her breath.

'You're still scared, aren't you? When you're quite used to the idea, I'll tell you why.' He smiled so kindly that she felt a lump in her throat. 'Mama wanted us to stay for dinner, but I thought we would go somewhere and dine together. Would you like that?'

Lucy nodded and then frowned. 'I'm not dressed for going out.'

'You look perfectly all right to me—we'll go to Dikker and Thijs, it'll be quiet at this time of year, we can stay as long as we like.'

It was a lovely evening. Lucy, lying wide awake in bed that night, went over every second of it, fingering the magnificent ruby and diamond ring on her finger. Fraam had taken it from his pocket during the evening and put it there and by some good chance it had fitted perfectly. It was old, he had explained, left to him by his grandmother when he had been a very young man; he had promised himself then that he would keep it until he could put it on the hand of the girl he was going to marry. Lucy sat up in bed and turned the light on just to have another look at it. It was so beautiful that she left the light on and sat up against her pillows and went on thinking about the evening.

Fraam's parents had been kind. They had welcomed her into the family with just the right kind of remarks, told her that she was to come and see them again as soon as possible and expressed their delight at the idea of having her for a daughter-in-law. And Fraam had been a dear. She repeated that to herself because right at the back of her mind was the vague thought that he still hadn't said that he loved her and his manner, although flatteringly attentive, had been almost like that of an old friend, not a man who had just proposed. She wanted too much, she told herself; more than likely she wasn't a girl to inspire that kind of feeling in a man. It was surely enough that he wanted her for his wife. She went to sleep on the thought and by morning her doubts had dwindled to mere wisps in her mind.

Mies was flatteringly impressed but disconcertingly surprised too. She exclaimed with unthinking frankness: 'I am amazed, Lucy—Fraam has had eyes only for Adilia, who is beautiful—when you returned to England he took her out many times. What will your parents say?'

'They're delighted.' Lucy tried to speak lightly, but she frowned as she spoke. Here was a new name and a new girl. 'Adilia—I don't think I've heard about her. Did I ever meet her?'

Mies thought. 'Fraam danced with her at the hospital ball, she was wearing a flame-coloured dress, very chic. They've known each other for ages. I quite thought...' She looked at Lucy's face and added brightly: 'But that means nothing; he has had so many girl-friends, but Adilia he sees more than the others. But not of course now that he is engaged to you.' She added hastily: 'You must not be worried.'

'I'm not in the least worried,' declared Lucy, consumed with enough worry to sink her. She would ask Fraam; he would probably see her during the day. She cheered up at the thought and went along to see how Doctor de Groot was and to break the news to him. He wasn't in the least surprised, indeed he suggested that she might like to leave then and there. 'I'm quite able to look after myself,' he told her, 'and Fraam did mention something about his sister paying him a visit—I daresay he plans for you to go and stay with him while she's there.'

'Well, yes, he does. But don't you want me here? I never did have much to do, I know, but you're not going back to work yet...'

He looked benignly at her. 'Just an hour each day,' he murmured. 'I've already discussed it with Fraam—I'll go away for Christmas as I said I would, but I just want to keep my hand in. Now run along, my dear, I daresay Fraam will be along to see you.'

But Fraam didn't come—he telephoned at lunch time to say that he wouldn't be able to get away but could she be ready if he called for her after breakfast the next day? He sounded remote and cool, and Lucy, anxious for her world to be quite perfect, put that down to pressure of work and perhaps other people listening to him telephoning. All the same, she thought wistfully, he could have called her dear just once. She shook her head to rid it of the doubts which kept filling it; just because Mies had told her about Adilia; probably it was all hot air...

She was ready and waiting when he arrived the next morning and his hard, urgent kiss was more than she had expected—a great deal more, she decided happily as they made their farewells and she got into the Mini beside him. Mies must have got it all wrong about Adilia. She responded to Fraam's easy conversation with a lightheartedness which gave her a happy glow.

His sister came into the hall the moment they entered the house and before Fraam could speak volunteered the information that her name was Lisabertha, that she was delighted to meet Lucy, that they were almost the same age and that she was quite positive that they would be the firmest of friends. She paused just long enough to give Lucy a hug and then throw her arms round her brother's neck. 'Dear Fraam,' she declared, 'isn't this fun? And may I ask Rob to dinner this evening?' She turned to Lucy. 'I'm going to marry him next year,' she told her. 'He works in Utrecht, but he said he could get here by seven o'clock.'

Fraam chuckled. 'So he's already been asked to dinner?' He smiled at Lucy. 'If you two like to go into the sitting room I'll get Jaap to take the cases up.'

He stayed and had coffee with them and then left them to their own devices with the remark that he had work to do and would see them that evening. Lucy, who would have liked to have been kissed again, got a friendly smile, that was all.

The day passed very pleasantly. Lisabertha was obviously the darling of her family and had a great fondness for her eldest brother; she talked about him for a good deal of the time and Lucy listened to every word, filling in the gaps about him with interesting titbits of information. He had been in love several times, his young sister informed her, but never seriously. They had all begun to think that he would never marry, and now here was dear Lucy, and how glad they were. Where had they met and when was the wedding to be and what was Lucy going to wear? To all of which Lucy gave vague replies. Their meeting had been most unglamorous and the less said about it the better, she decided, and she had no idea when they were to marry. Fraam had suggested that she left the hospital at once, but at the back of her mind she wasn't too sure about that. Supposing he were to change his mind? If she worked for another month, that would give him time to be quite sure. But even as she thought it, the other half of her mind was denying it. Fraam wasn't a man to change his mind.

Certainly there was nothing in his manner to give her any cause for doubt that evening. The three of them dined together and then sat round the fire in the drawing room, talking idly, until Lisabertha declared that she was going to bed, and when Lucy said that she would go too, Fraam begged her to stay a little longer. 'For I have hardly seen you,' he protested, 'and we have so much to discuss.'

But the discussion, it turned out, wasn't quite what she had expected: whether they should visit his parents on the following day or the one after, and had she any preference as to when she returned to England.

'Well, I hadn't thought about it,' said Lucy. 'If I give a month's notice I suppose the quicker I go back to St Norbert's the better.'

He frowned. 'You seem determined to do that,' he observed rather coldly. 'I told you that it could be arranged that you left at any time…' He got up and strolled over to the window and looked out into the dark night, holding back the heavy curtains. 'You are not anxious to marry me as soon as possible, then, Lucy?'

'Yes—well, no. It's…' she paused, at a loss for words. 'I mean, supposing you changed your mind and it would be too late.'

'You think that I might change my mind?' His voice was silky.

It seemed a good opportunity to take the bull by the horns. 'I'm not at all the kind of girl everyone expected you to marry; Mies said, and so did Lisa-

bertha, that you liked pretty girls—not like me at all.'
She drew a little breath and asked in a rush: 'Who
is Adilia?'

He didn't answer her for a long moment but stood
by the window still, staring at her. Finally he said:
'I have rushed things too fast, I believe. You are
uncertain of me, Lucy—indeed, possibly you don't
quite trust me. I will tell you who Adilia is and then
we will forget this whole conversation and return to
our former pleasant task of getting to know each
other. She is a girl I have known for some years; I
have never had any wish to marry her, just as I have
never had any wish to marry any of the girls I have
taken out from time to time.'

He walked over to her and pulled her gently to her
feet. 'I have never asked anyone to marry me before,
Lucy.' He bent and kissed her lightly. 'Go to bed,
my dear. I wish I had all day to spend with you
tomorrow, but I'm not free until the late afternoon.
We'll put off going to Mama's and we'll go out to
dine, just the two of us.' He put up a hand and
touched her cheek. 'You're a dear, old-fashioned girl,
aren't you? You need to be wooed slowly; I should
have known that.'

He was as good as his word. He came to take her
out the following evening and by the end of it Lucy
had almost made up her mind to leave the hospital
at once and marry him just as soon as he wanted her
to. They had dined at a quiet, luxurious hotel and

danced for a while afterwards, and she couldn't help but be flattered by the attention they received. Fraam was obviously a well-known client and although he took it all for granted, she was made a little shy by it. They had walked back through the quiet, cold streets afterwards, and when they had got back into the house she had actually been on the point of telling him that she would do as he wished, but the telephone had rung and when he had gone to answer it, he had bidden her a hurried goodnight and left the house.

She saw him at breakfast, but as he was on the point of going as she reached the table, there was no time for more than a quick kiss and an assurance that he would be home for lunch.

As indeed he was, but with a guest. 'Adilia,' he introduced her coolly, and Lucy, instantly disliking her, greeted her with a sweetness only matched by her new acquaintance.

'We met outside and since Adilia tells me that she is at a loose end I invited her for lunch.' He added carelessly: 'I told Jaap as we came in. And what have you two been doing with your morning?'

He sat down between Lisabertha and Adilia, opposite Lucy, and it was to her he looked. Lucy began some sort of a reply, to be interrupted gently by Adilia, who demanded, in the prettiest way imaginable, that she might be given a drink. And after that she kept the conversation in her own hands, and during lunch as well, even though Lisabertha did her best to start up a more general conversation so that Lucy might join in; for how could she do that when the talk was of people she didn't know and times when she hadn't even known Fraam. She looked composed enough, made polite rejoinders when she was addressed and seethed inside her. Adilia might only be a girl Fraam had known for years, but she was a beautiful one and she had a lovely voice, a low laugh and the kind of clothes Lucy had hankered after for years. She decided that the wisest course was to attempt no competition at all and was pleased to see presently that Adilia found it disconcerting. All the same they parted on the friendliest of terms, and Lucy, talking animatedly, managed to avoid Fraam, calling a casual goodbye as he went through the door with Adilia, who had begged a lift, beside him.

'You do not like her,' declared Lisabertha instantly, leading the way back to the sitting room.

'I can't say I do,' agreed Lucy, 'though I daresay I'm jealous of her; she's quite beautiful and she wears gorgeous clothes.'

'And you also will wear such clothes when you are Fraam's wife, and you may not be a beauty, but he has chosen you, has he not?'

Lucy said 'Yes' doubtfully and because she didn't want to talk about it, said that she had letters to write and had better get them done and posted.

And that evening, when Fraam came home and

they were having drinks before dinner, he asked her what she had thought of Adilia. It would have been nice to have told him what she did think, but instead she said rather colourlessly that Adilia was beautiful. He laughed then and added: 'So now you know what she's like, my dear.'

CHAPTER NINE

LUCY HAD SPENT an almost sleepless night wondering exactly what Fraam had meant. He hadn't said any more; dinner had been a pleasant affair, just the three of them, and the talk had been of the family dinner party at their mother's house the next evening. 'Have you got that green dress with you?' Fraam wanted to know, and when Lucy answered a surprised yes: 'Then wear it, my dear, it suits you very well.' He had smiled to send her heart dancing: 'There will be more family for you to meet; there are a great many of us…'

'Aunts and uncles,' chimed in Lisabertha, 'and cousins. I suppose that horrid Tante Sophie will be there.'

'Naturally, and you will be nice to her, Lisa, although I think that we must all take care that Lucy doesn't fall into her clutches.'

'Why not?' asked Lucy.

'She is malicious. Perhaps she does not mean to be, but she can be unkind.'

'Well, if I don't understand her…'

'She speaks excellent English. But don't worry, we'll not give her a chance to get you alone.'

All the same, Lucy found herself alone with the lady the next evening. Dinner was over, a splendid, leisurely meal, shared by some twenty people and all of them, it seemed, der Linssens. They had had their coffee in the drawing room and had broken up into small groups the better to talk, and someone or other had delayed Fraam as they had been crossing the room, and Lucy found herself alone. But only for a moment. Tante Sophie had appeared beside her and no one had noticed her taking Lucy by the arm and leading her on to the covered balcony adjoining the drawing room.

'I'm really waiting for Fraam,' began Lucy. 'He's just stopped to speak to someone...'

'He will find us here,' beamed Tante Sophie. 'I have been so anxious to have you to myself for just a few minutes, Lucy. Such a sweet girl you are, you will make an excellent wife for Fraam; so quiet and malleable and never questioning.'

'Why should I question him?' asked Lucy curiously.

Tante Sophie looked arch. 'My dear, surely you know that Fraam is what you call a lady's man? That is an old-fashioned term, is it not, but I am sure that you understand it. So many pretty girls...' she sighed, 'the fortunate man, he could have taken his pick of any one of them, but he chose you. You haven't known him long?' Her voice had grown a little sharp.

Lucy didn't answer. She wondered if it would be very rude if she just walked away, but Tante Sophie still had a beringed hand on her arm.

'Of course, my dear Lucy, we older ones find it difficult to understand you young people—not that Fraam is a young man…' Lucy opened her mouth to make an indignant protest, but she had no chance. 'You are permissive, is that not the right word? Why, I could tell you tales—but wives turn a blind eye these days, it seems, just as you will learn to do.'

Tante Sophie had small, beady black eyes. Like a snake, thought Lucy, staring at her and trying to think of something to say. The lady was so obviously wanting her to ask all the questions she was just as obviously wanting to answer. When she didn't speak Tante Sophie said tartly: 'Well, it is to be hoped that he won't break your heart; he's never loved a girl for more than a few days.'

Lucy felt Fraam's large hand on her shoulder. Its pressure was reassuring and very comforting. 'He's never loved a girl,' he corrected the old lady blandly, 'until now. Have you been trying to frighten Lucy, Tante Sophie?' His voice was light, but Lucy could feel his anger.

'Of course not!' The elderly voice was shrill with spite. 'Well, I must go and talk to your mother, Fraam.' Her peevish gaze swept the room behind them. 'Such a pity it is just family. A few of those lovely girls of yours would have made the evening a good deal livelier.'

They watched her go, and Fraam's hand slipped from Lucy's shoulder to her waist. 'Sorry about that,' he observed easily. 'Do you want to call our engagement off?'

He was laughing as he spoke and she laughed back at him. Now he was there beside her, all the silly little doubts Tante Sophie's barbed remarks had raised were quieted. 'Of course not! She must be very unhappy to talk like that.'

'Clever girl to see that. Yes, she is, that's why we all bear with her.' He smiled down at her and for a moment Lucy thought that he was going to kiss her. But he didn't—perhaps, she told herself sensibly, because someone might turn round and see them, but it didn't matter; he loved her and everything was all right.

All right until lunch time the next day. She and Lisabertha had been out shopping and while they were waiting to cross the busy street at the Munt, she saw the unmistakable Panther de Ville coming towards them. And Adilia was sitting beside Fraam. Lucy watched it pass them in silence and it was Lisabertha who exclaimed: 'Well, what on earth is she doing with Fraam? He told me he was working until at least three o'clock.'

'Perhaps he finished early,' Lucy heard her voice, carefully colourless, utter the trite words, and her companion hastened to agree with her. But Lucy didn't really listen; she was thinking about Adilia. In the few seconds during which the car had passed, Lucy had had the general impression of loveliness and chic and beautiful clothes, and an even stronger impression that Adilia had seen her...

By the time they got home she was in a splendid turmoil of temper, hurt, and doubt. She could hardly wait until Fraam returned so that she might unburden herself; men who were just engaged didn't go riding round the city with other girls, nor did they tell lies about working until three o'clock when they weren't. When he did get home she was sitting in the drawing room alone, for Lisabertha, sensing her mood, had retired discreetly to her room. Fraam barely had time to close the door behind him when she told him icily: 'I saw you this afternoon—at lunchtime—with Adilia. You said you would be working until three o'clock.' She added waspishly: 'I suppose you took her out to lunch.'

His expression didn't change at all and she couldn't see the gleam in his eyes. 'Er—no, my dear.' She waited for him to say something more than that and when he didn't she got up and started for the door. She knew that she was behaving childishly and that she would probably burst into tears in no time at all; she had been spoiling for a nice down-to-earth quarrel and Fraam had no intention of quarrelling. Was this what Tante Sophie had meant? Was this learning to turn a blind eye? A sob bubbled up in her throat and escaped just as she had a hand on the door, but she never opened it. Fraam had got there too and turned her round and caught her close.

'Now, now, my love,' he said soothingly, 'what's all this?' He kissed the top of her head. 'I believe Tante Sophie's hints and spite did their work, after all.' He turned her face up to his and carefully wiped away a tear. 'I told you I would be working until three o'clock, but what I didn't explain was that I had a list at another hospital. I was driving there when Adilia stopped me and asked for a lift. And I didn't have lunch with her—indeed, I haven't had lunch at all.'

'Oh, aren't I awful?' Lucy said woefully, 'jumping to conclusions, and you going without your lunch. I feel mean and a bit silly.'

'You're not mean and you're not silly, but supposing we get married as soon as we can, then you'll be quite sure of me, won't you?'

'You mean I'm not quite sure of you now?' she asked him quickly. 'Well, no, perhaps I'm not. But don't you see, while I'm not then how can I marry you?' She went on earnestly: 'I think I should go back to St Norbert's and—and not see you for a bit and then you'll be sure…'

'Sure of what?' His voice was very quiet.

'Well, wanting to marry me.'

'And you? Would you be sure then, Lucy?'

She looked at him in surprise. 'Me? Oh, but I'm sure—I mean, sure that I love you.'

'So it is for me that you wish to go back to hospital? Not for yourself?'

She nodded. 'Yes. You do have to be quite certain.'

'And you think that I am not. Shall I tell you something, Lucy? The world is full of Adilias, but there is only one Lucy.' He pulled her to him and kissed her slowly. 'I can't teach you to trust me; that's something you must do for yourself, and I think that you do trust me, only you have this ridiculous idea that every girl in the world is beautiful except you, and because of that you have this chip on your shoulder which prevents you from accepting the fact that anyone could possibly want to marry you.'

'I have not got a chip on my shoulder,' said Lucy pettishly. 'I'm trying to be sensible.' She wanted to cry again, but she didn't know why.

'All right, no chip.' He kissed her again. 'We won't talk about it any more now; I have to go back to my rooms after tea, but after dinner this evening we'll talk again, and this time I shall persuade you to change your mind and marry me as soon as possible.'

She leaned her head against his shoulder and thought that probably she would be persuaded because that was what she wanted to do really. She said quite happily: 'Yes, all right—I like being with you and talking, Fraam.'

They had tea together presently, and Lucy had felt utterly content. This was going to be marriage with Fraam; quiet half hours in which to talk and knowing that he would be home again in the evening. Just the sight of him sitting opposite her, drinking his tea and eating cake and telling her about his day at the hospital, made her feel slightly giddy with happiness. Her matter-of-fact acceptance of her plain face was being edged away by a new-found assurance stemming from that same happiness and after all not many girls had green eyes. When Fraam had gone she went upstairs and washed her hair and wound it painstakingly into rollers while she did her face. The results were not startling but at least they were an improvement. She would buy a new dress or two, she thought happily, and when later that evening they would have their talk, she would agree to anything he said. He had been right, of course; the reason why she wasn't quite sure of him was because she hadn't quite believed that he could prefer her to other girls. She skipped downstairs to wait for him.

He didn't come. There was a telephone message a little later to say that there had been an accident—one of the surgeons on duty—and Fraam would stay in his place until he could be relieved. The two girls dined alone and the evening passed pleasantly enough discussing the clothes Lucy would like to buy. 'Get all you want,' advised Lisabertha. 'Fraam has a great deal of money and he will pay the bills.'

'I'd rather not—at least, not until he suggests it, if he ever does. I've some money, enough to buy a dress.'

They went to bed presently and Lucy, thinking of Fraam, slept dreamlessly.

He was at breakfast the next morning, immersed in his letters, making notes in his pocketbook and scanning the newspaper headlines. He got up when she joined him, settled her in a chair beside him, declared in a rather absentminded way that she looked as pretty as a picture, kissed her briefly and went on: 'I have to go to Brussels this morning—there's a patient there I've looked after for some time and his own doctor wants me there for a consultation. I'm flying down, Jaap will take me to Schiphol, and I should be back this evening—wait up for me, Lucy, there is something I want to tell you.'

'Can't you tell me now?' She tried not to sound anxious. His 'no' was very decisive.

Lucy was alone in the sitting room after lunch when Jaap came into the room.

'There is a visitor for you, Miss Prendergast,' he announced uneasily.

Adilia looked lovely, but then she always did. She brushed past Jaap as though he weren't there and addressed Lucy. 'I've come to fetch some things I forgot to take with me.'

Lucy felt puzzled. 'Things?' she asked, and added politely: 'Well, I'm sure Fraam won't mind if you collect them—where did you leave them?'

Adilia gave her a wicked look. 'Upstairs, of course—where else do you suppose? In the Brocade Room.' She gave a little laugh. 'Fraam called you the parson's daughter, and you really are, aren't you?'

She sank down into one of the large winged chairs, apparently in no hurry, arranging herself comfortably before she observed: 'Why do you suppose Fraam is marrying you, Lucy? He needs a wife...' she glanced round the beautiful room, 'someone to run his household and rear his children. That's not for me,' she shrugged briefly. 'I'm all for freedom, so he can't have me—not on a permanent basis—and now he doesn't care who he marries. You will do as well as any, I daresay—probably better.'

Lucy felt cold inside and there was a peculiar sensation in her head. All the same she said sturdily: 'I don't believe you.'

Adilia got up, stretched herself and yawned prettily. 'It's all the same to me. You will be an excellent wife, for you will never allow yourself to wonder if Fraam is really in Munich or Brussels at some seminar or other, or ask where he has been when he comes home late.' She nodded her beautiful head. 'It is a great advantage to be a parson's daughter—he sees that too.'

Lucy was on her feet now, her small capable hands clenched on either side of her. 'I still don't believe you,' she said, and somehow managed to keep her doubts out of her voice.

'You don't want to. Fraam is in Brussels, is he not, or so he told you.' Adilia tugged the bell rope and when Jaap came: 'Jaap, you drove Mr der Linssen to Schiphol, did you not? We are both so silly, we cannot remember where he was going.'

Jaap marshalled his English. 'To London, Juffrouw—the ten o'clock flight.'

Adilia nodded dismissal and he went away, looking puzzled and a little worried; Miss Prendergast had looked quite ill when he had said that…

'You see?' asked Adilia when the door had been closed. She crossed the room and tapped Lucy on the shoulder. 'Jaap does not lie—you have to believe him. And now you will have to believe me; I am going to London too.'

She went to the door. 'There is one thing of which you may be very sure: I am very discreet. But what should you care? You will have what you want—this house, Fraam's money and a clutch of children—they will be plain, just like you.'

She had gone, closing the door very quietly behind her, and Lucy stood speechless, the strength of her feelings tearing through her like a force ten gale. Rage and misery and humiliation all jostled for a place in her bewildered head and for the moment at any rate, rage won. She tore at the ring on her finger and then raced from the room, up the stairs and into her bedroom, there to fling on her coat, tie a scarf over her hair and snatch up her gloves. She was in the hall and almost at the door when Jaap came through the little arched door which led to the kitchens.

'You go out, miss?' he asked. He didn't allow his well-schooled features to lose their blandness, but his voice was anxious.

'Yes. Yes, Jaap.' She looked at him quite wildly, still re-living those terrible minutes with Adilia. 'I'm going away.' She darted past him, got the heavy door open and was away before he could stop her.

She had no idea where she was going, but she wasn't thinking about that. She had no idea in which direction she was walking either; she was running away, intent on putting as much distance between her and her hurt as possible. She hurried along, thinking how strange it was that she had been so happy and that just a few words from someone could sweep that happiness away like sand before the wind.

She walked on, right through the heart of the city, without being aware of it, and when the street she was in merged into the Mauritskade, she turned along it and then into Stadhouderskade and so into Leidsestraat. She trudged down that too, and if it hadn't begun to rain she might have gone on and on and ended up at Schiphol; as it was she turned round and started back again towards the centre of Amsterdam. She was tired now and she wasn't really thinking any more, aware only of a dull headache and an empty feeling deep inside her. It had grown from afternoon dusk to wintry evening and she realised that she was cold and hungry and needed to rest, and over and above that, it was impossible for her to go back to Fraam's house ever again. She would go home, of course, but just at the moment she was quite incapable of making any plans, first she must have a meal.

She had reached the inner ring of the *grachten* again and there were hotels on every side. She recognised one of them; Fraam had taken her there to dine only a short time ago. She went inside and booked a room at the reception desk, for she had to sleep somewhere and she remembered that he had told her that it was a respectable hotel. She didn't ask the price of the room; her head was still full of her own unhappy thoughts and she brushed aside the receptionist's polite enquiry as to luggage, following the bell boy into the lift like an automaton and when she was alone in the room, sitting down without even taking her coat off. But presently she bestirred herself and looked around her. The apartment was luxurious, more so than she had expected, and the adjoining bathroom was quite magnificent. She washed her white face and telephoned for a meal. It was while she was waiting for it that she realised that she had no money. And no passport either.

She ate her dinner when it came because whatever trouble lay ahead of her, and there would be trouble, it would be easier to face if she were nicely full; all the same, she had no idea what she ate.

When the room waiter had cleared away she undressed, had a bath and got into bed. She already owed for her dinner, she might as well owe for a night's rest as well. She really didn't care what they would do to her, although she wondered what the Dutch prisons were like. But her thoughts soon returned to Fraam. She would have to send him a message or write to him—probably from prison. She chuckled at the thought and the chuckle turned into tears until, quite worn out with her weeping, she slept.

She woke in the night, her mind clear and sensible; all she had to do was to telephone Jaap in the morning and ask him to send round her handbag. All the money she possessed was in it, and so was her passport. It was a pity she would have to leave her clothes behind, but they weren't important; she would be able to pay the bill and go to Schiphol and catch the first flight possible. She wondered if she had enough money; as far as she could remember there had been all of fifty pounds in her purse, surely more than sufficient. She closed her eyes and slept again.

It was after breakfast, taken in her room, and an

unsatisfactory toilet that she went down to the reception desk. There was another clerk on duty now, a sharp-faced woman who bade her a grudging good morning and asked her if she wanted her bill.

It seemed the right moment to explain. Lucy embarked on her story; she had left the house without her purse and could she telephone to have it sent to her at the hotel. It wasn't until she had come to the end of it that she saw that the clerk didn't believe a word of it. All the same she gave her the number. 'It's Mijnheer der Linssen's house,' she explained. 'He is known here, isn't he?' And when the woman nodded grudgingly: 'Well, I'm his fiancée.' Too late she saw the woman's eyes fly to her ringless hands. She had plucked off her lovely ring and left it…where had she left it? She had no idea.

'I'll call the manager,' said the clerk, still polite but hostile. And when he came, elegant and courteous, the whole story was repeated, but this time in Dutch and by the clerk, so that Lucy couldn't understand a word. At the end of it the manager spoke pleasantly enough. 'By all means make your call, Miss…' he refreshed his memory from the register before him, 'Miss Prendergast. Perhaps you wouldn't mind waiting in your room afterwards?' He smiled. 'Your handbag shall be brought to you there.'

Lucy sighed with relief and went to one of the telephone booths. Jaap sounded upset, but she didn't give him a chance to speak. 'My handbag,' she urged

him, 'it's on the dressing table in my room, please
will you send it round as soon as you can? You do
understand?' She heard him draw breath and his hurried 'Yes, miss,' but didn't give him a chance to say
anything else. 'And Jaap, don't tell anyone I'm
here—not anyone. Here's the address, and do please
hurry. And thank you, Jaap.'

She went upstairs at once since the manager had
been so insistent; perhaps they thought it would be
easier and save time if they knew where she was. It
was a little irksome to stay there, though, for the urge
to get away was getting stronger every minute. An
hour passed and she became more and more uneasy;
she didn't think that it would take all that time to
come from Fraam's house, she decided to go down
to the desk and see if it had been delivered and forgotten.

She had been locked in. She stared at the door in
disbelief and tried the handle again, fruitlessly, and
when she lifted the receiver no one answered. Not a
girl to panic, she went and sat down and tried to think
calmly. In a way it was a relief to have something
to worry about; it stopped her thinking about Fraam.
She thought of him now of course and tears she really couldn't stop spilled from her tired eyes and ran
down her unmade-up face. If he had been there, this
would never have happened, she told herself with
muddled logic. But he wasn't there, he was in London, possibly even now waiting eagerly at the airport

for Adilia. The thought made the tears flow even faster and she uttered a small wail. The sound of the key turning in the lock sent her round facing the wall so that they shouldn't see her face. When the door was opened and shut again she cried in a soggy whisper: 'Oh, do please go away!' only to swing round at once, because of course if they went away she wouldn't get her bag...

Fraam was standing there with a white and furious face, her handbag in his hand. He said in a bitter voice she hardly recognised: 'You wanted this? Presumably you left home so fast that you forgot it.'

He looked enquiringly at her, his brows raised, but she didn't answer him.

'You should be more careful,' he told her. 'You need both money and passport when you run away.' His eyes swept over her tatty person. 'Make-up too, and a comb.'

Surprise had checked her tears, but at this remark they all came rushing back again. How dared he poke fun at her! She meant to tell him so, but all she said in a wispy voice was: 'They locked me in.'

His mouth twitched. 'And quite right too. They weren't to know whether you were lying or not, were they? And you were lying, Lucy. I found your ring in your teacup—an extraordinary place—so I must take it that you are no longer my fiancée.' He added sternly: 'There is a law against false pretences.'

It seemed to Lucy that she was getting nowhere at

all. She had the right to upbraid him, but she had had no chance. To point out his duplicity, confront him with his two-faced behaviour. Suddenly indignant, she took a deep breath and opened her mouth. She was dreadfully unhappy, but an angry outburst might help her to forget that.

'And before you launch your attack,' said Fraam in a surprisingly mild voice now, 'I want an explanation.'

She choked on the words she had been preparing to utter. 'You want an explanation? It's me that wants one!' Her voice rose to a watery squeak. 'Adilia said…'

'Ah, now we are getting to the heart of the matter.'

Her rage had gone, there was nothing but a cold unhappy lump in her chest.

'Don't joke, Fraam—please don't joke,' and when she saw how good-humoured he was looking now, she added pettishly: 'Why do you look so pleased with yourself? Just now when you came in you were furiously angry.'

He was leaning against the wall, his hands in his pockets, looking, she was shocked to see, as though he was enjoying himself. 'My dear girl, no man worth his salt likes to find his fiancée—ex-fiancée—locked in an hotel bedroom because she can't pay the bill. Over and above that, I was roused from a night's sleep by Jaap's agitated request that I should catch the next plane and return home because you had left the house rather more hastily than he liked. I've had no breakfast and I'm tired, and until a few minutes ago, the most terrified man on earth. And now tell me what Adilia said to cause you to tear away in such a fashion.'

'You went to London,' Lucy pointed out in a wobbly voice, 'and you told me you were going to Brussels, and Adilia said—she said that she was going to London too and that I was a parson's daughter and you only wanted to marry me because she wouldn't have you.' She sucked in a breath like a tearful child. 'And she said I'd have p-plain children, just like me.'

A spasm passed over Fraam's handsome features. He dealt with what was obvious to him to be the most hurtful of these remarks. 'Little girls with green eyes and soft mouths are the most beautiful of God's creatures,' he said in a gentle voice, 'and as for the boys, they will be our sons, Lucy, with, I hope, their mother's sweet nature and my muscle.'

He left the wall so suddenly that the next thing she knew she was wrapped in his arms. 'You silly, silly little girl,' he observed, 'did you not know that I would come after you wherever you went?'

Lucy sniffed. It was very satisfying to feel his tight hold, but they still hadn't dealt with the crux of the matter. 'Adilia said…' she began, and was interrupted by Fraam's forceful: 'Damn Adilia, but since you have to get her off your chest, my darling, let us hear what the woman said and be done with it.'

It was a little difficult to begin. Lucy muttered and mumbled a good deal, but once she got started the words poured out in a jumble which hardly made sense. But Fraam listened patiently and when she paused at last, not at all sure that she had made herself clear, he had the salient points at his fingertips. 'Dear heart, will you believe me when I say that Adilia has never, at any time, stayed at my house? There was nothing of hers in the Brocade Room or anywhere else in my home. Why should there be? You have been the only girl, Lucy. She was making mischief—people do, you know; they're bored with their own lives and it amuses them to upset those of other people.'

'Of course I believe you,' declared Lucy, and added after a moment's thought: 'You went to London—she asked Jaap, you know, and he told us. Because I didn't believe her.'

'I went to London, my dearest darling, to see the Senior Nursing Officer of St Norbert's, for it had become increasingly clear to me that getting married to you was more important than anything else and all this hanging around for a month until you could leave was quite unnecessary. I saw your father briefly too and asked him about a licence. If you would agree, we could be married within the week.'

'But you didn't say a word...'

'I was afraid you would have all kinds of arguments against it, my love.' He kissed the top of her
head. 'No time to buy clothes, you would have said,
certainly no time to arrange for bridesmaids, no time
to send out invitations…'

Lucy considered. 'I don't mind about any of those
things,' she told him, 'though of course I must buy
a dress…'

'My dear sensible girl, and so beautiful too.' And
when she looked at him she saw that he meant it.
'At your home? And your father, of course. My family can fly over,' his eyes narrowed in thought, 'I'll
charter a plane.'

'But that's extravagant!'

'Surely one may be forgiven a little extravagance
at such a time, my darling.' He loosed her for a moment, found her ring in a pocket and slipped it on
her finger. 'Why a teacup?' he wanted to know.

'I don't know—I don't remember, I was so unhappy.'

'You shall never be unhappy again, dear heart.'
He kissed her slowly. 'And now we're going home.'

Lucy received the manager's apology with a smile.
She was so happy herself that she wanted everyone
else to be the same, only she longed to wave her
hand with the ring once more upon it under the
clerk's nose.

They hardly spoke as Fraam drove through the
city. It wasn't until they were in the hall with a beam-

ing Jaap shutting the door on the outside world that Lucy spoke.

'Fraam, were you ever in love with Adilia, or—or any of those girls you danced with at the hospital ball?'

He turned her round to face him, holding her gently by the shoulders.

'No, my love, just amusing myself while I was waiting for you to come along, and when you did I was so afraid that you would have none of me...I think I am still a little afraid of that.'

Lucy flung her arms round his neck. 'The first time you saw me—at that lecture, you looked as though you wanted to shake me.'

'Did I? I wanted to get off that platform and carry you off and marry you out of hand...I fell in love with you then, my darling.'

She leaned back the better to see his face. 'Did you really? And I looked such a mess!'

His hands were gentle on her. 'You looked beautiful, my darling, just as you look beautiful now.'

She leaned up and kissed him. 'That's such a satisfactory thing to have said of one,' she commented. 'I'm not sure that it's quite true, but oh, Fraam, I'm so glad I'm me!'

Jaap, coming from the dining room, looked carefully into the middle distance and coughed. 'There is breakfast,' he mentioned with dignity.

They both turned to look at him. 'Jaap, old friend,

you think of everything,' remarked Fraam as Lucy left him to take Jaap's hand.

'Thank you,' she said. 'I hope you'll be my old friend too.'

Jaap beamed once more. 'It will be my pleasure, Miss Prendergast.'

He watched the pair of them go into the dining room and then closed the door. On his way to the kitchen he ruminated happily on the days ahead. Such a lot to do; a wedding was always a nice thing to have in a family. He nodded his elderly head with deep satisfaction.

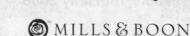

MILLS & BOON
100 YEARS
of pure reading pleasure

100 Reasons to Celebrate

**2008 is a very special year as we
celebrate Mills and Boon's Centenary.**

Each month throughout the year there will
be something new and exciting to mark the
centenary, so watch for your favourite authors,
captivating new stories, special limited
edition collections…and more!